You and Me

D0537734

7

Between You and Me

MARGARET SCOTT

POOLBEG

Published 2013
by Poolbeg Press Ltd.
123 Grange Hill, Baldoyle,
Dublin 13, Ireland
Email: poolbeg@poolbeg.com

A catalogue record for this book is available from the British Library.

ISBN 978-1-84223-596-6

Typeset by Patricia Hope in Sabon 10.75/14.6

Printed and bound by CPI Group (UK) Ltd, Croydon, CR0 4YY

www.poolbeg.com

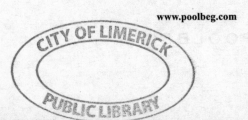

About the Author

Margaret Scott is a writer, an accountant and mother to two little girls. She lives in Kildare with her husband Keith Darcy, four dogs, two cats, two donkeys, a pony and a rabbit.

An avid fan of social media she can be found on Twitter @mgtscott and on Facebook at www.facebook.com/margaretscottauthor.

This is her first novel.

Acknowledgements

Publishing my first novel means the fulfilment of a lifelong ambition. But whilst writing is a solitary pursuit, this book simply wouldn't have happened without the support and friendship of a lot of people.

I have to thank the Naas Harbour Writers for all their encouragement with the early chapters and for convincing me to give Holly at least some redeeming features.

Trying to get published in Ireland today is an impossibly daunting task, but Vanessa O'Loughlin of Inkwell Writers helped me believe that dreams can come true. I would not be in this position today but for her untiring support, her inexhaustible knowledge and generous guidance.

I owe a massive debt of thanks to my agent Ger Nichol of The Book Bureau. We clicked from day one and I will never be able to thank her enough for her help in making this book the best it could be. Her enthusiasm was both exhausting and exhilarating, but at all times inspiring.

Writers are not always the most emotionally stable of folk (or maybe it's just this one). I'm not sure if it's the long hours spent at a desk, the endless search for inspiration, the racking self-doubt or the waiting (oh man, the waiting!). But this gang stuck by me through thick and thin: Anne Marie, Alan, Tracy, Sarah, Elaine, Maria, Becky, Niamh, Dee and anyone else who didn't avoid me in the last two years.

I also owe a huge debt of gratitude to Eibhlin of Alice's Restaurant, Naas, who has let me use her corner table every weekend for years, supplying me with tea and Luka Bloom CDs on demand, ensuring that I can no longer write anything without both . . .

The long hours at the computer would have been interminable were it not for the joyous distraction of both Twitter and Facebook, so a huge thank-you to anyone who chatted with me through those long, lonely nights. Yes, without you it might have been finished sooner, but there's no way it would have been as much fun.

To this end I also have to mention (or I'll be shot) the best group of female friends a girl could ever have: the Q107 Rollercoaster Mammies. Every last one of the thirty-eight of you is a gift. Inspirational, funny, generous, kind and unfailingly supportive – thank you, thank you, thank you.

I knew from the age of eight that I wanted to write books. But I'm a bit like Holly that way – if there's a long way around, I'll take it. Throughout all those years though, I always had the support of one of the best families in the world. Mammy, thank you for always encouraging us to be creative, be it painting, writing, dressmaking or engineering. We were never allowed to mention the word 'bored' in our house growing up, nor did we ever have the time! And thanks to Daddy for always being so proud, no matter what we achieved or what we decided we wanted to do, and for instilling in us all a work ethic that we'd achieve nothing without. And to Michele, Jim and David, no, you were *not* the inspiration for the family in this book. I promise.

A special thank-you too to my extended family: Hilda, Billy, Laura, Gemma, Anna, Lucy, Michelle, Matthew,

Ben, Emma, Kate, Aoife, Eimear and David. Thank you for stepping in to mind children and for being supportive in every way.

And to Mairéad and Michael, a very special thank-you for providing me with a husband that is the envy of the parish. I should add that thanks to you I can neither participate in 'bad husband' nor 'annoying in-laws' conversations, ever.

When people ask me how I write whilst working full time with two small children, there is no other answer but that I have the best husband in the world. Being friends with a writer is in the ha'penny place to being married to one. This man deserves a medal and I hope he knows that I know that. And how could I not thank my two beautiful, funny girls, Isabelle and Emily. I'd love to say you two haven't inspired any characters in this book, but I just can't. You inspire me every day.

Thank you also to my editor Gaye Shortland, an eagle-eyed, long-suffering genius.

Thank you to Kathleen Lambe of Stage Door & More. Someday, if it's the last thing she ever does, I'll speak as confidently as I write . . .

Finally a massive thank-you to Paula Campbell of Poolbeg Press for her unfailing knowledge, support, advice and guidance and for saying yes in a summer of turbulence in the world of women's fiction. I won't let you down.

To Mammy & Keith
The first for having me,
the second for keeping me . . .

MarshaG *posted today 20.51*
  Hi girls,
  Now one of my four-month-old twins is hardly sleeping
  at all at night. It's a nightmare and I'm not sure how
  much more I can take.
    All advice welcome.
    MG

Mum2Satan *posted today 20.55*
  Hi MarshaG
  I feel your pain – how long has it been?
    M2S

MarshaG *posted today 21.02*
  Hi Mum2Satan,
  Thanks for your quick response – well, it's been four
  nights now ...
    MG

Mum2Satan *posted today 21.05*
  Hi MarshaG
  I haven't had a full night's sleep in seventeen months and
  two days. In answer to your original question, that's how
  much you can take. Feel better now?
    M2S

Chapter 1

"That brings me to the gravel, Mr Baron."

"The what?"

"The gravel, Mr Baron," I repeated, while pulling an invoice from the bundle in front of me. "An invoice from Andersons Sand & Gravel, dated 18th July, in the amount of €18,000."

To my left I could hear my team leader Oliver Conlon clear his throat uncomfortably, but I ignored him. There wasn't a sound from my right where Seán, the team junior, seemed suddenly very interested in his biro.

I tucked a non-existent stray blonde hair behind my ear and waited.

Ger Baron looked at me blankly across the gargantuan mahogany table, its ostentation matching the faux wood-panelled walls and shelf upon shelf of books that had clearly been bought by the yard at some auction house.

Something told me that Ger Baron was probably not the reading type.

"It says it was delivered to the Drunken Duck?" I said.

He visibly brightened. "Ah yes, I remember now – that was for the smoking area."

"The smoking area," I repeated.

"Yes," he said happily.

I heard Oliver sigh. He had no choice now but to intervene.

"Eh, that would be a sizeable amount of gravel for a smoking area, Ger," he said.

"It's a sizeable smoking area," Ger Baron smiled.

The gall of the man infuriated me but, to be honest, two weeks into this assignment, nothing could surprise me about him any more.

Baron Entertainment had started life as two grotty pubs and a nightclub back in the eighties. Now, with a chain of swanky venues dotted all over the city, Ger Baron prided himself on still being a simple working-class soul – a man of the people, albeit one that dripped in designer labels, drove a Porsche and had recently finished building a palatial spread, complete with stud farm, somewhere on the outskirts of North Kildare.

He had strolled into this meeting with us, his company's auditors, all five foot two of him, like he hadn't a care in the world. Now he sat in front of us on what looked scarily like a giant throne, smiling smugly, and I just knew that if I looked under the table I'd see his little legs swinging like those of a bold schoolboy.

He reminded me of my dad's barrel-chested Jack Russell terrier that strutted around under the illusion that he was, in fact, a Rottweiler.

"Right. Well, that's that then," said Oliver.

I looked at him in disbelief. From the outset I'd known that he had a soft spot for Ger Baron. He'd worked on the

4

Baron Entertainment audit for several years now and the two seemed to get on. I also knew that it was Friday evening, we were way over budget on this job and that if we didn't get it wrapped up soon our manager, Catherine Taylor, was going to blow a fuse.

"Well, yes, of course," I glared at him, "if you are happy that the smoking area of a pub on Westmoreland Street would require the same amount of gravel as, let me see . . ." I paused as if trying to think, "the four-hundred-metre driveway and courtyard of a large country house . . ."

"Fine, yes, I'm happy with that." Ger Baron hastily pushed his chair back from the table.

"However," I continued, looking down at my list, "I'm afraid I still have a few other questions."

Oliver sighed. "Oh, right. Sorry, Ger, I'm sure this won't take long."

"Ask me anything – I mean, you know me by now, Ollie – an open book." Ger Baron threw a disparaging glance in my direction. "Obviously, there are a few new faces on your team this year and we can't expect them to be familiar with the way we do business."

The fact that I clearly wasn't his favourite person didn't bother me in the slightest. If popularity was important to me, I'd never have chosen auditing as a profession. As an auditor you can do no right. Clients see you as an unnecessary expense; their staff see you as an annoying interruption in their daily lives. The better you are at your job, the more they hate you.

And I was very good at my job.

"Great, let's talk about the hot tub then," I said pleasantly.

Oliver spluttered and even Ger had the good grace to look sheepish.

"Ah yes, well now, that might be a mistake alright." He chuckled in obvious forced amusement. "I'll have to get Ellen to check how that one got mixed up with the pub invoices." He smiled at his insipid bookkeeper who was by now looking very uncomfortable as she crouched in her chair beside him.

"Well, it was in the same bundle as the ones I have here for, let me see . . ." I shuffled through my pages, quite unnecessarily as I knew this list off by heart, "a four-poster bed, a chaise longue, a life-size self-portrait and, em . . ." I paused again, this time for pure effect, "two gold eagles and pillar mounts."

At this, any pretence at amusement faded, and he looked at me with thinly veiled hatred.

"I said we'll look into it," he spat.

There was silence as we eyeballed each other across the table.

But this paragon of nouveau riche-ness didn't faze me. Oh no, I'd known what was ahead of me as I got ready that morning so I'd dressed for the occasion. As a result, I could have taken that chancer's eye out with just one casual flick of an Armani lapel and then finished the job with a poke from a carefully applied Louboutin heel. He wasn't to know that I clad head to toe in purchases from the Niemen Marcus Fall '09 sale.

"Right so," Oliver said, "now that we have that mis-understanding sorted –"

"There's another matter, of a more serious nature," I interrupted.

My gaze hadn't shifted.

Neither had Ger Baron's.

Not even the loud click of Seán's biro broke the tension. He mumbled an apology but he needn't have bothered.

All eyes were on me.

"I'd like to discuss the seventh till at the Drunken Duck."

"You *what*?" Ger Baron sat back.

"I said, I'd like –"

"I know what you said," he leaned forward again, "and I'm saying I don't know what you're talking about."

"Allow me to explain." I reached once again into my briefcase. "I have here an analysis of the till rolls that were supplied to me by Ellen. An analysis of the six tills listed at the Drunken Duck."

"So what?"

"So where are the till rolls for the seventh till?"

"What fuckin' seventh till?"

"The seventh one I counted last Saturday night."

There was an audible gasp around the table. For a brief moment I thought Seán was going to fall off his chair.

"Well, you must have counted fuckin' wrong!" He leaned forward again, his eyes narrowed to little slits.

"D'you know, I don't think I did," I answered calmly. "You see, I was out with a few friends. We started off in the Drunken Duck, then went on to the Strawberry Bed, next the Liffey Arms and lastly Old Connell House – and guess what? In each of them I counted one extra till."

"You accountants really know how to tear up the town," he sneered. "Had you really nothing better to be doing on a Saturday night than going around pubs counting bleedin' cash registers?"

"Mr Baron, I think you're missing the point. If I was able to spot something like that, so could the Revenue, and the repercussions for both you and your shareholders would be huge."

"Fuck the Revenue!" he spat. "They get enough off me. And you want me to give them more?"

"You have to understand – it's nothing to do with what I want. All I'm trying to do is warn you that –"

"No, all you're tryin' to do is ruin me. I've met your sort before, and I'm telling *you* what I told *them*. Fuck off and work for the Revenue if you're that fuckin' worried about them!"

At this, Seán erupted into a volley of nervous coughing that threatened to choke him and the insipid Ellen had to assist him from the room.

"I think maybe that's enough for Mr Baron to think about for today," Oliver said, valiantly trying to call some order to the meeting. "Why don't we meet again early next week?"

"I'd rather finish this list if you don't mind."

"*Holly!*" Oliver said sharply.

I hesitated, then handed Ger Baron the sheet of paper.

"This outlines the queries we've covered today, and the ones we didn't get to." I shot Oliver a dirty look. "I'll be back on Monday morning, 9 a.m. sharp, to see if we can come up with some mutually acceptable answers."

"Well, I suggest you stay out of my pubs in the meantime," he snapped.

"Oh don't worry, Mr Baron – I've a quiet one planned for this weekend."

I gathered my stuff together, rose to my feet and left the room.

When Oliver joined me and Seán on the footpath outside I was too livid to look at him.

"Right," he said, "get in the car, the two of you."

"I'll get a taxi," I snapped.

"Just get in the bloody car, Holly." He sounded weary.

Seán slid into the back seat of Oliver's Audi, leaving me with no choice but to get in the front.

For several minutes there wasn't a sound but the drone of the engine and Oliver's somewhat violent gear-changes.

"You know that Catherine is going to kill you," he said eventually.

I wouldn't look at him.

"And then probably kill me for not having more control over you?"

I shrugged. "Pity she wouldn't kill you for being such a spineless lick-arse every time you're around Ger Baron. 'Oh, yes Ger, no Ger,'" I mimicked. "You're only short of jumping up to make a cuppa for him when he walks into the room. Pathetic."

"Whatever, Holly. The facts remain: we're already a week over on this job – now we're probably going to lose the client altogether – and, in case you haven't noticed, thanks to this bloody recession, clients of his size are fairly thin on the ground."

I sat, looking out the window – Seán mute in the back – so Oliver continued.

"I mean, it's okay for you – you're back off to New York in a few weeks – but you could try and leave a bit of business for the rest of us."

"What's that supposed to mean?" If he'd wanted to get my attention, he had it now.

"I think that's fairly obvious. I mean, for the love of God, Holly!" He was shaking his head now.

"I was right and you know I was!"

He slammed the wheel with his fist. "That's not the point!"

"Well, what is the point then?"

9

"The point is, there's an easy way and a hard way to do things. It beats the shit out of me why you always pick the bloody hard way!"

"Forgive me but back where I trained that's how you did a job properly!"

"Oh, don't start that again."

"Ah, that's right, I forgot. This is *Irish* auditing." I couldn't help the sarcasm dripping off my tongue. "I took a class in Irish auditing once. It was very short though – *because they'd taken the ethics section out!*"

"Well, you can explain all that to Catherine. I'm sure she'll find your theories very interesting."

There was no point in saying anything else. Since my arrival in Grantham Sparks on secondment almost five months before, Oliver and I had clashed on virtually every auditing issue that arose. He was right about one thing though – in six weeks I'd be back in New York and cocky little upstart Ger Baron would be somebody else's problem.

I turned and looked out the window as Oliver guided the car through the Friday-evening traffic back towards the IFSC. My apartment was one of several owned by GS in the adjoining development.

As we pulled up outside, he sighed and turned to me, "Look, I'm not saying that wasn't very impressive back there but –"

"Oh get lost!" I snapped, slamming the door then half waving to Seán who was cowering in the back seat.

Only when I got inside, kicked off my shoes, took the pins from my hair and poured myself a large glass of Pinot Grigio did I feel the tension start to leave my body.

Out of habit I turned on my laptop and it opened as usual

on the CNN website. It was nice to know what was going on back home. Well, back in the States, which I considered home. It was all a bit confusing really – well, confusing to everyone else, that is. I didn't let the fact that I'd lived in Ireland for nineteen years before moving to New York deter me from never expecting to call Ireland 'home' again.

Though, to be fair, this trip back to the old sod had turned out much better than I'd expected.

There was no denying that the Dublin I'd come back to was far, far different to the one I'd left behind nine years before. Pleased with what I'd found, I'd worked hard and, as a result, people took me seriously. They only knew Holly the Achiever. Holly the Problem Solver. I ran my eyes over the well-thumbed books lined up beside my laptop. Jack Canfield's *The Success Principles*, *Troubleshooting for the Medium-Sized Enterprise*, *Think on Your Feet – the Twelve Step Approach to Solving Problems at Work*. My babies. In fact, it was no lie to say that my favourite possessions in the whole world were my How-to books and my tiny, gleaming MacBook Air. Nothing symbolised the New Holly Green more than these possessions.

And that brought me to the best bit of all about Dublin: here nobody knew anything about me, and I'd never felt the need to fill them in.

Well, apart from one person.

Yes, there was one other reason why my stay in Dublin had been so very enjoyable.

I looked at my watch, feeling the usual twinge of panic starting.

He should be here by now.

I took another long sip of wine. I was being ridiculous, of course he'd be here.

11

I couldn't sit still. Switching on the television, I switched it off as quick.

By the time I was halfway through my second glass, a cold sweat had started at the back of my neck. I looked at my mobile.

Don't you dare.

I looked at my watch again. Only seconds had passed. He wasn't coming.

I looked at my phone again.

I could call . . .

You will not.

I picked up the phone.

Put it down. Put it down!

And then the door-buzzer went.

I flung the phone back on the couch and ran to the door. Looking at the hazy figure on the monitor, I almost punched the air with relief.

Thank you, God!

Pressing the switch that released the door, I knew I had only seconds to compose myself.

Be cool, be cool.

I opened the door, but despite my best efforts couldn't hide the relief that flooded through me.

"I thought you weren't –" I started to whisper.

But I never got to finish as Oliver Conlon pinned me to the wall, growling, "That fucking suit does it to me every time."

And then he kissed me in the way I'd waited for since he'd left my bed that morning.

12

Chapter 2

My finger hovered over the doorbell and, as was my custom at the front door of this particular suburban semi-d, I took a deep breath before pressing it.

It said it all that I didn't have a key.

Through the wavy amber glass panel in the door I could see someone approach. I released my breath, slowly through my teeth, timing the last tiny hiss to the exact moment the door opened.

"Oh. It's you. I was expecting Nancy Spillane's daughter – she's dropping me over this week's *Hello!*."

And breathe again.

Fourteen seconds and I'd disappointed her already.

"Sorry about that, Mam."

I walked past my mother, into what I called the Green Hall of Fame, stopping briefly, as was my habit, to see what new additions had been made to the collection of family pictures on the wall. And it was quite a collection, so vast in fact that it was hard to see exactly where the pictures ended and the pattern of overblown-roses on the

13

wallpaper began. Of course if my mother had removed the rather large picture of the Sacred Heart that looked mournfully down from the midst of us all she'd have been able to fit even more in, but that would take something like Marsha's inauguration as President of America. One thing for sure, nothing I'd ever do would be amazing enough to usurp the Lord.

Aha! Two new pictures of Aoife and Arann, Marsha's twins, on ponies. With rosettes. Good to see the over-achieving was continuing down through the generations . . .

"Aren't they adorable?"

Mum was beside me, wringing her hands with pride.

"They sure are," I had to admit. And they were. It wasn't their fault that their mother had been my arch-enemy ever since I was old enough to walk-later-than-she-had.

Leaving my mother fussing over some of the pics that weren't aligned to her satisfaction, I sighed and went through to the kitchen-cum-living-room where Dad was sitting with his usual Saturday paper on an enormous couch bedecked with yet more roses.

He looked up, smiling. "Ah Holly, isn't this a treat!"

"It is, Dad." I sank down beside him, cosying up to him.

It was the same every time I plucked up the courage to visit. With each stop that whizzed past the train window, the years rolled backwards until it felt like the last ten years had never happened.

Which is probably the reason that I didn't visit that often.

"And what divilment have you been up to these days?"

I was tempted to answer 'Oh, the usual – bank robberies, embezzlement, you know . . .' but I just smiled and said, "Busy working, Dad, believe it or not."

Dad had always regarded me in the same way you would a naughty puppy. When I was offered the placement with the Grantham Sparks New York office on graduating, he had slapped me on the back with glee and said, "Go on, ye chancer!" like I had just carried out the employment-equivalent of a jewel heist.

"Good woman yourself!" He shook his paper out. "Is there any good news in this thing at all?"

"Probably not." I snuggled into him, closing my eyes.

"This country's gone to the dogs. That's two construction companies gone into receivership this week alone."

"Yes, Dad, I know." I didn't like to tell him that I was only too well aware of the latest recession casualties – they were clients of ours and I'd been booked for both jobs.

"You'd be better off back in the States." Dad had worked for many years in America himself – in fact, of the four of us children, only Kelly, my younger sister, had been born in Ireland.

"Well, I'll be back there this side of Christmas."

"Good, good. You wouldn't like them to forget about you and give your job to someone else!"

"Oh Sweet Mother of Divine God! They've given your job to someone else?" My mother had entered the room, only catching the tail-end of the conversation. "Oh Holly love, what will you do now?" There was more hand-wringing before she continued in the mournful tone she seemed to reserve only for me, "Though, it's not surprising really, given all those shenanigans before you left. You could hardly blame the Good Lord, really . . ."

I rolled my eyes. My mother had a checklist of gripes with me that she seemed to need to tick every time we met:

- You haven't been to Mass and thus are going to Hell
- You've coloured your lovely red hair again – it's too blonde
- You've lost more weight – it doesn't suit you
- You still haven't been over to visit your sister Kelly in Sligo
- Do you remember how you embarrassed the whole family by having a very public affair with a very married colleague, who then very much left you and returned to his wife and children and thus you are going to Hell?

Same stuff every time. She occasionally tweaked the order to catch me out.

"Don't worry, Mother. I can always go back to waitressing. Or pot-washing – I was a pretty good pot-washer actually. It's all in the level of elbow-grease, I found."

My mother looked aghast and I smiled. It was a source of great family shame that, at nineteen, I still didn't know what I wanted to be when I grew up and had gone to live with Auntie Monica in New York while I decided. Every other member of the Green family had known from the age of four what they wanted to do in life, and definitely no other member of the Green family had ever done anything menial while they waited for inspiration.

"Oh Mother, relax, I'm pulling your leg. Tell me the news. How many times was Chad on telly this week?"

Dad gave me a warning poke, but it was too late. The light had returned to my mother's eyes as she proudly started rooting through video tapes to find the latest segment from *Tea at Three* or whatever other daily show my older brother had made a guest appearance on that week.

And yes, I'm aware that we were probably the only house in the universe that still used a VCR, but the poor woman couldn't get the hang at all of "those dreadful delicate disc things". It was an ongoing joke in the family that the best present you could possibly buy our mother was a fresh batch of blank video tapes, a gift now virtually impossible to source.

After much fumbling she found what she was looking for. And suddenly there he was, all six foot four of him, shoulders like a fireman, obligatory gleaming white smile, my brother, the Celebrity Dentist. This time he was schmoozing some middle-aged dear on a couch, making root canals sound like something she should queue for. Looking at him, I still found it hard to believe that someone whose giant hands once played basketball for Ireland, could make a living from carrying out intricate procedures in people's mouths. But his rugged good looks coupled with a chance appearance in a toothpaste television ad had catapulted him into the world of the media and now he seemed to spend more time on the TV than he did in the surgery.

"You know, he's going to be on the *Late Late* in a few weeks," my mother whispered almost reverently. "Some new initiative he's spearheading in schools."

"I'll watch out for it," I said dryly.

"I'll record it for you," she promised.

"Any chance we could eat sometime soon, Mary?" Like me, Dad could only take so much of daytime TV reruns.

"Okay, okay." With one last adoring look at the TV, my mother dragged herself over to the kitchen. "I need someone to set the table."

Dad poked me again.

I groaned and levered myself up from the couch.

"That's a good girl," he said, his eyes already back on the paper.

"Did I tell you Marsha's coming home for Christmas with the kids?" my mother shouted from the depths of the oven.

Yes, Mother, several times.

"Oh, it will be great, all of us together," she continued.

I didn't want to burst her bubble by reminding her that I'd be well and truly back in my lovely Manhattan apartment by then so I just kept setting the table. The fact that I wouldn't be around for The Great Marsha Homecoming was a relief to be honest. The eldest of us, Marsha had been seven when we'd moved back to Ireland. Her name said it all. Just as Americans embraced their Irish roots by using names like 'Colleen' or 'Shannon' my mother was likewise embracing her new life, and literally couldn't think of anything more American than 'Marsha'.

To date, her firstborn had yet to let her down. Beautiful, blonde and blue-eyed, she was also sunny-natured and gentle. This ensured that no matter how much you tried, you couldn't hate her.

Not that that had ever stopped me trying.

I'd long ago accepted that I was never going to come close to achieving Marsha-status in the Green household. Having returned to America to study medicine at John Hopkins, she was now a cardiothoracic surgeon based in Washington. Which would have been great, had it not happened that on the very day of my graduation, she was part of the team that carried out life-saving surgery on the American Vice President. It was almost more than Mam could bear to tear herself away from the hourly bulletins, such was her hunger to hear the Golden Child's name mentioned on TV.

Then, to add insult to injury, I'd caught her with a radio and headphones on during the ceremony . . .

"*Stop*!" There was a screech behind me. "What are you *doing*?"

I froze, cutlery in mid-air.

"Not *that* cloth!"

In an instant, my mother had whipped the tablecloth off and was examining it for possible cutlery-inflicted damage.

"It's a limited edition! It's not for *using*!"

I rolled my eyes. I knew exactly where this was going. My younger sister, Kelly, having floated through life in a blur of poetry and patchouli oil (not to mention more suspect vegetative odours), had been my only dysfunctional ally for a long time. But then she too let me down and, after getting a first-class degree in NCAD, was now running her own textile company in the wilds of Sligo. *Kelly Green* – so kitsch, it was never going to fail. And of course I'd seen her since I came back to Ireland. She'd come up to me in town and we'd had a hedonistic night out just like the old days. But it was easier to say nothing. My mother believed that where two or more of the Green family were gathered together there needed to be a roast, a camera and a Mass at the house at the very least. And poor Kelly was even less religious than me, constantly trotting out theories about evolution which thankfully my mother still thought were about learning to speak properly.

"Did I tell you what they called her in *Tatler*?" Mam said as she gently folded the precious cloth and put it away, replacing it with yet another rose-spattered concoction.

Yes, Mother, they called her the Irish Cath Kidston, but tell me again anyway . . .

"The Irish Cath Kidston. Would you believe, when I

showed it to Nancy Spillane she said Kelly obviously gets her eye for pattern from me, must get it from me, says I have great vision . . . Hang on – I kept a copy for you –"

"*Mary! Food!*" Dad roared from the depths of the vast couch, correctly envisaging another lengthy delay to dinner.

"Okay, okay, keep your hair on! I'll get it for you later, Holly love, not that you're probably that interested, given that you haven't even been down to visit your sister in the five months you've been home."

No, Mother, I'm not that interested because I have two copies already – the one you posted to me and the one you gave me the last time I was home for dinner.

I sank back down beside Dad. The couch really was cavernous. It was part of the array of furniture that my mother had insisted on shipping back from the States. My dad had tried to remind her at the time that our suburban American home, only deemed to be of average size compared to its peers, was almost three times the average Irish semi-d but she remained in total denial. The fact that the couch was now covered in a loud floral print always subconsciously made me check my skin for greenfly every time I sank into its depths.

"Any sign of a nice young man?" Dad asked, sensing my dejection.

Mam sniffed.

"Well, maybe there is!" I said, regretting my words the instant they left my lips.

"I hope this one doesn't have a wife!" My mother couldn't help herself.

For the hundredth time I reminded myself to enquire of Marsha why she'd seen it necessary to fill Mum in on that episode.

"He doesn't actually."

20

"A criminal record?" Dad poked his head from behind his newspaper, his interest piqued.

"No."

"Tattoos then?"

"*Daddy*!"

"And what's going to happen once you go back to the States?" My poor mother was clearly torn between the idea of me settling down with a nice young man and the thought that the Black Sheep might come back and be under her feet for good.

"Well, actually, he's going to go back with me!" I announced.

"And marry you? Oh thank the Lord!" Mam beamed. The perfect solution.

And I wasn't even lying. Okay, maybe the marriage bit was a tad premature but the rest was true. Oliver Conlon was going to join me in America, and not on some temporary secondment, but a full-time transfer. The triumphant return to New York was working out far better than I ever could have imagined. If everything went according to plan and he got the promotion he was hoping for before Christmas, it would be better again.

Just then my phone rang.

"Oh!" I couldn't help my surprise at the fact that Oliver's number was flashing on my phone. "That's actually him now. I'll take this outside."

"Hi, this is a nice surprise!" I said happily, as soon as I was out of earshot.

And it was a surprise. I'd been adamant from the start that the relationship be kept a secret as the last thing I wanted was another in-house romance on my CV. As a result we never phoned each other on impulse.

"Look, Holly, I had to let you know –"

21

"Sorry? Speak up – I can barely hear you!"

"Holly, will you just listen!" he hissed. "You won't be coming with me to Baron's on Monday."

"Oh. Okay. Why not?"

"It's Catherine. She's going to want to see you first thing instead."

"Oh," I said again, shrugging. "Well, it's not like I didn't see that coming."

"Holly, I'm serious. It's serious."

"How serious? What's she going to do? Take me off the job?" I laughed.

There was silence.

"She can't do that, Oliver! And let that little twerp win? No way. She can't – can she?"

"Look, I probably shouldn't have said anything. I have to go."

"What do you mean you shouldn't have said anything? Of course you should have! You're being crazy. I'll be back at the apartment in a couple of hours – come over then and tell me what's going on."

"I can't. Not tonight."

"Well, in the morning then."

"I can't. I'm – I'm away until Monday – look, I have to go."

"Fine, suit yourself," I said sulkily. Then it hit me, "Where did you hear all this anyway?"

But he was gone, leaving me with a silent phone and the start of an uneasy feeling in the pit of my stomach. The nightmare of the last time I'd been summoned to a manager's office was suddenly all too clear in my memory.

I rejoined my parents who were now at the dinner table.

"Now eat every bit of that – you're starting to fade away!" My mother handed me what could only be described as the largest plate of Irish Dinner I'd ever seen. Mountains of mashed potato soared over a huge slab of roast beef, swimming in gravy and, ugh, mushy peas . . .

And then, just as I thought things couldn't get any worse, she looked at me, fork in mid-air, and said, "Holly, I really wish you'd stop dying your lovely red hair – that awful blonde makes it look like straw!"

Chapter 3

"Back to New York? *This* Friday?"

I'd been gazing through the floor-to-ceiling window at the view out over Dublin Bay, waiting for my telling-off to finish. But with these words my eyes flew to the well-dressed woman sitting in front of me.

"Yes, well, they need you for next Monday." Catherine Taylor thought for a minute. "But you probably have a few things to finish up here so Friday seems the earliest you could go really."

"I'm not suggesting going *earlier*!" I almost laughed, "I'm still trying to figure out why I have to go at all!"

"Look, Holly," Catherine said patiently, "we've been over this. I've explained the dilemma I have and really this is the best solution I can come up with."

"It's a ridiculous solution!" I burst out. "In fact, it's not a solution at all. It's . . ." I struggled to find the right words, but they wouldn't come. "It's just ridiculous," I finished lamely.

"Be that as it may, that's the way it will have to be."

I looked across the table at her. Only a couple of years older than me, Catherine Taylor's position in the company was one I envied. A senior manager at Grantham Sparks Dublin Office was only one step from partner, and for a woman to have achieved this by her early thirties was nothing short of a miracle. Not that she looked young enough to be in her early thirties, to be frank. No, Catherine Taylor was blessed with the kind of timeless looks that were a great asset in your forties but deemed a disadvantage any earlier. However, her career success couldn't be disputed. The downside was that she wasn't viewed with much affection by her colleagues. Especially those she'd passed out on the way up. But, to be honest, the fact that her unpopularity didn't seem to bother her just made me admire her that little bit more.

However, in this instance, she'd got it very, very wrong.

"You can't punish me for doing my job! For doing my job *properly*!"

"I'd like you to stop looking on this as a punishment! Look, Holly, you may not have noticed but Ireland – Dublin – is in the mire at the moment. If one of my main clients threatens to leave unless a member of the team is replaced, my hands are tied! My biggest problem is that I've no other assignment to give you. Tuscon Construction and Cherryfield Developments have gone into receivership and God knows who else is heading that way. I'm really sorry, Holly, but I have no choice. I can't lose any more clients. New York only set up the Dublin office because of the Celtic Tiger – they could close us just as quick and then none of us would have a job."

I couldn't believe this was happening to me. Since Oliver's call on Saturday night I'd braced myself for the mother of all rows this morning, but nothing could have prepared me for this. The fact that Catherine was being calm and measured instead of just hauling me over the coals and screeching at me, actually made the situation far, far worse.

I sat there, shaking my head.

"Holly, let me assure you of something." She tried again to get through to me. "I don't like Ger Baron any more than you do. I certainly don't like getting irate telephone calls from him at nine thirty on a Friday night, so if it's any consolation I've been filled in on the issues you had with him and I'll be personally following every one of them up. I'll just be using more," she sighed, "how should I put this – diplomatic methods."

"I still think I'm being penalised." My initial shock had now turned to anger.

"I know it looks like that. And yes, your methods have caused us to clash more than once in the past few months. But of course I know how good you are at your job. And let me assure you, two years ago this wouldn't be happening. We'd have been able to tell Ger Baron to take his pubs and his gravel and get lost. But I can't do that now."

It was clear that nothing I could say was going to change her mind, not when she'd gone as far as ringing New York and arranging a project for me to start on the following Monday.

All I could do was summon up whatever dignity I had left, shake her hand and leave her office.

Once outside the door, my resolve started to slip.

I had three days left in Dublin.

Three days left with Oliver.

26

Oliver!

I scrambled for my phone.

"Look, it's not as bad as it seems," Oliver said, trying to console me as he sat opposite me in a crowded coffee shop in Dawson Street.

"It's worse!" I mumbled, my head in my hands.

"How is it? You were heading back soon anyway."

I looked through my fingers. "I had six weeks. *We* had six weeks. Now we have three days!" I groaned and put my hands over my eyes again.

"Look, it doesn't change anything – I'll be there before you know it."

I looked up. "When?"

"When what?"

"When will you be there?"

"Well, when we'd planned, after the promotions."

"What if you don't get promoted?"

"Oh, I will," Oliver said confidently, and then laughed. "Especially now that my maverick sidekick has been evicted from the country!"

"For God's sake, Oliver, there's no need to sound so relieved about it!" I wailed.

"Oh relax, I'm not relieved, honestly I'm not. I'm going to miss you like crazy." He stole a furtive glance around then leaned over the table. "I hope you have Skype in that lonely New York apartment."

I couldn't help smiling. "And you'll definitely come out at Christmas?"

"I will definitely come out as soon as I can."

"That's not what I said!"

"Oh come on, Holly, think of how good it'll be for us

27

if I'm manager before I arrive. Think of how good it'll be for you. I'm no one as I am now – it would be career suicide if I transferred as a team leader. What difference does a few weeks make anyway? We have the rest of our lives to make it up."

He had a point. In the bigger scheme of things, my having to return a bit earlier than planned really wasn't the end of the world. The problem was that, despite Catherine's reassurances, it still felt like I was going home to New York under a cloud, which was the very thing I didn't want. For this reason I hadn't even told my parents yet. My mother would wring her hands and then buy up every penny candle she could find in the church, whereas Dad would probably laugh. I was dreading the conversation so much I was even toying with the idea of not telling them at all.

I sighed again.

At this, Oliver put his hand on mine and, looking at me with the big brown eyes that still had the power to melt my heart, he said softly, "Trust me. It will be okay. I promise."

"So you're heading back *tomorrow*?"

Another colleague, the same question. These Going Away drinks were starting to seem like a bad idea.

"Yes." I smiled through gritted teeth for what seemed like the hundredth time.

"Wow, that's earlier than you thought!"

'Tell me something I don't know!' I felt like saying, but instead I smiled the when-you're-good-you're-good smile I'd been practising all day saying, "Oh, you know how it is when Head Office calls . . ."

I looked around. The drinks had been Oliver's suggestion, a solution to my fear that people would think I was slinking back to New York with my tail between my legs. In a way I was grateful that he realised how important this was to me. But, given that I hadn't made that many friends while I was in Ireland, I worried that it would be just me and him – but he'd assured me that no one would pass up the chance of after-work drinks. Especially after-work drinks on a Thursday as it heralded the unofficial start to most people's weekends.

And he'd been right. The bar was full. Hordes of slick city types were crammed together like penguins at feeding time, ties and tongues loosened.

"It wasn't the same without you today." Seán squeezed his way in beside me.

"Ah thanks, but I'm sure Ger Baron didn't miss me." Being resigned to my early return didn't mean I still wasn't bitter as hell about the reason behind it.

"Oh, I don't know, I think he was as bored as I was."

Seán looked so doleful that I laughed.

"Well, you'll just have to provide the entertainment instead! Where's Oliver?"

"On his way. I have to get the drinks in. What'll you have?"

"I'm fine at the moment." I gestured to my still full glass of white wine.

I was glad that Grantham Sparks had an area reserved. From my perch on a much-coveted high stool I had a clear vantage point over the crowded bar. I looked eagerly for Oliver. Maybe tonight was the night I'd throw caution to the wind and plant a big kiss on his lips in front of the whole company . . .

That would definitely ensure that I'd go out with a bang.

Hugging this new plan to myself, I sat contentedly with my drink, listening to the idle chatter that was going on around me.

It was the mention of Oliver's name that caught my attention. I looked around, wondering if he'd come in without my noticing. But still I couldn't see him. I listened more intently.

"Oliver Conlon? With *her*? That can't be true?"

I froze.

"It absolutely is. Don't ask me how no one spotted it before now."

Fuck!

"Well, you'd be waiting a long time to get any personal information out of Oliver – he never tells anyone anything."

"Well, he'd hardly be boasting about being with that grumpy cow anyway. I mean, would you?"

Eh, hello? I'm sitting right beside you?

I half-turned but the two girls who were talking had their backs to me. I turned back quickly. I was strangely excited that our secret was out, but also curious as to how we'd been caught.

"Ah, that couldn't be true!"

Oh, yes, it is!

"It is! I saw them with my own eyes!"

No way! We'd been so careful!

At that moment I saw Oliver approach and, smiling, I put my finger on my lips. Raising an eyebrow, he stopped.

"When?"

Yes, when?

30

"Saturday night, in Galway of all places, all over each other they were!"

Liar! I'd been in Celbridge on Saturday night, with my parents and that bloody big dinner.

I shook my head in puzzled amusement at Oliver who moved closer, leaning in to listen.

As he did there was a shriek of laughter.

"Oh. My. *God*! Oliver Conlon and Catherine Taylor? On a dirty weekend in Galway. That is just *too* good!"

I looked at Oliver as the blood drained from his face.

And at that exact moment, my glass hit the ground.

Chapter 4

And then it was morning. When I first woke, I lay still for a minute before opening my eyes, as if all my other senses were running through a system scan, assessing how bad things actually were.

It didn't take long to confirm that things were pretty bad.

The absence of a warm body in the bed with me, coupled with the fact that I was lying still fully dressed on top of my bedclothes, frozen into the rigor mortis of the devastated, meant that the first feeling to hit me was the cold.

And that was followed swiftly by the silence. No squawking alarm in my ear, prodding me to get up for work. Because there was no work to go to today.

Just a flight to catch.

And still I lay, eyes closed, letting the events of the evening before wash over me.

Oliver and Catherine, and I hadn't suspected a thing.

I mean, Catherine Taylor? It would have been funny if it hadn't been so awful. Okay, so she wasn't *that* much older than me but, seriously, she was a senior manager. Where did

32

she even get the time? And what in God's name did he see in her? I mean, she was good-looking in a career-driven-accountant kind of way, I'm sure she worked out and she could certainly afford killer clothes, but well, I couldn't imagine her letting her hair down enough to –

Stop, this is getting you nowhere!

Every limb cold and aching, I dragged myself over to the window and looked down onto the road below.

His car was gone.

Oh yes, Oliver had followed me home. When I'd run from the pub he'd sprinted after me but, despite my being blinded by tears, I was in a taxi before he'd managed to catch up. But not long after I'd arrived back at the apartment, he was buzzing the door. When I'd refused to answer, he'd sat in his car outside my window, and bombarded me with call, after call, after call.

I picked my phone up from the window ledge. Eighteen missed calls. There'd only been twelve when I left it there, tired of alternating between watching it flash and watching the car below, knowing that in it he was ringing me.

That bloody car.

I would never be able to see a black Audi again without associating it with Oliver Conlon. That car meant so much to him. I think, to him, it was a symbol of how far he'd come. It distinguished him from the old school pals that he still played five-a-side soccer with twice a week. It was the one thing he said he would miss when he moved with me to America.

That bloody car.

The night it had all started, we'd been on a job in Finglas and, boy, had we had a bad altercation that day! As always it had been his fault.

On my arrival in Dublin it had quickly become apparent that, for whatever reason, Oliver Conlon felt threatened by my presence. Not that I ever did anything to help my situation: I contradicted him at meetings, ignored the majority of his directions and met every disdainful remark with something equally assured and cutting.

Looking back, it has to have been uncomfortable viewing for the rest of the team. Had I not worked twice as hard and twice as efficiently as everyone else, I'm sure he would have had me shipped back to the States after that first fortnight.

And that fateful day was a particularly good example. We'd been working on site with a large building company, Sunrise Developments, and to my disgust Oliver assigned me the Fixed Assets section.

Allow me to explain: Fixed Assets was for Juniors – it was tailor-made for them. You assigned a Junior to Fixed Assets and came back to them in two weeks only to check that they were still breathing. They worked on drafting up schedules, verified that the chairs they were sitting on did actually exist and that any additions to last year's file could be vouched to invoices. A Junior with a bit of initiative might actually check a few lease agreements, but most left these to those higher up the ladder working on Creditors.

No, I wasn't happy.

Nor should the client have been. It didn't make sense to assign someone with my charge-out rate to such a lowly section, but I shrugged it off. There was another way to deal with this.

We were stationed in the Sunrise Head Office. Previously situated in a jumble of portacabins in Finglas, Sunrise had profited well from the building boom of the Celtic Tiger and now occupied a newly built premises in Parkwest Business Park.

Within two days I knew Oliver was under pressure. That often happens with jobs – you get there thinking it's all going to be plain sailing and then after a while you get the feeling that the deadline you felt was safely somewhere far on the horizon was starting to creep closer and closer.

So I happily ignored the first strains of pandemonium that were starting to filter over from his side of the bright, airy office.

Fixed Assets it was.

It didn't take long for my deliberate yet subtle tactics to take effect.

On day four Oliver walked by my desk and something caught his eye.

"Holly!" he barked.

"Mmm?" I didn't look up from the paper I was immersed in.

"Any chance you'd do some work? We're kind of under pressure here."

"I *am* working." I still didn't raise my head.

By now the entire team was watching. Oliver was known for two things: his good looks and his low threshold for adversity.

"Care to explain exactly how reading the *Buy and Sell* constitutes working?" He pointed to the open free-advertisement paper on my desk, the bright yellow pages of which were clearly visible.

"I'm valuing the Fixed Assets."

"I beg your pardon?"

"Yes, it's fascinating actually – I didn't realise that you could pick up a cherry picker for so little these days."

"A what?"

"A cherry picker – oh sorry, I should say a teleporter. Apparently they're the same thing."

"Put away that fucking paper!" He was apoplectic by now.

"No."

"*Now!*" he roared.

It was time for me to look up.

"I said no. Do you realise that Sunrise have overvalued practically all of their Plant & Machinery by at least 35%, and I haven't even started on their Fixtures & Fittings or Motor Vehicles yet." I dipped my head into the paper again. "I did however see an Audi A2 2005 here for 11k – what did you pay for yours again?"

"Right, that's it!" His face was by now white with rage, and he looked like he would willingly have swatted me over the head with the offending periodical, but even he knew when he had lost. With a look that would have unnerved a lesser mortal, he hissed, "Give that bloody paper to Angela. I'm moving you to Creditors."

I smiled sweetly at his retreating back and said, "No problem, you're the boss!"

And he'd stopped, turned slowly and while it was obvious he was trying to give me a warning look, it was even more obvious that he was trying to contain a smile.

Later that evening he'd offered me a lift home. I'd been about to say no, but if it came to a toss-up between a trip on a stinking Dublin bus or a spin in a cool car, I knew where my priorities lay.

As I'd sunk into the leather-upholstered passenger seat, there was no escaping the change in the air. He'd loosened his tie; I'd shaken the knot from my hair. Both of us knowing exactly what we were doing. Neither of us spoke until I saw the Dublin Mountains start to flash past my window. When I turned to question him coyly about his chosen route, he'd just laughed and told me he wouldn't charge me any extra for the scenery. Immediately I felt those first frissons of excitement raise the hair on my arms. That was Oliver all over, cocky, self-assured cheekiness.

I looked at the phone again. There were more messages too, as well as the calls – six of them, all unread. I couldn't remember how many there'd been when, at 5 a.m., I'd left the window and lain on the bed, wanting him to stop ringing, stop messaging, stop buzzing the door.

I put the phone back on the windowsill and sat back down on the edge of the bed, head in my hands, fighting back the tears.

You stupid girl.

And that was another funny thing. Deep down, I knew that I really should have answered the phone and told him that he was every form of two-timing-bastard-under-the-sun. But I hadn't. I hadn't because to speak to him, to answer his call, to read his messages, to let him in the door would have meant taking time out from berating myself.

Time out from the all-consuming self-loathing that was fast reaching dangerous proportions.

From the sinking feeling of déjà vu.

Because I was no stranger to romantic disaster. Oh no, we were practically old friends at this stage. It didn't matter that what had happened wasn't my fault. When these thoughts came to visit, all I could focus on was the fact that my life was once again a mess, and who else could possibly be to blame for that?

When it came to love, I ricocheted from one disaster to another.

Why do you fall for such horrible, useless men?

Why did you get involved with anyone at all? After last time . . .

Will you never, ever learn?

It was like a never-ending mantra going around in my head and, short of slapping myself, I couldn't stop it.

But I thought he loved me.

For a second I let the voice of reason have a say. I hadn't just thought he loved me. Oliver Conlon had said he loved me. He'd said it, and I'd believed him.

You'd think I'd have learned. After all, it hadn't been that long since Cain Hobson had uttered those very same words . . .

Chapter 5

The Cain situation had been textbook really. When I moved back to the States at the tender age of nineteen I had two goals: the first was to get away from my parents and Golden-Child siblings and the second was to have a think about my life, maybe write a little, you know, spend a bit of time taking stock . . .

Well, my Auntie Monica had other ideas on how best I could spend my time. A straight-backed, stern woman who worked for the Internal Revenue, she saw no reason why I also couldn't find myself some gainful employment while all this soul-searching was going on. She promptly got me a job waitressing in a downtown restaurant and didn't waste too much time worrying if the commute from West 72nd Street was safe for a young Irish girl virtually on her own in a strange city. This kind of freedom was new to me and that first day I'd kind of lingered at the front door waiting to be drenched in Holy Water but it just didn't happen.

And she was right. I never got mugged or raped or even frowned on and six months working in those sweltering kitchens was enough to make me realise that I'd better finish the taking-stock period, and fast.

I'm not sure who suggested finance first, but I'd say it was Monica who put it in my head then patiently waited for it to be my idea. So, to cut a long story short, I enrolled in grad school, then university, still waiting tables to earn a few dollars, and on graduation got the job at Grantham Sparks.

No one was more stunned than me to discover that accounting, then auditing, was to be my thing. I think that when I discovered I was good at it, there was no further question of where my future lay. After all, there was never a long list of areas in which I might excel.

Armed with my new talent, I became the rising star at Grantham Sparks. I got the best jobs, the best appraisals, the best opportunities and my whole being was charged with new-found confidence. I dyed my auburn hair blonde and jogged my way into an array of beautifully cut power suits. Even the fact that I was a Size 10 at home but a Size 6 in American sizing gave me a thrill. A Size 6, could you imagine? The world was my oyster.

And then, with no trepidation whatsoever I also launched myself onto the New York dating scene. I'd watched the programmes: no self-respecting girl went out with just one guy, so I was damned if I was going to. And, boy, was it fun! I was never, ever going back to Ireland . . .

So when Cain Hobson, a senior manager in the practice, bought me a Gin Martini at a company night out in The Plaza, it really didn't mean anything to me. When he then went on for ten minutes about how the best Gin Martinis were to be had at Cipriani's – they even froze the glass – I was only just short of yawning. I found his attempt at educating the new Irish girl clumsy and patronising and I believe I told him as much. So he offered to take me to Cipriani's there and then and I laughed at him.

I had a date, I told him.

Cancel it, he said, and I walked away.

It wasn't that he wasn't good-looking. He was. Tall, athletic, he had a long lean frame. Even his face was lean, his cheekbones angular, and his eyes dark and slightly restless. But the main thing about Cain Hobson was that when he spoke to you he made you feel like you were the only girl in Manhattan.

Which was rich, when it turned out you weren't even the only girl in his bed.

It took me two weeks to give in. Two weeks of cryptic emails, texts – he even passed me a piece of paper in a meeting which, when opened, turned out to be a torn-off map of Manhattan with Grand Central Station (which I'd since found out housed this famous Martini bar) clearly marked with a date and time.

I'm not sure what made me succumb in the end. I suppose I was dating so many other guys, one more in the pot didn't seem like too big a deal. I'd meet him, let him buy me one of the goddamn drinks and that would be it.

So in early November we had our first date. And on that date the first thing he told me was that he was married. And I should have been shocked. I should have chucked his frozen glass in his face and got on the next subway out of there but I didn't. There was something about his dark, brooding eyes and the way he looked so wounded about the situation that made me believe him when he told me it was all but over. But looking back, it wasn't just a matter of believing him, it was a matter of

MARGARET SCOTT

wanting to believe him. Because despite all my protestations and statements to the contrary, I fell for Cain Hobson that night – hook, line and sinker.

And as for the married thing? I shrugged it off. He had a wife, I had Richard and Juan, and – well, I told myself it didn't matter.

Of course there'd be nights where he'd cancel at the last minute because one of the kids was sick – oh yes, did I not mention he had kids too? Of course he did – as I said, this whole thing was textbook – but children were so far removed from my daily life that again I'm ashamed to say I didn't give them much thought either.

Of course the logistics of the relationship weren't easy. He lived with his family in the Village and I lived on Perry Street on the West Side with Auntie Monica. But she travelled a lot and, well, let's just say we managed . . . He didn't talk a lot about home and I didn't think a lot about his home, so we got along just fine.

And then suddenly I didn't want to see Richard or Juan or some other random "guy". I wanted Cain. I wanted him in a way that made my heart leap in my chest at a glimpse of him in a corridor. I wanted him in a way that made me sleep with my phone under my pillow so that when he texted me goodnight I'd know straight away. And slowly, the other guys drifted off the list.

And, anyway, me dating other guys made that muscle in the corner of his jaw twitch, and nothing was worth that. It was bad enough that his wife made him miserable without me starting . . .

Until I didn't see him for four days solid over Christmas and I got my first taste of the downside of dating a married man. Those four days seemed endless.

No clandestine lunches in the Polish Kitchen or clandestine suppers in Little Italy. No meeting at the Boathouse in Central Park on frosty Saturday mornings, strolling up through the Ramble, climbing Belvedere Castle to not notice the views and then ending up for hours in the Conservatory Gardens. No Knicks games in Madison Square Gardens. No phone calls, no texts, no nothing.

Yes, those days at Christmas without him were an eye-opener. It suddenly became painfully obvious that it wasn't just us.

That it was just me.

I moped around so much that even Monica could see there was something wrong. And on day four I decided that was it. Enough was enough. This sitting-around lark was a mug's game and I was no mug.

I picked up my cell and sent him a message: Just to let you know the Irish merger is no longer an option due to lack of interest.

Within forty-five seconds he phoned.

"What are you talking about?"

I could almost hear that muscle twitch from where I sat in Monica's apartment on Perry Street.

"You know what I mean. It's over. Not happening."

"Meet me. In thirty minutes."

"No."

"I've something to tell you. It's important."

"No. No, Cain, nothing you have to tell me will make any difference. I'm twenty-eight years of age. I've just sat in waiting for you to call for four days. That can't be the way I live my life."

"Look, there's a park at the end of Bleecker – that's not far from you – I'll be there in one hour."

He hung up.

And of course I met him. And there, in that tiny park, he pulled me close to shelter me from the foggy drizzle and told me he was leaving. That his marriage was over. That they'd discussed it over Christmas and it was mutual.

He told me that he'd fallen in love with me, that we would move in together, and that everything was going to be great.

And I believed him.

And so we continued.

And that was where I got cocky. There was a new bounce in my step and I suppose I no longer cared who knew that me and my dishy senior manager had a "thing" going on. I flirted a bit more openly and even hinted that my dating days were over. That I was going steady with a mystery man. The trouble was, I didn't have many close friends at work and, to be honest, this carry-on didn't make my female colleagues warm to me any further. But I didn't care. I had everything I wanted.

Exactly three weeks later Cain Hobson stood me up again. It was no biggie. We were meant to be going an exhibition at the Guggenheim and I waited outside for thirty minutes before huffily deciding to go ahead without him.

I'd read the best way to view the collection was to take the elevator to the top level and work your way slowly down the spiral ramp, so I did this, full certain we'd meet halfway down.

But he never showed.

Furious, I lingered in the Tannhauser room, standing in front of a huge Van Gogh, my mobile phone clutched tightly in my hand. But my phone remained silent and eventually I stomped out to Fifth Avenue and caught a cab.

There was still no word from him by the time I got to work the next morning and, by the time I reached my floor, I could feel my mouth was set in a thin line.

So it took a while to notice that people were looking at me, well, differently. Some were even smirking. I didn't have time to wonder much about it though as at nine thirty I was called to the office of Mike Preston, my team leader.

Where he asked me nicely to stay away from Cain Hobson as my harassment was damaging his marriage.

At first I laughed. I actually thought it was a joke. But then I noticed that Mike wasn't laughing with me.

"I've been *harassing* him? Did he say that?"

"Look, Holly . . ." Mike was clearly uncomfortable with the whole situation.

"Did he *say* that?" I almost screamed.

"He asked that you be taken off his assignments. Are you saying you have no idea why he would say that?"

"I'm not denying we were in a relationship, no. But his marriage is over. He said so."

"Well, it's not. This – this whatever it is has obviously caused some difficulties but it's not over. He's taking some time off, but . . ." he paused, clearly afraid that what he had to say next would tip me over the edge altogether, "he'd like you off his team before he comes back."

"But he can't do that!"

"Holly, please – this doesn't look so good for you right now. Cain is well thought of here – so's Melissa for that matter – if he wants to try and save his marriage, you should do the decent thing and stop whatever it is you're doing."

"What *I'm* doing? What has he said to you? He asked

me out – he – he – it was *all* him!" I knew I sounded like someone demented now and the look on Mike's face was starting to switch from discomfort to annoyance.

"Why don't you take the rest of the day off? This will blow over, teams switch around all the time . . ."

I could do nothing but nod.

But I didn't go home. I went to my desk alright, got my bag and wound my scarf tightly around my neck before leaving the floor, ignoring the smirks all around me. Then I left our building and started to walk and I didn't stop. Past City Hall, past the Flat Iron Building and on up Fifth Avenue towards the Park.

And all the time the conversation that had just taken place spun round and round in my head. And with every step I had to fight the urge to dial Cain's number. It was ironic but my months as a mistress had trained me well.

Then, as I reached the Park, my phone rang. I didn't recognise the number but I knew even before I answered that it was him.

"Holly, I'm sorry."

"Cain, what the fuck is going on? I've just been nearly fired for *harassing* you!"

"I know, I know. Look, it happened last night. She found out. I had to do something."

"Why? I thought it was over – you said it was over!"

"Look, Holly, it's not that simple – there's the girls –"

"What do you mean the girls – the girls were there all along – what? You're only remembering them *now*?"

"I don't expect you to understand."

"Damn straight I don't understand – why say anything at work? Why make up that ridiculous story that I'm harassing you?"

46

"Because she threatened to take the kids to Tampa to her folks. I couldn't let that happen, Holly – I couldn't."

"So why blame me?"

"Do you have any idea how bad this looks for me? I'm not meant to be chasing junior members of staff – and Mel, well, she knows all the wives – I had to try and save face for her somehow. This marriage is all she has – you're young, gorgeous – you'll be fine, the world is your –"

At that point I hung up.

By now I'd reached the Park. It was almost two hours since I left the office. And still I walked, round all our usual haunts, up past the Dairy towards the lake. Past the boathouse and on up towards the Ramble.

But the magic was gone. This time I wasn't Holly the up-and-coming financial whizz kid strolling hand in hand with her snazzy older man – no, this time I was Holly the Fool. The lonely, stupid fool. Suddenly this city that I'd loved so much seemed huge, busy and unwelcoming. When it started to get dark I left the Park and headed back along Fifth Avenue, past the Rockefeller Centre and found myself in front of Grand Central Station.

For old times' sake I ordered a Gin Martini in Cipriani's, then another, then another before finally stumbling into a cab and home.

For three days I stayed in my room. For three days Monica fussed, cajoled and finally threatened me with flying my parents over. At the end of day two I told her what had happened and could barely stop her from marching the entire way back down to the Financial District to give Cain Hobson what for. I should have let her. What she did instead was almost worse. She phoned Marsha, who insisted on flying down from Washington to talk some sense into me.

Marsha's visit did the trick.

On day four I got out of bed, went into work and requested a transfer to the Dublin office.

And for what? For the whole thing to happen all over again?

I parked the self-loathing for a second and wondered how long Oliver had been seeing Catherine. Had she known about me? Had they laughed about it?

Was it the real reason I was being sent home?

All of a sudden I felt sick. It was all starting to make a bit more sense now. Of course it was the reason I was going home. Maybe Ger Baron hadn't complained at all. Maybe Oliver had spotted an opportunity to hang me, and between the two of them they'd concocted the whole thing.

They couldn't wait until Christmas. Let's get her out of here, they'd planned. I'd left New York because of a man and here I was – on my way back because of one too.

I jumped as the phone leapt into life and started wobbling its way across the windowsill.

Go away, I moaned silently to myself, you have what you want, just go away. Your clever little scheme worked.

Just leave me alone.

And then it stopped. And there was silence again. I looked at my watch. It was hard to believe that later that day I would be on the plane home. I really couldn't believe it. I started to sob, great big, ugly, heaving sobs of disappointment and self-pity. Then, through my crying, I heard a knock on the door of the apartment.

Oh God no.

"Holly? Let me in!"

"Go away!" I screamed at the door, cursing whoever had let him up that far.

"Please, Holly, You're totally overreacting here. Just let me in for God's sake!"

"Go away." This time it was more of a plea. The knowledge that he was only feet away was suffocating me.

"Oh come on, just let me in for five minutes."

He could obviously sense the weakening in my resolve.

"No," I whispered.

"Holly, this is ridiculous."

I said nothing.

"Look, I understand you don't want to talk to me. I understand why you won't let me in. But please, you can't leave it like this. Meet me, somewhere, *anywhere*. I just need to explain something to you. Then you can go away and never talk to me again if that's still what you want."

'*None of this is what I want!*' I wanted to screech at the door but I didn't trust myself to speak.

"Right, Holly, I'm leaving now. In a few hours you'll be gone. And then it'll be too late, and you'll never know. It's up to you, Holl. It's whatever you want now."

And then there was silence again. I ran to the window and waited to see him leave the building below. There he was. My heart thumped in my chest. But then he turned and I had to duck back from the window. I'd seen enough.

Chapter 6

What was I going to do?

Of course I knew what I should do. I should continue my packing, wait for my taxi, and head to the airport, chalking another failed romance down to experience. But it was very hard not to replay his words over and over in my head: "I just want to explain."

And then the doubts started to creep in.

Could there be an explanation? What could he possibly say that might make it all better? That I'd imagined those girls talking? That what they were saying wasn't true?

But it had to be true. After all, he hadn't denied any of it. That was the killing bit: he hadn't denied it. So what could he possibly say that would make this horrible mess any better?

The thing was, I'd never know unless I met him.

No. No. No. Just go home. For once, do the right thing and just go home. You deserve better than a lying, cheating bastard like him.

I started to pack even more quickly, flinging things into

my suitcases, anything to avoid the sight of my phone, still lying on the windowsill, its silence now taunting me.

But I knew I wasn't going to go without speaking to him. It was the masochist in me.

I needed to know why I hadn't been enough.

I needed to know why he felt the need to turn to Catherine.

I needed to see his face one last time.

I picked up the phone.

Walking the short distance from my apartment to Harvey's, there was no escaping the irony that the only part of our entire relationship that would happen in public was its demise.

After that first night, our appetite for each other had been voracious, the flames fanned by the fact that during working hours our relationship never differed. We still sparred with each other during meetings, in fact possibly more so, and our propensity to out-do each other at every given opportunity never waned. All the mock-hostility however, only served to whip up a frenzy of intensity that had to be contained in our after-hour liaisons.

Well, apart from that time in the sixth-storey filing room.

Or the time in the lift of Goldthorpe Investments.

Or that lunchtime in – okay, let's just say it was *pretty much* confined to after hours.

The irony of it all now was that the initial attraction of the entanglement had been the total lack of commitment desired from either of us. I'd just had my heart pulverised in New York and to go through such heartbreak again was way down my list of priorities. And Oliver, well, he was a popular guy, and I assumed that he wouldn't be short of female company. God knows there was no escaping how good-looking he was. He had the sweetest deep brown eyes that seemed to be permanently peeking from under a thatch of thick brown hair. Like me, he was fiercely ambitious and I think, initially, we each expected the other to end it any minute, hence the lack of willingness to display any desire for commitment.

And then one ordinary Wednesday, he'd gone and completely moved the goalposts.

It was in early August and we'd been "seeing" each other for three weeks. That particular week Oliver was working in Monaghan on the audit of a large meat-packing company. I was back in the stifling office, finishing off a few files.

Then at 9.30 a.m., Amy, the gum-chewing secretary slapped a file on my desk.

"Oliver needs that file at Gro-Span."

I looked up at her.

"So?"

"So you have to take it up to him."

"Eh, I don't think so. Just put it in a cab."

"He said someone had to go with it. The taxi will be here in twenty minutes."

I looked at her. It was 35 degrees out. Did he really think I was going to get in a cab and make the two-hour drive to Monaghan, hand him a file and then travel another two hours back in this heat?

He had a cheek.

"Tell him I'm not going. I'm busy. He can drive down for it if he wants it that badly."

She threw her eyes up to heaven and sashayed her way back to her desk.

Twenty minutes later my phone rang. It was reception. "There's a taxi here for you."

I cursed but, looking around, could not see Amy anywhere. Picking up my bag and the cursed file, I stormed down to reception.

Having wrenched open the door of the taxi, I flung myself into the back seat. When my leg touched off someone else's I screeched.

"Hi," Oliver said.

"What the hell are you playing at?" I yelled. "You nearly gave me a heart attack there!"

"Sorry," he grinned. "Surprise!"

"*Surprise*? Why aren't you in Monaghan? What's going on?"

"Well, I decided I didn't want to spend my birthday amidst vast quantities of meat carcasses, so here I am."

"Your birthday?" My hand shot to my lips. "Oh Oliver, why didn't you say something!"

"I'm saying it now – surprise!"

"So I'm not going to Monaghan then?"

"No, Holly," he said with his usual trademark grin, "You're not. Don't tell me you're disappointed?"

"I don't know yet," I said coyly, my mind suddenly racing with all kinds of possibilities. "That depends on what you have planned. Your place or mine?"

"Neither," he said. "You'll have to wait and see."

Soon the taxi had left the city centre and was heading out the motorway towards Wicklow. I had no idea where we were going and I was so excited I didn't care. Then it swooped off the motorway, drove through some giant stone pillars and pulled up. The sign read *Powerscourt Gardens*.

"Oliver, we're can't go sightseeing – we're meant to be

at work!" I hissed, but he was already paying the driver. He then got out of the car and was taking something out of the boot.

A giant picnic basket.

I squealed in delight.

"Oh my God, a picnic? But won't we be missed? Get in trouble?"

Putting down the basket, he waved the taxi-driver on. Then he turned and put his hands each side of my face.

"Today, my darling Holly, is not about work, or about us killing each other, or even," he winked, "about what we get up to when we're not killing each other! It's about me and you."

"But I – I never even got you a present!"

"You are my present," he whispered, kissing me with a tenderness he'd never shown before. "Today we are going to sit in the most beautiful garden in Ireland, we are going to eat this delicious food, and the woman I love is going to tell me everything there is to know about herself."

I looked at him open-mouthed. This was definitely against the rules. In an instant, the memory of myself and Cain strolling down the promenade in Coney Island came rushing to my mind.

"Please don't say that."

"Why not? I mean it."

And as I stood there, warning bells ringing in my ears, my heart thumping so much I could hardly breathe, he'd held out his hand for mine, and taking a deep breath, I'd taken it.

More fool, you.

I pushed open the giant revolving door of Harvey's, the

business plaza's brasserie. I'd deliberately chosen it as the most public place I could think of, especially at this time of the day.

I cursed silently at the already forming queue at the *Please wait to be seated* sign, my foot tapping impatiently. I'd hoped to get seated and grab a coffee to steady my nerves before he got here.

"Is it always this busy?" a voice behind me asked.

Oh for God's sake, I really wasn't in the mood to be polite to strangers.

"Friday lunchtime," I murmured without turning around.

"Ah, I see. So, what do you recommend?"

Leaving me to hell alone? I almost snipped, but then I sighed – a distraction from incessantly analysing my failed relationship was probably no harm.

The voice belonged to a tall guy not much older than me. He was what could be termed "alternative-looking" with a shock of obviously highlighted hair falling over one of his eyes. Wearing the mandatory business suit for the venue, it somehow looked different on him, quirky even, as though he was really some kind of surfer dude masquerading as someone more serious. He was also weighed down with not one, but three laptop bags.

I smiled despite my misery. Not coming from a quintessentially financial background (those hectic years of waitressing in downtown New York never far from my psyche), it was refreshing to see someone a bit different.

"Do you always travel so light?" I asked, trying to make up for my earlier snippiness.

"Don't talk to me!" he groaned, shifting one of the straps further up his shoulder. "The smaller they make these things, the more of them I seem to end up lugging around.

I should be more like my brother and refuse to use anything other than a pen and paper."

Even his accent was different, Irish, but with a definite hint of someone who'd travelled.

"No way, in this day and age?" I said.

"I jest you not. Having said that, the bloke has never made a mistake in his life so he's probably on to something."

I couldn't help smiling at the glum note in his voice.

"A bit like my sister," I said.

"Oh, I'm sure he's worse. He's a vet, and I think Superiority is one of the compulsory subjects in their final year."

Just then my phone beeped.

I have a table at the window. O.

Damn him, he was already here.

I hadn't long to collect my thoughts.

I straightened my shoulders and took a deep breath. Suddenly I wished I'd made more effort with my appearance. At first, the temptation to kohl my eyes and subject him to a plunging neckline had been huge. *See if it's still Catherine Taylor you want now, you bastard!* But in the end I hadn't bothered. Partly because all my best stuff was already in a container bound for Manhattan, partly because I wasn't here to impress him, I was here to tell him to bugger off.

But mostly because I was just too goddamn tired and defeated.

Instead I'd spent an hour pacing my way around the apartment, rehearsing over and over again my bitter words of break-up. Muttering a brief goodbye to my queuing buddy, I headed for the window.

And then I saw Oliver, and my mind went blank.

Chapter 7

"Hey," he said as I sat in the chair opposite him.

My stomach twisted as he looked at me, as always reminding me of a Hollywood leading man. In fact, even more so this morning with his stubble and hangdog look.

Get a grip, Holly Green.

"Hi."

"Thanks for meeting me." His voice was hoarse, nervous. "I didn't think you were going to."

"I wasn't."

"Oh. Well, thanks anyway."

"Oliver –"

"I just –"

We both spoke at once. He gestured to me to continue, so I did.

"Oliver, I'm just here to say goodbye. I have nothing else to say to you."

He flinched. "Look, Holly, I know you're mad as hell, I'd be surprised if you weren't, but it's not as simple as you think. You have to let me explain."

"Explain what? From where I'm sitting, it's pretty simple."

"I wish it was. Look," he sighed, "I was going to tell you."

"Oh really? When? On your fucking wedding day?"

"Okay, okay. I know how bad this looks, but I was going to tell you. It just never seemed the right time."

"I think you're missing the point!" I hissed. "It's not that you didn't tell me, though yes, it would have been nice to hear the gory details from you instead of from random strangers. It's the fact that there's anything to tell!"

"I never expected . . ." he paused, looking down, ". . . you. I never did. This, us – it wasn't part of the plan, you know?"

"Sorry about that. Well, I won't ruin any more of your plans." I started to move my chair back from the table.

"No, wait!" Several people looked up, so he lowered his voice. "Can't you see? Your arriving changed everything. Suddenly what I had with Catherine seemed –"

"Whoa!" This time I was struggling to keep my voice to a hiss. "You were with her from the start?"

"Well, yes, for quite a while actually."

"You prick!" Suddenly my choice of venue didn't seem like such a good idea. How I'd thought I'd be able to conduct this conversation in public was beyond me.

"I would have told you – I should have told you. But I was afraid."

"I'll bet you were! Afraid of her!"

"No. Afraid you wouldn't want me."

"Well, you were right. I wouldn't have."

"Oh, come on, I just didn't know how to break up

with her. I tried, over and over, but she's under such pressure there never seemed to be the right time. And then as things between me and you got so good, and New York seemed to be an option, I thought: I'll apply for New York, it'll just fizzle out with Catherine and no one will be hurt. Not her –" he sighed, "and definitely not you."

"And you'd get your promotion," I said bitterly.

"Yes," he said, suddenly sounding defensive, "I'd get my promotion. And I don't feel bad about that, Holly. I deserve that promotion – I've been working for years towards it and it didn't seem right that I'd lose it because –"

"Because you were sleeping with me," I finished for him.

"Because I'd fallen in love with you," he said quietly.

I looked at him. This was not the conversation I'd rehearsed for.

"Well, that's all very romantic Oliver, but it doesn't change anything."

"Of course it does!"

"No, it doesn't!" I said. "You had a girlfriend. You should have told me."

"How could I? After everything you'd been through in New York?"

"No, Oliver! *Because* of everything I'd been through in New York!" I shook my head in frustration. "I had a right to know that it was happening again!"

"It wasn't happening again. He treated you like shit – I was trying to protect you."

"Well, you failed," I said sadly.

"How?"

"How? Are you insane? You have a girlfriend!"

"But I don't want her, I want you!"

"Oh Oliver, please! You've had months to break up with her. Months. And you want another month? What do you take me for? In a few hours I'll be on a plane out of Dublin, and before it lands you'll have forgotten all about me. I've been in this situation before, remember?"

"Stop!" he said, causing several people in our vicinity to look over again. "Stop," he repeated, this time more quietly. "I am not Cain Hobson."

I could feel the tears start to well up behind my eyes.

"Don't say his name," I managed hoarsely. "It isn't fair."

"Oh, for God's sake – this is exactly what I didn't want to happen. I've made a massive mess of the whole thing. But how many times do I have to say I'm sorry? You have to realise, I have never felt like this about anyone. And, after everything, I can't understand how you would even doubt that."

I tried to remember my speech, but none of it seemed relevant any more.

"I thought you were both laughing at me. I thought . . ." I shook my head as I remembered how humiliated I'd felt, "I thought that this was why she was getting rid of me."

"No," he said vehemently, "absolutely not. I couldn't believe it when she told me she was sending you away – that's why I rang you straight away to try to warn you –" He stopped suddenly.

I almost laughed. "Oh my God! When you rang me – you were in Galway with her, weren't you? Bloody hell, this just gets worse and worse."

"We were at her cousin's wedding. I couldn't get out of it."

"Stop! I don't want to hear any more."

60

"Right. Fine. You're right. Just go then." He sat back in his chair abruptly.

I looked at him, stunned at his change in demeanour.

"I beg your pardon?"

"I mean it. Just go. I'm not sure how into this you were anyway."

"What the hell is that supposed to mean?"

"Well, you didn't do a whole lot to stop yourself getting sent home, did you? Maybe that's what you wanted? Easy way out for you."

I stared at him, almost expecting him to smile and say "Only kidding" but one look at his face told me that wasn't going to happen.

"How could you say that? You think I wanted to be sent home? To leave you?"

"Well, can you blame me? I warned you, over and over again, that you were pissing her off, but you wouldn't listen. You knew best. Well, you have what you wanted now. Pity, I really thought we had something."

"We did have something! I mean –" I stopped. "You're not being fair, Oliver, you know you're not."

"I'll tell you what's not fair, Holly," he said, leaning forward, his tone low and quiet. "I've put my job on the line for you time and time again during the last few months. And this is how I'm repaid. She might have got rid of you, but she's not going to forget any time soon the way I've defended you. And where will you be? Out of the firing line, back in New York with your ex-boyfriend, up to God knows what." He sighed. "That's why I think you're right. It won't work. You'll be there, I'll be here. It's best just to say goodbye now."

He stood up as if to go.

"*Wait!*" I shrieked.

My head was spinning. This was a turn that I hadn't expected the conversation to take. Luckily he sat back down before I had to decide whether to run after him or not.

"I can't believe you're making out this is all *my* fault?" I said.

"Well, you having to go back definitely isn't mine!"

"And if I wasn't going back?" I whispered.

"Well, you are, so I guess we'll never know now, will we?"

"But – Catherine . . ." I grappled frantically to remember why we were having this conversation.

"Catherine has nothing to do with this!" He was getting really annoyed. "It was under control. We haven't been getting on for months – she knows there's something up. When it came to telling her that I was going to apply for a full-time transfer, it would have come to a natural end and I'd have left with you."

"Then come with me now." I looked at him, beseeching him to say yes.

"Oh yes," he said, sarcasm oozing from every word, "that's a great idea. I'm possibly four weeks from being promoted to senior manager but I'll hand in my notice. Leave with someone they've just sent away and start again from the bottom in a strange country, with a bad reference – if any – and the stigma of a sleazy office affair hanging over me. Great idea, Holly. Brilliant. Having said that, I notice you haven't offered to stay yourself."

"And live where?" Despite my distress I couldn't keep the incredulity from my voice. "I can hardly move in with you now, can I? What would you like me to do? Move home with my mother? Take a job in Tesco's?"

"Well, there you go. It's all just one big mess. But just

so you know, everything was fine, Holly, until you lost the run of yourself with Baron. You can't deny that. Your fault, not mine."

I felt like he'd slapped me in the face.

"You know that I was right about Baron," I hissed, "and I'm sorry that you think I should have licked his arse like you did, but at least I've got some principles."

"Oh, woopty-do for you, Holly, but at what cost?"

There was no point in answering that.

"So what do we do then?" I asked.

He shrugged and my heart plummeted in my chest at the look in his eyes.

"Look," he said then, "I need to head back." He looked me straight in the eye. "I guess it's up to you now, isn't it? You need to decide if what we had, what we could have, is worth fighting for. Call me sometime and let me know." He stood up and moved his chair back before turning and saying with a bitterness I'd never heard from him before: "Enjoy your flight."

And with that he was gone. I watched him wend his way through the tables but he never looked back.

Not once.

I sat, frozen in shock and disbelief.

Just as the tears of self-pity started to form at the back of my eyes, I was flung forward with a jolt. I looked up as a tall man shoved his way past me, towards Oliver's seat.

"Thank God – I thought he'd never go."

With a start I realised it was the surfer dude with the laptop bags again.

"I beg your pardon?" I scrabbled to regain some composure, wondering exactly how much this annoying, though strangely pleasant, guy had seen.

"Ah come on, you don't mind if I join you? I just can't

wait any longer for a table. If I don't get a bite to eat soon, I won't be able to open these goddamn computers let alone carry them."

He was already seated, tucking his bags under the table with the ease of someone who was obviously used to such a level of luggage. He held out his hand.

"Harry Fielding, Freelance Programmer to the stars! Your pal left in a bit of a hurry, didn't he? Not that I'm complaining, but I suppose it'd be manners to ask if you think he's coming back?"

I shook his outstretched hand. "Holly Green, accountant and auditor. And no, he's not coming back."

"Great, I'm starving – do you mind?"

He gestured towards Oliver's untouched club sandwich. I shook my head, watching, silent with disbelief, as he started to tuck in, all the time chatting away, oblivious to my horror.

This day was starting to resemble a very, very bad dream. *Your fault, Holly, not mine.*

"So, anyway, as I was saying –" The computer guy cleared his throat with mock vigour.

"Sorry?" I dragged myself back to reality.

"Had a bit of a row, did ye?"

"What makes you say that?"

He winked. "Ah, he didn't look the Mae West as he rushed past me, if you know what I mean."

I grunted.

"Ah, don't worry, you'll sort it out." He took another huge bite of sandwich.

"Not from New York, I won't," I answered, half to myself.

"New York?"

64

"It's where I'm heading," I said, looking at my watch, "in about four hours."

"Bummer."

Yes, bummer.

Just then his phone rang. After searching in four different pockets he eventually tracked it down and answered it, waving his hand apologetically to me.

He needn't have worried. I was glad of some time to get my head around what had just happened with Oliver.

I couldn't believe he'd been so angry with me, that he'd gone from begging me for forgiveness to washing his hands of me in just a few short minutes.

And I really, really couldn't believe that in just four hours I'd be on a flight back to the States. All of a sudden the reality of what was waiting for me back in the New York office hit me right between the eyes. It had taken a month for the transfer to Ireland to come through. A month of me pretending that I didn't care if the entire building thought I was the office bike. And of course Cain had arrived back for the final two weeks. I wish I could say I'd been professional about his return but I'd ignored him. Of the two options available to me, at least I couldn't go to jail for ignoring him.

I toyed with the idea of ringing Oliver but I knew there was no point. There was nothing new to say. He was right: I'd be in New York, and he'd be here. It was a fucking disaster and I couldn't help wondering whether he was right – if things would have worked out fine if I hadn't got myself sent home.

Now hang on! He's the one that had the affair.

I'm well aware of that, I answered myself back sharply, but it doesn't appear to be as simple as that.

Of course it is.

Oh bugger off! I can't think!

There's nothing to think about. Chalk it up. It's over.

If only I had more time.

"Hello?"

I looked up. My new companion had finished his phone call and was looking at me curiously. I hoped I hadn't been arguing with myself aloud.

"Sorry. I was miles away."

"So I see. Sorry for the interruption. It was my bloody brother, though why he's ringing me with his problems is anyone's guess."

"Problems?" I asked, glad to hear that someone other than me had some.

"Oh, another one of his bloody nannies has resigned. Wants me to put an ad up on the web – oh yes, he believes in the Internet when it suits him. I should issue a warning with it – I mean, anyone taking a live-in job with him deserves a warning."

I laughed at the look on his face and then stopped as the germ of an idea started to grow in the recesses of my brain.

Oh God. What if . . .

"Live in, you say?"

No, Holly. Absolutely no FUCKING way.

"Oh yes, it would have to be with the hours he works – sure he's hardly ever there."

"Where is he based?" I asked casually.

It doesn't matter!

"Duncane, a small village just outside Naas, an hour from here, I suppose. Why?"

"Oh, no reason." I looked down.

It wasn't the worst idea I'd ever had. I mean, there was

that week I'd helped Auntie Monica mind Marsha's twins while she was in California and I couldn't remember it being that taxing . . .

Yes, it was. You lasted two days and then practically went AWOL for the remainder of the week.

"Well, you're clearly not asking for yourself as you're an accountant," he said, smiling.

I didn't answer.

"Oh my God, you *are* asking for you, aren't you?" His eyes were wide in surprise.

"Oh, please don't tell him. That's all I need – the 'Oh, you're overqualified' excuse. The thing is, I used to be a nanny." The lie was out before I could stop it but I was too busy trying to remember how bad those two days had actually been. I mean, I was older now – surely that made a difference?

"Really?"

"Oh yes, for my sister and she has twins! Quite liked it actually."

The speed with which the lies were leaving my lips surprised even me. But seriously – how hard could it be? I mean no one gave Marsha any training prior to letting her loose on two tiny newborns . . .

"Can't imagine it, to be honest. Anyhow, go back to the drawing board," he said firmly. "Believe me, being an unemployed accountant is a far better idea than being a nanny for my brother."

Before I knew what I was doing I'd grabbed his hand.

"Harry. I need a job. I need somewhere to live. Just give me the number. He's hardly an axe-murderer, now is he?"

"Well, that's the thing!" He winked at me again. "He's not – but how do I know you aren't?"

I dropped his hand quickly. "I hate the sight of blood. And anyway, surely they'll have to interview me? Your involvement is over once you give me the number . . ." I looked at him coyly, resisting the temptation to bat my eyelashes, wary of appearing too psychotic.

"There is no 'they'. His wife died about eight months ago, though to be fair," he sighed, "she'd probably have left him in time anyway."

"That's an awful thing to say."

"No, it's not. Not about him. He's a grumpy, anal workaholic. I couldn't allow you to go near him."

"Well, I'm not exactly a barrel of laughs myself at the moment." I tried again. "Look, it's just to tide me over, for a few weeks, a couple of months, Harry."

He started to speak and I could hazard a guess that everything he was saying was an attempt to dissuade me from this maniac scheme. But I wasn't listening to him. All I could hear was Oliver's voice: "You need to decide if what we had, what we could have, is worth fighting for . . ."

I could stay. Let Oliver stew for a few days. I wasn't altogether convinced that this whole mess was my fault, but this way I'd have time to find out, give him a chance to put his money where his mouth was. Who's to say that we couldn't still return together as planned for Christmas? I'd have to make up some excuse for the New York office, but I'd worry about that later. At this stage I had nothing to lose . . .

"The number, Harry, please!" I interrupted.

He opened his mouth to object then shut it again.

"Okay, if you insist, but when this all ends in tears . . ."

"I'll only have myself to blame," I finished, swiftly handing him a pen and a napkin.

Sighing, he gave in and started to write out the number. I knew I should tell him to stop, that I should just get up, get out of there and get myself on that plane.

But before I could stop myself, I took the hastily scrawled number with trembling fingers.

This is total madness.

But it would buy me time.

And at that exact moment, that was all I wanted.

Chapter 8

It had taken a while to summon up the courage to dial Mark Fielding's number. And then, after the numbers were punched in, it took every ounce of my determination not to hang up when I heard the ringtone. Instead I'd clenched my teeth and run through my rehearsed opening sentence over and over . . .

I needn't have bothered. The phone rang out. Against my better judgement, I left a voicemail stating that I'd heard he was looking for a nanny and I was interested in the position, and left my number.

And then I'd hung up. And started to reason with myself.

There was still enough time to make my flight.

So if he didn't call back I was going to be on that plane.

He had twenty minutes.

Twenty minutes or I'd never see Oliver again.

It would be like the last six months had never happened, hardly the triumphant return I'd been dreaming about.

I looked at my luggage, a large but tidy pile of assorted cases and cartons stacked neatly at the door. I still had a few things to tidy up but the anger that had fuelled my earlier packing had dissipated and now I just couldn't be bothered.

So everything just sat there in limbo. A bit like me.

No home to go to.

Well, not for much longer. I had to leave the apartment in ten minutes. If I was staying I'd have to find a hotel, if I wasn't then I was airport bound.

Ten minutes.

I should have been relieved that the decision was being taken out of my hands. But instead, I just felt bitterly disappointed.

I'd got used to the idea of staying.

Okay, so it was at best too good to be true, and at worst a ridiculous harebrained scheme but at least I'd have known . . .

And it might have worked.

Two minutes.

I had a brainwave. I'd ring Kelly. She'd know exactly what I should do. Kelly was good with affairs of the heart. She'd probably tell me to get on the first train to Sligo which, when I thought about it, mightn't be too bad an idea. I dialled her number but from the dial tone it was obvious she was out of the country. I flung the phone across the room in frustration.

And then it rang. I dashed across the room to retrieve it but the number didn't look familiar. My hopes crashing around my ears, I answered it.

"Hello?"

"Hi, is that Holly Green?" It was a pleasant-sounding young female voice.

"Yes." I tried not to sound annoyed but I really hadn't time for random conversations with strangers.

"This is Tara Harper of Raven's Hill Veterinary Clinic. I'm phoning for Mark Fielding."

Holy shit!

I dropped the phone with shock.

"Miss Green, are you there?"

I could hear the voice as I grappled to retrieve the phone.

"Yes!" I called hastily. "Yes, I am."

"Oh. Okay. Well, Mark is in surgery at the moment, but he was wondering would you be available to meet him here at the clinic?"

"*Really?*" It probably wasn't good to sound so shocked.

"Well, yes – you did apply for a position with him?"

"I did, yes, of course – when would he like to meet?"

"Well, he's aware it's short notice, but if you didn't mind coming here, he could fit you in between appointments late this afternoon?"

As she was speaking I tried frantically to do some quick calculations in my head. I could cancel my flight, meet him, and know today if the whole thing was viable. That left me enough time to get another flight tomorrow or, worst case scenario, on Sunday.

And if it was a roaring success, I'd have time to phone HR in New York and give them an amazing-reason-that-I'd-yet-to-think-of for not coming back for a couple of weeks, possibly months . . .

"Miss Green?"

I realised with a start she'd been talking and that I hadn't a clue what she'd been saying.

"It's perfect!" I said, trying yet again to sound calm.

She started to give me directions to the veterinary clinic and I forced myself to focus.

This was getting serious.

The phone beside the bed rang and with a deep intake of breath I walked towards it.

"Your taxi, Miss Green."

I recognised the monotone of the receptionist that had

checked me into the Melrose Hotel just fifteen short minutes previously.

"I'll be right down," I answered.

I went to stand in front of the full-length mirror, exhaling at the sight of my reflection. I had taken care to choose the right suit. There was a time and a place for killer lapels and this definitely wasn't it. Not that I was entirely sure what kind of suit a nanny would wear to a job interview, which was entirely fitting given that I wasn't remotely sure what a nanny did, full stop.

Leaning towards the mirror I examined my face anxiously for any signs of the madness of the previous hour. Thanks to the wonders of *Touche Éclat*, an unblemished complexion looked back at me, devoid of flushed cheeks and tear stains. I looked at my watch: 3.50 p.m.

My plane had just left the runway at Dublin Airport.

At this thought the room started to spin around me and I reached out to steady myself against the mirror.

I tried to console myself with the fact that I'd done nothing irreversible yet.

You cancelled your flight.

I postponed my flight – that's different!

Between the bed and the wardrobe sat the now not-so-neat assortment of cases and cartons, the transference of which from my apartment to this tiny city-centre hotel bedroom had been largely to blame for my earlier ruddy complexion. Where in God's name it was going to end up next was anyone's guess.

One thing at a time. I took another deep breath.

First of all, I had an interview to do.

An hour later I was still in the taxi, anxiously looking at my watch. Apparently we were stuck behind some "bleedin' accident" which had managed to take every car this side of the Red Cow Roundabout and knit them together into a big, snarling mess.

"Will we make it on time?" I anxiously asked the taxi driver for possibly the sixth time.

"We'll be grand, love," he assured me. "As soon as we get through this bleedin' roundabout I'll get off the main road and I'll have you there before you know it."

He wasn't joking. Within fifteen minutes we'd left the dual carriageway and were tearing at breakneck speed along windy, potholed country roads. By the time we slowed to turn down an even worse by-road, I wasn't sure what was making me sicker, nerves or motion-sickness.

I'd had time to google Raven's Hill Veterinary Clinic back at the hotel, as much to give myself some idea of where I was going as anything. It appeared it was situated on the property of the senior partner, a Mr Fenton Harper, which all sounded very *All Creatures Great and Small* to me.

I wasn't far wrong. We finally pulled up outside what appeared to be a turn-of-the-century country house, flanked on either side by outbuildings and fenced paddocks. Getting out of the taxi, I made my way cautiously through the gloomy dusk up to the badly lit front door which was at the top of a short flight of steps.

Nervously, I rang the bell.

Suddenly a volley of barking erupted inside the house and something huge started to fling itself against the far side of the door. I jumped, almost falling backwards down the steps.

"*Nero!*" a woman's voice roared from behind the door. "Get *back*, you fool of a dog!"

There was the sound of more jostling as the door cracked open and a pretty female face peered out. Long blonde hair framed her face and her eyes were the brightest blue I'd ever seen.

"Hi?"

I recognised the voice from the telephone call earlier.

"Hi, you must be Tara," I said, trying to sound more confident than I felt. "I spoke to you on the phone. My name's Holly Green. I'm here to meet Mark Fielding."

"Oh hi! Sorry, no one ever uses this door! *Get back*!"

It took me a second to figure out that this last bit was not directed at me but at the giant black dog that her slight frame was grappling to keep inside the house.

"Sorry about this – would you mind going around the back to the clinic – he should be there somewhere with Dad."

"Of course," I said, only too pleased to get out of reach of the slobbering beast.

Back I went down the steps and onto the gravelled driveway. As I crunched my way around the side of the house I couldn't help feeling relieved that I'd decided against wearing the Louboutins.

It was hard to figure out where exactly I was meant to go but a commotion in the buildings to my left seemed to consist at least partly of human voices so I made my way tentatively in that direction. Before I could get to the door there was the sudden roar of some sort of machinery and a tractor started to trundle past me.

With a squeal I jumped back from its path, and then I noticed what it was pulling.

A huge, dead, horse.

Or at least I assumed it was dead – to be honest I'd turned away before I could make a proper diagnosis.

"Hey there! Sorry about that, can I help you?"

I turned tentatively, but the tractor and its gruesome cargo had moved on around the corner. I stared in its wake, open-mouthed in horror.

"You must be Miss Green. Mark Fielding, nice to meet you."

I looked in the direction of the voice and jumped, my hand shooting to my mouth to stifle a scream. I'd been expecting a man resembling Harry, at least in looks – hopefully an easy manner – and a warm handshake.

I wasn't expecting a creature that looked like he'd stepped straight from *Night of the Living Dead*.

I wasn't expecting someone whose vast frame, enveloped in a huge scrub-like garment, was spattered with blood, who stank of something noxious, and whose steely blue eyes peered out from a blood-smeared face, unsmiling, into mine.

Yes, his hand was out, but it too was covered in something unmentionable.

He clearly wasn't expecting my horror. He looked puzzled until, withdrawing his proffered hand, he caught sight of his bloodstained fingers. "Oh, fair enough." He wiped the offending digits on his trouser leg, then, catching sight of the look of horror that still remained on my face, decided against offering it again. "We're in the middle of surgeries."

Looking slightly defiant, he gave the impression that I should be grateful he'd come out to me at all. The fact that he was covered in some animal's insides was clearly a small price to pay.

"What happened to that one?" I asked, referring to the corpse I'd just seen dragged across the yard.

"You can't save them all," he answered, his voice

76

suddenly cold. Stepping back, he gestured for me to come inside the building.

Once in the tiny hall, he closed the door and seemed to take a breath before saying, "Allow me to start again. Mark Fielding. You must be Miss Green."

"Please. Holly." Without thinking, I went to hold out my hand, but then remembered and pulled it back quickly to my side.

He had the manners to pretend he hadn't seen, though a flicker of a smirk caused his lips to purse slightly.

"We have one more to do and then I'll clean up, I promise. Make yourself a cup of tea and if you're so inclined you can watch through the window."

He opened the door into a tiny tearoom and then vanished.

I looked around me in disgust. Several cups were stacked in the sink, their insides brown with dirty tea stains, and an opened carton of milk sat on the counter. No sign of any cup I'd consider putting near my lips. I automatically picked up the milk and opened the fridge before shutting it quickly when I got sight of the pack after pack of labelled blood bags that were crammed onto its shelves.

I put the milk back on the counter, resolving not to touch another thing for the duration of my visit. A huge rumbling caused me to turn around towards the window he'd been referring to, which looked out onto what I presumed was the surgery. Huge lights hung from the ceiling over a long low table. Wondering what the rumbling could be, I peered in. For a second I could see nothing, then I looked up and to my amazement another horse, hanging upside-down from what looked like a giant hoist swung into view. I could see Mark and another gowned man guide it onto the table, where a smaller gowned figure started to clean down its huge belly. Another figure moved to the head of the horse to attach some kind of breathing apparatus.

It really was quite a remarkable sight. I was even more amazed by the fact that, in direct contrast to the untidy muddy yard and equally grubby tearoom, the surgery looked shiningly clean. Even Mark seemed to have changed into a spotless set of scrubs. Forgetting the fact that there was a taxi sitting outside waiting for me, I moved a stool to the window and gazed, entranced, at the spectacle before me.

When the obsessive cleaning of the stomach was finished by what I assumed was a nurse, she moved to the side and rolled over a metal trolley. Then the two men moved in. They worked deftly for almost twenty minutes, the nurse seeming to anticipate their every move by constantly handing instruments and swabbing the site with huge wads of gauze.

With a start I remembered that my own sister carried out these kinds of procedures on humans every day, and I suddenly felt an unexpected dart of admiration for her. Too soon, it was over and the men stepped back as the rumbling recommenced and the horse swung once again out of sight.

Seeing Mark say something to the other man and gesture in my direction, I moved quickly from the window, embarrassed now at my open-mouthed wonder. Within minutes the door opened and he stood once again in front of me.

The offending scrubs were gone and he had changed

into a clean shirt. While his perfunctory wash hadn't quite caught all the smears on his face, at least now I was able to get a good look at him without my stomach churning.

Obviously older than Harry, there was very little resemblance between the two men. Yes, they were both tall, but where Harry was willowy, Mark was broad, his wide shoulders further dwarfing the small room. Even their blond hair held no similarities: Harry's was highlighted and swept carefully into a "mess" while Mark's was tinged with grey and cut very short.

But the biggest difference was in his demeanour. From the start Harry had been chatty, friendly, and almost too familiar. I knew instantly I was going to have no such problem with Mark.

"Sorry about the wait – we're never sure how long these things are going to take."

"At least that one lived." I tried to sound pleasant.

"For now, yes." He smiled as my face dropped. "I'm joking – it's going to be fine. So welcome to Raven's Hill. I presume you've never been anywhere similar before?"

I shook my head, without clarifying that the audit of Sculpting Inc, a private New York plastic-surgery clinic, was the closest I'd come.

"Well, this place belongs to Fenton Harper, my partner. Not exactly how we'd like it, but my dream would be to build a purpose-built clinic myself someday."

Unsure of what to say next, I said nothing.

"So you're a friend of Harry's?" he said.

"Well, an acquaintance." I might as well start with whatever truth I could.

"Well, let me explain a few things. I work long hours. Long, anti-social hours. If you have a social life that requires you to be out Thursday to Sunday every week then there is no point in us continuing this conversation. It's not going to happen if you work for me."

"I don't," I said, surprised that my second answer was also the truth, given that anyone I knew in Ireland thought I was in New York.

Outside the window the rumbling had started again.

"Good. Well, when can you start?"

I looked at him open-mouthed. "Start? But you haven't –"

"What? Oh I'm sorry, I haven't told you anything about the children, have I?"

Ooops! I'd forgotten all about the goddamn children.

"So what do you need to know?" He stared at me and I struggled to think of an intelligent question.

"Well," I stuttered, "what ages are they for a start?"

"Five and two and a half."

"Right."

There was a silence.

"Girls or boys?" I asked.

"A girl and a boy."

There was another silence as I wondered how in Christ's name it had come to me interviewing him instead of the other way around.

"So, anything else?" he asked. "I presume the rate of pay in the advertisement is agreeable to you?"

I nodded, not wanting to tell him that I had never seen the ad. However, I had a feeling I might be better off not knowing what meagre amount of money was on offer.

He seemed to take a breath then before he said, "Look, I'm not sure how much Harry told you about my situation . . . but their mother, well . . ." He trailed off uncomfortably.

"It's okay," I interjected quickly, sensing that this topic

was obviously still very distressing for him. "Harry filled me in. I'm very sorry."

"Yes." He brightened. "Well, look, I've got to head back in there. I'm guessing you wouldn't have come the whole way down if you didn't want the job. You look capable enough . . ."

"But what about references?" I'd spent a crazed half hour creating an amazing reference from my sister – I couldn't help feeling disappointed that this work of fiction might have been composed in vain.

"Leave them with me," he smirked. "I'm sure they're glowing."

I nodded, speechless at his blasé attitude.

He turned to leave the tearoom.

"Eh, I could start tomorrow?" I called after him.

"Oh, yes, well, that would be perfect." He turned. "And don't worry – we'll know quick enough if it's going to work out."

And with that he was gone.

I had a job.

I was one phone call away from staying.

Chapter 9

"Oh Oliver," I groaned, "I've missed you too, I really, really have . . ."

My pulse was racing, my eyelids heavy with lust, my heart pounding in my ears . . .

Oliver was here. I was in his arms at last. Now we could be together forever. I wondered how I had ever doubted that this ridiculous plan would work.

But then, above the sound of my heart thumping, I could hear a piercing wail, at first quiet, but then louder, closer.

Ignoring it, I wound my fingers in his hair and he nuzzled deeper and deeper into my neck . . . but there it was again. And then, without turning, I knew Catherine was standing behind me, holding a screaming baby, a victorious gleam in her beady blue eyes . . .

"No!" I was groaning again, but this time it wasn't the throaty mumblings of passion, but the guttural moan of loss.

No! Not this again. It wasn't fair. Oliver was mine now, no matter what scheme that strait-laced bitch had thought up, and she wasn't getting him back this time . . .

But, despite my best efforts, I could feel him slipping away. Well, sort of . . . something was still digging into my neck, something still wasn't quite right.

I opened one eye and squinted at the rain sliding down the skylight above my head. For a moment, unsure of where I was, I rolled over searching for the strong arms of the man I loved, but it was too late, he was gone.

But if he was gone, then what in God's name was . . . I reached behind my head and extracted a copy of *Childrearing, A Labour of Love* from where it had been digging into my neck behind my left ear.

Oh Christ, it was all coming back to me now. Stretching out, I flung the useless tome to the far side of the room in disgust.

And then I heard it again, the soft but persistent wail coming from the room below me.

Sweet Lord. It only seemed like a nanosecond since that cry had interrupted my sleep at four thirty that morning. And that had been for the third time that night. Did that child ever sleep?

Resisting the urge to heed my heavy eyelids and slide back into a deep slumber, I sat upright. Then swinging both legs from under the warm duvet while taking care not to hit my head on the sloping attic ceiling, I rolled grumpily from the bed.

Automatically, though it had only been two days now, I tiptoed down the creaky attic stairs, picking my way carefully around the piles of laundry, and made my way along the narrow hall.

What in God's name had possessed me? Sitting in Harvey's, face to face with Harry Fielding, it had all seemed like such a good idea. I would take a step back from the hamster-wheel of Dublin life, bury myself in the countryside, work on my plan to get Oliver to New York and, oh yes, mind a few children in my spare time.

On my return from my bizarre trip to the veterinary clinic, I'd rung the HR department in New York before I could change my mind. I needn't have worried; it had been like taking candy from a baby. They'd swallowed my family emergency story without hesitation, and simply asked that I keep them in the loop about my plans.

Like that was a loop they really wanted to be part of.

I then had to figure out what to do with all my stuff. I couldn't arrive, purporting to be a nanny, with six months' worth of business clothes, a laptop and several How-to-be-the-best-accountant-in-the-world books.

No, I had some decisions to make, the first of which was easy – there was no way I was being parted from my laptop. It just wasn't an option – no matter how crazy a nanny sporting a shiny MacBook Air looked.

I folded my suits carefully, for a moment wondering what in God's name I was going to replace them with. I had two pairs of jeans, neither of which were designed with housework in mind but they, alongside my four pairs of yoga pants, would have to do.

In the end, I packed everything I deemed to be surplus to requirements into three cardboard boxes. Now, what could I do with them? Again I considered ringing Kelly but now that the ridiculous plan was underway I was less enthusiastic about getting her involved. Chad lived in Foxrock – he was another option but, again, a plausible explanation would be required. So, instead, I rang the only gullible person I could think of: Seán. And told him I'd ring him in a month's time to instruct him what to do with them at that stage.

Poor Seán – he'd taken the boxes, all parcelled up with my new address on them, without question.

My new address: *Meadowlands*.

It had a nice ring to it. Heavily influenced by Fenton Harper's stud-railed paddocks, I'd imagined it might be a similar sort of Pemberly-type country pile, where giant friendly dogs loped on the lawn. The same lawn where I would likely indulge in picnics with the children, bedecked in florals, assorted pastel cupcakes haphazardly arranged on mismatched china.

I toyed briefly with the notion of a quick trip to Laura Ashley on Saturday morning to acquire some suitable floral dresses but I was too afraid of bumping into anyone. At this stage, I definitely needed no further complications.

True to his word, Harry collected me at 3 p.m. Again, my paranoia required that he pick me up in the underground car park of the hotel.

"Ha, you haven't chickened out then?" he said as I sat in beside him.

"Several times," I confessed, "but beggars can't be choosers."

"You'll be fine. Mark's not that bad. Well, if you're not related to him, that is."

"You two don't get on then?"

"Ah, we get on okay, better now than we used to, to our mother's relief. Our dad died when I was twelve and Mark was fifteen, and really the problems started then."

"Well, that would be a hard time for anyone, I suppose."

"True but, to be honest, Mark was always intense."

He sighed. "Becoming the man of the household was never going to help that. He thinks I'm a waster. He was always the brain-box who got enough A's to do veterinary – I was the budding computer-hacker who found someone foolish enough to employ me. But anyhow, enough about our dysfunctional family – tell me about this Oliver guy and why you are not, right now, living it up in ole New York."

I settled back in my seat. Harry was easy to talk to – in fact, as I began my tale it occurred to me that this strange man was the first person I'd confided in, in a long, long time. It was nice to talk and it certainly helped that he wasn't the type of person that would judge me.

It was a far more pleasurable journey than the one of the previous evening. In no time at all he pulled into a small housing estate just outside the village of Duncane. I was confused. What were we stopping here for?

Then I saw the pretty granite plaque on the verge that read, very clearly, *Meadowlands Close*. By the time we pulled up to No 12, all notions of escaping to a country retreat had well and truly evaporated. It was all too evident that Mark was the junior partner in the whole veterinary arrangement. I looked in dismay out the window at the row of pretty semi-d's that fanned out around a small green. And then I looked at No 12, which was definitely the least pretty in the row. The garden looked like it might have been picturesque at one stage, but now the beds were overgrown with weeds and the window boxes cracked and broken.

"So, here we are," Harry announced cheerfully as he swung his nifty Golf in behind a mud-spattered Land Cruiser whose giant wheels straddled the narrow driveway, digging into the straggly lawn on either side. "I'll see you Friday then!"

"What – you're going?"

"Ah, well, you see, I've got to be back in town by five." He made a point of looking down at his grossly over-sized diver's watch. "So I'd best be on the road."

"Gee, thanks," I muttered sarcastically.

I nervously got my bag from the back seat and swung my laptop bag over the other shoulder. There was nothing for it but to pull myself together, assume my best straight-backed Mary Poppins pose and ring the doorbell.

A clean, un-blood-spattered Mark answered the door. He looked beyond me at Harry's rapidly disappearing Golf.

"I see he didn't hang around."

"No. He – he had, important business back in town."

"I bet he did. Very important, I'd say."

Harry was right; the brotherly disapproval was obviously mutual. Just then Mark's telephone rang and he disappeared down the hall, allowing me to have a nervous look around.

It was – different. The hall had a terracotta-tiled floor, a wise decision given the assortment of giant work-boots and Wellingtons that were lined up along one side. However, it would have looked better had the walls not been painted a deep ox-blood red which only served to make the small area very dark indeed. On top of a small rickety hall table, which appeared to be carved out of some kind of bog oak, lay a stack of unopened post. Children's toys littered the floor and a strange smell permeated the air, a blend of joss sticks, surgical spirits and something else. Nose twitching, I looked down. At my feet were two small plastic bags labelled *Leinster Stud – Stool Samples*. Something about the smell emanating from them told me that the labels weren't referring to anything of a furnishing nature.

Then he was back.

"Right then, your room is on the third floor – it's a partially converted loft – you can't miss it and I'll be back around nine."

I almost choked. "Excuse me?"

"Well, you'll be okay, won't you? The kids are with our neighbour Mrs Murphy. She said she'd drop them over around half six, to give you time to settle in."

"Oh, I see."

Clearly there wasn't going to be any small talk, let alone the grilling I had been dreading. This was most bizarre. As I stood there, abandoned by a second Fielding brother within ten minutes, I couldn't help thinking that they'd more in common than they thought.

Chapter 10

I paused for a second outside the nursery door in the vain hope that the wailing had stopped and that by some rare miracle Amber had gone back to sleep, but no, and to make matters worse, I could now hear stirrings from the room next door as five-year-old Jamie started to make his presence known.

However terrifying meeting their daddy for the first time had been, meeting his two precious children had been infinitely worse.

Throughout the whole decision-making process leading up to this point (which, granted, had not been the most thorough) I'd kind of overlooked the whole having-to-actually-mind-children aspect. I'd just decided that it couldn't really be that hard. After all, my mother had raised four of us and she was definitely a few sandwiches short of a picnic.

It was only when the doorbell rang that first evening and I realised that I was about to come face to face with my new charges, that the first goose-bumps started to rise on my arms.

Mrs Murphy was a rotund, middle-aged woman who clearly looked like she knew what she was doing as she shepherded the two children through the front door.

"You must be Holly. Mark's told me all about you." She proffered her hand politely.

"Em, y-yes," I stuttered, wondering what he could possibly have told her, given his limited interview technique. Then I hastily pulled myself together and added with a giant fake beaming smile, "And this must be –" I stopped as it occurred to me that I'd no idea of their names.

"Jamie and Amber," said Mrs Murphy.

"Of course! Hi guys, it's lovely to meet you both."

The little boy looked up – a nervous-looking five-year-old, who seemed so afraid of me I decided that he just might be manageable. He had the same colouring as his father, blond hair and blue eyes, but where his father's eyes had been vacant and cold, his were huge pools of worry.

His sister, on the other hand, was a lively-looking toddler, with cheeky brown eyes and a tangle of golden curls. At just over two years of age, the seriousness of the situation had clearly swept right over her head. Her eyes held none of the worry of her brother's, quite the opposite in fact. She smirked at me as if she knew exactly what I was up to.

Could this be the first child to ever actually scare the crap out of me?

In front of the pleasant Mrs Murphy I decided to adopt a kind of jolly-hockey-sticks approach, having already ruefully accepted that my plan of adopting an English accent for the duration of my appointment was obviously not an option.

"So," I said brightly, clasping my hands together, "here we all are!"

The children looked at me blankly.

I was in serious trouble.

"They've had their tea," Mrs Murphy interjected helpfully.

Oh Christ, it had never occurred to me that I was going to be expected to feed them. Let's hope they weren't too fussy.

"Great!" I beamed.

More blank looks.

I could feel Mrs Murphy's eyes bore into me and under her eagle-eyed scrutiny I couldn't breathe. There was nothing for it, she had to go.

"Rightyo, Mrs Murphy, I'll take it from here." My firm tone belied my panic. "Thank you very much for your help. Say thank you to Mrs Murphy, children."

Jamie mumbled something under his breath.

"No!" Amber said, and giggled.

I gave her a look that I hoped implied I would deal with her later.

Just as soon as I figured out how.

I walked Mrs Murphy to the door. When we were out of earshot of the children, she turned to me.

"It really isn't my place to say –" she started.

My heart stopped. It was never good when a sentence started that way.

She was on to me.

"But I'm very glad those children finally have a professional to look after them."

She definitely wasn't on to me.

"Jamie is a little dote but he has taken the whole

91

business very hard," she continued, clearly not noticing my discomfort. "Amber, on the other hand, is –"

"Wilful?"

"Spirited."

"Lively?"

"Bold," she finished. "She definitely needs someone with a strong hand, she's at that age. I'm sure you've seen it before."

I nodded sagely.

"And it's just that her daddy, well, with the hours he works . . ."

I placed a reassuring hand on her arm, hoping she wouldn't feel it shaking.

"I understand, Mrs Murphy – you just leave it with me."

As a very relieved Mrs Murphy left the house I took a deep breath before heading back to the children.

Jamie was sitting on the couch, staring vacantly into space. Amber was nowhere to be seen.

"Jamie, where's your sister?"

He shrugged, looking as if he might burst into tears.

I moved quickly back out to the hall. No sign. Throwing a quick eye up the stairs I ran to the kitchen.

Christ!

She'd clearly scrambled up a strategically placed chair, and was now wobbling precariously on the counter top, one foot on an upturned pot, one chubby arm stretched out towards an open press.

"Amber!" I screeched, lunging towards her.

"Choc-choc!" she gurgled, just as the pot started to slip from under her foot.

I reached her just in time and swung her down to safety.

And then it started.

When I say that the child went ballistic, I mean ballistic times ten. She flung herself on the ground and screeched and kicked and stamped.

I was stunned. The golden-haired cherub was nowhere to be seen and in her place was a Tasmanian Devil.

"Amber! *Amber!*"

I knelt down and tried to placate her but she kicked and punched like a she-devil. As I struggled, I hoped to God that there wasn't a hidden camera in the room. But, amateur and all as I was, I knew that giving in could prove fatal.

"Amber, stop that right now!" I desperately injected an attempt at authority into my tone.

The screeching continued.

Two minutes later I was kneeling, spread-eagled, vainly attempting to pin her two flailing arms in cruciform on the floor, while she delivered kick after kick to my gut.

"Shit!" I cursed as her knee made contact with my forehead.

Just then, Jamie quietly entered the room behind me. Wordlessly he went over to the chair, climbed up on to the counter, reached into the open cupboard and took out an open packet of biscuits. He then climbed back down, as if this kind of activity was perfectly normal, and handed one of the biscuits to the shrieking toddler who instantly stopped her histrionics.

"That's what Daddy does," he said.

Then he reached into the under-the-counter freezer, pulled out a well-battered bag of frozen peas and gave it to me.

"For your head," he said, before turning and leaving the room just as quietly as he'd come in.

I sat there holding the peas. Speechless. This was going from bad to worse.

It was by now seven o'clock and I started to tentatively make noises about bedtime, though to be honest my motives were mostly selfish. I badly needed to regroup before Daddy came home and saw what a mess I was in.

Again, Jamie was no trouble. He silently went upstairs and came back down in his Spiderman pyjamas, got himself a glass of milk and then, whispering "Goodnight" padded back upstairs again.

I looked at Amber.

"Right – bedtime," I said firmly.

"No," she said. Just as firmly.

"Yes."

"No."

Christ.

It took exactly forty-five minutes to get her undressed and into her pyjamas and up the stairs. It took another hour and fifteen minutes before she finally passed out, exhausted, in her cot.

I trudged wearily back down the stairs, and sank down on the bottom step. Taking out my mobile phone I stamped in Harry's number.

Funnily enough, there was no answer.

Harry Fielding, I am going to kill you.

Just then I heard a key in the front door. I shot to my feet and pushed my hair back behind my ears, hoping the exertion of the previous hour and a half didn't show too much on my face.

Mark Fielding looked at me.

"They're both in bed?" he asked, clearly surprised.

"Eh, yes, they're in bed."

"Oh." He looked at his watch. "Right, that's early, isn't it?"

Is it?

"They were exhausted," I said firmly.

"Right. I see. Well, I brought back something to eat." He held up a brown-paper bag with giant grease stains on the side. "Have you eaten?"

I thought about saying no just to get up to my room away from this uncomfortable situation, but the fact that I was starving prevented me. And so, despite being slightly sceptical about what could be lurking inside such unappetising packaging, my stomach overruled my head.

"Eh, no, I haven't actually."

"Well, you can't be expected to cook on your first night," he smiled.

I surely wasn't expected to cook for him too?

I followed him into the kitchen. He dumped the paper bag on the table and got out some plates and cutlery. I hovered trying to help, but his huge frame didn't leave much room.

"Sit down," he said as I bumped into him for the third time.

I sat.

Now that I had a chance to look at him properly, he didn't look quite as scary as he had earlier. For one thing, there was no blood visible on his person. In fact, he was quite good-looking in a kind of Army-Marine kind of way.

Definitely not my type though.

Not like Oliver, tanned, brown-eyed, silky-haired Oliver.

"Ketchup?"

I jumped in my seat as he put a giant plate of what

appeared to be proper chipper-chips in front of me. My eyes widened. There was no way I could have eaten that many carbohydrates in two years, let alone one sitting.

"Eh, no, thanks," I stuttered.

"Mayonnaise?"

Just in case there's any room left in my arteries after the chips?

"I'm fine."

"Fair enough." He squirted a large blob of mayonnaise on his plate.

I sprinkled mine with salt and vinegar, then tentatively picked up one of the giant, greasy chips and put it in my mouth.

Mmmm . . . Goddamn but they were good.

"Onion rings?" He held out a small white bag from which the most delicious odour was seeping.

"Oh, okay," I nodded. I was fast remembering that I hadn't really eaten properly in days.

"So your last boss was a heart surgeon?" he asked.

"Um, yes." I almost smiled. I'd expected that the fake reference from Marsha would impress him.

"In New York?"

I nodded, glad my mouth was still full of chips.

"I hope you won't find it very boring around here."

I shook my head.

"As I said yesterday, I work a lot," he said.

No shit, Sherlock. Arriving home at nine thirty on a Saturday night kind of gave that away.

"So that's why I need someone like you. Of course the main problem is I can't give you set hours. I'm on call every second evening and every second weekend, but an emergency can happen at any stage. Obviously that's why your pay is a bit higher than the normal rate – you know, to reflect the inconvenience."

I nodded again, this time onion rings preventing speech.

"And you're sure that's okay with you?"

"Yes," I managed at last. "Of course."

"It's just that it became a problem with the other girls."

Well, as you'll find out, me and those other girls are not going to have very much in common.

"Well, it won't with me," I said truthfully. "I have friends in Dublin, but fitting around your schedule won't be a problem."

After all, I thought, with the first twinges of guilt, it was the least I could do for the six weeks I'd be here. I was suddenly reminded of the something I'd prepared that morning in advance of my new role. I reached into my bag and took out my laptop.

"Wow, that's a fancy piece of equipment!" His eyes widened at the sight of the brushed steel casing.

"Um, yes, it was a present." I lied. "From my parents."

"Very generous of them."

"Yes, well, anyway. I was thinking about the house-keeping situation." I spoke rapidly in an attempt to get off the subject of my thousand-euro laptop. "I did up a spread sheet and –" I swung the screen around to face him, "you'll see here I've divided all the expenses into categories, so you can see at any stage where the money is going and what it's being spent on. Then you can direct-debit an amount into the household account and, at the end of the month, I can total it all up for you and give you your balance." I obviously left out the fact that this task would be someone else's in month two as I'd be long gone.

"Oh." He went very quiet.

"Or I can do it weekly? I just thought monthly might be often enough, but it's no trouble . . ."

"Mmm . . . yes." He frowned, still looking at the screen. "The trouble is, it wouldn't be quite the same level of detail we'd be used to."

What? What did he want? Graphs? Shit, I should have done graphs, pie charts – some kind of averaging . . .

While these thoughts were flying through my brain, he got up from his chair and unearthed a terracotta jar from behind the bread bin.

"I usually just chuck a few quid into this whenever I have it and the nannies spend it whenever they need to."

I looked at my multi-coloured spread sheet on my all-singing, all-dancing computer and snapped down the lid, flushing bright red.

"Or we could definitely just do that," I muttered as I witnessed Mark Fielding laugh for the first time.

Chapter 11

And so here we were. Monday morning and still winging it.

And I was already exhausted.

Sunday had passed in a haze of domestic chaos, the like of which I could never have imagined. Every time I started to do something, I had to stop to extricate Amber from some death-defying stunt or other. As a result, the house was like a tip and I still hadn't even managed to tackle the vast backlog of washing that seemed to envelop every room. I resolved to make a start as soon as I had Jamie safely in school.

This mission alone had very nearly come between me and my sleep. I'd had problems getting myself out to work in the mornings – how on earth was I going to manage with a five-year-old?

I needn't have worried. On opening his bedroom door that morning, I was stunned to see him sitting quietly on his bed, already fully dressed in his uniform.

"Wow, Jamie, you look eager!"

He shrugged, getting up from the bed and walking past me towards the stairs.

I followed him, mesmerised. I had never before met a child so keen to get to school on a Monday morning. Not even Marsha the Golden Child. But I hadn't time to dwell on Jamie right then. I had way bigger problems on my hands.

Amber.

She seemed to sense that I was under pressure and her behaviour was even more horrific than normal. She flung her breakfast from her high chair and gleefully tipped her beaker onto the floor.

"Right so," I muttered under my breath as I dragged her out of the chair, "you can starve."

Big mistake.

Her newfound freedom went to her head and she tore out of the room and into the TV room.

"*Barney!*" she hollered, flinging herself on the couch.

I ran in after her brandishing a clean nappy. Having spent the first twenty-four hours trying to figure out the correct way to put one of these horrific items on, I now no longer cared if they were back to front.

Two pinched arms and a bruised knee later, I decided she could suffer a while longer in her wet nappy and pyjamas.

By now, Jamie was standing patiently at the front door. I couldn't blame the child. A day at school was infinitely more inviting than what I had ahead of me.

As Amber sprinted another lap of the house, it occurred to me that I had no chance of controlling her on the mile-long walk down the main road to the school. I clutched my forehead and sought frantically for a solution.

Aha – stroller!

There must be one somewhere.

"Jamie, where is Amber's stroller?"

"Her what?"

"Stroller. Pram. Pushchair – you know –" I frantically made a pushing motion with my hands.

"Do you mean her buggy?"

"Yes! Buggy. Whatever."

"She doesn't go in one any more."

"Well, she is today – now where is it kept?"

Jamie shrugged again.

I dashed around the house. It wasn't under the stairs, or in the back kitchen. I wondered if there was a garden shed and ran outside to check.

Sure enough, there was and in it, trapped under a pretty, vintage-looking bike which I presumed to have been Emma's, was a very battered contraption that looked like it might just serve my needs.

Thank God.

Sweeping the compost and cobwebs off the front, I dragged it down the side passage and around to the front door, rapping my shins violently at the same time.

Now I just had to get the possessed child into it.

To my shock and relief, she seemed to view her new vehicle as some kind of treat and clambered in gleefully. With such enthusiasm, actually, that the goddamn thing collapsed.

Crap.

I cursed.

Amber screeched.

Jamie rolled his eyes to heaven.

"*Cooeee!*"

The next house's front door had opened.

"You must be the American!" a high-pitched voice trilled from over the hedge.

Double crap.

This wasn't happening.

"That must be me," I replied sarcastically without looking up. Amber was still screeching as I untangled her from the dusty wreck but she seemed to be unharmed.

"I'm Bernadette Foley, Mark's neighbour."

Please go away, I pleaded silently, mindful of the fact that Amber was still very obviously in her pyjamas with a sodden nappy swinging low between her knees.

"Teresa Murphy was telling me all about you."

Great.

"Are you having a spot of bother?" the shrill voice continued.

What does it bloody look like, you stupid woman?

"You do know that Emma didn't use a buggy? She didn't believe in them, used a sling. Said it formed a better bond."

I really hadn't time for this but there was nothing for it but to look up and make eye contact with the irritating Bernadette Foley. She was just as I had envisaged. Middle-aged, arms folded across an ample bosom, little bird-like eyes taking every in every single mistake I was making.

"Really. That's very interesting but –"

"Oh yes, Emma-God-rest-her-soul –" she whispered this bit, gesturing towards Jamie with her beady eyes, "was a firm believer in the sling."

I had never heard such rot. If she thought I was going to strap that banshee to my person like I was some kind of pack horse, she had another think coming.

"Well, I'm not." My voice was firm. "It's very bad for the child.

"No!"

"Oh yes," I shook my head sagely. "For their posture. A disaster."

"Never!"

Aha! Now she was showing me some kind of respect. I started to warm to my subject.

"Oh yes, all the latest research says so – no one in New York uses slings any more."

"Oh!" she gasped, clasping her hands together. "Isn't it as well she never knew! She was such an angel, you know, a beautiful, beautiful girl. Such a tragedy, such a –"

"Good morning, Mrs Foley," interrupted a cheery voice.

Thank God, someone to distract her. I needed to make my escape – Jamie was starting to shift from foot to foot beside me.

"Good morning, Dawn!" Mrs Foley called out to the woman on the footpath. "Have you met Mark's new nanny!"

Oh please, I begged, the last thing I needed was another old biddy to quiz me.

But I needn't have worried. The girl was about my age and winked at me as she held out her hand.

"Lovely to meet you. I'm Dawn Kinahan. I live in No 9, three doors down."

"Holly, Holly Green." The relief of meeting someone semi-normal swept over me.

"Holly's from America," Mrs Foley announced.

I rolled my eyes. It was too late now to explain.

"Oh lovely, what part?" Dawn smiled.

"Eh, New York." I answered in an I'm-totally-not-from-New-York accent.

"Well, welcome to Duncane!" Dawn winked again. "Are you having buggy trouble?"

I nodded, looking down at the cursed contraption. "I don't think it's been used in a while."

"No," Dawn said, "I don't remember ever seeing Emma with it – I think she used the sling."

"Oh! I was only just saying, isn't it better she never knew?" Mrs Foley was bristling with excitement.

"About what?" Dawn looked up.

I could feel the blood rushing to my face. Now I was for it.

"About the damage she was doing!" There was no stopping Mrs Foley.

"Damage?" Dawn looked at me in confusion.

"Yes," I couldn't look her in the eye, "to their posture."

"All the New York research says so!" Mrs Foley said knowingly.

Dawn looked back at me and then smiled, her eyes practically dancing with mischief.

"Oh, *that* damage!" she said. "Sure I was only reading about that the other day, in *Parenting Weekly* – very serious it is too! All those poor teenagers, walking around like hunchbacks."

I shot her a look. After all, there was no need to overdo it, but she was on a roll.

"And as for breastfeeding – who would have known –"

"It was lovely meeting you, Mrs Foley." I put out my hand firmly before the older woman's eyes could get any bigger. "Dawn, would you mind giving me a hand with the buggy?"

"Of course!" she grinned, "and then I'll walk you to the school, just to show you the way. Bye, Mrs Foley!"

Mark's next-door neighbour retreated reluctantly back into her house, and it wasn't long before the buggy was righted with Dawn's help, Amber was reinstated in it and we were on our way to the school.

"So, New York, eh?"

"Yep."

"What brought you over here?"

For a brief minute Cain flashed into my mind and the fact that I had come to Ireland to escape the shame of that entanglement.

"Ah you know, nothing like a change of scenery." I almost smiled as I thought of Oliver.

"True," Dawn nodded. "The furthest I've travelled was from Cork to Dublin and then down to here. I often wondered about working in a different country, but I couldn't help feeling it would be the same thing only with different weather."

I froze.

Cain Hobson. Oliver Conlon.

My American married lover, my Irish also-in-a-relationship lover.

Cain, Oliver. Oliver, Cain.

She was right. What the hell was I doing?

Chapter 12

I couldn't get Dawn's words out of my head as I trudged wearily back towards the house. Not even the fact that Amber had fallen fast asleep in the buggy could cheer me up.

Cain Hobson, Oliver Conlon.

Oliver Conlon, Cain Hobson.

Same shit, different weather.

So blown by Dawn's words had I been, that I had even agreed to attend a Mother and Toddler Group with her on Thursday morning.

A Mother and Toddler Group?

Man, had I lost my way!

With a heavy heart I plodded wearily around the kitchen, scraping cereal off the ground and gathering up dirty breakfast dishes. What in God's name was I doing? I could feel a wave of panic start to spread through my body as the reality of the situation I now found myself in started to rear its ugly head.

Surely this was my worst mess ever. Even Kelly, in her

wildest imagination – and Kelly had a very wild imagination (I blamed the years she'd spent loved up on Ecstasy . . .) – wouldn't believe all this if I told her.

Just then Amber appeared at the kitchen door.

"Barney?" she suggested, her little eyes huge with hope.

I hadn't the energy to fight. Whatever Barney was, she could have it.

"Why not?"

She ran into the television room and came back brandishing a DVD case.

"Awan dis one," she said.

Ah, so Barney was a television programme. You're probably surprised I didn't know that. Don't be. When I told you I had very little to do with children before this venture, I wasn't joking.

I sat on the couch with her as the opening credits rolled and to my surprise she snuggled into me. A huge purple dinosaur leapt into view and still I sat, beyond caring any more.

"*Gee, boys and girls,*" he bellowed, "*what would y'all like to do today?*"

Fancy that, Barney was American!

To my horror a fat tear started to slide down my cheek at the familiar accent. And that was all the encouragement I needed. Five minutes later, I was sniffing furiously, to disguise the fact I was crying from Amber, and it was all I could do to stop myself climbing into the TV to join the multi-racial smattering of overly happy kids for a big fat dino-hug. Surely the purple monstrosity would tell me everything was going to be okay?

Or would he? Might the cuddly pillar of wisdom look me in the eye and tell me to call it a day?

Head back to New York and admit that I'd made a huge mistake, write Oliver off to experience and tell nobody, ever, that I had ended up in a three-bed semi in a small Irish town watching inane children's programmes because of a man.

The more I watched, the more certain I became that what I was watching was essentially Dr Phil for toddlers. It could be only minutes before he'd come out with something like: "*All together now, kids: There are no victims – only volunteers!*"

And sure enough he was bursting into song now. Some rubbish about raindrops being lemon drops and gum drops. But I wasn't really listening. I was still thinking about Doctor Phil. He'd been Auntie Monica's guilty pleasure and she'd make me sit through his show over and over again. Well, no prizes for guessing what he'd say to me if I was on his couch right now.

'Holly,' he'd drawl with his Texan twang, 'Sometimes you make the right decision, sometimes you make the decision right.'

Oh my God.

That was it.

Sometimes you make the right decision.

Sometimes you make the decision right.

On and on Barney sang, with the hordes of annoying overly animated children chanting along with him.

I started to hum along.

At first in my head: *Sometimes you make the right decision.*

Then under my breath: *Sometimes you make the decision right.*

Then louder: *Make the decision right!*

And then louder and louder until I had scooped a

bewildered Amber up into my arms and was waltzing around the room screeching: *Make the decision right!*

Round and round the room we went, Amber by now in hysterics of laughter.

Round and round until my purple saviour stopped singing.

I flopped back down onto the couch. My moment of hysteria over.

But it had worked. I was no longer longing to sob in the arms of a dinosaur, and miraculously my head was definitely clearer. There was no doubt but that I had made some seriously dodgy decisions in the last few days but there was no point in thinking about that now.

Now was the time to make it right.

As was my habit in a crisis, I started to think about my time in the kitchens in downtown New York. While my family firmly believed I had squandered those years of my life, I knew better, as had Monica when she sent me to work there. Those years had been the true foundation of my education. College had simply built upon them.

For it was in the grimy kitchen of Fontaines Grill, on the corner of 42nd Street that I had first come in contact with Fat Tony Abadesso.

Fat Tony was Portuguese and not only was he fat, he was gargantuan. The head chef at Fontaines, he was primarily responsible for its rise from a measly fifty covers a night to two hundred plus. In fact, I was there for its all-time high of two hundred and eighty and it was this experience I found myself thinking about now.

There were definitely better chefs in New York than Fat Tony, but you have never seen a man to mobilise his troops with such vigour, such energy and such determination.

But his main talent was his insurmountable ability to

pull his team out of the shit – or *le merde!* as Tony would bellow – no matter what problems arose.

Fifty orders of monkfish when we had only catered for twenty-five? With a roar he would stride from the kitchen and come back with a box of monkfish on his shoulder.

Or the night that Anton, the broiler chef, had broken the handle off the giant grill in the middle of service, and Tony had plunged his huge ladle into the slot, twisting it until it did just as good a job. Which was lucky for Anton as Tony's next solution was for the tiny Italian to stick his own hand in instead.

Yes, someone's head would always roll later but, at that moment, while food had yet to leave his kitchen, all Tony was interested in was *fixing* the problem.

Which brings me to that memorable Saturday night.

The kitchen was already at bursting point. I was on wash-up with two Mexicans, but the chefs were a man down. Anton had done the unmentionable: he had phoned in sick. I remembered thinking it had better be terminal.

Then, at about eight o'clock, from the far corner of the kitchen, came a guttural scream. Now, injuries were nothing new in Fontaines, in fact, they were almost welcomed, worn as a badge of honour, the more stomach-churning the better.

So I knew when I heard the roar that this was serious. Raising my head from the sink I saw Louis standing, white as sheet, cleaver in one hand, severed little finger in the other.

Tony strode down from where he'd been checking the dishes as they were handed to the waiting staff.

"*Fuck*!" he roared.

Next thing, he shoved Louis towards the back door. "You go, get seen to."

"Should I go with him, Chef?" Jermaine the pastry chef stepped forward.

"Is it his fucking *tongue*?" roared Tony.

"Eh, no, Chef," spluttered Jermaine, retreating rapidly back to his station.

Frederick, the front of house manager, ran to ring for an ambulance.

Tony looked wildly around the kitchen.

"You!" He stabbed a huge index finger in my direction.

I looked around, hoping in vain there was someone in close proximity to me that he was gesticulating at.

"Me?" I stuttered.

"Yes, you!" he hollered. "Get a hat and an apron and get back here. You can do starters – Juan, you move up to the broiler – now everyone else *back to work*!"

He had turned his back and was striding back up to his station.

I stood speechless.

He turned.

I ran. Quickly.

Three and a half hours later, service was over. Two hundred and eighty covers. I sat in the staff room, unable to move. My clothes were saturated, the veins in my forehead throbbed relentlessly and my fingertips were so burnt and raw that the FBI would never be able to print me.

There was a noise behind me.

I looked up to see Fat Tony enter the room. I made to get up but I couldn't – my poor body had seized. Luckily he gestured to me to stay sitting.

He pulled a chair over and sat down facing me. Too close for comfort.

It was just me and him. Like that time when I had

shared a lift in Bloomingdales with Brooke Shields, I could think of nothing intelligent to say.

"That – was – mental," I eventually managed.

Fat Tony shrugged. "It was good, yes."

"Good? It was *horrendous*!"

Fat Tony shrugged again, then looked at me.

"Vat is your name?" he asked, lowering his giant head towards mine.

"Holly," I said warily, his huge bloodshot eyes and dripping forehead far too close for comfort.

"Vell, Polly, vat would you have recommended? That we close for the evening because one stupid foocker couldn't keep his pinkie from under his tools?"

"Well, no not exactly but –"

"But nothing, Polly, but nothing!" He moved even closer and I could smell his intensity. "The true mark of a man is not the trouble he gets into, but the way he gets himself out of it. You remember that, Polly – it will get you far."

He heaved his giant bulk from his seat and went to leave. At the door he turned.

"You vant to be a chef?"

I shook my head silently.

"Pity," he muttered, then turned and left.

No, I didn't want to be a chef, but I never, ever forgot Fat Tony's words. It wasn't the trouble you got into, but the way you got out of it.

I was slap-bang in the middle of the weeds now, but like that fateful Saturday night in Fontaines, now was not the time to analyse how I got there, but to start to plan how in hell I was going to get out.

112

Chapter 13

Resolutely I got up from the couch. Three days were enough to know that while Amber was engrossed in her DVD right now, it was unlikely that this respite would last very long.

The thing was, I just didn't know where to start.

A sudden craving for coffee reminded me of the way I started most projects. For a second I thought longingly of the home-roasted coffee in Abraco on East 7th Street, before remembering that I was standing in the kitchen of your average house in your average small Irish town. Without opening the cupboard door, I knew that all I would find would be tea bags, and plenty of them, or even worse a dried-out half-jar of instant coffee . . .

That's where I could start.

I scrabbled through the cluttered worktop, looking for a pen and paper. A few minutes later, chewed pencil and a torn envelope in hand, I sat down.

I needed a list and I needed it now.

At the top I printed neatly: *SHOPPING LIST*

And below that: *decent coffee*

Let's face it, there was no chance of making it through this without it. I smiled briefly as I wondered how long Mark's terracotta jar would last under my jurisdiction.

The thing was, the maximum amount of time I'd be here would be six weeks. Six weeks – how bad could it be? And I really hoped that I'd manage to meet up with Oliver by the weekend. If I found out then that he wanted nothing to do with me, I wouldn't even be staying six weeks.

But that wasn't going to happen.

It couldn't.

Pulling myself out of yet another Oliver daydream, I looked around the kitchen. The grim reality was that I couldn't last even one more day in such a mess, let alone six weeks.

While I might not have seen much of my illustrious new employer in the last few days, there were signs of him everywhere. He had clearly swept through the kitchen like a whirlwind earlier that morning. It was actually possible to pinpoint his exact movements by the used teabag stuck precariously to the side of the sink, the toast crumbs on the counter and the crummy knife still embedded in the butter. Nice.

And it didn't stop there.

Granted some of it was my responsibility: the breakfast things were still caked in half-eaten cereal, and even Amber's beaker still sat upside down in a puddle of juice on the floor.

But it went further than that. The Formica worktops were sagging under an indescribable amount of clutter, most of it of veterinary origin. Bundles of periodicals balanced carefully on dog-eared docket books, and bottles of multi-coloured potions nestled side by side with the half-eaten loaves of white bread. The microwave was in danger of toppling off the work top with the volume of unopened (or opened and hastily reclosed) post that was stuffed behind it. And on top of the washing machine was the biggest load of laundry I had ever seen. In fact it loomed so large that I had my doubts that any of the clothes at the bottom would actually still fit anyone, let alone be still in fashion.

The thing was, even if this kitchen was spotless it would still look cluttered. There were handmade pots on the windowsill overflowing with now-dead herbs. Chunky woven baskets held a combination of eggs, tape measures and half chewed pencils. Art was obviously a great love of Emma's as it appeared that every single scribble the children had ever created was still stuck to the door of the fridge.

Just as I could feel my resolve starting to droop, my mobile rang.

Could it be Oliver?

No, it was my mother.

"Holly! I tried your office extension just now, but I just got a funny tone."

Damn. I had said nothing to my family of the more recent developments in my life. It had all happened so quickly. I scrabbled frantically to remember what country she thought I was in.

Ireland. I thought.

I needed to think fast. At least she hadn't phoned the main number, given that the Dublin office was probably still under the illusion that I was back in New York. I wasn't really sure how long it would take for news of my 'family emergency' to filter through.

"No, Mum, I'm out on a job at the minute."

"Oh, I thought you said you were spending this week at your desk?"

Gosh, there must a lull in Marsha's achievements for her to remember that kind of detail about me. I'd had to remind her I was sitting my finals at Stern practically every day for six months.

"Yeah, well, I'm subcontracted out to a company for the next few weeks . . ." I scrabbled frantically for a plausible story. "It's kind of like I'm working for a client."

"Oh." For a moment she sounded impressed, but then added, "They didn't want you themselves then."

Now that's the Mum I know and love.

"Well, of course they did, but it's a very good client, and they wouldn't take no for an answer."

So there! I almost snipped, before remembering the truth . . .

"Oh." She still wasn't sure.

Time to change the subject.

"So how are all the others?"

"Well, Marsha and Steve have gone to Florida with the kids for a few weeks, and then Marsha is bringing the kids home here for Christmas –"

Ha, I knew there had to be a reason for her to think of ringing me . . .

I walked with the phone to my ear to the door of the TV room in the hope that Amber wasn't up to anything death-defying. But to my astonishment she was still glued to the TV. That Barney show was a miracle.

"And you know Chad is coming too, so that just leaves you . . ."

"And Kelly?" I interjected, ducking quickly back from

the TV-room door as the Purple One burst into song again.

"Yes, Kelly too of course, though she's in Paris at the moment."

Aha, that explained the overseas ringtone.

"Didn't she mail you?"

Yes, probably to my GS email account.

"She was talking about meeting you in Dublin."

Shit.

"Maybe even staying a few days with you?"

Double shit.

"But now she's to go to that trade show in London."

Thank God. My life stopped flashing before me.

Though if I had to explain my current situation to any of my siblings, Kelly would have been my preferred choice. We'd been thick as thieves as children but, in a funny way, even though she was younger than me by a year, Kelly always seemed to need to mother me. Whereas the others, if they knew of my present predicament, would just roll their eyes and say they really hadn't expected any different from me, Kelly would just look at me with big teary, soulful eyes and tell me how I deserved so much more. To be fair, I'm not sure which would be worse.

"So when are you going back?"

Not this again.

"I'm not sure, Mum – a month, six weeks maybe. I'll know more after the weekend – I mean, in the next week or so," I hastily corrected myself. "Look, I'd really better go, I've a conference call with Brussels in fifteen minutes, and I need to talk to a few people first."

"Oh, okay – don't forget your brother is on the *Late Late* this –"

But I'd hung up. I really couldn't cope with her today.

Sitting at the table I lowered my head into my hands. It was a good job she couldn't see me now. All those years of trying to prove her wrong, wasted.

Stop! I banged the table with my fist.

I had to be positive about this. I would somehow track Oliver down so that he could see me across a crowded bar, and promptly burst with happiness. So much so that he would then drag me from the bar, to the nearest hotel room (or car, or bus stop – I was warming to this) and I might never even have to come back to this dreadful house, with its dreadful children and horrible father.

In fact, given that this scenario was so eminently possible, it was the least I could do to bring some order to the house so that my replacement would have some chance of survival.

I did this kind of thing with companies all the time.

Why should an untidy house be any different?

Resolutely I stood up.

Get off your ass, Holly Green – get this place sorted, get your man back then get to hell out of here.

I started to work.

Chapter 14

Two hours and three Barney DVD changes later, the kitchen looked worse than ever. Tidying had had a snowball effect. As I moved about I kept finding more and more that had to be done. Cupboards full of out-of-date food, drawers that once opened spewed their contents in such a way that made closing them again virtually impossible. I felt like binning every useless hand-woven teacloth and crochet oven glove that I came across but frustratingly had to be mindful that their owner was no longer with us.

And of course it wasn't just the kitchen that needed urgent attention. I had walked slowly around the entire house to assess the full extent of the situation.

It was a not a big house by any stretch of the imagination but yet should have had ample room for such a small family. Downstairs was the kitchen/dining room, a TV room and, behind a locked door, what I assumed was a "good" sitting room.

Upstairs was the master bedroom, Jamie's room,

another smaller bedroom and a nursery for Amber. I was housed in a converted loft, beside which was jammed a tiny attic for storage. However, once I'd established on arrival that the wireless broadband network stretched that far, this arrangement suited me just fine.

No, it wasn't the lack of space that was the problem, but rather the clutter that trickled out of every room. There were clothes everywhere, bundles ran into other bundles and it was no longer possible to see where the clean heaps ended and the dirty began. The mere fact that every bed was strewn with a beautifully handmade but hideously gaudy patchwork quilt did not show the already small rooms in the best light, nor did the fact that every room was painted a different dark sludgy colour, the ox-blood red of the hall, the olive green of the TV room, even the kitchen was a dark midnight blue, enough to put anyone into a gloomy mood.

The TV room was strewn with toys. The carpet was splotched with stains and encrusted food and tiny multi-coloured plastic bricks crunched underfoot no matter how carefully I made my way from one side to another.

I was almost sorry I'd started. The only break I'd taken was to shoehorn Amber into the buggy again so that I could collect Jamie from school and right now he too was plonked in front of the TV with a cheese sandwich.

But, it had to be said, I was really starting to warm to my project. Only falling short of actually writing Terms of Reference for myself, my idea of treating it like a problem company had really grown legs. The shopping list now ran to three pages, which in turn looked nothing compared to my to-do list, which I'm proud to say featured several spider diagrams.

As I sat cross-legged on the floor with the entire contents of the under-the-sink cupboard scattered around me on the floor, a voice suddenly boomed across the kitchen.

"*What the hell is going on here?*"

From my position on the kitchen floor I looked up. Mark Fielding, a grinning Amber on one hip, glowered down at me.

"I'm sorry, I-I didn't hear you come in," was all I could stammer.

"That much is obvious."

Wincing at the sarcasm, I scrambled to my feet, furious I'd been caught at such a disadvantage.

"Well, I wasn't expecting you home just yet."

Like not for another six hours, going on your normal working routine.

"Let me make something clear, Holly," his eyes were like blue steel as he glared at me, "it's never a good sign when someone tells you they weren't expecting you home yet. I will come home, when, and as often, as I like, so if you are to stay here it would do you good to remember that."

I was so stunned by the unfairness of his attitude I could feel tears prickling at the back of my eyes.

"And as for this chaos?" He waved an arm around the kitchen. "I can't imagine for a second what you were thinking."

Okay, that was enough. Insulting me was one thing, insulting my afternoon's work, a whole other issue.

I drew myself up to my full height.

"Well, Mr Fielding, I'll tell you exactly what I was thinking. I was thinking that it might be nice for all of us if this kitchen was a little more organised. That maybe you might prefer to be able to open a drawer or cupboard without having its contents puked over your head every time. That, as you obviously don't intend to ever deal with that pile of post, we might come up with a different place to store it so that the chance of the microwave falling on one of the children's heads isn't so high. That maybe you weren't intending eating all of the out-of-date food that's lying around and that maybe, just maybe, it might be a better idea to keep your veterinary paraphernalia in a more suitable location!"

He glared at me but I matched him, eyeball to eyeball, before continuing.

"And yes, it doesn't look much at the moment, but that's because it was such a goddamn mess to start off with. Which leads me to another thing, Mr Fielding. It would do you good to remember that, if I *am* to stay here, I will expect order to be kept on the house, and any changes I make to be adhered to."

He had the grace to rein in his glare momentarily at my outburst but recovered quickly enough to bark back with, "Well, maybe to facilitate your bringing order to my house, it might be an idea for me to take the children out for a while. Clearly their supervision is hindering your effectiveness."

His tone didn't faze me, I had dealt with worse than him before and, if it was sarcasm he wanted, I was more than able to dish it out.

"Well, that would be very helpful, Mr Fielding, perhaps you might bring those bags to the launderette on your way and I'll be needing cash for that shopping list. I'm not sure that the €3.50 in the jar will accommodate my current needs. Now, if you'll excuse me, I have work to do."

I turned back to the sink, my hands shaking. The whole altercation had stunned me but, now that I had time to think, I couldn't help wondering if I had overstepped some kind of boundary? Maybe I should have asked him first before I tore his kitchen asunder? I had no idea what nannies were meant to do. Should I have just sat on my ass and watched television for the week? Who'd have thought it would be this complicated?

I stubbornly ignored the chaos that ensued as Mark grappled with Amber to get her ready for their outing. To be honest, it wasn't exactly clear if my help would have been appreciated. Up and down the hall she ran screeching as he strode behind her, bent double, brandishing a tiny pink jacket like a matador's cape.

The silence when the door shut behind them was a massive relief. It was the first time I'd been alone in three days. I looked around again. Whether my project was right or wrong, one thing was for sure, I couldn't leave it as it was now.

And I only had an hour.

With no children underfoot, I zoomed around like a woman possessed, mentally dividing tasks into what should be done now, and what could be done later. I turned a blind eye to the mouldy food in the back of the fridge, but scooped armfuls of toys up from the floor. Up and down the stairs I ran, all the time ticking things off my mental checklist while swiftly adding others in their place.

Counter tops cleared – tick!

Grubby skirting-boards – tomorrow

Bins emptied – tick!

Change children's bed linen – tomorrow

And so on.

I would show that insufferable man that there was method to my madness.

As I struggled out the back door with the last two black garbage bags, I heard the front door bell ring.

Oh crap, who could that be?

I took a quick look around the room and cursed, I could have done with one last burst of activity before anyone else arrived.

Squaring my shoulders I opened the door, hoping it was someone I could get rid of quickly.

To my dismay it was that nice girl Dawn that I'd met earlier. She was pushing her buggy and holding up a paper bag that said *Maguire's Bakery* in pink writing on the side.

She must have noticed my face drop.

"I-it's okay," she stammered. "It was just an idea, if you're busy . . ."

I instantly felt like a bitch. Torn between getting my work finished and the unexpected longing for some friendly company, I said, "No, of course not, come in!" and practically pulled her in the door.

I could see her eyes widen as she looked around the hall.

"I've never been in here before," she said. "Interesting colour scheme."

"Unfortunately the paint is the least of my problems," I said wryly.

Her face dropped as she caught sight of my clearly unfinished business.

"Holy Mother of God, what's happened here?"

Oh, goddamn it, I'd nothing to lose. I filled her in on the project, Mark's reaction, and my whole feeling of regret that I'd started at all.

"Right then!" She took off her coat and rolled up her sleeves. "Shout."

I looked at her blankly. "I couldn't expect you –"

"Daniel is asleep – we'll have it finished by the time he wakes. It might mean that you'll have to hold him while I eat my cream slice. Now, what do you want me to do?"

I couldn't help thinking that Grantham Sparks could have done with a few Dawns on the team. I handed her a mop and bucket before struggling upstairs with the vacuum.

And she was right. In twenty minutes we had done enough for my point to Mark Fielding to be well and truly made, and the kettle was on. I even had developed a longing for whatever was in that paper bag.

True to her prediction, six-week-old Daniel woke just as the kettle boiled and was duly plonked in my arms as Dawn deftly made a pot of tea.

I might have been more comfortable making the tea.

He really was very small.

"He won't break, you know."

I turned and saw her looking at me out of the corner of her eye as I balanced him carefully on my knee.

"I've never held one so small." It was out before I remembered.

"Oh?" She sounded surprised.

"Well, not in a long time," I stammered. "Most of my charges have been toddler-aged upwards."

That's why I'm so successful with that particular age group, I thought sarcastically, thinking of Amber.

"Did you always want to work with children?"

"No," I answered truthfully, "I wanted to be a writer." I laughed, that was the first truthful sentence I'd spoken in a week.

"That's a bit of a change."

You don't know the half of it, darling . . .

"How about you?" I thought I'd best quit with my life story before the lies started again. "What do you do?"

She looked at me blankly, then at the wriggling baby in my arms and then back at me.

"Oh, yes, sorry." Oops!

"Well, I used to work in the bank – I was assistant manager actually, and that's where me met – but Graham, well, he thinks it's better, well, *we* think it's better if I don't go back. It took us a long time to have Daniel and, well, now that he's here I prefer to be with him."

"Don't you miss working?" I asked with a sinking heart, wondering would I ever find anyone that I had anything in common with ever again.

"Well, I do actually. I miss the chat, the interaction with other adults. But you see, I had two miscarriages before Daniel and I swore that if we were ever lucky enough, well, that there was no way I was going back." She smiled brightly. "So here I am."

I couldn't help smiling with her.

"Yes, here we are."

Chapter 15

I clicked the mouse and waited. Luckily the broadband in the house was excellent – I'd have gone insane altogether without it. After all, it was my last remaining tenuous link with my old world. Reading the financial pages with my laptop balanced on my knee at six thirty every morning was the only time of the day I could pretend to myself that everything was normal. So adamant was I that this sidestep was temporary, I kept religiously to my old routine: *Financial Times*, *New York Times* and then the *Irish Times*. A quick skim through each and then my reward: Facebook.

Facebook was my other way of pretending that everything was normal. Not that I could post on it myself, mind you. No, not when half my friends thought I was in New York, and the other half thought I was in Ireland. No, I'd become the type of Facebook user I'd always sneered at – a lurker – and simply used it for keeping an eye on everyone else.

And by everyone else, I mean Oliver.

Trouble was, he also seemed to have vanished off the radar.

Initially I comforted myself with the assumption that he was too upset to post anything, but now I was starting to get worried. I'd been hoping to get some idea of his plans for the weekend and I was fast starting to run out of time.

I closed down my laptop. Nothing today.

For God's sake, Oliver – help me out here! I really didn't want to ruin the whole surprise by ringing him. But if this information-drought went on much longer I'd have to.

I needed some hope. A goal. A sliver of some sense of purpose . . .

And I needed it this morning more than any other morning so far.

Today was the day of the Mother and Toddler Group.

Why I'd agreed to it I'll never know. Well, I suppose I do know . . . Dawn had caught me in a moment of weakness. Moments that prior to my moving to Meadowlands had been few and far between . . .

I braced myself.

How bad could it be?

Dawn called for me at ten and after much deliberation we decided to walk down to the Community Centre. Driving was just too complicated what with the whole palaver about car seats and whether or not Amber was big enough for a booster, whatever in God's name that was. My efforts to hide my total lack of knowledge regarding the pinning of a rambunctious two-year-old to the back seat of a car were admirable but I couldn't help feeling I'd only just got away with it.

It didn't bode well for the rest of the morning.

I did however console myself with the fact that Amber was due her nap, and with any luck would fall asleep on the walk down and not wake until we were safely home again.

Given her 'issues' that really would be best for all concerned.

The walk down was perfectly pleasant. The small town was built on a series of hills through which flowed a wide, lazy river. A pleasant change from the frantic traffic of Dublin, not to mention Manhattan. Everyone seemed to just amble along in the sunny October morning, casually going about their business. There were very few shops. I counted a rather modern-looking butcher's, a florist's, a purple hairdresser's with *Kutz n Kurlz* written above it in lilac script, and a smallish supermarket.

Obviously you needed to go further afield for anything outside of bread, milk, steak or a blue rinse.

Noticing Amber's blonde curls lolling back, I could feel the tension leave my body.

Maybe this wasn't going to be so bad after all.

The Community Centre was built overlooking the river, a pretty building clad in old stone. I was glad that we hadn't driven as its car park was already full to overflowing with giant SUV's and station wagons.

"Quite a crowd this morning," Dawn observed.

"Mmm," I murmured, thinking this could go one of two ways: either I wouldn't be noticed in the crowd, or I would have a cast of thousands knowing instantly that I was a fraud.

I took Dawn's lead and navigated the ancient stroller through the front door and into the airy hall beyond. Inside were about two dozen women in various groups dotted around the hall, each group bearing a startling resemblance to old wagon circles in the Wild West with their buggies fanning out around them.

"Dawn!" a voice from one of the larger groups called and my heart sank.

So much for sneaking a quick cup of coffee and then sidling out the door before anyone had noticed us.

As I rolled reluctantly over behind her, I noticed that each of these ladies had a buggy identical to Dawn's, but for the colour: various acidic shades of pod-shaped contraptions with futuristic brushed metal frames and matching diaper bags.

Shit. These women meant business.

"I want *ooooouuuuuut*!" Amber rose from her sleep and started grappling with her straps.

Double shit.

And it wasn't just me that looked instantly uneasy.

The lime-green-buggy lady automatically pulled her contraption closer to her, easing the blankets up around her charge's ears as she did so. Another lady, her vehicle burnt orange, swiftly zipped up her diaper bag and stuffed it under her chair, and yet another, candy pink this time, cautiously slid several half-full coffee cups towards the centre of the table.

"You must be Mark's new nanny!" The lime-green lady held out her hand.

"Umm, yes, I am." I attempted to shake her hand while pinning the squirming Amber down.

"Let her go over to the play area," Dawn suggested, helpfully gesturing towards a matted area with blocks and other various plastic toys where several bigger kids were playing. "She'll be fine over there."

The sigh of relief around the table was audible as Amber tore off across the room. I could see out of the corner of my eye several other mothers throw a wary glance in her direction as she reached their children but I ignored them. Their kids were bigger. If she didn't kill them she would make them stronger.

"So, how are you finding it?"

The question originated from the lime-green way but instantly five heads leaned forward in anticipation of the answer.

"Fine. So far so good," I lied.

The five heads simultaneously leaned back out in disappointment.

"But you've not been there that long," the lady with the turquoise steed consoled herself.

"True," the others nodded sagely.

There was an awkward silence.

"Where are my manners?" Dawn exclaimed. "Girls, this is Holly Green. Holly, this is Ellen . . ." (lime green) "Rachel . . ." (bubble-gum pink) "Karen . . ." (turquoise) "Sarah . . ." (burnt orange) "and last but not least Hannah . . ." (black – must have been half-price) "Holly, let me get you a coffee – back in a tick!"

Shit, she was gone.

There was another awkward silence.

"So," Ellen started, clearly not satisfied with my previous answer, "no problems so far then?"

I was about to answer when a shriek came from the play area. Amber had a grip on the back wheels of a rather large farm vehicle with a much bigger boy tugging on the front, and was screeching "*Miiiine!*"

"If you'll excuse me . . ."

131

I dashed over but the little boy had let go, flinging Amber flat on her back with the huge green tractor plonked on her chest. I waited for the howl but it didn't come. So thrilled was she with her victory, the fall meant nothing. I scanned the room to see if the little boy's mother was glaring at me, but luckily no one seemed to be watching, so I sidled back to my seat, in front of which Dawn had thankfully put a steaming cup of coffee.

"So what do you think of Mark?" Rachel flushed as pink as her buggy.

"I expect she hardly sees him," Karen snorted. "Remember what Tonya said."

"Tonya?" I questioned.

"Mark's last nanny," Dawn answered helpfully.

"No, Katerina was his last one," Hannah corrected. "Tonya was the one before that, just after Eva."

Aha! Hannah was clearly some kind of sharp-minded professional which explained the black choice of vehicle.

"I didn't realise there had been so many!" I shot a look at Dawn as if to ask why I was only hearing this now.

"Oh God, yes, poor Mark hasn't been very lucky." Rachel had a dreamy look in her eyes.

"Our Rach has a bit of a crush . . ." Hannah winked at me. "She thinks Mark is rather –"

"It's not just me!" Rachel shrieked, now pinker than her buggy. "Let's face it, *you* wouldn't kick him out of bed!"

I listened. Aghast. Could they possibly be talking about the same man I knew? Mark the stony-faced asshole that barely had a word to throw to a dog?

Dawn caught my look of incredulity and patted my arm. "Apparently he wasn't always so grumpy," she explained.

"Oh, no!" Rachel was still rolling her eyes. "Always quiet, but in a strong tall manly way."

Cue more shrieks of laughter, until Hannah added solemnly, "To be fair, you can hardly blame him, after . . ." Her voice trailed off.

The others stopped their shrieking instantly.

"Such a tragedy." Now Rachel looked like she might cry.

"So you all knew Emma then?" I enquired, grateful for the slight change in subject. The thought of anyone finding that man attractive was a bridge too far for me.

"I didn't really," Dawn answered. "I was never really around until I went on maternity leave, and that was after, well, you know . . ."

"Myself and Rach knew her," answered Karen. "We weren't close or anything, but that didn't matter to Emma, she treated everyone as if they were her best friend. She was lovely, so full of life, always dashing around."

"They were such a sweet couple," Rachel sighed. "They just worshipped each other."

The others all nodded in silence.

As if on cue, there was another squeal from the play area. I made my excuses and dashed. By the time I got back, having wrestled some other poor child's doll and pram off Amber, they had moved onto an argument about weaning, whatever that was.

It seemed to have all kicked off when Rachel had produced some dreadful-looking gloop called baby rice for cherub-faced Fiona, which drew shrieks of derision from both Karen and Sarah. Apparently at four months Fiona was not the "recommended age for solids". Judging by the fact that Sarah was breastfeeding a child that looked to me like it should be at school, I could see how she might be of the opinion that any other food was bad. Back and forth went the arguments and I sat petrified in case my "professional opinion" was sought.

"So how's Jamie these days?" said a voice in my ear. Thank God. I turned my back on the warring females. It was Ellen.

"Eh. Okay."

"Good, good. I always worry about poor little Jamie."

"Oh really? Well, actually now that you mention it, he's, well, a bit . . ."

"Quiet?"

"Well, yes. Quiet. Not that I'm objecting." I gestured towards raucous Amber who was flinging coloured balls out of a pit across the room.

"Oh, I wouldn't worry – he was always quiet. My Oisín is the same age, you see, but Jamie always seemed like a child with the weight of the world on his little shoulders."

"Really?" I was surprised. "Even before his mum . . . well, you know . . ." Jamie had barely spoken two words to me since my arrival and I had just put it down to all the upheaval in the last eight months of his life. It never occurred to me that he'd always been like that. To be honest, I'd been kind of glad. Compared to his sister he was delightfully low-maintenance.

"Oh yes, he was always quiet. I saw him a lot as he and Oisín used to go to Little Kickers together."

"Little what?"

"Kickers – it's football training for pre-schoolers. Jamie was quite good too."

"Was?"

"Well, we haven't seen him in months. It's a pity really – it was the one time of the week you'd see any kind of life in him at all."

"Oh."

"But, quietness aside, you don't notice anything, well, odd about him?"

Clearly this question was aimed at my 'professional capacity' and I tried frantically to formulate an answer that would get me off the hook.

"Well, in any period of change one requires a period of adjustment," I rattled off sagely. "In Jamie's case, it's really to be expected, especially now that I realise how many nannies he's had before my arrival."

"True. The poor little mite, I just always felt there was something not quite right with him though . . ."

Christ, now I felt really bad. How could it be that the quiet, well-behaved child had now overtaken his maniac younger sister in the problem stakes?

Jeez. Was there to be no end to the complications?

One hour later, I sank down on my bed. I had some time before I had to collect Jamie and a spent Amber was back napping in her buggy. I had a million things that I knew I should be doing, trying to figure out what delightful oven-baked ready-meal I could give them for the tea being possibly the most urgent.

But I just wanted one little look first . . .

I flipped open the laptop and waited for the Facebook page to load.

What a horrendous morning.

What a horrendous life.

What a – wait! My hands started to shake as they hovered over the keyboard, afraid to move in case the words I was reading vanished.

Oliver Conlon: Anyone for pints tomorrow night?

Chapter 16

"*Nooooooo!*"

"Yes."

"*Nooooooo!*"

"Yes."

Amber stopped howling and looked at me, incredulous at the fact that I was smiling. The poor child didn't know what way to take me today. Even her reaction that morning to the fact that I was a completely different colour, the San Tropez having had its desired effect, had been hilarious.

Oh yes, I was going all out in the preparations and was actually on my way for a blow-dry in *Kutz n Kurls*, the purple preening palace. Thank God my roots didn't need doing as there was no way anyone in that salon was getting near my honey-blonde highlights.

"No," she said quietly one last time, looking at me semi-defiantly from under ridiculously long eyelashes.

"Yes." I smiled again and proffered the sleeve of her coat one last time.

She started to laugh at me and I knew I'd won.

Thank God. The last thing I needed was to have to explain a black eye to Oliver later on . . .

Oliver, Oliver, Oliver . . .

My stomach did a flip at the mere thought of his name. Nothing was going to get me down today. I got dizzy every time I thought about that evening.

Out.

In the city.

In a public bar.

With alcohol.

Correction – with a lot of alcohol.

To see Oliver.

I'd kept an eye on his Facebook page, and had ascertained with glee that it was a solo run (i.e. Catherine the Great was in London) and that the guys he was meeting were not GS staff, which just made things so much easier. I was also blessed that not only had Harry volunteered to come along on the mission but he had agreed to collect me at six thirty. The plan was to be already in the pub – which I now knew to be McGuire's on the quays, before Oliver arrived.

Oliver. Oliver. Oliver!

Oh, the excitement!

And the nerves too, of course. A little part of me had to keep reminding myself that this was it. If this didn't work, I was screwed.

It would be back to the drawing board.

It would be back to New York alone.

Enough.

This was going to work.

"So you all set then?" Harry enquired as I opened the door to him later that day.

All set? Was he being sarcastic? I'd been "all set" since brushing the last of the super-hold hairspray from my fringe at midday.

There was just one problem.

"Bloody Mark is still out on an 'emergency'!"

Harry laughed at my furious face as I hooked both fingers on the word 'emergency'.

"Stop panicking. There's no way that bloke you're hoping to bump into will be there before eight. We've loads of time. Stick on the kettle."

"Oh for the love of God, not you too. What is it with the Irish and your need for hot liquids in times of crisis?" I flung a teabag into a mug for him.

"Nothing like it!" Harry winked, before delving into his coat pocket. "But this, my dear, is just for you – I think you might need it!"

In his hand was a small bottle of vodka.

"Harry! It's only six o'clock!"

"Shush, for the love of God – down it quick before himself gets here . . . I never met such a dry shite when it comes to drink. Go on, it'll take the edge off yeh."

"Eh, hello? I'm technically still on duty here!"

"Sure isn't Uncle Harry here now!" He scooped a whooping Amber up into his arms and spun her around.

"Not so sure that's seen as a good thing around here," I said dryly.

"Oh come on, there has to be someone fun in their lives!" He looked around. "Where's the young fella?"

"Upstairs. I'm a bit worried about him actually, he's –"

"Drink!" He pushed a can of Diet Coke from my stash in the fridge across the worktop.

I didn't put up any further argument. He was right. I needed something to calm my thumping heart. I quickly sloshed the vodka into a glass, added a splash of Diet Coke and downed the lot.

Just as the front door opened.

"So you're here then?" Mark grunted as he stooped to remove his boots – a new rule.

"I said I would be!" Harry answered cheerily.

"And that would guarantee what exactly?"

Harry rolled his eyes but I hadn't time for a brotherly war so I grabbed him by the arm and said, "*Car. Now.*"

Mark looked at me for the first time since entering the house.

"You look different."

My cheeks flushed scarlet, thinking the vodka had started taking effect, but remembered my hair and tan just in time.

"Thanks!" I answered chirpily, deciding to assume that different meant better. "Harry – *car!*"

"So you two heading out then?"

"Yes," Harry smirked. "On a date. She mightn't be back till lunchtime. Sunday."

"No, we're not!" I thumped him. "Harry's just giving me a lift. I'm going to meet some friends. I won't be late."

"Be as late as you like," Mark said bluntly. "I'm here in the morning anyway."

"Oh yes, about that." I took a step back in from the door. "I was talking to a girl called Ellen the other day – Ellen Higgins? Anyhow, she mentioned that Jamie used to go to Little Kickers, and well, I was wondering . . ." I hesitated, trying to gauge if I was overstepping the mark, "if you'd like to take him."

I could see his huge shoulders visibly stiffen.

"Who says he wants to go?" he said defensively.

140

"Well, I don't know – has anyone ever thought of asking him?" Now it was my turn to square up.

"Right, folks, you can continue this in the morning," Harry interrupted. "Holly, you're going to be late for your 'friends', and that would be a dis*aaaaas*ter!"

He manhandled me out the door and into the car.

"That man drives me crazy!" I spat.

"Now you know how I feel!"

"Easy now – you're no walk in the park either – it was you that got me into this mess, remember?"

"Pardon me?" Harry stopped reversing the car for a moment and put a finger to his lips in mock astonishment. "From what I remember, I was getting you *out* of a mess."

"Okay, okay, just drive!" I giggled.

Harry was such easy company. Nothing ever seemed to get him down.

"Damn, it feels good to be out!" I sighed, nestling back into the leather bucket seat.

"Domestic life not all it's cracked up to be?"

"On the contrary, it's every bit as bad as I could have imagined. Emma must have been a saint." My hand shot to my mouth in horror, "I mean . . ."

But Harry was laughing.

"I know what you mean, but while she may well be a saint now, she certainly wasn't back when I met her first. Before my brother turned her head, that is."

"You knew her before Mark?"

"I introduced them, my dear! For all the thanks I ever got," he added with a trace of bitterness.

"You weren't tempted yourself then?"

"Wouldn't have mattered, she wasn't for tempting. Once

she set eyes on my charming brother that was the end of that."

"Charming? I just don't get it." I was still flummoxed at the general consensus that Mark was a "catch".

"Oh come on, don't try to tell me you don't fancy him just a little bit!" He laughed at the look of horror on my face. "Obviously, I mean personality aside."

I thought for a minute. I wouldn't say looks didn't matter to me at all, but it was hard to judge someone on them alone. Especially when their personality was as lacking as Mark Fielding's was. Yes, he was good-looking in a tall, broad, caveman-like way, and his eyes, when not glaring at me, were a nice, steely blue, and that day I'd caught him smiling at Amber his smile was kind of cute if only on a what's-seldom-is-wonderful basis . . . But no! I gave an involuntary shudder. Just *no*!

"Aha! I have you thinking now!" Harry goaded.

I thumped him.

"Hey, stop! I'm kidding. So tell me all about your mission tonight."

Phew. Familiar territory.

"Well . . . I suppose it's less a plan than a play-it-by-ear scenario. To be honest, I don't know if I'll be playing hard-to-get or falling into his arms."

"Why are you so interested in this pathetic guy anyway? Oh, that's right – I forgot you have a pre-existing habit of falling for people you work for."

I was about to thump him again, but then I remembered Cain and my fist unclenched and fell to my side.

"I'm joking." Harry had spotted my discomfort.

"I know. But yes, I suppose I do have a habit of repeating my mistakes. No! I don't mean your brother," I added hastily as his eyes widened. "Trust me, he's safe."

"To be honest, I can't see him ever being interested in anyone again, not that anyone would put up with him for that matter."

"I hear they were a lovely couple."

He thought for a minute.

"They were an odd couple. Emma was so full of life – she was really good fun, always up for a laugh – and well, you know what he's like."

"Even then? I presumed this was all as result of, well, you know, everything . . ."

"Huh. You'd like to think. Mark has been Mark for many a long year. We always clashed. As I told you before, when Dad died I was only twelve, which made Mark fifteen and, well, it was like the weight of the world descended on his shoulders. He was such a martyr – and no one asked him, you know, he took it all on himself. And couldn't understand why I wasn't the same."

"What did your mum think?"

"To be fair to Mam, she was tired of telling him to relax. He just wouldn't listen. He was unbearable."

"So what happened?"

"I fucked off travelling any chance I got."

I laughed. "I knew you looked like a surfer dude!"

"Snowboarder dude, my dear!" he corrected me. "God, it drove Mark mad. '*You're never around for Mam – you're such a waster*'," he mimicked his older brother.

"Where's your mum now?"

"She's living it up in Kilkenny, would you believe?

Took a transfer down there about seven years ago. She's very independent. Still works away in the Civil Service and lives in a lovely apartment five minutes from her job. If Mark had his way, we'd still all be living together in some farmhouse in Laois, holding hands around a pot-belly stove. But seriously," he sighed, "this topic wears me out. Tell me about your family – I bet they're great."

I snorted. "Let me see, where do I start?"

Chapter 17

By the time we arrived, the bar had conveniently slipped into that Friday night lull stage where the after-work-drinkers had gone home and the night-time-revellers hadn't yet arrived. Therefore we had no problem finding a seat at a perfectly placed table midway between the door and the bar.

"So what's the deal?" Harry asked as we took our seats, me sitting facing the door. "Am I your brother, your cousin, your lover, your husband or . . ." he winked, "your new boss?"

I laughed. "As I said, let's just play it by ear – he mightn't even come."

A wave of panic engulfed me as the worst-case scenario sped through my mind.

"He'll be here," said Harry. "Now, what about a drink?"

"Oh no, let me, I think it's the very least I owe you." I made to get up but he stopped me.

"Easy now, we can't have this accountant-guy thinking I'm some sort of tight-ass."

"Well, at least let me pay." I shoved a twenty into his fist.

I settled back into my seat as he made his way to the bar. If I hadn't been so uptight about Oliver, it really could have been quite an enjoyable evening. The easy friendship that had sprung up between myself and Harry was a welcome side-effect of this whole mess. But I really was on edge. This was not a pub I'd been in often, but it still felt that any minute I was going to hear Seán, or someone else from the team, roar in my ear and ruin everything. I willed Harry to come back. The last thing I wanted was to be sitting on my own when Oliver arrived.

"So what about you then?" I asked on his return.

"What about me what?"

"Well, we've dissected my relationship history – what about yours?"

"Feck. My history won't keep you entertained for long."

"You haven't got a girlfriend then?"

"No. You offering?" He leaned forward and gave me a big cheeky wink.

"No!" I squealed.

"Good. Cos you're not my type."

"Gee, thanks!"

"Ah, don't be offended. It's your age."

"My age! I'm only twenty-nine, for crying out loud!"

"I know. Too young. *Waaayyy* too young. I like my girls with a bit of mileage on them – if you catch my drift."

"Harry Fielding! I'm shocked!"

"Ah, you know it makes sense. Sure what do you young wans want only rings and babies, and sure I'm still a baby that needs a bit of minding myself. Now, unless a girl is early twenties and too young for that whole settling-down business, but," he sighed wearily, "that's no good any more either. Cos then I feel old and they just want to stay out all night partying. I'd rather be curled up with some grateful ould wan –"

"*Harry Fielding!*" I screeched again and swung to thump him yet again.

And at that moment, Oliver walked in.

For a second, my arm froze mid-swing but I recovered in time and managed to pretend I had no knowledge of his arrival. But eagle-eyed Harry guessed correctly from my expression that Oliver had just walked in behind him.

"Are you okay?" He slid closer down the seat towards me.

"Yes." I hoped my smile wasn't too wide and glassy-eyed.

"Do you want me to go or stay?"

"Don't you fuckin' dare leave me yet!" I hissed through gritted teeth. I took a breath. "Shit. I think I'm going to faint . . . Just keep talking!"

"About what?"

"Anything! Tell me about your latest lady-friend."

"Well, her name is Bernadette," he whispered conspiratorially into my ear, "and she's eighty-four . . ."

This time the laughter was real, and I could breathe. I knew that Oliver was at the bar and I could only presume that he had seen me too. And I had no idea what I was going to do next. In my fantasies he always swept me into his arms on sight. Thank God for Harry who kept me regaled with outlandishly exaggerated tales of his past conquests. Eventually, though, our glasses were empty and it was time for him to go for refills.

"Are you sure you'll be okay on your own?" he hissed.

"Positive," I said, in a far from positive voice.

"Well, at least you won't do what Sylvia did," he whispered, as he slid out of his seat.

"What was that?"

"Well, she forgot where she was and started looking for the matron. Thought it was games night in the home. She couldn't understand why no one had a chessboard . . ."

I was still giggling when I felt someone at my shoulder.

"Do you mind me asking what exactly you're doing here?"

Crap.

It was him.

Double crap.

I took a deep breath and turned.

"Oliver! Oh my God! How *are* you?"

He looked slightly taken aback at the gay formality in my voice. Considering the last time he'd seen me I was a cross between a gibbering mess and a spitting ball of fury.

"I'm fine. How are you? More to the point, why aren't you in New York?"

"Because I changed my mind. I, eh, got a job actually, and decided not to go."

"A job? Where in God's name did you get a job?"

"Don't look so shocked. I'm perfectly employable as you well know." I tried to rein in my offense and the temptation to flirt. Light and airy, light and airy, light and airy, I kept telling myself.

"Fine then, well, thanks for letting me know."

And with that he was gone.

I felt a wave of panic surge up through my chest but in an instant Harry was back at my side.

"You were *fantastic*!" Harry hissed.

"I'm shaking!" My glassy smile was returning. "Is he looking over?"

"Absolutely!" Harry smiled, then he reached forward and tucked a strand of my hair behind my ear, saying in the cheesiest attempt at a sexy voice I've ever heard, "Let's get out of here, babe . . ."

"Really? Do you think?" I was starting to panic. What if that was it? What if I'd overdone the disinterest? Maybe I should . . .

"Absolutely," Harry repeated. "Trust me – grab your coat – you've scored!"

I took a deep breath, grabbed my coat and followed him to the door.

And out the door.

Where I paused to slowly fasten my coat.

And down the street.

Where I paused again, willing the green man to turn red. Anything to delay . . .

To the junction, where I –

Heard someone call me.

"*Holly!*"

I froze.

Harry hissed "Yessss!" under his breath and threw his arm around my shoulders. "Keep walking!"

"But –"

"Holly! Hang on!" Oliver had broken into a run now.

"Wait – don't look yet," Harry hissed at me under his breath. He turned first, and then made a big deal of elbowing me to turn around. "It's your friend!" He motioned to Oliver who had by now caught up with us.

"Oh! Hi, sorry, Oliver, I didn't realise – what's up?"

Light and airy, light and airy, light and airy.

He looked from me to Harry and back again.

"Oliver?"

"I'd prefer to have a word with you on your own actually." He looked at Harry again.

My heart leapt.

"Oh! Should I be worried?" Harry puffed up his chest in mock machismo.

"No, Harry, of course not! You go on to Houlihan's, and I'll catch up with you."

Harry shot Oliver an excellent dirty look and shuffled off down the street.

"Well?" I asked.

"*Well?*" he practically shouted. "What do you mean 'well'?"

"Sorry, Oliver, what exactly is the problem?" How I kept my voice level was a miracle.

"You've no idea?" He swung his arm back towards the front door of McGuire's. "Could you explain what the hell is going on?"

"Going on? I still don't know what –"

"For fuck's sake, Holly – 'I changed my mind, I got a job'!" he mimicked.

I almost laughed aloud at the vitriol in his voice.

This seemed to enrage him further. "I'm glad you find the whole fucking thing so funny!"

"Well, I'm sorry that you don't! I still can't see what your problem is. At the end of the day, I'll do whatever makes me happy."

"Happy? With that fuckin' Neanderthal?"

"What do you want, Oliver?" I asked quietly. The peculiar sense of loyalty I felt towards Harry wouldn't allow me to let Oliver ridicule him in the street.

"You know what I fucking want!"

He turned and kicked the wall behind him.

My hand shot to my mouth. Now would not be the time to laugh. But this episode seriously could not be going any better.

I resisted the temptation to speak.

He turned to face me. "Why didn't you tell me that you were staying in Ireland?"

"I was going to, but I wasn't sure if there was any point – and, well, then the week got away from me. It all happened very quickly, you know."

"So I see." There was no escaping the sarcasm.

"I'm not so sure that I need to apologise for that," I said and turned to walk away, every muscle in my body resisting.

But before I could go two steps, he grabbed me from behind and spinning me around, started to kiss me with a force that shook the breath from my body. I couldn't help reciprocating before a warning voice in my head screeched *stop*.

So I screeched, "*Stop!*" and shoved him back with a force I didn't know I possessed. "What in hell do you think you're doing?"

"Meet me. Later. Tomorrow. Next week. Whenever. Just meet me!" he pleaded.

"I can't," I said, looking back up the street after a fast-disappearing Harry.

"You can."

"Well, you certainly can't!" I snapped. "You've a girlfriend, remember?"

"Let me worry about that. Just call me."

"No." I started to walk away, afraid he would see the sweet smile of victory etched on my face.

"I'll ring *you* then!"

"I won't answer!"

"You'd better, or I'll come looking for you."

I turned and laughed, all pretence at seriousness gone now.

"Good luck with that!"

Chapter 18

"Amber!"

"Noooooo!"

"Amber!"

"Noooooo!"

I turned and buried my sore head in the pillow but I could still hear the all-too-familiar exchange of words.

Damn you, Amber! Actually no – damn you, Mark!

It was my morning off. Did I really have to go down there? I'd had a late night . . . I groaned.

Damn you, Harry . . .

Then I remembered in one glorious rush exactly what Harry and I had been celebrating until the early hours of the morning.

Oliver.

Mission accomplished.

"Noooooo!"

The screeches were still audible from below. I pulled on my Gap hoodie, dragged a toothbrush across my teeth and stumbled downstairs.

"Holleeee!"

A semi-naked Amber tore across the room, almost knocking me off my feet.

My gaze traced her steps to where Mark sat on the couch, surrounded by an assortment of children's clothes. He looked so helpless and miserable that I started to laugh. I knew I was less than effective when it came to controlling her, but I'd credited him with a higher level of competence – after all, he was her dad.

"Man! You look worse than I do," I said without thinking.

"I think I feel it," he said glumly.

"What's the problem?" I asked, trying to swat away a whooping Amber who was doing a good job of tugging down my pyjama bottoms.

"I can't get her dressed. Not that it matters – Jamie says he's not going to the football."

"Oh?"

"So that's that then." He looked at the mess around him and sighed.

"Whoa – not so fast!" I shoved Amber onto his lap and, pulling together everything I learnt in one week of dealing with her, clicked on the TV in front of them. "Wait there a minute."

I knocked softly on Jamie's bedroom door. He was sitting on his bed. Just sitting there, not playing with anything.

Just sitting there.

He didn't look up when I came in so I sat beside him.

"What's up, sport?"

No answer.

"I hear you don't want to go to football?"

No answer.

"It's a pity. Oisín's mum said you were real good at it."

154

He sighed.

Okay, it wasn't much, but it was a start.

"Want to talk about why you don't want to go?"

He shook his head.

"Someone annoy you at it?"

He shook his head again.

Suddenly there was a screech downstairs, followed by a roar.

Jamie flinched, and then sighed again.

"She's pretty loud, isn't she?" I said.

He nodded.

"She doesn't mean it – she's only a baby really," I said softly.

"Huh. She's always like that. It's not fair."

"No. I suppose it isn't."

"We can't do anything cos of her."

"I see."

"Everyone laughs at me when she starts screeching. It's not fair."

He had now spoken more words in five minutes than I'd heard from him in five days.

"You're right. It's not fair." I sighed. "But, you know, I have a sister too, and she embarrasses me in a different way. She's so good she makes me feel like the bold one, all the time."

He looked up at me.

"So you see," I continued, "that's the thing with having brothers or sisters – it's never going to be plain sailing. And maybe, when you two get older, you'll annoy her by being so good all the time!"

He looked up from under his heavy fringe and I thought I saw the first trace of a smile on his lips.

"So then I can get my own back?" he whispered.

"You bet!" I decided to chance putting my arm around his shoulders and giving them a little squeeze. "I tell you what though, until then I've got a better idea. Let's do a deal. I'll keep Amber here at home with me, and you and your dad will go to soccer."

"What do I have to do, in the deal?" He looked at me suspiciously from under his long lashes.

"You," I winked, "just have to tell me *all* about the soccer when you come home. Do you think you could do that?"

He smiled. A shy smile, but a smile nonetheless. And a nod.

"Right so – you put on your gear, and I'll see you downstairs."

Morning off, gone.

Lucky I was in very, very good humour . . .

I went back downstairs.

"He's going."

"What? How?"

"I'll talk to you later about it." I took Amber off Mark's knee where she sat chewing on his phone and sat down with her on my lap.

"Why? Is there something I should know?" The stern look was back in his eyes.

"I said I'd talk to you later!" I looked pointedly at Amber who had by now scrambled off my knee and was immersed in picking a Barney DVD from the stash under the TV.

"Oh."

I gestured to him to come out into the hall where she couldn't hear us.

"He's embarrassed." I said. "She's not the quietest toddler in the world."

"She's only a baby!" He was defensive now.

"I know. But you know, maybe it's never just about him. Why don't you spend the day with him, take him for lunch or . . ." I tried to think of something a father and five-year-old son could do, but drew a blank, "I don't know, go somewhere, just the two of you."

"But it's your day off!"

"I know, don't remind me. I might change my mind," I said gruffly, trying not to blush.

"Oh." He looked at me. "That's very kind of you. I know you probably have a million things you'd rather be doing."

And then he smiled at me.

For the first time.

And for a second I really wished I wasn't in my Garfield pyjamas.

"I hadn't that much planned really," I stuttered over what were possibly the first words of truth I'd ever told him.

"Well, thanks. I mean it. I appreciate it."

"It's fine, it's fine!" I could feel my cheeks flame as he stared at me. "Have fun. Come on, Amber!" I called into the TV room. "It's time for Holly to get dressed!"

I fanned my cheeks as I headed for the stairs, Amber in tow. It was definitely easier when we hated each other. He needn't think he was going to start being all nice and smiley at me now.

And then I caught sight of myself in the hall mirror.

And the first thing I saw were two long black streaks of mascara leaking down my cheeks and I cursed my stupidity.

He wasn't smiling *to* me, he was smiling *at* me.

Well, that was a relief.

Wasn't it?

Oh forget it! I really was too hung-over to figure it out now.

Chapter 19

Yes, it was a good job I was in an amazingly good humour.

Because Amber certainly wasn't.

She seemed to realise that Jamie had escaped without her and literally went insane. Running up and down the hall, throwing her dolls at the wall, all the time screeching at the top of her voice.

And all I could think of, through my thumping headache, was Oliver.

And when he was going to phone.

And if he was going to phone.

And if it could possibly be even the teeniest bit okay if I phoned *him*. Harry said he would kill me with his bare hands if I did, but I was still secretly toying with the idea.

Amber did another lap of the kitchen as I attempted to tidy it. It was definitely time for Barney.

"Come on, my little Child of Satan, time for the big purple monster!" I called sweetly.

I seriously couldn't be expected to put up with any

more. Besides, I wanted to bring my laptop down to the kitchen table and sit and gaze at Oliver's profile on Facebook.

Mmmm . . . Facebook . . . Harry didn't say anything about Facebook.

I finally got Amber into the TV room, lugged my laptop downstairs and sat down with a huge mug of coffee. I flipped open the screen.

And there he was.

Phone me, I willed his photo, *phone me!*

Suddenly there was the most horrendous screaming noise coming from the TV room.

I rolled my eyes. For Christ's sake, Amber . . .

I reluctantly dragged my eyes away from the screen and wearily walked to the TV room. But, as I approached the door, I could see Amber on the couch, still sitting quietly watching TV.

So how could I still hear her screaming?

Okay, so it obviously wasn't her . . .

Then who was it?

Could I really be so unlucky that another toddler had broken into the house especially to go off on one?

I entered the room and the puzzle was solved. The DVD drawer had spat open, leaving the TV to flick back onto some random channel where a toddler the exact same age as Amber was throwing the biggest tantrum I'd ever seen. No, wait, it was two toddlers. Aha! That explained how it was louder than Amber.

I reached for the controls just as some lady in a suit came on screen and a voiceover said with a very authoritative English accent: "*It was time for Supernanny to take control.*"

I'd like to see her try, I thought sarcastically.

Then I stopped, controls in mid-air.

I actually wouldn't mind seeing her try . . .

And so I stood and Amber sat and we watched, both open-mouthed, as a rather robust-looking lady in a bizarre business suit whipped those two screaming, lunatic toddlers into shape. Not literally whipped obviously, which, while it would have been a solution I'd have wholly approved of, would hardly have been suitable for broadcast before the watershed. But still, by the end of the programme they were happy and smiling and the sun was shining and Mum had stopped crying (actually Mum had had a haircut too, but I don't think that Supernanny took the credit for that).

The better the children got, the more disinterested Amber became and by the time Supernanny was saying her goodbyes to the Ratchet family, she had wandered off – for all I knew to play with knives in the kitchen.

I didn't care. I was in a Supernanny-induced stupor and I wanted to know more. To my delight I discovered it was a double bill. I ran out to put the kettle back on and grab a notebook.

An hour later, Amber had gone down for her nap and the second episode of *Supernanny* had come to an end. A strange sense of euphoria had enveloped me. Who was this Supernanny and why didn't I know about her? Okay, well, seeing as I had only heard of the global phenomenon that was Barney six days before, I suppose it was kind of predictable that I'd never heard of Supernanny. But come on, the woman was clearly a genius. For the first time it occurred to me that Amber's behaviour, while obviously not unusual, definitely wasn't "acceptable" – Supernanny's words, not mine . . .

I thought of Jamie's little face that morning as he sat on his bed, willing to give up his football because of the embarrassment of his sister's tantrums.

Imagine if there was something I could do.

I'd be here for at least another week if Oliver phoned.

When Oliver phoned.

If I phoned Oliver.

And Harry didn't find out and kill me.

It would be just another project.

And I loved projects.

I definitely needed to know about this woman. I remembered my laptop, sitting open on Oliver's profile page. And I wondered why I hadn't thought of it before.

I flew out to the kitchen and started to type into Google.

Who is Supernanny????

A mere twenty minutes later my head was starting to spin.

There wasn't just a Supernanny that I hadn't heard of, there was a Toddler Tamer, a Toddler Guru and somebody called a Toddler Whisperer. I didn't investigate the Toddler Whisperer any further as I figured Amber was probably way past anything that whispering could accomplish.

The thing was, they all seemed to be saying the same thing. That the average toddler's problems all stemmed from lack of routine, lack of discipline, poor diet and bad sleeping habits.

And we had all of those.

Throw in a deceased mum and a workaholic dad and I reckoned there could be several TV companies jostling in a bidding war for the Fielding family.

My head was spinning. It had never occurred to me that this thing could be a science. Something that could be solved by charts, lists, plans and *other stuff I could do!*

And the solution seemed to be pretty simple. All these 'experts' had basically the same edict. Routine + discipline = happier child. Happier child = happier parents/fraudster nanny.

This was amazing stuff. For the first time in weeks I felt the stirrings of work-related excitement. Okay, so it wasn't Assets & Liabilities, but there was still a formula, a formula that these people promised would work.

I got totally immersed in the whole thing. Then my mobile beeped and, still with one eye on an episode of *Nanny 911* (Supernanny's American cousin), I opened a text.

I'm serious. Meet me. O

I looked at it. Then put down my phone.

And reached for a second notebook.

Wooohooo!

I was definitely here for another week.

Chapter 20

By four o'clock there was still no sign of Mark and Jamie. Not that I was worried. Why would I be? I'd only sent a recently bereaved borderline psychotic man with his recently bereaved borderline psychotic son off together for the day, which was undoubtedly the longest they'd spent together in five years.

No. I wasn't worried.

By five, I still wasn't worried. So why did I keep going to the front window to subtly check for the giant Land Cruiser to come rumbling down the estate. If it definitely wasn't worry, then what was it? Ha! Well, it might have been the same reason why, as soon as I'd surfaced from my Supernanny-induced stupor, I'd put Amber to bed and literally raced to the shower.

I was not happy to have been caught off guard with the pj/hoodie/hangover ensemble that morning, and needed to eradicate it fast from everyone's memory.

So I straightened my hair. My poor hair, screaming to be highlighted, but there was only so much I could achieve in the tiny bathroom of a rural semi-d.

And chose my jeans carefully. And my brand-new Ralph Lauren T-shirt.

And stuffed the shameful Garfield pyjamas into the laundry.

But still there was no sign. There was more than one reason for my impatience though. Yes, I was dying to know how the two of them had got on, but there was also another reason. That morning I had seen a chink of light in my relationship with my new employer. A chink I wanted to nurture, if for no other reason than it would make my life a whole lot easier. Now that Mission Oliver was underway, it looked likely that I would stay until he was available to return with me, and wouldn't that be easier in a house with a pleasant atmosphere?

Wouldn't it be easier if we just, well, got along?

What my carefully applied make-up that had been checked seven times between the hours of four and five had to do with just 'getting along' was anyone's guess, but one thing was for sure, if they didn't get back soon, all my efforts would be for nothing. My squeaky-clean look was starting to fade.

I heard a key in the door.

And in burst Jamie, running down the hall before flinging himself on me.

"Holly, Holly! Guess where we were?"

"Oh, let me guess – the movies!"

"No!"

"The toyshop!"

"No!"

"The zoo!" I was starting to run out of suggestions given my total lack of knowledge of a) the surrounding area and b) children in general.

"No, silly! We were to see the horses!"

"Oh, wow! You went horse-riding!" I was impressed.

I looked at Mark as he came in the door behind Jamie, and the fake, breezy smile I'd been practising all afternoon was way outdone by one of genuine surprise. "That was a great idea!"

"What?" Mark looked at me cautiously.

"The horse-riding! He's thrilled." I looked from the blank face of one to the other.

"We didn't ride the horses, silly!" Jamie laughed.

"Oh?"

"We *fixed* them!"

"You *what*?"

"Eh, I'm just going to get some stuff out of the jeep."

"We fixed them. Oh Holly, it was great – Dad let me hold the 'jections and everything!"

Mark visibly winced, one foot almost out the front door.

"Great!" I smiled through clenched teeth. "Jamie, sweetie, why don't you take off your coat and fly upstairs to wash your hands. Then we'll have tea."

As soon as Jamie was gone, Mark turned with a sheepish look on his face. "I can explain."

"You went to *work*!"

"Yes – but –"

I could feel all my carefully rehearsed resolutions slip away. One afternoon. That was all the child was asking from him. Just one afternoon. There I'd been, imaging them up to all sorts of bonding activities, and all this time . . .

Then I stopped.

The child was on cloud nine.

What was the problem?

I took a deep breath and felt my shoulders relax. This was not the end of the world. Baby steps.

Exhaling, I looked up and said, "Well, it looks like he had a ball."

"Eh, yes, he did. Actually, we both did." Mark was cautious now, not quite sure how he'd gone from zero to hero in quite such a short space of time.

"Well, great then."

"Eh, right."

And so we stood there. Awkwardly.

"You were getting something from the jeep?" I reminded him.

"Oh. Yes. I was, wasn't I?"

"Tea will be ready then."

"Great." He turned back towards the door.

"Oh, and Mark?"

"Yes?" He swung back again.

"Maybe don't let him hold the injections?"

"Oh. The lids were on the syringes though."

"Mark."

"Oh, okay. I suppose you're right. Scalpels only then."

"*Mark!*"

But he was gone. And I could have sworn he was laughing.

The positivity continued on into teatime. And what a tea!

Earlier that afternoon, when three o'clock had passed and there'd been no sign of them, I'd occupied myself with trawling the internet for some delicious recipe for tea that would appeal to both adults and children. I was a pretty good cook. Asian stir-fry, wild mushroom risotto, pan-fried scallops with minted pea purée – whenever Monica entertained I was her personal chef. But cooking for children? Cooking for these children? I'd met my Waterloo. They didn't like rice, they didn't like meat, and don't even approach them with anything resembling a vegetable. I'd had to re-educate myself completely and today Nigella's Luscious Lasagne was the best I could come up with. I did however couple it with chips and salad and the end result was a veritable feast. I'd even got carried away while I was at the butcher's buying the minced beef and there was currently a plump chicken sitting in the fridge and the makings of an Irish Breakfast for the morning.

And bless Nigella and Brophy's Butcher's but that lasagne smelled out of this world. With its delicious aroma wafting around the kitchen, it was hard not to muster up an amicable atmosphere.

And we actually chatted – I mean, like a real family. At one stage I looked around the freshly scrubbed pine table and thought we might have been the Waltons themselves, only with fewer children and better clothing.

And at least once, if not twice, Mark nearly laughed again. He was actually quite handsome when his face wasn't pinched with stress and bad humour. And I was glad I'd made an effort too, if only for the ego boost I got when I caught him looking at me once or twice.

Yes, I was in a very good place indeed.

The meal was almost over when Amber picked up her bowl of pasta and looked me straight in the eye. With a sinking heart I knew exactly what she was planning to do next.

"Amber – no," I said, using the quiet but firm voice I'd been practising all afternoon.

"Ess," she said, her chubby arm reaching higher.

"Amber, if you throw that bowl, you are going straight to the time-out area. Do you understand?"

"Ess," she said, chubby arm suspended in mid-air.

"The what?" Mark asked.

"Good girl." I turned to answer her dad. "The time-out area. It's something new we're trying. Trust me, it works."

"Oh, sounds a bit drastic."

"Well, not really. You can see how effective even just the threat of it is," I said smugly, just as Amber's half-eaten bowl of lasagne crashed down on Jamie's shoulder.

Brat.

Conscious of Mark's eyes boring into my back, I got up and calmly walked around to Amber's chair.

"Now, Amber, Holly said that if you threw your bowl, you would have to go to the time-out area."

"Holly – I don't think she meant it –"

"Mark," I interrupted him with the same firm voice I'd used on his daughter, "could you look after Jamie, please? You'll find a clean T-shirt in the press under the stairs. We'll be back in a minute."

I went to unstrap Amber from her booster and where that afternoon she'd been almost comical in her acceptance of the punishment, she now started to scream "*Daaaadaaaa!*" at the top of her lungs.

"No, Amber. I told you. Now come with me."

"*Daaaaadaaaaaa!*"

"Holly – please – I –" Mark jumped to his feet, but I turned on him.

"Mark! I'd like your support on this!"

"*Daaaaaadaaaaaa!*"

"I'm sorry, Holly, I can't let you –"

But I pretended I couldn't hear him. Grappling with the screeching toddler, I practically dragged her over to the cushion in the corner of the room and placed her on it firmly.

"Holly – I said –" he tried again.

But I was on my knees, holding Amber firmly by both arms, down at her level, looking her straight in the eye.

"Now, Amber, do you know why you have to go in time out?"

"*Daaaaaadaaaaaa!*"

"You're in time out because I asked you not to throw your dinner, and you did, so you have to stay here for two minutes and then you have to say sorry to Jamie. Do you hear me?"

"*Daaaaaadaaaaaa!*"

I got up but before I could even turn around she was off the cushion. So I grabbed her and plonked her back on it again.

"Holly!"

"No, Mark!"

"I said stop!"

"No."

"*Daaaaaadaaaaaa!*"

"This is barbaric! She's only a baby!"

"No, she's not, Mark! She's two and a half! She understands every single word we say. She knew exactly what she was doing. I need you to trust me on this. And could you please get me that top for Jamie!"

"*Daaaaaadaaaaaa!*"

She got up.

I put her back.

She got up.

I put her back.

"Holly, I can't see how this will achieve anything!"

"Don't tell me how to do my job!"

To be fair, thinking about that one afterwards, I did wonder where I'd found the nerve. It sounded the death knell for our family dinner but it worked in that Mark turned away, muttering, "I can't watch this – I've got a call to make."

And before I could even snap, 'Well, isn't that just your solution for everything!' he was gone, the kitchen door slamming in his wake.

And instantly Amber stopped crying.

And sat on her cushion.

And I looked at my lovely Ralph Lauren top, terminally smeared with Nigella's Luscious Lasagne, knowing without looking that my mascara was once again streaming down my sweating, puffy cheeks.

And, as I sank to the floor beside Amber, I felt two arms around my neck as Jamie hugged yet more lasagne into my no-longer-straight-but-still-in-need-of-highlighting hair. Tears of frustration and disappointment rolled down my cheeks.

And then I heard: "Saweeeeeee, Jamie."

I stopped, and looked up, certain I couldn't have heard correctly. But sure enough, Amber, two chubby arms outstretched, was reaching out to her brother. Who looked dubious, and understandably nervous.

I wiped my tears away hastily.

"Jamie, say 'That's okay, Amber'," I prompted quietly.

"Eh, that's okay, Amber."

And as the two children clumsily hugged, I started to smile. Victory clawed from the jaws of defeat was still very, very sweet . . .

Take that, Mark Fielding, you insufferable prick!

Chapter 21

I woke next morning at seven thirty with the sinking realisation that it was Mark's weekend off. This meant it was my day off too but I was definitely not looking forward to being under his feet for the next twelve hours. I had some shopping I needed to do but, given my tiny victory the night before, was anxious to hang around and proceed with the new technique.

So I lay there, guiltily praying for some giant veterinary emergency to hit one of his clients. Then I heard Amber wake up but, before I could move, I also heard Mark go in to her and take her downstairs. Oh, I thought, well, fine then. At least that gave me time to get up and get dressed. And, boy, did I definitely need my make-up well applied today!

As the lukewarm water dribbled down onto me, I tried to decide what way to play it with him this morning as I'd made a point of being in bed before he got home the night before. I thought of the sausages and rashers that lay expectantly in the fridge and wondered would a good fry-up put him in good humour. Not that I was planning on grovelling to him, definitely not.

I'd be professional, pleasant, and non-confrontational. After all, that's what Supernanny would do . . .

Then I heard the front door shut. Turning off the shower, I listened, but there was silence.

I ran out to my room and peeked from behind the blind just in time to see the Land Cruiser pull out of the driveway. That was strange, I thought.

Tiptoeing downstairs, I crept into the kitchen and sure enough there was a note for me on the counter.

I've taken the kids to my mother's, so you can enjoy your day off without them.

Mark

Oh.

Well, that was that then.

I read the note again, trying to pin down its tone.

Sarcastic? Probably.

Penitent? Not so much.

Oh, God help me but that man really did my head in. The sooner I could head back to New York the better. I really wasn't sure how much longer I could put up with this.

And then I calmed down. There was no point in getting upset. I had committed to a project and I might be a lot of things, but a quitter wasn't one of them. I needed to look at this practically. I had been gifted a child-free day, so I should really make the most of it.

Running back upstairs, I got dressed and day off or no day off, started to whip like a dervish around the house, giving myself a target of thirty minutes to get the place straightened out before I started some serious studying.

With the dishwasher and washing machine on and the vegetables peeled for later, I finally sat down at the kitchen table, laptop and notebook at the ready.

By 10 a.m. I'd compiled a list of seven books that I couldn't do without another day, which, had I still lived in Dublin city centre, wouldn't have been a problem. According to Google, the nearest bookshop open on a Sunday was in the neighbouring town of Newbridge. There was probably a bus at some stage but, as time was of the essence, I called a cab.

Less than thirty minutes and fifteen euro later, I was standing in front of a bigger array of childrearing books than I could ever have imagined existed. This was obviously a growing market, though to be fair as it wasn't an aisle I'd ever frequented before, it was hard to tell if this was a recent craze or the norm. I was leaning towards the former, though, as I couldn't really imagine my mother's generation having had much truck with titles such as *Top Tips for Fussy Eaters*. She'd had her own solution to that problem: it was called *Eat or Starve* and its sequel *I Haven't Poisoned You Yet*.

Still though, for someone like me who really hadn't a clue, there was no possible child-related issue that someone hadn't written a book about. Without moving more than four feet in any one direction, I could have found out how to predict my ovulation, do the deed in the most effective manner (apparently it made a difference *how* it was done), map every single nanosecond of my pregnancy, choose from over four billion baby names before giving birth in any one of thirteen different ways. To finish the process off, I could then rear my child to the point of wedlock, literally feeding them a different menu every single night along the way.

I was truly stunned, but I hadn't time to flick through them all. I was on a tight schedule. This schedule was made tighter still by the fact that I'd seen a large discount clothes shop on the way in and it had occurred to me that maybe a few new jeans and T-shirts might be an investment worth making. The memory of my ruined Ralph Lauren top was still very fresh in my head.

By four, I was back from my little shopping expedition, with three heavy shopping bags and one considerably lighter wallet. Raiding the terracotta pot for recompense for my purchases was not an option, so I decided these were balance-sheet items, investments . . .

By five, my head was in my hands. I had gone from positively brimming over with ideas and plans, to the sinking feeling that Mark Fielding was going to hate all of them.

But if he'd only let me explain. It was clear where this family was going wrong – there was no routine, no discipline, no proper eating habits, way too much TV – the books had only reinforced what I'd learned from *Supernanny*. And surely knowing what was causing the problem was half the battle?

I could do it, I knew I could. It was just so frustrating.

Wearily I tidied my books from the kitchen table and moved them up to my room. Exactly twenty-four hours previously, I'd anticipated Mark's return with excitement whereas now I found myself anxious, completely on edge. What a difference twenty-four hours could make.

The story of my life really.

Well, he wasn't joking about being gone for the day. When there was still no sign of him by eight I put the vegetables into containers, wrapped the roast chicken and put it all in the fridge for the following day. Wherever he was, he'd have had to feed the children by this time so presumably he would have eaten too.

It wasn't until eight thirty that I heard his key in the lock. I listened for the ensuing madness. But there was none. Sticking my head out into the hall, I saw him heading up the stairs with a sleeping Amber over one shoulder and Jamie trailing in his wake.

I'd been so determined to give Mark a wide berth on his return, but I couldn't help myself. I grabbed Amber's nightclothes from the radiator and followed him up the stairs.

She looked so tiny in his huge arms. As he gently laid her down in her cot, I had to admit there was no escaping the similarities between her and the picture of her mother on the stairs. I glanced sideways at Mark and, by the bittersweet look on his face, I knew he'd seen it too. He leaned down and stroked her cheek gently.

Embarrassed by the raw emotion on his face, I dragged my eyes away and started to slide off the sleeping child's coat. He reached down to help me and working together with the smooth cautious movements of two army bomb-disposal experts, we managed to get her nightclothes on and then both just stood there, awkwardly.

Out of nowhere he stunned me by saying softly, "About last night –"

I gestured towards the sleeping child and ushered him out the door. Outside, I turned and said, "Look, Mark, I'm sorry, but –"

"No," he interrupted me, "*I'm* sorry. I've been thinking about it, and of course you're right."

177

My mouth, already open with all the reasons why I was right, shut tightly as he continued.

"Obviously you're the experienced one, so I'd like you to do whatever you think is best."

I was stunned. This was not what I had been expecting. There had been no sign last night that he in any way thought I was doing the right thing, nor this morning when he'd virtually snatched the children out of my care before running to his mammy.

"Well, Mark, I don't know." I wasn't for letting him off the hook too easy, so with a tone that even I found absurdly confident, I said, "It's very hard to instill discipline without the parent's support."

"You have my support."

"Well, I didn't have it last night."

"I know, I'm sorry."

"Are you sure? Because there's a lot of stuff round here that needs to change."

"Of course."

"You need to be sure."

"I am. It's just that," he paused, looking back at Amber's bedroom door, "I'm not very good at that sort of thing, you know? Her mother, well –"

"Did all that," I finished for him without thinking. "I know, it can't have been easy –"

The soft look on his face vanished, and his voice was instantly cold. "With respect, Holly, you couldn't possibly know." Then he stopped and, sighing, said, "But that's not your fault. I'm sorry, I'm just tired, and it's been a long day."

"You've eaten, I suppose?" I asked suddenly.

"I ate with the kids earlier, yes."

"I could fix you a chicken sandwich?"

"Yes, that would be lovely actually." He smiled although the weary look was still in his eyes. "Thank you."

I have to say, as I followed him downstairs, I couldn't help feeling a sense of elation. At last I had free rein to get Project Amber underway. And Mark's change of heart gave me a strange kind of confidence. I felt vindicated by the fact that he'd obviously seen something in the way I took charge of her the previous night. Then it occurred to me that maybe she'd behaved fantastically well today as a result. Yes! That must be it, I thought, and I let the new sense of power wash over me.

A little later I dropped into Jamie's room to tuck him in.

"Holly?" he said.

"Yes, love?"

"What does 'get your act together' mean?"

"Oh," I said, still not used to him actually speaking to me, "well, it means get better at something. Why?"

"Well, today at Nana's, Amber was being really bold –"

Well, that blew that theory out of the water then.

"And Nana shouted at Daddy that she was a nightmare of a child and that he needed to get his act together."

Well now, that put a whole new slant on things.

"Really? And what did your dad say?"

"He said he was doing his best. But he's a bit rubbish, isn't he, Holly?"

"No, Jamie," I smiled as I tucked him in, "your dad *is* doing his best. We just need to help him, that's all."

Mark Fielding, you sly, sneaky coward!

Chapter 22

The next morning my clock went off at six thirty and I bounded out of the bed. Organisation was key in my mission to bring order to the house and, to be organised, I had to be up at least an hour before the children.

– Get up an hour before the children – tick!

God, it felt good to be achieving again.

The previous evening I had spent an hour drafting out a timetable for our day, complete with scheduled naps, meals and activities all broken into fifteen-minute timeslots.

In true *Supernanny* fashion, my first task was to tape this masterpiece to the newly cleared fridge door.

– Tape daily routine to fridge – tick!

Then, humming softly to myself, I put the kettle on. I then started my stock-take on the fridge and food cupboard as a big grocery shop was pencilled in for 12.45 p.m.

– Stock-take of fridge & store cupboard – tick!

"Hi!"

Holy shit.

I jumped, smashing my head off the top shelf of the fridge, causing it to dislodge and upend its contents onto the kitchen floor.

"Shit!" I said, rubbing my head and looking at the mess.

"Sorry, I thought you knew I was here."

Mark was leaning against the kitchen door, steaming cup of coffee in his hand.

"Clearly not."

"Well, sorry."

"No need to apologise – it is your house after all."

"Indeed." He smirked as he handed me a dishcloth, then added, "You've, eh, got something in your hair."

"Oh, thanks." I pretended not to care while inwardly wishing he would just bloody well bugger off and go to work.

"It's a strange time of the day for fridge-cleaning – or is that one of your new routines?" He was still smirking.

I drew myself up to my full height, suddenly thanking God that the fridge was still wide open which meant he couldn't see the new routines in all their glorious Technicolor stuck to its door.

"I'm changing the children's diet. I need to see what you do and do not have."

"Oh."

"Diet has a huge effect on behaviour, you know."

"I'll take your word for it." He threw the rest of his coffee in the sink and, still smirking, put on his coat.

"Yes. You do that." I tossed my head and went back to my fridge-cleaning, mentally adding another task to the list.

– Put smile on other side of Mark Fielding's face

God, but I couldn't wait for that "tick".

Two hours later I was leaving the house, the kids having had their very last breakfast of Chocco Krunchies.

Dawn looked surprised to see Amber dressed and with a clean face.

"New week, new us!" I told her confidently.

"Oh. Well, good luck with that!" she grinned.

"Thanks. Oh, I need to ask you, where's the best place to get paints and stuff?"

"Don't tell me you're doing up the house too?"

I had to laugh at the mixture of shock and admiration on her face.

"No way! Though I'm thinking of suggesting to him that the good front room is a complete waste and should be turned into a playroom."

"Does he not use it at all?"

"No, it's literally just sitting there. The door is even locked. But anyhow, it's paints for Amber I need and, you know, other stuff for her to play with, educational stuff like, well, you know, stuff . . ." I trailed off lamely . . . 'paints' was as much thought as I'd given the idea.

By now we'd reached the school gates, and Dawn went to greet the other mothers. Then she beckoned to me.

"You remember Ellen, don't you?"

I looked blankly at the lady she was standing with.

"From the Mother and Toddler Group?"

My eyes searched frantically for some clue, then lit on the lime-green buggy at her side.

"Ah yes, Ellen, of course!" Mentally I was doing the maths. If she was at the school gate, then she clearly had a child in school. I presumed there was another in the

Day-Glo contraption, but what stunned me was that there seemed to be yet another on some kind of step attached to its rear.

"You have your hands full!" I couldn't help but comment.

"Oh I know, busy busy."

"Ellen was telling me about just the shop for you, for the paints," said Dawn.

"Yes, you need Johnson's, down near the church. They sell all that sort of stuff – crayons, wall charts – it's a kind of teachers' supply store but they sell to everyone. They only take cash though, so have plenty with you when you go. So how are you finding it at the Fieldings'?"

"Great," I answered with a wide smile.

"Jessica and Amber were born about a week apart," Ellen continued, gesturing towards the cherubic-faced toddler clinging to the back of the buggy. "I remember being pregnant at the same time as Emma – such a lovely girl."

"So I believe," I said automatically.

"A wonderful, wonderful mother."

"Yes, again, so I believe."

"And you know that child," she indicated a glowering Amber, "never made it easy for her."

"Well, I don't think –"

"Not a bit like our Jessica, who was always so – willing."

"She's not that –"

But she'd moved on already. "Oh yes, Jess is just such a sweetheart, and it's not easy for her, you know, not with Robert crying half the night –"

"Robert?" I asked.

"My son, he's only eleven months younger than Jessica."

She gestured towards the child sleeping in the lime-green pod. "I think we took our eye off the ball on that one. But, anyway, for the life of me I can't get him down in the evening."

"Obviously you've tried Controlled Crying?" I asked without thinking.

"Controlled what?"

Shit. What did I say anything for?

"Crying, you know, where you keep going in at regular intervals, reassuring him until he drops off." I racked my brains to try and think what else I'd read about it.

"Never heard of it, sounds a bit harsh."

"Nonsense. Make sure you wind him down first – stories, bath, whatever –" I started to recite what I knew while inwardly cursing my stupidity. "After a few nights he'll see that you're serious."

"Well, I don't really believe in those strict rules. I think he just needs reassurance that Mummy and Daddy love him and that we'll be there when he wakes up."

"Nonsense," I said briskly. "Children need boundaries – you'll find that's sometimes all the reassurance that they need. Anyhow," I continued, "thanks for the tip about the school shop – we'll head that way now."

"You're taking Amber with you?" Ellen looked incredulous.

"Of course," I answered confidently.

"I can't bring mine to any shop," she sighed. "It's just not worth it – they'd drive me mad."

"Oh, we have a system, don't we, Amber?" I cooed. "Amber is my special helper. It's called the 'Involvement Technique'. I give her little jobs to do and it all gets done in jig time. Now we must go – Amber is scheduled to have her nap at ten thirty sharp and we must be home by then!"

I swung the buggy confidently around, feeling quite pleased with myself. A quick stop-off for some educational toys and then maybe I'd treat myself to a takeaway latte on the way home to sip at my leisure while Amber slept.

That would mean two more ticks for the list.

Sure enough we found the shop, which lived up to Ellen's recommendations. Crammed full of art materials, wall charts, wooden toys and puppets, it didn't take long for me to realise that I hadn't a clue what children Amber's age played with. All I did know was that the first thing she picked out, an incredibly uneducational-looking sword, wasn't quite what I'd had in mind. Luckily for me, the owner was a kindly faced man who clearly knew a fish-out-of-water when he saw one. A man on a mission, he soon had my arms full of paints, flashcards, wooden blocks and jigsaws and had even managed to wrestle the sword away from a very determined Amber, replacing it with a giant purple parrot puppet.

This job was costing me a fortune. But then I was getting very used to putting the whole money issue to the back of my head. For starters my 'salary' was a joke. I'd known it wasn't going to be in any way comparable to what I'd been earning in Grantham Sparks but like seriously? People *lived* on that amount of money? And I was getting over the usual rate. Incredible. Thank goodness, due to my workaholic tendencies (and my rent-free accommodation in New York), I'd built up a nice little reserve for myself over the years. Which was just as well – these new purchases were on me too – a gift to the kids, I told myself.

By the time I struggled home with the load, it was almost eleven. I consoled myself with the fact that the timetable was not going to go completely to plan on the first day and thirty minutes was not too far to be behind.

However, I reckoned without Amber who had absolutely zero intention of leaving her new toys and going upstairs to bed.

We faced each other. Me, rapidly cooling latte in hand, her with two chubby arms full of purple parrot, two jigsaws and a bag of bricks.

I sighed. And opened the first jigsaw.

Forty-five minutes behind schedule would be fixable. Just.

Sixty minutes behind schedule was not as fixable.

One hour and fifteen minutes behind schedule was fast becoming a disaster.

At one hour and thirty minutes behind, I decided that the paint-spattered Amber didn't need a nap and that stifling her creativity would be far more disastrous.

And *voilà*! We found ourselves back on schedule. This routine thing was a piece of cake: you just removed the items that you didn't get a chance to do.

And so at 1.30, bang on schedule, we found ourselves in the supermarket.

Me, Amber, the giant purple parrot puppet and my list.

But as the first whiff of freshly baked bread wafted in my direction, I remembered, with a sinking feeling, that neither of us had had lunch.

Thirty minutes later, there was no escaping the fact that grocery shopping with a hungry, tired toddler was a recipe for disaster. I could practically sense Supernanny watching me on her stupid laptop, shaking her head and tutting, "I left her to her own devices for one morning and look what happens!"

Up and down the aisles we went. I threw items into the trolley, Amber threw them out. As I went to pick them up, she replaced them with random items off the shelves. When I took her stuff out of the trolley, she went insane.

Not quite the serene shopping trip I'd had in mind.

There was nothing for it, though, but to keep going. Get the key items I needed and then get the hell out of there.

Ah yes, the key items I needed.

The book had made it look so simple but they'd reckoned without the stock of a rural supermarket. I hadn't expected it to be quite like the Food Emporium on 68th and Broadway, but come on! Okay, so they had plenty of rice that you could boil away merrily in a bag – but wholegrain basmati? Quinoa? Buckwheat? Their fruit and veg looked dull and tired and chicken that had seen any kind of fresh air throughout its life was an exorbitant price. The only fish to be had was breaded, and the bread itself came in two varieties – white or used-to-be-white-before-it-was-dyed-brown. It was futile. I needed a trip to a better supermarket but that would necessitate borrowing a car, a complication I couldn't resolve that simply.

By the time we got to the checkout, I was exhausted and Amber was roaring. In desperation I grabbed a neon bag of crisps from the shelf and shoved them at her. I knew that they were probably steeped in saturated fat and dredged with salt but if she didn't stop crying soon I was going to start wailing myself.

Then behind me I heard a voice.

"*Cooeee!*"

It was Ellen. Fresh-faced and beaming from ear to ear.

"Somebody doesn't look very happy," she said, looking at Amber's blotchy red face and teary eyes.

Thanks for pointing that out, you silly bitch.

"No. But you know how they are at that age," I forced through gritted teeth, noticing the cherubic Jessica was sitting up in her seat, nibbling away delicately on a small box of raisins.

"Yes, well, you can never rely on them not to show you up, that's for sure."

Oh, piss off!

"Boundaries," she said sweetly, looking directly at the crisps. "You're right – sometimes that's all they need."

Chapter 23

"One spoon, Amber, like a good girl."

"No."

I sighed. I really needed this morning to go well. My ecstatic high from Sunday had taken a severe bashing in the supermarket yesterday and had by now well and truly vanished. I looked across at Jamie who was quietly swallowing the last spoonful of porridge-scattered-with-delicious-ground-flaxseed into his mouth. Which was great, don't get me wrong, but there was just something very peculiar about that child. Even with our new early-morning start, he still managed to be sitting on his bed, dressed for school, every time I went up to wake him.

"Oh, feck the whole lot of ye ungrateful psychotics!" I muttered to myself.

Here I was, shovelling mucky porridge into the most belligerent child in Ireland, when I should be – I stopped. What would I have been doing?

Let's see, Tuesday morning – I even had to think about that for a minute – one day of mindless domestic drudgery was hard to distinguish from the next. I looked at my watch: 8.20 a.m. Well, if I was in Dublin I'd be just coming back from the gym that was attached to my apartment complex. There'd be a spinning class, or Pilates, or else I'd just speed-walk 5k on the treadmill. I froze for a moment, as I realised how little physical exercise I'd done lately. The last thing I wanted was to start piling on the pounds. Then it occurred to me that the relentless pushing of a hefty toddler the length and breadth of a small village was probably giving me better arm definition than a whole season of Grunt & Grind.

Anyhow, after the gym, I'd come back to the Dublin apartment and have a light breakfast of poached egg, and one slice of grilled bacon – Size 10 figures didn't maintain themselves, you know. And coffee, proper coffee from proper freshly ground coffee beans.

I'd then put my plate and cup carefully into my dishwasher-for-one, run a cloth over the marble worktop and give the sink one last shine. I prided myself on the fact that my kitchen looked like that of a show house permanently.

Then, after my carb-free breakfast, I'd pad, barefoot, across my cream carpet to the shower where I'd stand under its needle-sharp jets and let the Molton Brown shower gel infiltrate my senses. I'd check my legs for the first signs of stubble and tweeze any stray hairs from my eyebrows. My clothes, usually a suit/shirt combo still in plastic from the dry-cleaner's would have been laid out the night before, so I'd sit for five minutes after my shower, wrapped in my snow-white dressing gown and read the financial pages on my laptop.

Life in New York had been slightly different. I was

happy to live in Monica's Perry Street apartment, as to afford somewhere on my own would probably have meant moving out to the Boroughs. As it was, Monica's apartment was three doors down from Carrie's 'stoop' in *Sex and the City* and, every time I walked past the tourists queuing for photographs on the famous steps, I couldn't help the thrill of feeling I'd arrived. In Manhattan, I made a point of walking to my office at least three mornings a week, chucking my sneakers in my bag when I reached the building. I got such a kick from that city. I really hadn't thought I'd ever, ever move anywhere else.

Oh, how the mighty had fallen!

Here at Meadowlands there was no such glamour. I'd either squeeze in a shower when Amber was still in bed, or I'd have to plonk her on the bathroom floor with her blocks and grab a quick one while she was awake. There was never any temptation to linger either as it was a rubbish shower with only a handful of un-lime-blocked jets and the only senses ignited by the own-brand shower gel was the sensation of dry skin stretched tight over my hairy shins. Breakfast was usually a hastily grabbed slice of – albeit wholegrain – toast and my clothes selection revolved around what was clean, comfortable and to be found.

To be fair, my mornings in the apartment in Dublin needed to be that relaxed and serene because I worked bloody hard for the remainder of the day. From 8 a.m. to 8 p.m. most days, often not even stopping for lunch, the hours flying by in a haze of meetings, deadlines and, on occasion, meetings about deadlines.

Being a part of the team at Grantham Sparks was almost like being back at college. We worked hard but, boy, did we party hard too! We tended to socialise only with fellow employees as no one else would have appreciated either our hours or the effect the stress and strain of our work had on our temperaments. As a result, work-based relationships were common enough.

Especially illicit ones.

Because, of course, there was no denying the one thing that had made the previous six months so worthwhile.

Oliver.

Unlike myself and Cain, we'd worked on practically every one of my assignments together. When I skipped lunch, so did he. When I worked until midnight, so did he. And all that time, even though we were rarely ever alone together, our awareness of each other and of our 'thing' was palpable. I knew without looking when he was listening to me and I could feel without looking when his eyes were boring into my back. When he wasn't with me, I needed to know where he was, and when he entered the room the hairs on the back of my neck stood on end.

The away jobs of course were the best. We'd work until late, and then the team would eat together before heading back to our separate hotel rooms. And then I'd hear the soft knock on my door, and there he'd be. Leaning jauntily against the door, his brown eyes twinkling. On nights that he couldn't join me until later, I'd slip a key card into his pocket and I'd go to bed and fall asleep, not knowing any more until I felt his arms around me and then I'd sigh and curl into him, falling into the deepest of sleeps, knowing that finally I had everything I wanted in life.

I hadn't imagined any of that.

And that was what I had to keep reminding myself.

I stood up to see what other cereal I could offer the child. The choice was limited thanks to my overzealous dumping of anything unhealthy. I sighed, and turned back towards the table to see Amber engrossed in making patterns in the spilt juice on the table of her high chair.

I hadn't imagined my time with Oliver.

The nights that we'd lain there and planned our future.

The nights where we didn't sleep, but chatted for hours on end, our bodies entwined, my head on his chest. Again, the fact that I had my own apartment meant all this was so much easier – no waiting to hear Monica's key in the lock, no strolling around a freezing park because we'd nowhere else to go.

And I'd never forget that first night when he'd suggested that he'd return to New York with me.

Up to then I'd assumed this was one, long, glorious holiday romance. That at the end of the six months I'd go my way and he'd go his.

And then, that night in late July he announced that my leaving without him was definitely not in his plan. And my heart had leapt from my chest and the room had begun to spin in long, glorious swoops.

I hadn't imagined any of it.

I never could have imagined it. That kind of optimism just wasn't me, especially not after New York. Such was my scepticism at the start, I'd taken some persuading that he was serious.

Because I'd been burnt badly in New York. And yes, of course it was my own stupid fault. A relationship with a married man was only ever going to end one way. But for those few glorious weeks with Cain Hobson, I'd managed to fool myself that this one was different, that this one was going to have a happy ending – for me at least. But of course it hadn't. Cain Hobson got caught, went back to his wife and children, and I'd been made to look like a home-wrecker. Not that I expected any sympathy, which was just as well, as I definitely didn't get any. I'd taken my punishment on the chin. Public humiliation and, what was almost harder, the knowledge that people were saying a lot worse in private.

Yes, I'd learnt a valuable lesson and had definitely not been looking for another relationship from Oliver Conlon. And I think that was why I had tried to keep my head throughout the early days. It hadn't exactly been a Mills & Boon type romance. We argued a lot. We had a very different way of doing things. He laughed at my ways, and I, in turn, replied that people like him gave accountants a bad name. As a belated birthday present I'd bought him a vintage abacus and wrote in the card that it was from the same era as his accounting methods. He told me I was unorthodox, a rebel, but I insisted that I just knew how to think outside the box, that he'd have been a better auditor if he'd had more imagination. But all the bickering only added to the tension between us. And that was never a bad thing.

We had a remarkably enjoyable way of dealing with tension.

And all that time, he had been sleeping with Catherine Taylor.

All that time he'd let me walk blindly back into the same situation I'd fought so hard to leave behind.

And he hadn't said a word.

Yes, why didn't he just tell you? It's not like you would have finished it.

I would have!

But you haven't, have you?

I sat down at the kitchen table. What was I doing? Why was I giving him a second chance? Had I learnt nothing? What kind of a fool gives a liar a second chance? What kind of a fool lies to an entire village to give a liar a second chance?

I looked at Amber again and realised with a sinking heart that my real reason for all this effort with her was not to try and help this family out.

It was to ease my guilty conscience.

In a twisted way I was trying to make up for my lies by improving the household a little before I went on my way. In fairness I could have let the two of them munch away on Chocco Krunchies for a month, but I needed to give something back to make up for my deceit. I was sugar-coating my lies, no point in denying it.

Sugar-coating.

That was it.

Okay, maybe not sugar – that would kind of defeat the process, but surely to God there was something here I could add to the bloody porridge to get it into the little terror.

I flung open the fridge and the first thing I saw was a punnet of blueberries.

Bingo!

"Amber?"

"Ah?"

"Would you like Holly to make your porridge the same colour as Barney?"

"Yaaaay!"

You see, Oliver? Sometimes you just have to think outside the box . . .

195

Chapter 24

The fire crackled as I sank into the cream sofa. I took a deep breath and then exhaled slowly, closing my eyes.

"Holly?"

I opened one eye to see Dawn standing over me, glass of white wine in hand.

"Oh yes," I murmured, taking the icy-cold glass from her, "I have to say, this is just bliss, Dawn. This room, the wine and . . ."

"The fact that Amber, Jamie and Mark are four doors away," Dawn finished for me.

"And that. Mostly that." I laughed, taking a long, slow sip of the beautifully chilly Chardonnay.

Dawn had invited me over for supper as Graham was away on business for the evening, and between the heat of the open fire and the sensation of icy-cold wine trickling down my throat, any reservations I'd had about saying yes were swiftly melting away.

"I can't believe how different your house is to ours –

sorry – Mark's," I corrected myself, blushing at my mistake, "even though essentially they're the same house."

It was true. Dawn's house, while warm and homely, was decorated in various shades of cream and ivory, making everywhere look so clean and bright. The honey-coloured oak boards that covered the entire ground floor were scattered with deep pile rugs. We were in the sitting room, the same room that was locked up in Mark's house, and I looked around with interest. Huge scatter cushions were artfully flung on the giant L-shaped couch, and delicate wood carvings hung on the cream walls. The giant glass-and-oak coffee table had obviously been expensive and gave the room a look directly out of an interiors magazine. Dawn had a lot better taste than I would have given her credit for – there wasn't an item or colour out of place. The finishing touch was the sweet aroma of a Jo Malone candle wafting in from the hall.

Mark's house on the other hand, despite the myriad of colours it was painted, seemed dark and cold compared to this haven of honey. And while it smelt of a myriad of things, magnolia was never one of them.

It was the clutter in Mark's house that really drove me insane. Of course Daniel was too small to have toys scattered to the four walls but, still, any sign that a baby existed in Dawn's house was so tastefully done. For example there was no garish plastic highchair on view: Daniel's was walnut with a cream leather-lined seat, and not splattered with congealed food like Amber's. I imagined that Dawn would be the type to purée organic food for her precious baby, and then store it in tiny, pastel-coloured containers, lovingly stacked in a frost-free freezer. No baby-food jars in this house! I also caught sight of a chart on the back of the kitchen door which seemed to chart Daniel's sleeping and eating pattern since he was born – well, that's what I assumed the hours and ounces were referring to.

But then Dawn seemed to be a girl who liked to keep records. I looked around at all the photographs. There were so many photographs – on the walls, on the mantelpiece, on every available surface. Spanning from obvious early-relationship snaps through to very artful wedding photos to a giant portrait of the gorgeous Daniel, whom I could now see was the picture of his good-looking dad.

Again I couldn't help thinking of the Fieldings' house. Apart from that one family shot on the stairs, and a small picture of Emma in each of the children's rooms, there were no photographs. Plenty of paintings, but no photographs.

"You're frowning?" Dawn said.

"Am I? Sorry."

"What's the problem?"

"Oh, nothing really. I'm just admiring your photos but, I've just realised, there are no photos in the Fieldings'."

"What – none?"

"Well, one of the family in the hall, and then the kids have one each of Emma, but no others. Strange."

"I suppose." Dawn was thoughtful. "Maybe he took them all down, after the accident."

"I didn't think of that. I suppose that makes sense."

"Well, it wouldn't be easy still seeing her everywhere."

"No. Definitely not. Did you know her at all?"

"Not really, actually. I was still working then, you see, so I'd never have been around much during the day. It's funny, though, she was kind of famous around here, so I feel I knew her even though I didn't really. People were always talking about her. They all kind of adored her even though I've heard some of the girls say that you'd either see Emma all day or not for weeks. And she was certainly very good-looking."

"Yes, stunning," I agreed, before continuing curiously, "Do you know how, well . . . what happened? I mean, I know it was a car accident, but was there anyone else involved?"

"Well, I know as much as you. It was a car accident, early one Wednesday morning – not really sure of the details but it was at the junction of the Kilkenny road – but no, no one else was involved. Apparently there were a lot of wet leaves on the road and her car skidded into a wall."

"Jesus. Where were the children?"

"Well, that was the lucky thing. Teresa Murphy – you've met Teresa, haven't you? Well, she had them – I think she often kept an eye on them for Emma. Her grandchild is about Jamie's age – they used to play together a bit."

"Thank God they weren't in the car."

We both paused, lost in thought for a few seconds. Then I noticed the look of misery on Dawn's face and felt guilty.

"Look at us! Could we find anything more depressing to be talking about? Tell me all about that handsome man up on the wall there!"

It worked.

"Oh, that's my Graham." Dawn blushed. "We've been together for almost six years now, married for four."

"Wow, that's lovely! I didn't realise you were married that long."

"Yes, well, as I was telling you before, it took us a

while to have Daniel." Dawn looked embarrassed. "We were about to give up trying actually."

Ah yes, I remembered that story now. No wonder there were so many photographs of the child. Then it occurred to me that maybe most married couples had houses like this, peppered with snapshots of their happiness. With a start it hit me that Cain Hobson probably had a sitting room just like this. Wedding photos, baby photos, arty family snaps . . .

I suddenly felt very strange.

Like an imposter. I didn't fit in with this kind of domestic bliss, all this cream and ivory and perfect photographs of perfect people. It was all starting to make me feel a bit ill actually.

Suddenly I wondered if I would ever have this kind of room. Or ever want one for that matter.

It didn't seem likely; at the very least the scatter cushions would drive me insane.

Dawn was looking at me funnily again.

Just then I felt my phone vibrate in my pocket. "Well, lucky you didn't stop trying!" I said, fishing it out of my pocket in case it was Mark.

It was a text from my dad.

Holly, pls contact your mother 2 further confirm extension not necessary to sunroom 4 your sister's Xmas visit.

I smiled, slightly impressed at Dad's attempt at texting. "What's up?" Dawn asked curiously.

"It's my dad – my sister is coming home for Christmas and I take it Mam is up to her usual tricks of trying to overhaul the entire house prior to her arrival."

"Rolling out the red carpet, eh?"

200

I rolled my eyes. "You better believe it. Marsha is the Golden Child – a visit from the Pope is the only thing I can think of that would create more fuss."

"So that's where you're spending Christmas then?"

Before I had to answer we heard the front door open. Dawn shot up in the couch.

"Who's that?" I asked.

She shook her head slowly, then the sitting-room door opened and she squealed, "Graham!"

A face that I immediately recognised from the photos on the wall looked around the door.

"What are you doing home?" Dawn was still squealing.

A flash of annoyance crossed his face as he noticed me on the couch, instantly making me uneasy.

"Oh, last-minute cancellation – you know how these things go."

For someone who had just got out of a boring business conference, he looked incredibly grumpy, but Dawn didn't seem to notice. She immediately started fussing around him like a mother hen, taking his coat, offering him a glass of wine and then finally remembering my presence.

"Oh, where are my manners!" she shrieked. "Graham, this is Holly – she's just started work with the Fieldings, as their nanny. Holly, this is the famous Graham."

"Hi, Holly, nice to meet you."

"Hi, Graham." Seizing my opportunity, I stood up. "Dawn, I'm going to go and leave you two to it."

"Well, nice meeting you." Graham sank down on the couch.

"Oh Holly, no! You haven't even eaten yet! *Graham*!"

"What? I'm joking! Of course you should stay. Don't mind me, I'm tired."

Graham was smiling now and, while it looked relatively genuine, the whole domestic-bliss air to the house was starting to make me feel claustrophobic. First the photographs, then this whole 'Hi, honey, I'm home' routine – Jesus, it was just too much. Mark's house might be cluttered with annoying bric-à-brac and painted in those dreadful garish colours, but its chaotic ambience was exactly what I craved at that moment.

I just couldn't take the perfection of Dawn's house. Not for another second. Even the smell of her bloody candle was starting to turn my stomach.

"No, seriously, I'll be off. If it makes you feel any better you can give me a portion of that delicious curry to take home!"

While Dawn protested further, I knew that really she was thrilled to have her husband home and was dying to get him to herself. He seemed to travel a lot with work, so a night like this was rare enough without me sitting in the middle.

I eventually got out the front door and drank in the cold night air in huge gulps. I looked down the street at Mark's house. There were lights on downstairs. Mark was still up.

My pace quickened. Then I noticed the strange car parked behind his on the driveway. Visitors? At this hour?

I let myself in and, assuming the guests were in the sitting room, tiptoed into the kitchen, bemused at my disappointment that a coffee alone with Mark was no longer an option.

I jumped when I saw the pretty blonde sitting at the kitchen table, looking very much at home.

"Hi, Holly!" she said, smiling.

"Hi?" was the best answer I could muster before Mark came into the room behind me.

"Ah Holly, you know Tara, don't you?"

"I do?"

"Tara Harper, Fenton's daughter – you would have met her at the clinic that day?"

Tara Harper. Oh shit – the girl that had opened the door, with the giant black man-eating dog.

"With the dog?"

"Yes, that was me." Tara smiled a perfect smile at Mark. "Nero was doing his usual."

"Ah." Mark smiled back.

Obviously Nero's "usual" was a private joke. I was surprised at the dart of jealousy that was starting to niggle at me.

"Sit down, Holly, I'll make you a cuppa." Tara had jumped to her feet and was over at the kettle before I could say what-the-hell-are-you-doing-in-my-kitchen-bitch?

"I'm fine, thanks." I shocked myself with my iciness.

"Oh come on, sit down – we're finished with all the shop talk." Even Mark was being unusually pleasant.

"God, yes, we promise no vet-discussions." Tara smiled again. "Mum says there's nothing worse than a couple of vets around the table."

And then the two of them were laughing again.

Mark Fielding. Laughing. Like he hadn't a care in the world.

What was her secret, I wondered.

I had no choice but to sit down with them.

"So you've settled in okay?" asked Tara.

"Fine, thanks."

"Well, the kids are such dotes."

"Angels." I couldn't keep the sarcasm from my voice and to my delight I could hear Mark snort beside me.

"But then, you'd be so used to the little ones – nothing you haven't seen before I bet."

"Nothing." God, I had to stop these monosyllabic answers. She was going to think I'd no command of the English language at this rate. I struggled to come up with something intelligent. "So you're a vet too then?" was the best I could do.

"Well, I'm still at college, but that's the plan, yes." Tara flashed another beaming smile at Mark.

"It'll be no bother to you." He smiled back.

Christ, I had to get out of here – at this rate I was starting to miss Dawn's pungent candle.

I stood up, taking my tea with me.

"I'll leave ye to it, I've an early start in the morning."

"Oh, us too!" Tara smiled, "Best be off myself, or I'll be falling asleep on Mark's shoulder tomorrow."

She gave him a playful poke in the arm and with that I was gone.

I'd had enough of other people's happiness for one day. It was only when I got to my room and felt the first pangs of hunger that I remembered I'd left my portion of Dawn's curry on the kitchen table downstairs.

Well, it could stay there. I hoped they choked on it.

Chapter 25

The bus shuddered to a stop yet again and I remembered all too well why I'd shunned Irish public transport for most of my adult life. We were only five minutes outside the village and I was already feeling ill.

The only positive thought I could cling to was the fact that with every lurch and shudder, we were leaving Duncane village further and further behind.

Because, frankly, I'd had enough.

I'd had enough of three-bedroomed semi-d's, of tiny village stores that never stocked anything I wanted, and of cooking, cleaning and spending my days constantly listening for something to go wrong.

I'd especially had enough of small-minded village women whose only thoughts seemed to revolve around what colour vomit their child had spewed up and how it was still a better colour than anyone else's.

So what had brought on this particular bout of self-pity? Oh, only another session at the Mother and Toddler Group . . .

I hadn't wanted to go to start with. I'd woken up feeling

surprisingly low after I'd been in Dawn's. It didn't help that I'd stayed awake for an hour the night before listening for the noise of Tara Harper's car starting up. I mean, what was that all about? It was stupid really but, given the circumstances in which I found myself, I suppose I was entitled to one bad day. Plus, the last person I needed to see was Smug Ellen, who, I was quite sure, hadn't forgotten my supermarket disaster.

"Oh come on, it'll be good for Amber!" Dawn insisted. "What else had you planned for today? Meal plans? Artwork for a new timetable?"

"Eh, like you can talk Miss-I'd-Give-Gena-Ford-a-Run-for-Her-Money Kinahan."

I'd nervously shared some of my plans for the Fieldings with Dawn who, despite her constant teasing, was actually quite receptive. Being a new mother, presumably she was still at that fresh-faced stage where she'd every intention of doing everything right and of course, with only one, idealism was probably that much easier. And, boy, was Dawn idealistic! I reckoned not only had she read the controversial *Contented Little Baby* but she'd followed its routines to the button since Daniel was born. Which was fine – I was all for a bit of order in the house – but seriously? I was doing it as a job – it was Dawn's *life*!

"Maybe." I smiled.

"Oh come on, we'll have a laugh! Anyhow, I need back-up. Maureen Costello is probably back from her holidays and she's a woeful pain in the backside."

Great, that was all I needed. Another pain-in-the-backside mum.

"And that will make us laugh how?"

"Oh come on," she cajoled.

I gave in. Dawn was one of life's nice people, and it just wasn't possible to stay grumpy for long in her presence.

"We'd better laugh!" I warned her.

Off we'd set. And it had been okay at first. Only three of the girls I'd met before were there – and none of them was Ellen. There was, however, one new mother, who I quickly established, without any help whatsoever, to be Maureen Costello.

Dawn had not been kidding.

She was one massive pain in the arse.

A pain in the arse whose favourite thing in life was the sound of her own voice.

My least favourite type.

So she'd been on holiday. And not just any holiday. A holiday that we definitely all had to do next year. There was simply no other way of going on holiday to any other location on the planet. It had to be where she went. It had to be how she did it. We had to pack the way she packed, and eat exactly where she ate.

Then Sarah happened to mention that her Julie had asthma. Off Maureen went again. The only doctor in the country they should bring her to was in Tipperary. Absolutely no substitutes should be accepted. Everyone else was a quack, especially the one that poor Sarah was currently attending.

Like seriously.

To be honest, after five minutes I zoned out. I'd come up against women like her before. In Dublin, in New York, practically everywhere. This breed of bitch was universal. They were the best at everything; their children were the best at everything. They might have been bad at something once, but boy did they get better at it and now, you guessed it, they were the best.

So there I was, doing fine, sitting there minding my own business, until she turned her attention to Dawn.

"I see Daniel is getting bigger."

It was obviously a statement, not a question, so Dawn just nodded.

"That would be the formula."

Dawn visibly paled as if she knew where this was going.

"I'm sorry?" I asked.

Maureen turned to look at me as if seeing me for the first time, her eyes narrowing slightly, clearly viewing me as a second-class citizen.

"Formula," she said slowly and carefully as if she was speaking to some sort of uneducated slave, "makes babies fat. Obese. Fact."

"Oh, really?"

"Absolutely. There is just no substitute for breast milk."

"Well, it's not like I didn't try," Dawn said chirpily though she was clearly embarrassed.

I knew without ever even discussing it with Dawn, that had she been able to breastfeed, she would have. God knows, she'd handed over every other aspect of her life to that child.

"Oh piffle! It's the most natural thing in the world. You don't see cows giving up, do you?"

"Well, now, hang on." I wasn't finished. "It's not like she liquidises McDonald's and tubes it into him and, anyhow, surely it should be the mother's choice?"

"Well, I just fail to see who would choose what wasn't best for their baby? I mean, you call yourself a childcare professional – surely you know the health benefits?"

"Of course I do, I'm not saying –"

"I mean, apart from the bonding issues," she had the cheek to say this while looking directly at little Daniel snuggling into his mother's neck, "breast-fed babies are so much more intelligent."

"I see," I said, the calmness in my voice totally belying the fact that I'd just lost all patience with this bullshit. "In that case you won't mind me asking – were you breastfed yourself?"

Maureen's mouth opened, then closed.

"I didn't think so," I said sweetly, ignoring the gasps of shock from the group. "Now, if you'll excuse me, I think it's time for Amber's Mensa class."

I stood up to leave but then heard a voice shriek behind me.

"*Oh, Holleeee!*"

Fuck.

It was Ellen. I couldn't believe my luck. Just when I thought I had the upper hand on this motley crew of fanatics.

I pretended I didn't hear her and kept packing, but she wasn't for swaying.

"Holleeee! Just the girl I wanted to see!"

I could ignore her no longer.

"Ah, Ellen, what can I do for you?"

"Oh Holly, it worked! It really worked!"

Oh, so she was going down the sarcastic route? Well, good for her, I'd had enough.

"Great, Ellen, thanks."

"Wait!" she shrieked. "Do you not want to hear all about it?"

Eh, I was there, remember?

"All about it?"

"The Controlled Crying! I mean, I really didn't believe you, to be perfectly honest – I thought it was a bit, well, you know, extreme, and I mean I did nearly give up, on night one, but then just as I was about to cave – there was silence!"

I looked at her blankly, then the penny dropped.

"Really?" I asked, before quickly reining in my incredulity. "I mean, of course it worked, it's a method I've been using for years."

By now the other mothers were firing questions at Ellen, who was only too pleased to tell all about her Controlled Crying. Well, all except Maureen who was just sitting there with a face like thunder.

"Well, bye all! We must dash!" I decided to quit while the going was good.

Dawn was on her feet in an instant.

"I'd better go too – I've got to show you that thing."

"Thing?" I asked, puzzled, before registering the furiously nodding and face-making Dawn. "Oh yes, that thing. Right, we'd better head off quickly then!"

When we got outside Dawn grabbed my arm.

"You – were – amazing!" she hissed, practically jumping up and down on the spot.

"Oh please, someone had to shut her up – she is an awful woman."

"Come on, let me buy you a proper coffee – it's the least I can do!"

"You know what? I think I need one."

Thirty-six hours later, here I was. Sitting on a bumpy bus, the smell of stale vomit making me feel queasier and queasier . . . But neither that, nor the fact the journey that had taken Harry's Golf forty-five minutes exactly a week ago seemed ten times as long aboard this rumbling dinosaur, could keep me in a bad mood for long.

I was on my way to see Oliver. No ifs or buts this week. It was a definite arrangement: eight thirty at the Axis Hotel at Newlands Cross.

A hotel. The bloody cheek of him! Okay, it was a meeting place, with a bar, but I'd almost choked when he'd suggested it, imagining he was planning all sorts. After pacing up and down the room ranting to myself about his text, I eventually calmed down. We obviously couldn't meet at his apartment, and I didn't have one any more, so what choice did he have? Any of the pubs in the centre of town were out. So, while it may have looked presumptuous on his part, I had to give him credit for finding somewhere relatively out of the way and, conveniently, on my bus route. But, if he thought for one second that we would be availing of any of services other than the bar, he was well mistaken.

Life with the Fieldings was so busy that this rendezvous had kind of snuck up on me. In a way I was almost glad that I had the bumpy duration of the bus journey to try and sort my head out.

Because I had actually no idea of what I was going to say when I saw him. All my planning and scheming had been to get me to this point.

So what now?

I had no idea. I'd have to play it by ear when I got there.

Squinting out the now rain-spattered window, I tried to figure out how much more of this torture I had yet to endure. But it was hard to tell – one view of the Naas dual carriageway looked just as bleak as the next.

I sighed and looked around me. There weren't too many more on the bus. No surprise there – I mean, who took buses any more? Two hairy students down the back, one drunken auld lad up the front, and me the out-of-work-faux-nanny-and-dater-of-married-men.

This whole positive-mental-attitude thing wasn't going so well. I took my compact out of my bag for one last check. I couldn't help wishing I had Harry with me to tell me how utterly divine I looked. But no, he was down the country with friends though, bless him, he'd texted me twice to wish me good luck. The second time to reassure me that although he was far too drunk to come and collect me himself, I was still to ring him if I had any trouble and he would get a taxi up to "put that plonker in his place".

I smiled. While he was definitely one of the few good things to come out of this whole mess, I was really hoping that phoning him wasn't going to be necessary.

"*Newlands Cross!*" the bus driver roared.

Feck! I bundled my stuff back into my bag but, as I tried to stand up, the bus lurched to a stop and I fell back again.

I couldn't believe it had just stopped. Without even pulling in, it had literally stopped on the side of the dual carriageway. I looked around in disbelief but there was no one to consult. Then with another lurch he started to pull off again.

"*Wait!*" I squealed.

I could hear him curse under his breath as it lurched to a stop again. Luckily I'd flung out an arm to save myself this time and managed to sway down the aisle.

I opened my mouth to complain as I drew level with him but he just looked stonily ahead so I knew there was no point.

It was also pretty apparent that if I didn't get out soon he was going to pull off again.

I made my way gingerly down the steps.

And just as I stepped off the bus, the heavens opened.

For Christ's sake.

So there I was. On the side of the Naas dual carriageway, the rain running in rivulets down my face. I turned to get back on the bus. I don't know where I was planning on going – into town or back home or, well, anywhere to avoid running the five hundred yards to the huge hotel.

But it had groaned into action again, and was gone. With an anxious look at the headlights of streams of oncoming cars bearing down on me, I stepped off the road. Straight into a rather large puddle, ensuring any part of me that wasn't rained on was now soaked in an oily, gritty mess.

"For the love of God, Holly, this is the final straw!" I actually shouted as I stood there.

What in hell was I at? Travelling on a stinking bus, getting dumped on the side of the road in the pissing rain, and all to meet a two-timing git in a seedy hotel on the outskirts of town!

I thought of Dawn and her honey-coloured house and her bloody nausea-inducing photographs and I knew she'd never had to go through anything as humiliating as this.

That did it.

I'd had enough.

Suddenly I wasn't winging it any more. I knew exactly what I was going to say to Oliver Conlon when I saw him.

I was going to tell him to stuff it. Whether he was single or not.

I'd had the worst goddamn week of my life and looking forward to this *fiasco* was what had got me through it?

Was I insane?

Resolutely I started to march towards the hotel.

You are going to walk in there and tell him that you don't care what he has to say. It's over. Then you are going to go back to that godforsaken village and tell Mark Fielding that you are leaving. You are going to pack and then get yourself back to New York and forget this whole sorry mess ever happened.

I was mad as hell.

I strode into the lobby of the hotel.

And there he was. The first person I saw. And the cheeky low-down fucker was at reception, clearly checking in.

To a bedroom.

But, goddamnit, it felt good to see a familiar face.

He took one look at my dripping form and said, "Come on, let's get those wet clothes off you."

And I should have said it. I should have told him to go to hell.

But I didn't.

Instead I followed him into the lift.

Chapter 26

"So what are you going to tell Harry about this?"

"Exactly the same thing you're going to tell Catherine, I guess."

"That would be nothing so!"

He laughed and I had to stop myself from slapping his smug face.

What was I after doing? Lying in his arms, clothes strewn all over the room – how had I forgotten everything about the last nightmarish two weeks so easily? It was unbelievable really, yet I couldn't help feeling that what was even more unbelievable was that I'd been so near to telling him to go to hell. Everything was so familiar – his smile, his smell – that for a while I could hardly remember why we'd broken up.

"She's still around so?" I asked, not able to help myself.

"Don't ruin it, Holly," he answered, stroking my hair, but I could detect a warning tone in his voice.

I struggled out of his hold and leaned on one elbow.

"Ruin what, Oliver? I think it got kinda ruined the day I found out you had a girlfriend. A girlfriend that was also my boss. Why do you think I met you tonight if not to discuss it? It's what we're meant to be talking about! This other –" I gestured wildly around the room, "*stuff* was not in the plan!"

"Mightn't have been in *your* plan," he said cheekily, trying to tickle me to make me laugh. "Ah, come on, Holls, admit it, this is great."

"I never said it wasn't great," I struggled to fend him off, but I knew I was failing, "but clearly it was never great enough for you!"

He groaned and rolled away.

"How many times do I have to tell you? It wasn't like that."

"Oh come on, you really expect me to believe that?"

"Yes. I do. Why would I lie to you? If it was her I wanted I'd never have begged you to stay in Ireland. I mean, why would I? I'd just have let you go back to bloody New York, wouldn't I? For the love of God, would I be listening to all this shit if I didn't have to? Would I even bother lying?"

I almost laughed at the desperation in his voice, but I still couldn't resist one last dig, tinged with bitterness.

"Oh I don't know – that's what men do, isn't it?"

"You know that's not fair. When have I ever lied to you before?"

"How am I supposed to know? I didn't realise you were lying to me this time until I overheard those smug bitches gloating in the pub that night!"

He started to laugh. "Okay, fair enough. I'm not really surprised you went mad at me in Harvey's that day."

"Went mad? Have you any idea of how insanely angry I was?"

"Well, the fact that you were here for a whole week without telling me gives me a fair idea."

"What else was I meant to do?"

"Oh, I don't know, Holly – given me another chance?"

"For what? You were in a relationship with Catherine Taylor!" I slammed my head back into the pillow, before continuing almost to myself, "Maybe I should have guessed when you were so good at keeping us a secret."

Now it was his turn to get indignant.

"Ah, hold on, you wanted it kept a secret too, remember? In fact, you were every bit as keen as me that no one find out."

He was right. It had suited me. After the public humiliation of my failed romance in New York, I knew only too well that another in-house relationship would not do my professional credibility any good. And anyway, I had to admit, the secrecy had been half the fun . . .

"Again, how very convenient," I mumbled grudgingly. "Still, you should have either told me, or broken up with her, or both."

"Holly, she's also my boss. What was I meant to do? Tell her by text to eff off? 'Oh, hi, Catherine, it's all off, but if you don't mind I'd still like that promotion you've promised me'?"

"Well, why not?"

"It was a very tricky situation."

Okay, so he might have another point there. But before I could feel my resolve start to soften I had to go for the jugular.

"So you're going to break up with her now then?"

He pulled the sheet up over his head and muttered something.

"What?" I asked.

"Yes," he repeated.

I dragged the sheet down.

"Say it like you mean it," I demanded as his hands went up to cover his face.

He winced as if anticipating my reaction.

"Yes, I am going to break up with her. Or you. One of you, soon, I promise."

I shot up in the bed.

"*What*?" I screeched.

He dove under the sheet again. "I'm joking!" he shouted.

"Tell me why I should believe you!"

"Because you love me?"

He peeped with one eye from under the sheet and I thumped him.

"Love you? Are you mad? I'd love to bloody well kill you right now!"

"I promise. I'll sort it all out. Just give me a bit of time."

I sat, my shoulders starting to sag, wanting so much to believe him.

And it was like he could see the chink in my armour.

"All those plans, Holls, I wasn't bullshitting – just give me a bit of time."

His arm snaked around my waist and started to tickle my ribs, further and further up until I started to squirm, then laugh, and then slide down the bed until we were face to face.

"I want to believe you," I said quietly.

"Then do."

To him it was simple and before I could say any more his lips were on mine.

"This is how it should be," he whispered as he started

218

to kiss my neck. "We have all night, then in the morning we can get a taxi out to Dalkey – I'll even treat you to a posh brunch, your favourite . . ."

"Wait!" I shot up on one elbow again. "A taxi? Where's your car?"

"My car? At home. Why?"

"What's it doing at home?"

"Cos I had a drink with the lads earlier. What's the problem?"

"The problem? The problem is you've got to drop me home, thicko!"

"Home?"

But I wasn't listening – I had my phone out and was frantically trying to access the hotel's Wi-Fi.

"Come on, come on!" I muttered.

"Eh, Holly, we were kind of in the middle of something there?" he tried to remind me.

But I had shot out of the bed and was hopping around on one leg trying to get my jeans on while looking for my bra.

"What the hell is going on?" he demanded.

"The earliest bus in the morning is too late!" I panted. "If I hurry I'll just make the last one home tonight."

"What the hell are you talking about? You're not going home tonight!"

"I am, I'm sorry, it's Jamie –" I stopped myself, there was no way I could explain to Oliver that I had to bring a five-year-old to football in the morning as his daddy, my boss, was working. "I just have to be somewhere," I finished lamely.

"Who in God's name is Jamie? I thought that hairy fucker's name was Harry?"

"It is. Jamie is – his nickname?" This didn't sound

plausible, even to me, but by now I was almost dressed and had given up trying to find the offending bra.

"Holly, is this some kind of joke? How can you go home? I booked a room for us. For the night!"

I almost laughed at his woebegone face and, kneeling on the bed, took it in my hands.

"I had a great night. But I have to go. I'm sorry. But we can meet again, really soon."

"Wednesday?" he asked, his face lighting up.

"I promise!" I kissed him before grabbing my bag and heading for the door, and then as I put my hand on the door handle I turned –

"Oh but Oliver, one thing . . ."

"What?" he asked sulkily.

"Next time bring the car, will you?"

Chapter 27

"Come on, Jamie! You can do it! *Shoot!*" I held my breath, almost afraid to look, then screamed, "*Yessss!*" as the ball rolled into the back of the net.

"*Yaaaay!*" yelled Amber from her buggy, her little open mouth full of half-eaten raisins.

I was thrilled. Cold, tired, but definitely thrilled.

Yes it would have been nice to have woken up with Oliver this morning, to have strolled through Dalkey Hill Park, sat on 'our' bench that looked out over the sea, and then had Eggs Benedict together in the tiny but delightful World Cafe. Instead here I was, standing on the side of a football pitch, the November wind whipping around my ears, my cheeks getting redder and redder by the second.

However, watching Jamie come alive on that very football pitch was the perfect consolation prize.

I wound my scarf tighter around my neck and looked at my watch. There couldn't be much time left to go.

"Hasn't he come on in leaps and bounds?" I heard a voice to my left. I looked around to see a kindly-faced, middle-aged woman standing beside me.

"Ah, Mrs Murphy! I didn't recognise you for a second."
I held out my hand as I realised it was the woman who had
dropped the children around on that first night.

"Well, I almost didn't recognise any of you!" she said
smiling. "And little Amber, sitting in a buggy, a sight I
haven't seen too often."

"Don't remind her," I whispered conspiratorially. "It's
a new development and one that takes a lot of bribery!"

"I'll say nothing!" She winked. "So it's all going well
for you then?"

"Well, we have our moments," I admitted. "I'd be
lying if I said it was all plain sailing."

"How's Mark?"

"He's – he's fine." I hesitated. "You know yourself."

"Oh I do, only too well."

I thought I detected a slightly grim note to her voice.

"Well, I'm sure the last year hasn't been easy for him."
I wasn't sure why I should defend him but a bit of
employee/employer loyalty seemed in order.

"Mark was Mark before things ever got difficult," she
said, again with just a touch of bitterness to her voice.

"Well, he does work a lot," I admitted.

"Far too much. He always did. That poor girl, as if she
didn't have enough on her plate."

I didn't know what to say now. I was never one for
gossip and this conversation just didn't feel right. So I just
nodded and wondered aloud how much of the game could
possibly be left.

Mrs Murphy seemed to sense my discomfort and put a
hand gently on my arm.

"Listen to me going on," she said. "I'm sorry. I don't
want you to think that I'm some old gossiping biddy like

that Bernadette Foley. It's just that I got very close to Emma and, well, I just feel very strongly about some of the things that happened in that house." She sighed. "Mark's not a bad lad – I suppose some people just don't cope well when things go wrong."

I had no idea what she was talking about; I just knew it was definitely time to start making an exit.

"Well, it was very nice meeting you, Mrs Murphy. I have to say you were the last person I expected to bump into here."

"Oh, my grandson is on Jamie's team. They used to play together all the time before. We should organise something someday. You should bring Jamie over. I often mind Peter for my daughter."

"Oh, the Grannies of Ireland!" I said, smiling, glad of the change of subject. "What would we do without them?"

And with that, the final whistle went and the children started to stream off the pitch.

A glowing Jamie ran into my arms, stunning me with a big hug.

"You were fantastic, sweetie!" I squeezed him tight. "Just wait till we tell Daddy."

"When will he be home?"

My heart sank at the eagerness in his eyes.

"Well, not till later, love," I said. Then I thought of something. "But we could try phoning him if you like?"

"Oh, could we?" His face lit up.

"I don't see why not – if he's busy he just won't answer and he'll call us back."

I dialled Mark's number; it rang for a second then clicked onto his paging service.

I looked at Jamie and his face fell.

And then I had another idea.

"Come on, I know your dad has surgery this afternoon – let's go and tell him ourselves!"

"At the clinic?" Jamie's eyes widened with awe.

"Yes, at the clinic – he'll probably kill me but, hey, what'd be new?"

"But how will we get there?"

"Oh." I hadn't thought of that. I tried to think about how far it was to Harpers' from the pitch. By my calculations, it wasn't *that* far, and we did have a buggy and Mark could drop us home . . .

"Well, we could walk – do you think you could manage that?"

"I could! I really could!"

"*Yaay!*" Amber screeched from the buggy, caught up by Jamie's excitement while having no clue what we were talking about.

So off we set, me only now wondering if, now that I'd relayed my mad idea to the kids, I would actually be able to find the clinic. Twenty minutes later I also started to wonder would the skin on my heels ever heal as I started to feel the toll of the long walk on the backs of my feet.

But by some fluke or miracle, aided by Jamie's directions, it actually wasn't long until I recognised the wooden fencing of Fenton Harper's farm.

Down the gravelled driveway we trundled, the buggy grinding so deep down into the stones I was practically ruddy-faced by time we reached the top. This time I avoided the whole big-dog-debacle and circumvented the house, heading straight around the back towards the sheds that housed the surgery. It did cross my mind briefly that the last time I was here there were dead horses being dragged around by tractors but I reckoned surely Mark didn't have fatalities every week.

"Dad! I scored a goal!" It was Jamie's roar that alerted me to the fact that Mark was crossing the yard towards us.

"*Go!*" shouted Amber, pudgy arms flung open wide as she too spotted her daddy.

"I hope this is okay?" I pushed a stray, sweaty tendril of hair behind my ear, knowing that my face had just got even redder. "We're only here for a minute. It's just that he wanted to tell you his news . . ."

"Of course it's okay – a goal? Come here to me, son!" he grabbed the delighted child and swung him up into the air. "Now tell me all about it – did the keeper even get a hand to it?"

"No! He didn't, Dad, I swear, he went like a totally different way. And it was Barry Murphy, Dad, he's like usually totally *awesome!*"

Watching the two of them chatter so animatedly I suddenly forgot the blisters on my heels and the fact that the sweat was dripping in rivulets down my back.

Then hearing a whimper at my side I looked down and poor Amber was looking totally dejected at the lack of attention. I reached down immediately and, unclipping her straps, swung her up onto my hip.

"Hey, Dad – wait till I tell you how good this girl was all morning!"

The minute Mark turned towards her, her little face lit up.

"Oh Amber, love, I'm so *proud!*" he said, taking her from my arms into his.

And, I swear, she actually blushed.

"Why don't we all go inside?" Jamie asked, clearly wanting to make the most of this unusual visit.

"Well, only if Daddy says that's okay."

"Of course it is. We've finished for today and I'm sure there's biscuits in the canteen."

I wrinkled my nose, not sure if there could be anything I'd let past the children's lips in the canteen I remembered.

"Oh come on, we've cleaned it up a bit since you were last here, it's not *as* bad!" Mark gave me a little push.

For some unknown reason I jumped away from his touch.

"Oh – sorry – I didn't mean –" he said.

"No! I'm sorry!" My face flushed scarlet at my ridiculous reaction.

He looked at me quizzically, but I just looked away and followed the children into the clinic.

You fool, I hissed at myself.

Inside, Mark was busy showing the children around and I could take some time to pull myself together. I suppose it had been a pretty strange 24 hours, what with the Mother and Toddler Group, then the hotel with Oliver and now, well, I suppose this was the weirdest bit – seeing a soft side to Mark Fielding. What girl wouldn't be all at sixes and sevens?

Wandering around on my own, I came across what seemed to be a small library. Trying to ignore the selection of horse's skulls, jawbones and what seemed to be freeze-dried severed legs labelled with various ailments, my eye was caught by a selection of drawings on the wall. They seemed to be CAD drawings of a large building, like a school or large house.

"That's the dream."

I leapt again at Mark's voice behind me.

"Dream?"

"My own clinic."

"What's wrong with this one?"

"Oh come on, you're allowed say 'apart from the obvious'."

I smiled. He was right – I was trying to be charitable. And I did in fact remember him mentioning this dream the first time I had come to the clinic.

"Well, firstly," he said, reaching up to smooth one corner of the drawing back, "it's not mine, it's Fenton's and, secondly, he's hoping to retire in the next few years and I'm sure he won't want me pottering around in his back yard. Thirdly, it's not purpose built. It kind of grew and is not exactly state of the art."

"So you'll go out on your own then?"

"Well, that's the plan. Of course, plans go astray and, well, this hasn't been the easiest of years." A muscle flicked in his jaw and suddenly I knew who he reminded me of. Tall, lean, muscular Cain. Another man with the weight of the world on his shoulders.

"Of course," I nodded, "but hopefully things will get easier for you, for all of you."

"Maybe they have already." He looked directly at me and then blushed, and I knew the words were out before he'd realised what he was saying.

I stood open-mouthed, not really knowing what to say or do. This was a moment I hadn't been expecting. And for some insane reason, it was one I didn't mind lasting.

But then there was a crash at the door and somebody shouted "*Watch out!*"

But it was too late – a huge black dog had run in and buried his head in Mark's knees.

"*Oi!* Nero, get out!" Mark shoved him away, clearly relieved at the diversion.

"Oh sorry!" It was Tara.

Great.

"Hope we're not interrupting." She beamed up at us from where she crouched, restraining the giant dog in her arms.

"Of course not," Mark said, a little too eagerly.

"Definitely not." My response was a little cooler.

"Oh good – I was wondering if I could borrow Mark – I need a little favour?"

Goddamnit, if she wasn't definitely batting her eyelashes.

"Oh. Right. What's up?" said Mark.

"Any chance you'd do the bandage change on Elite Dancer – you know how he tosses me around the stable?"

Oh please. I tried to restrain myself from rolling my eyes – 'Poor little old me, could big strong Marky Warky protect me from that mean old horse?'

"Well," Mark looked at me and hesitated, "I was going to drop Holly and the kids back home."

"Oh no, we're fine," I answered quickly. "We'll walk. In fact, I'd love to walk. Honestly, you go do whatever it is you have to do and don't worry about us."

"Really? It's quite a way . . . you'd better wait for me."

The backs of my heels screamed in agreement but I was cross now and wouldn't hear of waiting for a lift. I rushed around, gathering together the children, and before they knew what was happening we were trying to push the buggy through the deep-gravelled driveway again.

"But I wanted to stay," whined Jamie.

"Yes, but Daddy's busy and, anyway, I've got a surprise," I said, racking my brains valiantly for an idea for a surprise.

"What surprise?" Jamie asked huffily.

Then it came to me. "Who'd like to go for a bun?" I asked with exaggerated excitement.

It worked. They whooped with excitement, and even Jamie announced that this just might be "the best day ever".

Twenty minutes later we were safely ensconced in Myrtle's Coffee Shop, a treasure trove of a place on one of the back streets. It reminded me slightly of the Magnolia Bakery that myself and Monica used to go to on nearby Bleecker Street before the cupcake craze had swept through New York City, resulting in queues down the block. I wondered how long it would take before one of the Mother and Toddler Mafia walked in and caught me feeding my charges giant e-number-laden buns. Well, stuff them, I thought as I picked up my equally giant latte – everyone deserved a treat every now and then.

"This is delicious," Jamie said, his mouth full of bun.

"Lishish," said Amber, not to be outdone.

"Say *dee – lish – us*, Amber," I coached. I had decided from observing other children at the school gate that Amber's speech was quite poor for her age. Perfectly natural given the turbulent nature of the last year but, still, I was determined to bring it on.

"Dee – lish – iz," mimicked Amber happily.

I smiled, looking at the two contented children sitting in front of me. Every now and again, I'd have a moment like this and think: *Another thing you thought you couldn't do!*

"So are you glad you're back playing football then?" I asked Jamie as he took a huge sip from his carton of orange juice.

He nodded. "'Cept I wish I could go every week," he said.

"Of course you can go every week. Why couldn't you?"

"What if you can't bring me?"

"Well, if I can't bring you, your dad will."

"Oh." This seemed to come as a surprise to him. "Will you tell him to bring me when you're sick?"

I laughed. "I won't be sick. Why would I be sick?"

"I dunno," he shrugged. "Mummy couldn't bring me when she was sick. And then I missed it and Eamon Murphy used to get to be the striker."

"Now, Jamie," I smiled at his solemn little face, "I'm sure your mummy wasn't sick that often."

He nodded, his little eyes like saucers. "She was, you know. She was sick a lot. And she'd stay in bed and I'd have to mind her and Amber *and* miss football."

I ruffled his hair affectionately. "I'd say your mammy just wanted a lie-in. And, while I can't say I blame her, I promise I won't be sick and, if I am, I'll make sure Daddy takes you. Deal?"

"Deal." He smiled.

"Dee!" said Amber.

I started to clean up the debris around us.

"Five more minutes now, guys, then we've got to hit the road. Daddy said he might try and get home early and imagine if he got home and we weren't there."

Jamie giggled. "Daddy might go mad!"

"It's a definite possibility," I said wryly, "and we don't want that, do we?"

"Excuse me," said a voice from the table behind me.

I turned around to see another woman sitting there, a small child in a buggy beside her.

"You must be the American lady minding the Fielding children."

Gosh, word travelled fast around here.

"Eh yes, I suppose I am," I said, "though I'm, well, I'm actually not American although I did live in New York for quite a while."

"Oh, I beg your pardon!" The lady looked embarrassed. "It's just when they said you were a nanny from New York, I assumed –"

"Oh it's not a problem!" I smiled. "Happens all the time!" I held out my hand, "Holly Green."

"Well, I'm Noreen – Noreen Costello."

"Nice to meet you, Noreen."

The woman blushed again and looked around as if to make sure no one was listening.

I waited. Clearly she wasn't finished with me.

"The thing is," she whispered, leaning in towards me, "well, he's nearly three . . ."

I looked at the child asleep in the pushchair and nodded, wondering where this was going.

"Yes?"

"And Ellen Higgins said that you'd know."

"Oh. Right."

"Well, it's just that this is our seventh day, you know?"

"Know?" I whispered back, afraid to raise my voice. "Know what exactly, Noreen?"

"He just won't do it. I mean this is the seventh day and he's just refusing. Wants nothing to do with it. I've tried Superman underpants and no luck. Soaked."

Oh Sweet Jesus, what could she be on about?

"How, Noreen?"

"How?"

"How did he get soaked?"

"Well, from the wee, of course! I mean I tried to get him to go on the potty, but he won't! Not even a teaspoonful. And then the little fecker stands up in front of me and just does it! On the kitchen floor! All over his socks!"

The penny dropped. "Oh – you're trying to toilet-train him!"

"Well, yes, I mean he's almost three! And I've tried everything – stickers, star charts – everything!"

I looked at the poor child sleeping in the buggy.

An underachiever and not even three years of age!

"Well, maybe he's just not ready," I said quietly, more to myself than to the anxious woman sitting in front of me.

"Not ready?" Noreen Costello looked at me. "My sister's fella is a month younger and he's doing poos and all!"

"Be that as it may, Noreen," I said, a slight defensive tone in my voice, "all children are different. He'll do it in his own good time and the worst thing you could do is put him under pressure."

"I never thought of that." Noreen Costello's shoulders visibly relaxed. "Maybe I should just leave him for a while."

"Well, what's the rush?" I asked.

"There's none really. I just thought as Sally's young lad seemed to be –"

I held up my hand. "Stop, Noreen! You'll get nowhere by comparing them!"

Except a lifetime of insecurity for him.

"You're right!" she said happily. "Anyway, I suppose they are all different. I mean he has way more words than Sally's young lad."

She seemed delighted with this thought and I smiled.

"I'm sure he does, now go home and stick a nappy on him and get yourself a takeaway and a bottle of wine!"

She grasped my arm and shook it.

"You know, I think I will. Ellen was right. You're a real expert!"

She started to pack up her stuff, still beaming from ear to ear . . . then suddenly turned towards me again.

"Now that I have you . . ."

Shit.

"Well, it's about his naps. How many should he be having?"

Double shit.

"Ehm." I looked at the sleeping child, "What age is he again?"

"Well, he'll be three in two weeks."

"Mmm." I had no idea what answer to give her. I racked my brains to try to think of something to say. "You know, Noreen, I'd like you to leave that with me. I mean, I could give you an answer but the guidance on these things changes all the time."

"Oh, don't talk to me!" The disappointment was obvious in her tone. "They tell you to let them sleep on their front, then they tell you no, that'll kill them, so you put them on their side and sure then –"

I had to stop her. This could go on all day.

"Well now, luckily enough, Noreen, I was at a conference of the Sleeping Association of America just before I came over here and I'm nearly certain I have the notes back at the house somewhere. Let me look them up for you."

What? Of all the lamest . . .

"Would you?" Her eyes were wide with awe. "I would be so grateful!"

233

"No problem at all, Noreen!" I couldn't believe my stalling had worked. "Write down your number and I'll give you a shout when I dig them out. In fact, I'll go home straight away and look for them!"

I got up hastily, put Amber back in her buggy and bundled Jamie into his coat. The last thing I wanted was for her to think up some other kiddie-conundrum for me.

I wasn't sure I could wing any more questions.

The Sleeping Association of America.

Like really.

Chapter 28

I was still chuckling at my hard-neck response to Noreen Costello when we got back to the house. How had I gone from a hotel bed with Oliver to doling out parenting advice to an anxious mother in just twelve hours?

"Right! Jamie, up to the bath – Amber you too – come on. Let's all be nice and clean for when Daddy gets home."

The two children scampered up the stairs ahead of me. I knew it was only lunchtime, but I needed to get to my books to see if I could come up with some answers for Noreen Costello. Within minutes they were in the bath and I was sitting beside them on the bathroom floor, books spread out around me.

"Is that your homework, Holly?" Jamie asked.

"It kind of is, Jamie."

All those years of studying financial methods and theories and here I was, cross-legged on the bathroom floor with the Toddler Whisperer.

Nice work, Holly.

"Homework?"

I jumped as I heard a voice behind me.

"*Daddy!*" screamed the children.

Feck. I'd been caught.

"Eh, yes," I stuttered, my cheeks flaming. "For my CPD, you know, Continuing Professional –"

"Development," Mark finished, towering over me like a virtual giant from my lowly position on the bathroom floor. "I didn't realise you had to do that."

"Well, you don't *have* to," I said, scrambling to my feet, wondering how many more lies I was going to have to tell just to get through the day, "but I like to, to keep abreast of changes and, well, stuff."

"Ah, stuff, of course, very important. I agree."

Damn it, he was laughing at me again.

I hastily bundled the books into the corner.

"Don't stop on my account," he said. "In fact, why don't I take over here and you go study for a while – you've had them all morning."

I looked at him, not sure if he was still teasing me – after all, I had them all day every day but that was what he was paying me for.

"I'm serious," he smiled, "I can handle bathing them. Probably." To be fair, he looked slightly wary of Amber who was at this stage firing all of Jamie's toy boats out over the edge of the bath. "And anyway, you never know, I might get called out again later and this way I won't feel too bad."

This Mark-with-a-conscience was a whole new concept for me but I wasn't going to look a gift horse in the mouth.

"Oh. Well, okay then, I'll go upstairs to my room for

a while if you don't mind." I grabbed my books and then remembered. "Oh, I met Mrs Murphy earlier, at football."

"Did you now. Full of chat, was she?" He turned and started to pick up the boats.

Instantly, I knew from his tone that I shouldn't have mentioned it.

"Well, no, not really," I said, my cheeks flushing at yet another lie. "She was asking for you, that's all."

"I'd say she was, alright." He threw the boats back in the bath.

"She was, seriously."

This time he said nothing so I just turned and, after warning the children to behave, went upstairs.

I had no interest in whatever might be up with him. After all, I had bigger issues. Somewhere out there was a mother expecting me to phone her back with the findings of the latest study by the Sleep Association of America on the Napping Patterns of the Three-Year-Old.

Once up in my tiny loft I flopped on the bed and looked at the books beside me. Really I had neither the time nor the energy to leaf through them page by page. I sighed wearily, then spotted my laptop lying on the bed.

Oh my God, how had it not occurred to me before now – surely the internet could help?

I typed "naps three year old" into Google and hit search. *Whoosh!* And there it all was.

My son won't nap – HELP . . .
Refusing to nap – why it happens & what to do . . .
All about sleep – who needs it and when . . .
Do three-year-olds need a nap?
How long should a three-year-old nap . . .

The list went on and on and on . . . I couldn't believe my eyes. All postings from what appeared to be different forums and websites such as *practicalparenting.com*, *successfulparent.com* and even *ultimateparenting.com*.

Three clicks and I had all the information I needed. It was so easy that I couldn't figure out how it hadn't occurred to Noreen Costello to do the same. But then it hadn't occurred to me either and I used to live with my laptop practically attached to me. Back in the good old days, before this godforsaken village made me feel like I was living in a time warp. I mean, how much trouble would I have saved myself if I had thought of the internet? There was a wealth of information out there for the asking. I suppose I had never connected the internet with such mundane things – high finance, yes – toddlers' naps, no.

I jotted down a few answers and then, out of curiosity, typed "parenting websites" into Google.

Again, another list that seemed to go on and on forever.

My eye was drawn to the first on the list though, partly because it wasn't called giftedkidsareus.com, but mostly because it was Irish.

> Ireland's Number One site for pregnancy, parenting and everything in between. The babyline is on call twenty-four hours a day, because you are!

Now this sounded like a resource I could use.

I double-clicked on its name.

Up came a bright screen divided roughly in four. One square had a picture of a beautiful blonde girl, caressing a giant bump, and was titled 'Mums-to-be'. To the left of it was another square with a cute baby wrapped in soft blue blanket with the title 'Babies, Toddlers & Beyond'. Below this was another, showing two women, presumably mothers, having coffee, titled 'Discussions' and then the final square was aptly called 'Everything Else!'.

I decided to take the discussions option. Clicking on the square brought me into a screen showing a long list of topics to choose from. These seemed to range alphabetically from Adoption to Weight Loss, including all sorts of topics like Finance, Recipes and What's On. I came back out and clicked on the 'Mums-to-be' square. This time a new window opened up but instead of a list of topics, you had to choose how pregnant you were by selecting the month you were due.

Out of curiosity I randomly picked January. When I spotted the first topic entitled 'Anyone else with piles?' I exited rapidly to the home screen.

So next was 'Babies, Toddlers & Beyond'.

You had to choose exactly how new your baby was: newborn, toddler, preschool or school-going. I selected toddler.

What came up then was literally a list of every question I'd asked myself over the last week.

> Constant whinging and seeking attention
> 18-month-old won't sleep
> Recipes for fussy eaters – please!
> Which car-seat for 2-year-old?
> Help! My three-year-old is violent

The list went on and on and on.

I scrolled down to find a topic that interested me. Aha! **Activities for 2.5-year-old**. Pity I hadn't seen that the other day before my trip to Johnson's.

It appeared to have been posted by someone with the username Babylicious. I wondered if the username referred to her child or herself, or rather some image she'd had of herself prior to Baby's arrival.

Anyhow, Babylicious had posted the following request:

> Wondering if u could suggest some activities for 2.5-year-old which we can do indoors or else in garden. Due new baby in a week and want to be organised to be able to give her time too. We normally do painting, tea parties, drawing, jigsaws … Anything else? Tks B

Fair request, I thought, scrolling down to the replies with interest.

The first was innocuous enough.

> Hi Babylicious
> Huge congrats in advance on the new arrival.
> Wow, you are so organised, sorting all this out well in time. The activities my dd loves are painting, making towers with blocks and of course Play-Doh.
> Don't put yourself under too much pressure though, remember a bit of communal TV-watching can sometimes be a great thing.
> Hth
> Star7

Okay, so I'd no idea what a 'dd' or a 'hth' was but apart from that it was a nice friendly answer.

On to the next one.

> Hi Babylicious
> The last thing you should do is plonk your dd in front of the TV. She'll feel lonely and left out and it will lead to all sorts of problems down the road.

Whoa! Don't hold back, tell us what you really think!

> In our house we try to avoid the TV and really enjoy the following activities: card-making (ds and dd both love glue, glitter, paints, cutting out and stencilling). Then we like to act out little plays and stories from our books, baking, jewellery-making and dance-related activities.
>
> There's lots more but we're on our way to music class now so I'll come back on later with other ideas.
> ZoeyB

Eh don't bother, ZoeyB, I thought – I was exhausted just reading your list. Are you forgetting this woman will also have a newborn baby? You have her tidying up after glue, glitter, baking and beads – she'll be a basket case!

I read on. Oooh, Star7 was back and she was mad as hell!

> Hello again ZoeyB
> If you read my post again I did say *communal* TV watching.
>
> I wasn't suggesting she lock her dd in a different room for 24hrs with just a TV for company! I see nothing wrong with snuggling up on the couch to watch a bit of Peppa Pig, new baby in one arm, toddler in the other. A bit of bonding for everyone. What you're suggesting means the house will be like a tip and poor Babylicious will be stuck at the kitchen table while new baby screams for a feed.
>
> Not the first time you've twisted my words like that. Why don't you follow someone else on here and annoy them instead!

241

Wooo-hooo!

I was intrigued now. These girls obviously knew each other, or at least had crossed swords on this site before.

Just as I started to think that this parenting-forum stuff was better than the TV, there was a knock on the door.

I jumped guiltily and slammed the laptop shut.

"Come in?" I said.

The door opened and in stepped Mark, cautiously, hampered by the fact that he had to lower his head coming in the door while trying to hold a tray with both hands.

"I thought you'd like a coffee while you're studying," he said.

I was flabbergasted. This was not the Mark I knew.

"I'd – well, I'd love one, eh – thank you," I stuttered. "Thank you very much."

His huge frame made my tiny room seem even smaller, and I flushed with the sudden realisation that he, a 'strange' man, was in my bedroom. Without looking, I hoped that there was none of my underwear on show. But I needn't have worried. He stood there, head forced sideways by the sloping ceiling, and looked awkwardly at me.

With a jolt I realised he was still holding the tray.

"Gosh. Sorry – let me take that from you."

"Thanks," he said, looking like he couldn't get out of there quick enough. "I'll, eh, see you downstairs in a while then."

"Em, yes, I shouldn't be too long."

"Right."

He turned and stooped again to go through the door.

"Thanks again!" I called after him, but he was gone.

Well, it was the nicest coffee I'd had in weeks – and chocolate biscuits too.

Good man, Mark, you're not all bad!

An hour later I was completely hooked. It seemed that thebabyline.ie was like Facebook for mothers, albeit all under a thin veil of anonymity. They all seemed to know each other or at least each other's on-line personas, and the depth of information that they supplied about their daily goings-on was incredible.

While it seemed most contributors dipped in and out, one lady, who went by the name 'simonfan', seemed to be around to chat at any hour of the day or night. Anyhow, by the time my hour was up, I knew how many children she had, what she was having for dinner, that she hated her mother-in-law and that she 'dtd' with her husband that morning. Despite the fact that 'did the dishes' was the best I could come up for that abbreviation, I had my doubts that that was what she meant.

A whole new world was opened up to me and I literally had to drag myself away when the smell of cooking started to sneak under my door. Mark was an absolute disaster in the kitchen. There was nothing for it but to close my laptop and head downstairs.

I counted in my head how long it would be until the kids were in bed and I could return to my new discovery. The things that got me excited these days . . .

Chapter 29

Wednesday found me on a bus again. Really, I hadn't taken as much public transport in my entire life as I had these past few weeks. This time I was bound for a country pub, just off the beaten track, a trip that would involve two buses. But I didn't care. It seemed like forever since the last time we'd met and I couldn't wait to see Oliver again.

And, as this time he was bringing his car, I was hoping he'd suggest the scenic route home . . .

A shiver of excitement ran through me at the thought.

A bit of romance was exactly what I needed.

Mark's crisis of conscience on Saturday had predictably not lasted long and since then he'd been working round the clock. Apparently his practice partner Fenton was away which meant he had to be on call for several days on the go as Tara was not yet experienced enough to handle the calls on her own. She hadn't been to the house since the night I'd been to Dawn's but it was obvious by his tone when he was talking to her on the phone that she was about the only person he didn't bark at.

Including me.

Anyhow, Fenton had arrived back on Tuesday night, meaning Mark had no excuse for not staying home this evening.

I badly needed the break. Minding the children was exhausting. To be fair, Amber had come on in leaps and bounds since 'the methods' had been put into practice. But I was fast discovering that staying home with children, no matter how well they behaved, was a demanding and thankless job.

There was also another slight problem that had arisen. And I had no one to blame but myself.

The school run.

Actually, anything that involved leaving the house and bumping into other people.

Other mothers.

Other mothers who wanted advice.

Seriously, it was like I'd gone viral.

It had all started harmlessly enough. Well, I suppose it really started with Ellen and that first fateful foray into dispensing child-rearing advice about Controlled Crying. Then of course I'd had the near miss with Noreen Costello. When I'd rung her that evening with my Sleep Association 'findings', she'd been ecstatic. I had been sorely tempted to tell her that all this and so much more was hers for the taking if she just fired up her computer and got Googling. But if it was one thing I'd learnt over the last few days, it was that Irish mothers seemed to have an aversion to anything that might possibly have been gleaned from a book. I was assuming that a website would be treated with equal vitriol.

"Don't talk to me about those baby books!" they'd hiss with pure venom. "Sure what would they know?"

But for some bizarre reason, they didn't mind taking the advice from me, who had, ironically, just taken it from a book.

Not that they knew that of course.

No, I was the American Nanny.

The Oracle.

Which was okay if I could answer whatever question they sprang at me. And to be fair, my knowledge was accumulating. When I wasn't spending my spare time reading, I was on the internet, plundering the babyline for nuggets of wisdom. Let's face it, there wasn't exactly a vast array of ways to spend my spare time these days.

But then I came up against little Rosie Fagan and her messy poos.

Oh yes.

And I should have said, 'Do you know what, Mrs Fagan, I have no idea why your daughter has up to three messy poos a day. Go to your doctor.'

But I didn't.

I looked at the woman's anxious face and stupidly said, "Oh, Mrs Fagan, that's quite interesting. I could chat to you about it now but I have to take Jamie to the dentist – leave it with me though – I promise I'll get back to you."

And home I went. No point in going to the books on this one – it was definitely a case for the internet.

"*Messy poos, messy poos, messy poos,*" I hummed to myself as I surfed.

"Meh-meh ooos!" chanted Amber beside me.

"Yes, Amber, meh-meh ooos indeed," I smiled. But I wasn't having much luck. Plenty of posts concerning 'no poos' but none relating to the 'messy' variety.

Then I had an idea. I closed out to the home page. My mouse hovered over the register button for a second.

Come on, what harm will it do? You can de-register just as soon as you get the info you need. No one will know you!

Then I inhaled deeply and started to type.

> Hi girls,
>
> I'm new to this board but I was wondering if anyone could help me. I have a three-year-old dd who well, sorry if tmi, has messy poos.

Tmi meant 'too much information'. I had discovered a glossary on the site that explained all the abbreviations: dd meant 'darling daughter', ds meant 'darling son', dh was 'darling husband', hth was 'hope this helps'. . . oh, and dtd was 'did the deed' . . .

> I'm quite careful about what she eats, but not obsessive iykwim.

That meant 'if you know what I mean' – boy, was I getting into this!

> I've had her at the doctor and he said to keep a food diary. The thing is I'm not noticing it relating to any food in particular.

Thankfully, I'd got into the habit of cross-examining the mammies so that I'd be armed with as many of the facts as possible when it came to trying to find the answers.

> Any help or advice would be gratefully accepted.

I liked the last bit. Nothing like a bit of humble gratitude to get them onside.

I signed off: MarshaG

I especially loved my username. It kind of made up for that time she wouldn't let me borrow her ID for the local disco.

And now there was nothing left to do but wait. I closed the computer and got started on the dinner.

As it happened, it was bedtime before I managed to get back to the PC that night. Mark, surprise, surprise, was working and I had a mountain of laundry that simply wasn't going to iron itself. To be honest, I wasn't even sure if laundry should come under my remit but, as I felt increasing guilt that my tenure as Nanny of the Fielding Household was reaching an end in literally weeks, I was willing to overlook the small print of my contract.

So at almost ten I opened my emails to see if I'd had any replies.

You have seven new messages.

And all seven were notifications from the babyline.
I couldn't believe my eyes.
Logging into the site, I started to read . . .

Hey MarshaG,
First of all welcome to the babyline! Great to see a new face around here.

Now wasn't that nice.

Sorry to hear about your dd, nappies are bad enough without that kind of issue! Do you mind me asking has she always been like this?

Feck. I don't know.

The thing is, if she is then I'm wondering could it be some kind of allergy or intolerance?

Oh. Hadn't thought of that.

> I think you should definitely take her to see
> someone, if not your doctor then maybe an
> allergist or paediatrician.
> Let us know how you get on.
> Suki10

I kept reading. This was good stuff.
Next up was a nice lady called Dingdongdell (like really?).

> Hi MarshaG,
> I've no experience of this but I just wanted to
> welcome you on board – as Suki says, tis great to
> see a new face!

Girls – what are you doing to me! I'm nearly crying here.

> Just one thing though, pooing like that all the
> time isn't normal. You should definitely go back
> to your doctor and demand some answers.
> Dingdongdell.

Well, thanks, Dingdongdell, but you're not giving me
much there.

It wasn't until I read the next reply that the discussion
got going in earnest.

FunkyMunky knew her stuff . . .

> Hi MarshaG
> I totally feel your pain. My dd was the exact same.

Brilliant. Now we were getting places.

> I'd almost stake my life that your dd is lactose-
> intolerant just like mine.

Really?

It started when she was born. Always had huge issues with milk, throwing up all the time, never finishing bottles, always either constipated or with a runny bum. Has your daughter got a constantly runny nose too?

Em. I don't know. Maybe?

Anyhow, I took her to the doctor and to be honest, I think he thought I was overreacting. But I knew something was wrong. Anyhow, I did what you're doing, kept a food diary, but like you just couldn't spot a pattern. Then one day I spotted a thread on here.

I already knew that 'thread' was the name used for a discussion on internet forums.

I can bump it up for you if you like.

That meant updating it so as to move it up the discussion board to where I could find it.

Anyway, it mentioned a new milk that you could purchase called Lacto-free and I decided to give it a try. All I can say, Marsha, is NEW CHILD.
No runny nose, no constipation, no eczema.

I practically punched the air. *FunkyMunky, you little beauty!*

And on it went: two more people agreed with FunkyMunky, another gave me the name of her allergist, another suggested goat's milk.

In literally half an hour I had all the information I needed. I went to bed that night exhausted and dreamt of messy poos the whole night long.

Any wonder a girl was in need of a bit of romancing?

Chapter 30

"I've missed you." Oliver reached across the table and stroked my face. "It's just not the same without you."

"Yeah, right," I smiled. "You just have no one to blame everything on now."

"Well, there is that too," he admitted. "I didn't realise quite how much flack you took. But I'm serious – it's so boring."

"We won't always get to work together, you know."

"I know, but at least we'll get to live together when we're in New York."

"Oh really? When did we decide that?" I teased.

"Well, I just presumed . . . I mean, it makes sense, doesn't it?"

"Yes, I suppose it does. We'd have to get our own place though – it's not like we can both move back in with Monica."

Apartment-hunting together in New York! My heart gave a flutter at the thought. In a few weeks that's exactly what we'd be doing. Deciding between a studio in East

Village and a brownstone in the Upper West Side. There were days now where my former life in the most exciting city in the world seemed a million light years away. It was so hard to imagine that in a few short weeks we'd be there. Together.

I sighed with pure happiness and looked at my menu.

A menu.

That alone was a treat. I'd almost forgotten that there were people out there who got to pick what they were going to eat *from a list*.

And have it handed to them.

And not have to wash the pots.

"Oh, this is heaven," I murmured.

"Eh, Holly, it's pub grub?"

"I know. But it will be handed to me. Cooked. And I don't have to wash up."

"Why, are you living in a cave? Don't tell me you have to go out these days and hunt for your food? I'd have thought that, at the very least, that Neanderthal you're going out with would catch it for you."

"Ha ha, very funny," I answered, hoping he didn't keep this up. I'd been deliberately hazy about my exact living arrangements and had no desire to fill him in.

But he wasn't giving up.

"So how is Hairy these days?"

"Harry," I corrected him. "He's fine. And I've told you before: I'm not going out with him."

Oliver grunted. "I'm sure that's not his choice."

"Well, what does it matter whose choice it is?" I couldn't help being coy, there was no harm in him thinking he had a bit of rivalry. "Harry has been very good to me. He got me a job and a place to live and without him I wouldn't be here right now, so the least you can do is get his name right."

"Let's talk about something else," Oliver yawned. "I'm bored with him."

"Okay so. Any word on the promotions?"

He immediately looked down at his menu.

"Eh, no. Not yet."

"What's up?"

"Nothing, nothing."

"Are they out? Did you not get it?" I was torn between alarm that this might be true and elation that, if so, there would then be nothing stopping us heading to America.

"No. No, seriously, there's no word yet. It's looking good for me actually. That's the good news . . ." He trailed off.

"And what's the bad?" I demanded.

"Oh look, it doesn't matter."

"It obviously does matter!"

"No. You're going to go crazy and the evening will be ruined."

"Try me." My voice was icy, and totally belied the panic that was choking me inside.

"Well, my lease is up. On the apartment."

"And?"

"And, well, it's hardly worth me getting somewhere else, if I'm going away with you in a couple of weeks."

I didn't like where this was going.

"And?" I said again.

"Stop saying 'and'!"

"I will, when you tell me exactly what's going on!"

"Well, it's just that Catherine's offered –"

"*No!*" I shouted, standing up.

"Holly, sit down!"

"What kind of a fool do you take me for? Goodbye, Oliver!" I scraped my chair back from the table and, tears springing to my eyes, I rushed from the pub.

"Holly, come back!" Oliver was out after me immediately.

But I was almost running now, to where I don't know.

He grabbed my arm and swung me around.

"Let go of me!" I cried, tears streaming down my cheeks now.

"No! For the love of God, Holly, I'll hardly even be there. It's only for a few weeks!"

"I can't," I sobbed, "I can't do this any more. I can't believe you're moving in with her."

"And I can't believe you're being so unreasonable!"

"*Unreasonable?*" I screamed at him. "*Unreasonable?* You're moving in with her. How fucking reasonable do I have to be? In God's name, Oliver, I can't fucking take this any more!"

"Well, do you know what? Neither can I."

He let go of me and stepped back.

"What's that supposed to mean?"

"You're not the only one under pressure here, Holly. Let's just forget it."

I froze, my stomach feeling like it might hurl itself onto the footpath.

"You mean it? You want to break up?"

"No. I don't. But I'm sick of feeling like the baddie in all of this. If I don't feel bad about her, I feel bad about you. Quite honestly, I've had it."

I looked at him. He was white, and very, very angry-looking.

254

"Oliver, I –"

"You know what annoys me the most, Holly? I didn't have to tell you about this. You'd never have known. But I was trying to do the right thing. I thought, best thing to do is just to tell her. More fucking fool me, because nothing is ever enough for you, is it?"

"Now, come on, you can't blame for me for being upset!" I couldn't believe the direction the evening had taken. It was like a nightmare.

He wanted to break up with me.

"*Yeah, well, I'm upset too!*" he shouted at me, stamping his foot, for all the world like a toddler about to throw the mother and father of all tantrums. "But it has to be all about you, doesn't it, Holly! I wouldn't mind but I had other news for tonight and, now, well, there's just no point, is there, because there's just no pleasing you these days!"

"What news?"

"Forget it. I'll drop you home and we'll just leave it at that, alright?"

"Oliver, please." I couldn't leave it like this. I hated rows. I especially hated rows that were turning out to be all my fault.

"No, Holly, please. You're right. This isn't working for you. And it's a pity, because we only had to muddle through for three more weeks. That was all, Holly. Three weeks."

"What are you talking about?"

He scratched his head as if wondering whether to tell me or not.

"I was talking to Jeff Peterson in New York this morning. I don't know if you know him or not, but he's heading up this new division. I met him last year at a think-in. Anyway, he has a job for me, if I get manager."

"Why didn't you tell me?" I cried, forgetting my tears in my excitement.

"I'm not meant to tell anyone yet! It's all hush-hush. He's agreed not to say anything to Dublin in case it affects the promotion. But look. Forget it. We tried. It didn't work. I don't blame you for wanting out."

"I don't want out," I whispered, "you know I don't."

"No, Holly, there is no point in you pretending. If it's too much for you, just say it. I won't bother you again."

I reached up and held his white, tense face in my hands.

"I can handle it. I promise."

But he looked away, his jaw still tense with fury.

I reached up to kiss him. And then, almost reluctantly, he kissed me back, softly at first then hungrily, then crushing me against the stone wall of the building behind.

"You are killing me, Holly Green," he muttered hoarsely between long, passionate kisses. "Like seriously killing me."

"I love you too," I whispered, tears streaming down my cheeks again, only this time tears of relief.

It was happening. New York was really happening.

His hands were in my hair now, grabbing fistfuls, tearing my head back.

"Oliver – wait!"

We were on a main street, after all.

"Come on, let's get you to the car," he said, still kissing me as he bundled me along.

"Hey!" I squealed. "What about dinner!"

"I'll get you McDonald's on the way home." His voice was hoarse. "Now get yourself into that car before I change my mind."

Chapter 31

"What could you possibly have to tell me that's so funny?" Dawn asked as she opened the door.

"I'm sorry, but it's definitely a story that needs wine," I giggled, going past her into the kitchen.

Graham was away again, and Mark was home. This kind of night was starting to mean only one thing.

Drinkies with Dawn!

She went straight to the fridge.

"You know," she said, uncorking an ice-cold bottle of white, "when the evenings get longer we'll have to start going walking instead of sitting in my sitting room drinking wine or we'll end up being twenty-stone alcoholics!"

My smile froze.

I wouldn't be here when the evenings got longer. I'd be back in New York.

"What's wrong?" Dawn asked, noticing my change in mood.

"Oh nothing," I said, trying to think on my feet. "It's just that maybe Mark will have got sick of me by then."

"Well, hopefully not. Anyway you'll hardly be a million miles away if he does, will you?" She laughed. "I'll just have to hand over the reins to Graham and meet you somewhere!"

Hope you like flying.

"I suppose."

"Anyhow, why would Mark get sick of you – aren't you his lifesaver?"

I started to giggle again. "After last night, he might not think so any more!"

"Come on! Spill!"

I took my glass of wine from her and we went into the sitting room. Sinking down in her beautiful cream couch I could feel my good humour coming back.

"Well, it happened last night. At about ten thirty I heard his phone ring. I was actually still downstairs, in the sitting room, watching TV. He was up having a shower. Anyhow, I heard him answer it and next thing he was hopping around upstairs like a lunatic, getting dressed."

"Oh really, and how do you know that?" Dawn teased.

"Because a) he's not exactly light of foot, and b) by the time he got downstairs he was still half naked."

"What?" Dawn squealed. "Now that's a sight I wouldn't mind seeing!"

"Oh please!" I wrinkled my nose in disgust, though I still couldn't stop the flush coming to my cheeks. There was no denying that the sight of Mark crashing down the stairs naked to the waist had been pretty impressive. For someone who couldn't have had time to work out, he had an amazing physique. Giant shoulders, broad chest, tapering down into the flattest stomach and . . .

Of course what had happened next wasn't long in banishing all of those thoughts from my head.

"Anyway, there he was rushing around trying to find an ironed shirt. And of course all the laundry was still in the kitchen."

"An ironed shirt? Why in God's name was he being so fussy if he was in a hurry?"

"Well, it was Hannah Tuttlebury-Smythe on the phone, you see."

"Lady Smythe? Wow! Is he her vet?"

"Yes, she's his biggest client. A bit high maintenance apparently, though she seems to adore him."

"Why wouldn't she? Can't see anyone else being at her beck and call twenty-four hours a day!"

"True." I started to giggle again. "Anyhow, there he was hopping around the kitchen, trying to ask her exactly what was wrong, all the time trying to find something decent to wear. And he kept saying, 'Colic, are you sure you think it's colic, Lady Hannah?' And he was on one leg trying to get on his boot, and his shirt was halfway over his head." I paused to catch my breath. "And I could actually hear her screeching at the other end. And for a second, he took the phone from his ear and hissed at me to ring Fenton – that Lady Smythe's stallion had colic and that he'd better get the surgery ready and call in the nurses. So I had just picked up the house phone to ring Fenton when . . ." I could hold back the laughter no longer.

"Oh come on! Finish the story!" Dawn was on the edge of her seat, puzzled that I could possibly find a story about a sick horse so funny.

"When I heard him ask had they been walking him, and she obviously said 'Yes, around the house' because he said in a strange tone, 'Around the house? Well, I suppose, anywhere that you can . . .' and then I heard –" I wiped the tears from my eyes.

"What?"

"I heard him roar 'Calpol!'"

"*What?*"

"I know! And he shouted 'Jesus Christ, Lady Hannah – why would you give a horse Calpol?'"

The look of puzzlement on Dawn's face was hilarious.

"And then he stood still, his shirt half on and half off and he said, "Lady Hannah, let's take it from the start. Who exactly are we talking about here? And when she answered he said very slowly, 'Who, might I ask, is Tristan?'"

"And what did she say?"

"It's her grandson!" I shrieked.

"What? Her *grandson*?"

I nodded. "She was baby-sitting, and it was him that had the colic."

"Oh! *That* kind of colic!" The penny dropped with Dawn. "Even still though, why would she ring the *vet* about her grandson?"

"She wasn't!" I screeched. "She was looking for me!"

"Oh. My. God." Dawn was open-mouthed in amazement.

"Apparently her housekeeper had heard in the village that I knew all there was to know about babies and when she couldn't get Tristan to sleep she rang looking for me. Of course Mark was panicking so much when he heard 'colic' he totally missed the bit where she asked for me."

"Oh Sweet Jesus, what did you do?"

"What could I do? He just looked at me and handed me the phone. And I got to talk to Lady Hannah about her colicky grandchild."

"Oh God, I can't believe it!"

"I know! Oh, it wasn't funny at the time but I haven't been able to stop laughing since."

"Is he really cross?"

"I don't really know – you know Mark, he kind of has only one facial expression. Anyhow, it was hardly my fault. He just left the room and I've hardly seen him since."

"He's probably mortified."

"I doubt it. I wouldn't say Mark does mortification."

"Oh God, I think that is the funniest story I've ever heard!" Dawn sank back into the couch. "Wait till I tell Graham."

"Where is he anyway?"

"London. He'll be back tomorrow."

"Oh. He really is away a lot, isn't he?"

"I know. But I don't mind at the moment. It will all have to change once –"

She was interrupted by the sound of my phone ringing in my pocket. I took it out and looked at the display, not recognising the number I answered.

"Hello?"

"Hi, Holly? Is that you? It's Kelly. I'm outside your apartment but there's some guy in there and he says he doesn't know who you are!"

Chapter 32

For the seventh time that morning I ran up the stairs with a handful of clothes and toys. I'm not sure why I was so concerned that the place be tidy – it's not like any of that kind of stuff mattered to Kelly.

Yes, my sister was coming for lunch. Turns out she had a meeting about setting up a new shop in Kildare and was only too happy to stop by for lunch en route. Great. I wasn't sure if I was relieved to be seeing a friendly face or petrified at what she was going to say to me. Because I could do a lot of things, but I couldn't lie to my younger sister.

When she'd phoned the night before, I'd looked open-mouthed at Dawn standing in front of me, not knowing what to say.

When I eventually pulled myself together I said "Hang on, Kelly." Then I hurriedly excused myself to Dawn and left.

I leaned against the wall outside Mark's house.

"Kelly, I'm not in Dublin any more. You'd better sit down . . ."

At the end of my sorry tale, she'd insisted on coming down to me and so here I was, cleaning like a dervish in advance of her visit. Like a tidy house was going to make my ridiculous situation look any less ridiculous.

At exactly twelve the front-door bell rang. I looked out the window and despite all my nervousness my stomach leapt with excitement at seeing Kelly's cherry-red Mini Cooper in the driveway.

"*Woohooo!* She's here! Come on, Amber, come and meet my little sister!"

I flung open the door and there she was. My darling sister. Slightly shorter than me, and ever so slightly plumper, she hadn't changed much from when she was six. The masses of ginger curls that had prompted the nickname 'Little Orphan Annie' were still there in profusion as were the dancing eyes and cherubic lips.

"Well, look at you," she grinned. "Did I ever think I'd see the day that you'd open a door to me with a child on your hip!"

"Oh, don't start!" I had to laugh. "At least not until you get inside the front door. Some of us have to worry about the neighbours, you know."

"Hang on – I come bearing gifts." Kelly ran back to the boot of the car and took out a large bag.

"Ooooh – samples?" I squealed with excitement.

"Do I ever let you down?"

She stepped into the hall and looked around.

"Oh, interesting colour scheme . . ."

"Don't talk to me! I thought Mum's was bad."

"It is. If *Tatler* ever gets hold of Mum's sitting room, my reputation is ruined."

I laughed, feeling all the tension of the last few weeks

leave my body. Having Kelly sitting at my kitchen table was great, even if she did have a grinning Amber sitting on her lap.

"I suppose you've had the Chad reminder?" I asked as I put on the kettle.

"Yes, almost daily at this stage. I hope nothing of major consequence happens between now and Friday that the *Late Late* decide to run a whole show on. Mam will go mental if they cancel Chad. But anyhow, enough about him. Explain all this to me again?" She waved an arm around the small kitchen. "You've really done it this time, haven't you?"

"Hey! You're hardly in any position to lecture me, seeing as you haven't dated a man the legal age for years."

"Now, now," Kelly adopted a prim look, "I'll have you know that my current squeeze is twenty – well above the acceptable age."

"Marginally above, Kelly. Remember you're twenty-seven. You definitely only get away with this because Mum doesn't know."

"Oh, could you imagine? Though all she'd be worried about is whether he'd be after my money."

"And is he?"

"Holly, I won't lie, my bank account is looking quite healthy, but if a couple of packets of Marlboro and a pint of cider is what it takes to keep that delicious boy happy, then I'm happy enough to contribute."

"Kelly Green!"

"I know – I can hear the advertisement now . . . 'This is Adam . . .'" She changed her voice to an exaggerated, low, serious, tone. "'For just two euro a day, you could keep this penniless student in your bed and grateful . . .'"

"Kelly! It's so not fair! You're way more morally depraved than me!"

"I am. But I'm also ridiculously successful." Kelly flicked her red curls. "And I think I could shag the President himself in full view of Ireland and my mother would forgive me at the moment."

"Why, what have you achieved now? Go on, don't hold back on my account."

"Oh nothing much, just that you might want to watch the English papers tomorrow. I believe Kate Middleton is going to be carrying one of these!" She reached into the bag and pulled out a large umbrella embellished with her now famous KG logo.

"Oh, you *bitch*!" I squealed. "How did you manage that one?"

"Oh, Paulo knows people who know people. I don't get involved in all that business stuff."

Paulo was Kelly's long-suffering business manager, a dishy Italian who clearly adored the ground she walked on.

"Good old Paulo. The brand will go through the roof after this."

"So he says," she sighed, trying to look nonchalant, "but you know me, I'm all about the art."

"Go away, you don't fool me!" I flicked a tea towel at her and she giggled. "So when are you going to give up those boys and make an honest man of Paulo?" I asked.

Kelly sighed. "Oh, some day. He really is the love of my life, you know, but the boys are so much fun – they let me do lots of stuff that Paulo wouldn't approve of. Anyway, look how good I am with children?"

She was right. The usually rambunctious Amber was

still sitting quietly on her lap, by now happily going through the contents of Kelly's rather large, multi-pocketed handbag.

"There's nothing in there she might put in her mouth and get high on, is there?"

"Not today," Kelly grinned.

"You are incorrigible, Kelly Green."

"Eh, hello, Miss Hiding-down-the-country-as-a-nanny!" she shrieked. "This Oliver guy must be some piece of stuff."

"He is – even Mam would approve if she met him. He's good-looking, successful, charming . . ."

"See, that's the difference between you and me, Holls – you worry too much about what Mam would think. I couldn't give a hoot."

"That's easy when she thinks the sun shines out of your arse!" I bit back indignantly.

"Oh whatever! So does this mean you'll be around for Christmas? Please say it does . . ."

"Well, the plan is that we'll be in New York for Christmas so probably not."

"Oh Holly, go after Christmas! Stephen's Day if you like – just don't leave me with them on my own!"

I giggled. "They're all yours, sweetie. You should bring what's-his-name – Adam – I'm sure we could arrange for Santa to bring his presents there."

"Oh stop! Can you imagine the look on Marsha's face? Though I suppose he could keep the twins company!"

"Oh boy! I sure can imagine her reaction!" I'd seen the Older-Sister-look-of-disapproval once already this year and I wasn't going to forget it in a hurry.

"Well, he won't be there so we'll just have to find some

other way to shock Marsha." Kelly sniffed the air. "What is that delicious smell? Is it my favourite? Please tell me it's –"

"Would I let you down?" I took the vegetarian quiche from the oven and placed it on the table in front of her as she pretended to swoon at the delicious aroma.

"Oh Holly, I love you!"

"I love you too." I ruffled the chestnut curls as I went to get the salad.

Just then the kitchen door opened and I leapt in shock as Amber squealed "Da Da!"

"Why, hello," Mark said when he saw Kelly sitting at the table.

Oh shit.

"Mark, this is my sister. She's just here for some lunch. I hope that's okay?"

"Of course it's okay." Mark smiled at Kelly, who was sitting open-mouthed looking up at him, and then took an excited Amber from her arms. "I'm Mark, and you are . . . ?"

"Kelly. I'm Kelly." Kelly's mouth was still hanging open and I almost laughed to see my chatterbox sister so seemingly lost for words.

"How's everything?" Mark asked me as he went through his bundle of post.

"Great," I answered. "We'll be heading shortly to go and get Jamie."

"Well, I can get him and drop him back if you like." Mark looked at Kelly and smiled again. "Give you girls more time for lunch."

"No, it's fine –" I started but Kelly, who seemed to have recovered, interrupted me.

"That would be lovely, Mark, thanks."

Oh God, that was all I needed, Mark and my sister

bonding. I frowned at her in what I hoped was a meaningful way.

"Though I won't be under Holly's feet all day. I have to be at the Kildare Outlet by three," she added hastily.

"Oh, shopping?" Mark asked pleasantly.

"No, I've a meeting about a shop."

I kicked her violently under the table.

"I mean, well, it's not really a meeting, It's a – a job interview. In the sunglasses shop." She smiled. "Have to take the jobs where we can these days – isn't that right, Holly?"

"Yes, dear." I shot her another warning look but Mark, who seemed to have found whatever piece of post he was looking for, wasn't listening.

"Would you like some lunch, Mark?" Kelly asked sweetly.

Mark looked at his watch. "Smells good but I have to be off if I'm going to collect Jamie at one thirty. I'll grab a sandwich on the way."

"Holly could pack you a takeaway. Couldn't you, Holly?"

"Yes, of course." I made a face at Kelly and got up to get a plastic container. I put in some quiche and salad and handed it to Mark, who handed me Amber in return.

"Why, thank you," he said, smiling. "I guess I'll see you later."

"I suppose you will," I answered, feeling a flush start to rise on my cheeks.

"Bye, Mark!" Kelly called sweetly from the table.

"Lovely to meet you, Kelly." He smiled at her. "And best of luck with the interview."

The minute he was out the door Kelly grabbed my arm.

"Who was that?" she hissed.

"Eh, my boss, I would have thought that much was obvious."

"And, eh, why have I heard nothing about him before?"

"What's to hear? He's my boss. Oh, and don't be fooled by all that smiley-smiley stuff – he's not like that all the time."

"Jesus, Holls, he's a fine thing!"

"Oh, come on! I think my life is complicated enough at the moment without you throwing Mark Fielding into the mix."

"Well, janey, you could throw him into my mix anytime you feel like it. And I do declare I might have seen the hint of a blush on your cheeks when he smiled at you."

"Start eating, Kelly!" I slapped her with the tea towel again. "I think your blood sugar must be low."

"All I'm saying is, you sure don't do things by halves, do you?"

"Tell me something I don't know," I sighed. "Tell me something I don't know."

Chapter 33

I woke on Saturday morning and, looking at my phone, saw it was only nine o'clock. Cursing, I closed my eyes and rolled back under the warm duvet. It hadn't been all that long since I'd gone to bed so I willed myself to go back to sleep.

But it was no use, I was wide awake now – ironic, given it was Mark's turn to do the football-training run. So I just lay there, replaying the previous night over in my head.

Wow.

From the very start of the evening, Oliver had been so attentive. He'd even offered to collect me. Which, in turn, gave me a new dilemma. He thought I was sharing a house with Harry, so how could I explain Mark and the children? So I spun him some story about the directions being complicated and instead offered to meet him outside the butcher's on the main street. Luckily he didn't question me any further.

"Where are we going?" I asked as I hopped into the passenger seat.

"It's a surprise," he said, "to make up for starving you on Wednesday."

"Oh goodie, I love surprises!"

Instead of then turning and driving back towards Dublin, he took the Carlow road and drove the ten miles or so to Rathmoylan House, a small hotel set in a beautiful country estate just off the Carlow Road. A further mile down a winding gravel driveway, it couldn't have been more secluded.

"Oh, this looks wonderful!" I gasped.

"Well, I'm glad you're impressed – it even has one of those fancy stars they're always talking about," he answered, looking very pleased with himself.

"Definitely better than a drive-through McDonald's," I teased.

"We can only hope."

Just then my phone buzzed. It was another text message from Dad.

Chad on Late Late 2nite. Pls ring your mother after show to tell her he was great whether U saw him or not.

I rolled my eyes and shoved the phone back into my pocket. Poor Dad, she really must have him under pressure. I made a mental note to do as he asked later.

"Well, does this make up for the pub-grub fiasco?" Oliver asked as I finished my last, luxurious bite of chocolate marquise.

I nodded, too intent on savouring my final mouthful to talk.

"Well, I'm glad you enjoyed it – and that you appreciate the effort I've gone to."

I looked at him in surprise. "Of course I do! That's a silly thing to say. I'd have been just as happy with a bag of chips in the car as long as I'm with you, though."

He grunted.

"Oliver! I would! It's lovely!"

"Well, I'm glad you enjoyed it, that's all I'm saying."

After dinner, we took our coffees out to the library, where we snuggled in front of an open fire. Thankfully, the tension seemed to leave his body and I could feel him relax.

"I can't believe I'm off tomorrow and you have to work! You never usually work on Saturdays," I sighed.

"I know, but I'm trying to make a good impression, you know – promotions could be any day now . . ."

"I bet you're just spending the day with her?" I said, regretting the words as soon as I'd uttered them.

"No, Holly, I'm not. She's not even around this weekend. Anyhow, I thought we weren't going to talk about her any more." Oliver's voice was uncharacteristically sharp.

"I know, I'm sorry." I looked down, annoyed with myself for saying anything.

"You're forgiven." He kissed me. "However, I don't have to be in work until nine." He kissed me again, this time on my neck, just behind my ear.

That man knew exactly what to do.

"So?"

"So, the night is young, that's all I'm saying." His lips were now tracing my jaw-line . . .

"What exactly are you suggesting, Mr Conlon?" I smiled, relieved that my earlier surliness seemed to have been forgotten.

"That I ask that nice girl on reception if she'd have a room?"

"What? Oliver!" I pushed him away, looking around at our sumptuous surroundings. "I doubt this kind of place lets you pay by the hour and you know I can't stay any longer than that!"

"Well, maybe I won't mention that we'll not be needing breakfast!" he muttered, before getting up.

"Oliver – no way – I am not booking into a hotel for a couple of hours."

"Why not?" he said sharply. "I'm sure you did it in New York all the time."

"That's a horrible thing to say," I said quietly, stunned at his nastiness. "Why are you being so horrible?"

"Well, why are you being so difficult?"

"I'm not being difficult, but we've had a lovely evening, really lovely – we don't need to –"

"Oh, so you've eaten and now you want to go home? It's like that now, is it?"

"There you go again – what is with you tonight? If either having sex or fighting is all you're interested in then why don't you just take me home?"

He sighed. "I'm sorry – that was uncalled for. I'm sorry."

"Well, so you should be – what in God's name is wrong with you?"

"I'm just under a bit of pressure at the moment – you know, the promotions and stuff. I suppose I just look forward to our evenings, you know, and I wanted this evening to be special."

"Well, it is – of course it is," I said, in relief at his remorse. "I look forward to seeing you too, you know." I put my hand on his arm but he shrugged it off.

"You're right, it's getting late, I'll drop you home."

"Well, we don't have to go just yet." There was something about his tone that was really starting to make me uneasy.

"Look, it's fine – I was just trying –" He stopped. "It's fine. Let's go."

I looked at him and before I could change my mind said, "If we stay we'll have to be gone by six in the morning . . ."

"Ah come on, it's not that far, and it'll be Saturday, remember? No traffic?"

"By six, Oliver, or I'm not staying!" I said firmly. There was no way I was arriving home any later than that, in the same clothes I'd gone out in. It wouldn't look right in front of the children, let alone Mark bloody Fielding.

But he was gone, already chatting animatedly to the receptionist. I looked away, my cheeks flaming. I couldn't believe we were booking a room basically just for sex.

Shit. With a sinking heart I remembered I hadn't phoned my mother. I toyed briefly with the idea of ignoring Dad's request, but I just couldn't do it to him. Stealing another glance at Oliver's back, I took a deep breath and started dialling.

"Green residence." My mother got more like Hyacinth Bucket every day.

"Hi, Mum, it's Holly."

"Oh Holly dear, well, what did you think?"

"Oh, he was fantastic, Mum, you must be really, really proud."

"Oh well, you know, I don't like to go on but . . ."

She clearly did want to go on.

"Well, Mum, I just thought I'd let you know I'd seen it – I'm sure you want to keep the line clear for all your other callers." My duty was done and I could see Oliver walking back towards me, swinging a key card cheekily in his hand.

"Wait – how did you think he looked?"

Shit – how had he looked?

"I thought he looked . . ." I wondered quickly how he could have looked any different than suave, confident Chad always looked but could come up with nothing, "good?" I finished tentatively.

"Did you not think he looked tired?"

Shit. He'd looked tired.

"Just a little, but you know, Mum, he works so hard."

"Yes." My mother still didn't sound happy. "I suppose. He was always so hardworking."

I waited for her to say 'Not like you,' but was surprised when she instead launched into an attack on the colour of his tie. A debate I really couldn't enter given my scant knowledge of the evening's appearance.

Meanwhile Oliver was now sitting beside me, kissing my neck.

"Mom, I really need to go," I tried to interrupt her while pushing Oliver away with my non-phone-holding hand.

"No, wait – I want to talk to you about Christmas –"

My heart sank. This conversation could go on all night. Meanwhile my boyfriend was still doing his level best to get me up to a bedroom that we'd virtually rented by the hour for pure unadulterated carnal pursuits.

"But, Mum –"

"Now, Holly, you're just like your dad – you want all the celebrating with none of the hassle. I've had to do everything – your dad won't even make the builders a cup of tea."

Builders? So the extension had gone ahead. I guiltily remembered Dad's text looking for my intervention, which of course I'd forgotten about until now.

I opened my mouth to reply but suddenly she was shrieking about there being an incoming call and with all her flapping she managed to cut me off.

In a swift move Oliver took my phone from me and turned it off.

"Now, come on, let's go!"

And up the grand staircase we scampered like two naughty schoolchildren, to a room more sumptuous than I could ever have imagined.

"There's one of those old-fashioned baths!" I squealed.

"Never mind the bath," Oliver grinned. "I'm more interested in having a go of that four-poster bed . . ."

My cheeks flushed again now just thinking about it. About how hours later we'd crept down the grand staircase, nodded sagely at the night-watchman and ran giggling out the front door.

Oliver had laughed at my shame. "For God's sake, you'll never see any of these people again."

And I knew he was right, but still . . .

Again I wouldn't let him drive me to the house, this time truthfully telling him that I wasn't having the noise of his car wake the entire neighbourhood – especially at that hour. So he'd left me at the entrance to the estate and I'd walked the walk of shame alone to the front door.

Now, with a long Saturday stretching out in front of me, I wondered would the lack of sleep come back to hit me later. There was nothing for it but to get up. I dragged on my jeans and a sweater and headed downstairs.

"Morning," said Mark. "You look remarkably fresh for someone who had such a late night – or was it an early morning?"

My cheeks flamed again. Damn it, he'd heard me come home.

"Sorry, I didn't mean to wake you," I muttered, turning to put on the kettle, unable to meet his eye.

"It's okay – I was awake."

"Oh. Right. Well, sorry anyway."

"So. What are you doing up? I've everything under control here. For once."

And he had. Amber was sitting up at the table eating her porridge and Jamie was, as usual, already dressed for football.

"I'm not very good at lie-ins," I said. "Actually, seeing as I'm up, there's something I've been meaning to ask you."

"Fire away."

"Well, it's your sitting room – you know, the room you don't use?"

He visibly froze, a warning look coming to his eyes, but it was too late for me to stop now.

"Well, I was wondering how you'd feel if I turned it into a playroom. It would give you more space and would tidy up the place a lot."

"No," he said.

"But –"

"I said *no*." He was so abrupt this time that I subconsciously took a step back.

"Right. That's obviously that then. Sorry for asking." And I took my cup of tea, left the kitchen and started to head for the stairs.

"Holly, wait!" He came out after me, shutting the door

behind him. "I'm sorry. I didn't mean it to come out like that."

"It's fine. It doesn't matter. I just thought it might be a good idea, that's all. But I shouldn't have said anything. It's your house."

"It's just that I can't do it."

"Well, I was suggesting I do it actually – well, as much as I could manage – but I thought you might give me a –"

"It's not a sitting room," he said.

"It's not?"

"It's – well, it was – a study. Emma's study."

"Oh. I see."

"And that's why I can't. I just can't. Because," he took a deep breath, "because there's stuff in there. Stuff that I just don't want to see." He exhaled. "That's why."

I could have kicked myself.

"Oh my God, Mark, I'm sorry. Of course. I didn't realise. It's just that when I was in Dawn's house, I saw her room, and I thought of your room and what a waste it is and . . ." I was babbling now, but this conversation was just awful.

"It's okay, you weren't to know. I know it's ridiculous but I just can't."

"Forget it. Forget I mentioned it." I literally didn't know what else to say.

"No. I don't want to forget it. It's a great idea. I often thought it myself. But I can do a lot of things – I mean, before twelve yesterday I'd shot one horse and castrated two, but just don't ask me to –"

He turned his head away so quickly that for one awful moment I thought he was going to cry.

I had no idea what to do. Deciding rapidly against

reaching out to comfort him, I did my usual and chose the practical route.

"Look, Mark. This is not a big house, and one whole room, one large room is completely wasted." I took a deep breath before continuing. "What would you think if I packed up the stuff for you? I'll box it and seal it and you can put it in the little attic beside my room or somewhere else until you're ready to deal with it. Maybe you'll never be ready but there's probably stuff the kids might want – you know, when they're older."

I braced myself for an onslaught of abuse, but it didn't come.

"I couldn't ask you to do that," he muttered.

"You're not asking me. I'm offering. Let's face it, I'm not going to be able for much else on two hours' sleep, am I?"

He nodded and turned his head to look at me, the devastation on his face heartbreaking.

So I continued. "And when the stuff is gone, it might be easier for you to consider the idea of a few minor modifications. It would be a lovely room for the kids, and you'd get your TV room back. Imagine, no more Lego embedded in the soles of your feet!"

At that he smiled, and I heaved a sigh of relief. The moment had passed. He wasn't going to cry.

"You know, I've got a load of empty cardboard boxes at the surgery," he said, visibly cheering up. "If you could mind the kids for ten minutes I could fly and get them?"

"Perfect. You've loads of time. I'll have Amber dressed when you get back. In fact, I'll pack a few things and why don't you go down and visit your mother? Show her the improvement in Amber. I bet she'll be amazed."

He nodded again and, taking his keys off the hook, he turned to me and said, "Thanks, Holly."

"No problem."

"I mean it. Thanks, you've no idea how –"

"Go!" I said.

After all, the last thing I wanted was to cry myself.

Chapter 34

As soon as they were all gone, I braced myself, took the key down from over the door and unlocked the sitting room.

Or, sorry, the study.

I'm not sure what I was expecting really, but at first it just looked like any ordinary room. Except it was dusty, and very, very dark. Of course the fact that the walls were painted in deep aubergine didn't help. Nor did the closed curtains.

I went over to the window and dragged across the heavy brocade material. Then I stood back and looked around. I was going to need every one of the boxes Mark had brought back.

Sorry, that Mark *and Tara* had brought back. It still amused me that the level of vitriol that poor girl brought out in me was so strong.

Because she was actually really nice. She was helpful, sweet, and didn't seem to have a bad word to say about anyone.

Maybe that was the problem.

Very hard to like someone you'd nothing in common with . . .

Anyhow, I'd no time to be worrying about her now. I was just realising what a mammoth task I'd set myself.

One wall was completely taken up with bookshelves, and there was a large desk in the corner. Against the other wall was a small couch, though it was covered under a mountain of what seemed to be clothes.

Emma's clothes, I realised with a start.

Oh God, what had I let myself in for?

Not sure I could either emotionally, let alone physically, do this on my own, I took my phone out and scrolled down to Harry's number.

He sounded sleepy when he answered.

"Holly, it's ten o'clock on a Saturday morning," he groaned.

"Don't tell me you're still in bed?"

"Don't tell me you're not!" he answered.

"I need a favour. Actually, no, your brother needs a favour."

"No to both of you."

"Harry! Come on, pleeease!"

"Speak." He sighed. "You have three sentences to persuade me."

And that had been an hour ago.

For a moment I'd stood in that dusty room, not really knowing where to start.

Eventually I decided to tackle the clothes first. It soon became apparent that they had literally been lifted from a wardrobe in a hurry and draped on the couch. Each item was even still on a hanger. I lifted a garment carefully and held it up. A long, flowing dress. She'd obviously been a lot taller than me and, surprisingly, thinner.

The whole pile consisted of flowing skirts, scarves and pretty lace tops. Every time I touched a garment, to my horror, the scent of her perfume wafted towards me and the goose-bumps rose on my arms.

Oh Harry, hurry up, I pleaded, but I knew there was nothing for it but to continue. I tried to use my judgement but in the end I was afraid to throw anything out. So I just packed all the clothes neatly into boxes, all the time trying not to inhale.

I moved the packed boxes and bags into the hall with relief, and turned to the desk. Oh God, but I felt like such an intruder. She was obviously some kind of writer. There were what appeared to be two unfinished manuscripts and several large yellow notebooks full of notes. Funnily enough, there was no sign of a computer and everything was written in the same flowing style of handwriting, beautifully consistent, on every page.

There was handwritten poetry too, again in yellow notebooks. I couldn't resist flicking through. Most were about the autumn winds or the spring frosts, but one in particular stood out.

It read:

> *With every kick, gurgle, hiccup,*
> *That rides high between my ribs,*
> *Or weighs down upon my hips,*
> *I thank God,*
> *That you are safe,*
> *Where I still know*
> *How to protect you.*

That was dated almost six years ago. It must have been written for Jamie. A lump rose in my throat. The poor, poor woman! Little did she know that she would only have a few short years with her beautiful children.

The masochist in me made me keep reading. More nature poems, a few about childhood memories, and then another that stood out, mostly because it was the only one where the beautiful steady handwriting wavered.

> *Alone*
> *The house is quiet.*
> *And I wait, and I wish*
> *That he'd change his mind,*
> *And go elsewhere.*
> *Because I've run out of*
> *Strength.*
> *And I know that when he knocks,*
> *There'll be nothing for it,*
> *But to open the door.*
> *And let the death of a thousand cuts*
> *Claim me for his own.*

I read the last two lines again.

What could she possibly mean?

"Eh, hello? Are we working or reading?"

I leapt with fright, dropping the notebook with a crash.

"Harry! For God's sake – what are you trying to do to me?"

"Sorry!" he laughed. "Did you think I was a ghost?"

"Yes! I should never have started this. She's just so – *here*!" I shivered.

"Yes, Emma always had a certain 'presence'," he said, looking around him. "I can't believe Mark hasn't been in this room since the accident."

"He must have been – all her clothes were in here."

"That wasn't him – that was Fenton's wife, Marian. He was deranged at the time, couldn't have even contemplated doing anything like that." He looked around. "Where do you want me to start?"

"Well, those boxes of clothes have to go up into the little attic. I've marked clearly what's in each box though I doubt they'll be opened again any time soon."

"Right. I'll get started. Now, don't let me catch you dossing again!"

"Okay, okay!" I closed the notebook and put it with the other notes. I then boxed them all carefully, hoping that someday Amber might like to see them.

It was then time to start on the bookshelves. She must have been a voracious reader. I was presuming the books were all hers as I doubted Mark ever had the time to pick up anything other than a veterinary journal. All the classics were there nestled alongside creative-writing books and a selection of plays. Harry was definitely going to put out his back hefting these up into the attic, I thought, as I lifted each book carefully down and into a box.

And then there was only one book left, on the top shelf, on top of a large box. I reached up and carefully took both down.

Ah, *Wuthering Heights*. I knew this one. I'd studied it at school. I opened it to see how much I remembered and saw that there was an inscription on the inside cover.

To my darling Mark, my Heathcliff,
"Now, my bonny lad, you are mine! And
we'll see if one tree won't grow as crooked
as another, with the same wind to twist it!"
From your ever loving Emma

Wow, I thought. Dreamy, romantic Kelly'd have a field day with this kind of stuff. The emotions were so powerful – they must have been so in love . . .

I then opened the box that the book had been sitting on. Inside was a large leather-bound book nestled on top of a pile of photographs. The fact that the photographs were all in frames led me to think that they'd probably been on the walls at the time of the accident.

Hands shaking, I sat down on the couch. I opened the leather-bound book, knowing before I did so that it was their wedding album.

Taking a deep breath, I turned to the first page.

Smiling back at me was possibly the handsomest couple I had ever seen. It took me a second to realise that the man was actually Mark, so fresh-faced and gorgeous did he look. And there was Harry, who looked about fourteen in the photograph even though he had to have been much older. And a nice-looking woman who must surely be their mother.

And Emma.

Ethereal, pre-Raphaelite Emma. Long golden hair flowing over her shoulders, her cheeks flushed, her eyes bright with happiness.

It was no wonder really that Mark never wanted to see these pictures again.

"Are you slacking off *again*?" Harry asked on re-entering the room.

"I think she's the most beautiful woman I've ever seen." I couldn't take my eyes away.

"She was pretty gorgeous, alright." Harry sat down beside me. "Good God, look at the state of me in those pictures! Put that album away, for God's sake!"

"Where did they get married?"

286

"That little church on St Stephen's Green. It wasn't a big wedding – they hadn't really been going out that long at the time."

I closed the album reluctantly. Harry picked up some of the pictures that were underneath it.

"My God, how young does Mark look in these!" he laughed.

He was right, Mark was unrecognisable. But it was more than just looking younger, he looked so much happier. There was no sign of the constant frown, or the stony glare.

I mean, I could have fancied *this* Mark.

Harry held up another picture of Mark and Emma. This time Mark was in a tuxedo, and Emma was wearing the most beautiful pale-blue chiffon gown, looking for all the world like a young Grace Kelly.

"I think that was Mark's graduation. I remember that dress. That's the night they got engaged."

"Oh, wow! How long after that did they get married?"

"Only a couple of months. Mark got the job down here, you see, and, well, Fenton could be a funny fish about stuff like 'living in sin' so Mark wouldn't move Emma down until he'd made an honest woman of her. To tell the truth, I'd say he actually wanted to get a ring on her finger quickly before she changed her mind!"

"But she must have been crazy about him too though." I thought of the inscription on the *Wuthering Heights* book.

"I don't doubt she was, but they were a crazy couple."

"Mark – crazy? Can't see that!"

"Trust me, I'm not talking crazy-good. Emma was a real free spirit. She'd studied English Literature and was always working on some epic novel or play. They were like chalk and cheese really, you know – he could have chosen better vet's-wife material."

"And they met through you, you were saying?"

"They did. She hung around with friends of mine and we all ended up out for my birthday one night. Funny thing was, Mark never usually went out with us. But he did that night and *boom*! He was smitten and that was the end of that."

"Obviously opposites attract. Oh look! Baby pictures!"

And so there were. Lots of pictures, mostly of Jamie and Emma. I guessed that was normal. Loads of pictures of first baby, not so many of the second.

"So what about Emma's family?" I asked, suddenly thinking it strange that there'd been no mention of other grandparents or aunties and uncles.

"There's only her mum. She was adopted and her dad is dead. Her mother, well, she's not well. Suffers a lot with her nerves apparently, and of course the accident nearly finished her off altogether."

"How sad," I sighed, looking back at the photographs. "I wonder would Mark mind if I kept a few of these down here for the children?"

"Mmm . . ." Harry looked at the photos. "He's funny about stuff like that. Maybe just a few and put them away for a little while. The right time will come along sometime."

I packed the album, the novel and most of the photos away, hiding the rest in an envelope. There was a sideboard in the TV room that I could put them in for now.

"Right, so these books up to the attic and that's nearly it?" Harry looked around the almost empty room.

"Yes. Then you have to take me to buy paint!"

"Oh come on – are you serious?"

I nodded. The room definitely needed to look as different as possible. I was even going to take down the curtains. The blinds that were there would do fine, and the room without that huge, heavy brocade pattern could only look brighter. Luckily the floor was already wooden, so all I needed was Harry to help me take out the giant mat.

"I'm not painting! So don't even think about it!" Harry warned me as he almost buckled under the weight of the first of the book boxes.

"No, you're not," I agreed. "I'm going to paint and you're going to put together the shelves we're going to buy. Now get a move on with those boxes!"

Chapter 35

"Oh Harry, I'm so pleased! I never thought we'd get it all done!"

It was six o'clock and I was standing at the new playroom door, surveying our work. It did look pretty good. The walls were bright yellow and, as I'd expected, the absence of the heavy curtains allowed the light to flood in. The furniture was all washed and waiting in the hall to go back in and I'd taken a bright green throw from one of the bedrooms for the couch. I knew Kelly had recently brought out a bright range of throws specifically for children – I made a mental note to ask her to send me one.

"Me neither." Harry came to stand beside me, trying to sound grumpy, but I knew he was secretly pleased. "Remind me never to answer the phone to you again."

"Ah, but what would I do without you!" I put one arm around his neck and pulled him in for a hug. "My lifesaver!"

"Well, isn't this cosy?" Mark had arrived through the

open front door and was staring at us with a quizzical but definitely stony look, a tired-looking child on either side.

"Oh, you're home early!" I said, remembering too late the row we'd had the last time I'd uttered those words.

If he remembered, it wasn't obvious as he sidestepped the furniture piled up in the hall and walked towards us. I couldn't help looking behind him to see if the lovely Tara was with him. But she wasn't.

"Uncle Harry!" Jamie hurtled himself towards Harry when he saw him.

"Ungo Howeee!" Next on top of him was Amber.

Harry scooped them both up and swung them around.

"Well, how are my favourite niece and nephew today?"

"We're good," Jamie answered. "We were at Nana's today."

"Nana – cake!" said Amber.

"Shh, Amber! That's a secret!" Jamie looked horrified at Amber's indiscretion.

"They were only allowed it after they'd eaten their dinner!" Mark said, looking at me defensively.

"That's okay," I smiled. "I wouldn't be telling any nana that she couldn't give her two favourite grandchildren cake! Have they had their tea?"

"Well, no, we thought . . ." He stopped, suddenly looking sheepish.

"We're going to bring you to a restaurant!" cried Jamie.

"*Yaaay!*" said Amber.

I looked at Mark who was now looking more than a little embarrassed.

"Oh!" Harry winked at me. "I'll get out of the way so!"

"No, Harry, wait!" I looked at Mark. "Why don't we get takeaway for us all tonight, and maybe we could go to the restaurant another night? I kind of wanted to get this finished today."

"Believe me, I'm happy to go back to town," said Harry.

"No, Uncle Harry, stay!" Jamie looked tearful at the thought of his playful uncle going already.

"Holly's right," said Mark. "It would be great to get this finished today. We'll get a takeaway in a while."

"*Yippee!*" shouted Jamie, "Uncle Harry, you have to stay until the bedtime story!"

"I will." Harry ruffled his hair. "But only as long as I can tell a really, really scary one."

"No way, Harry!" said both Mark and I at exactly the same time.

"Now, guys, go in and take off your coats and hats and I'll be with you in a tick," said Mark, before turning to Harry. "I wasn't expecting to see you here."

"I wasn't expecting to be here," Harry answered.

I realised with dismay that getting Harry to help with such a delicate mission might have been a mistake.

"I asked him to come, Mark. I hope that's okay. It's just that I didn't want this job to go on for days."

Mark looked at me and then at Harry, and sighed. "Of course it's okay. Thanks, Harry. Though, actually, maybe I should inspect your work first before I thank you."

"No!" I squealed. "It's not finished! We have to move the furniture back in!"

Now Harry put his arm around me and, giving me a squeeze, said, "Holly, darling. If you think that I am going to refuse help from a grown man and let you make me move all this stuff again on my own, you have another think coming."

292

"But the surprise will be ruined!" I said dismally – but I couldn't deny that he had a point.

Stepping back from the door, I let Mark look in.

He was silent for a second then his shoulders visibly loosened as he said, "It's great. Looks so different."

"Well, that was the idea!" I had the words said before I remembered the reason it had to look so different.

But Mark had already turned from the door and was fighting with Harry about the best way to lift the bookcase.

One hour later we were standing in the finished room surveying our handiwork.

"Oh, Dad, it's amazing!" was all that Jamie could keep saying.

"I know, son." Mark smiled. "But you have to say a really big thanks to Holly – it was her idea and it took a lot of work. Her biggest job was getting Uncle Harry to come down and do a bit of physical labour."

"Thanks, Holly!" To my surprise Jamie put his arms up for a hug. "And I'm sorry about the restaurant but this is *waaaay* better. I'd forgotten this room was even here! It's like magic!"

I looked up at Mark but he looked away.

"Well, maybe tomorrow Dad might see about getting you a TV for in here." I'd have said anything to change the subject. "What do you think, Mark?"

"Well, the children in this house would have to be awfully good!" he said, trying to sound serious, but I could tell that he too was glad of the change of direction.

"We are, Dad! Even Amber's not as bold. Nana said so!"

I have to say I was secretly thrilled at this remark, but I just smiled and said, "Now, now, Jamie, I think we should leave your dad and Harry to organise our tea, and why don't me and you see if there's any more of your toys we could bring in."

"Hands up for chips!" shouted Harry, shooting his long arm up into the air.

I smiled and, going next door to the TV room, started to pick up Lego from the carpet. I was so pleased with the new room. The whole house already seemed brighter, partly because a lot of the toys that had littered every inch of floor space were now ensconced in brightly coloured plastic tubs in the new room, but mostly because a door that had always been shut was now open, and the room within a bright sunshiny yellow.

"So what's going on?"

I paused as I heard Mark's voice in the room next door.

"Sorry?"

"Don't 'sorry' me – you and Holly, and all that huggy-huggy stuff."

My cheeks flamed. I didn't know whether to make my presence known or not.

"Would you ever relax? We're friends – that's what friends do, Mark."

Mark grunted. "Well, don't get any ideas," he muttered.

"Eh – she has a boyfriend?" Harry was getting cross now.

"Never stopped you before," Mark snipped.

"What's that supposed to mean?"

I didn't have to be able to see them to know that they were about to square up to each other so I leapt to my feet and crashed into the room with the plastic box of Lego.

"So, who's going to go for the food?" I asked innocently,

pretending not to notice that you could cut the atmosphere with a knife.

"Actually, I think I'll head off home," Harry said, staring at Mark.

"Mightn't be a bad idea," said Mark, equally coldly.

"No, you're not," I said firmly. "The kids would be very upset. And so would I. Whatever is wrong with you two, get over it and start acting like adults."

"I don't know why you're including me in that!" Harry looked affronted.

"Takeaway!" I said sharply. "Both of you. Now!"

To my shock they instantly looked sheepish and there was no further talk of Harry going home. In fact, the rest of the evening passed off pretty well.

Good old Supernanny! I wondered if she knew her methods worked on children of every age?

Chapter 36

And before I knew it, it was Wednesday again.

The days were starting to fly by. We'd settled into a nice routine. Yes, the mornings were still chaotic, but I was sure that was normal in any house with small children. Once Jamie was in school, myself and Amber usually walked home via the river. She adored the ducks and the fresh air always knocked her out.

And while her behaviour had come on in leaps and bounds, there was no escaping the fact that my favourite two hours of the day were during her nap time.

While she was asleep I ran around the house, straightening the beds, putting on washes and preparing the dinner. Then she'd wake and we'd have our lunch together before taking out her paints or jigsaws. She really thrived on having one-on-one time. In fact, the more she thrived, the more I hoped that whoever replaced me would give her the same attention.

Every time I thought of leaving, I felt sick with guilt. All I could do was console myself with the thought that the house I would be leaving was very, very different from the one I'd come to.

I'd be like Mary Poppins, sailing into the air with my magic brolly, leaving a scene of domestic bliss on the pavement below . . .

And yet, despite this aura of domestic bliss that had settled around No 12 Meadowlands, I still lived for Wednesdays and Fridays.

On these nights I gave the children their tea, Mark would arrive home, and I would race upstairs to "de-child" myself, attempting to get some way back to the old, glamorous me.

This was proving harder and harder to do. I hadn't appreciated how much time looking good had required out of my busy day.

Until the days got busier.

And yes, it felt slightly ridiculous to get so glammed up only to ride two buses to a rural pub in the back end of nowhere. But then Oliver would walk in, and I would be so glad to have made the effort, and of course, it was all worth it for the journey home . . .

I simply couldn't have coped without the excitement of looking forward to those two nights.

This particular Wednesday night I really pushed the boat out. I took a notion and pulled my Alexander McQueen handkerchief dress from the back of the wardrobe, and in a moment of high giddiness, decided to risk giving it an outing.

Calling back over my shoulder lest my outfit draw derisory remarks from the surly Mr Fielding, I slipped from the house and practically skipped to the bus stop, pulling some loose change from my pocket for the fare.

As usual, there weren't very many people in the pub. Of course the only other customers, two old men, stared at me as I walked in. Pulling my by-now-feeling-very-skimpy denim jacket closed, I strutted my way to my usual seat and waited for Oliver to arrive.

And waited.

And waited.

At first I wasn't too worried. Any minute now he would ring to say he was nearly there. I reached into my bag to check my phone wasn't on silent.

It wasn't there.

I rummaged around again.

It definitely wasn't there. I remembered now where it was. It was in my other bag.

With my wallet.

Shit. I really, really hated to be without my phone.

And I'd used up the last of my change on my by-now-half-empty glass of wine.

Fine, he would be here shortly and as he was late the drinks would be on him.

Twenty minutes later I checked the change in my pocket again to see if I could even stretch to a fizzy water.

No.

Shit.

Where was he? For a brief moment I wondered had he been in an accident, but I dismissed this as just being melodramatic. The other thing that lurked in the corner of my mind was the night Cain had stood me up at the Guggenheim, and it was this memory that was making me nauseous.

What followed were thirty of the longest minutes of my life, and with each minute the sense of panic in my gut rose, and rose.

From the corner of my eye I could see the two old men

in the bar looking at me, smirking. My earlier cockiness was starting to fade and I deliberately made no eye contact with anyone.

Oliver was now forty-five minutes late.

I would give him one hour and then I was leaving. I raged silently at the thought of having to get two buses home. I would kill him.

The bastard.

And then I remembered I couldn't get two buses. I had no money.

At this point I would have burst into hot, angry tears had I not been so aware of every eye in the pub being on my by-now-ridiculous figure.

What was I going to do?

God help me but the tears were coming anyway . . .

I heard the door open behind me but, before I could turn, one of the old men had waved his arm in recognition.

It wasn't him.

Great. Some other asshole to make fun of me. I was definitely going to kill Oliver Conlon when – if – I got home.

As my audience was currently distracted, I got up from my stool to slip out.

Then the newcomer stepped to my side and, kissing me on the cheek, said, "Holly, darling, I'm so sorry. I got held up in surgery."

I looked up, my hand to my cheek.

"Mark?"

"I know, I know, I'm so sorry – come on, we can still make dinner."

Mark Fielding.

Mark Fielding was *here*.

Mark Fielding was here and had *kissed me*.

My poor brain couldn't get over which element of what had just happened shocked me the most.

Before I could open my mouth he took my arm, calling to the two by-now-open-mouthed old men, "Night, Tom, night, Mr Benson!"

"Night, Mr Fielding!" they choroused.

I blushed at the impressed looks on their faces, wondering how on earth Mark didn't mind the rumours that would no doubt be circulating the farming circles in the morning.

Once outside he stopped.

"Sorry about the kiss – it seemed like a good idea at the time!"

I looked at him in shock, my cheek still on fire. "Never mind that, what are you doing here?"

From his pocket he produced my phone.

"You left this behind."

I looked at him blankly.

"He sent a text. Hang on, I'll show you." Pressing a button on my phone, he read: "'*Can't make it, will phone tomorrow. O.*' That's one charming gentleman you've got yourself there." The sarcastic look was back in his eyes.

"But how did you know –"

"Where you were? I called him."

I nearly choked as my breath caught in the back of my throat.

"You *what*?"

"I called him. To be fair, he didn't answer. Some girl did."

Catherine.

That's why the fucker had stood me up. He was with Catherine.

I suddenly felt so sick I couldn't even look back up at

300

Mark. This was fast turning into the worst night of my life.

"What did you say to her?" I whispered, not really wanting to know the answer.

"Well, obviously I didn't know what name to ask for, so I said I had a missed call from this number, and she put me on to him. Oliver, isn't it?"

I nodded. "And what happened then?"

"I told him that you had forgotten your phone. He sounded surprised and not best pleased really, but he's a good man for speaking in code – said he couldn't help me at the moment, but would phone from the office tomorrow. I expressed my concern again that you were somewhere waiting for him – again he said his hands were tied. As I said, charming. Anyhow, at that stage I called him an inconsiderate prick and explained that if he didn't send me a text in the next five minutes, letting me know exactly where you were, then I was going to call around, and even if it took tying his legs as well, he would have to tell me in person. And so here I am."

"Oh Jesus Christ."

I didn't know what was worse, the embarrassment of Mark having to come and get me, or the sheer terror of what Oliver was going to say to me tomorrow.

I climbed into the Land Cruiser in silence. I had never been in it before, and couldn't help noticing how tidy and organised it was.

Mark climbed into his seat. And suddenly we were alone together.

And I wasn't sure if it was because he'd kissed me, or because we were sitting so close in a dark car, but I couldn't take the silence a second longer.

"Your jeep, it's so tidy," I said stupidly.

"That surprises you?" he asked.

"Well, yes, given the state of the house."

"Well, nobody's perfect, Holly," he said sharply. "I mean, look at you, an intelligent girl who's wasting her time on some married asshole."

"He's not an asshole!" I snapped before I could help myself.

"Ah, so he *is* married."

I didn't answer him. Both cheeks were now flaring red. I should have kept my stupid mouth shut.

He turned in his seat, and in the light of the streetlamp I could see his eyes were full of disdain – as much for me as for Oliver, I suspected.

"And he *is* an asshole! He was quite ready to leave you stranded in the middle of nowhere."

"I'd have been fine! I'm able to look after myself, you know!"

"Really? Well, you are certainly appropriately dressed for this neck of the woods!"

I pulled my jacket around me. I was sure my face was by now puce with embarrassment.

"Just how exactly were you going to get home?"

"I was going to get the bus!"

"Oh, were you now?" His eyes were blazing with sarcasm. He reached into the glove compartment, took something out and held it up. "Here's your wallet. It was with your phone!"

What could I say? The hot tears finally came and, mumbling thanks, I turned to the window so he couldn't see the first of them slide slowly down my cheek.

It was going to be a long drive home.

Chapter 37

"What the *fuck* was that all about?"

Oliver didn't phone until lunchtime the next day, but he was every bit as incandescent with rage as I'd predicted. In fact, I'd considered not picking up the phone at all but I knew that avoiding him was only prolonging the agony.

"Excuse me? I was the one left sitting in a pub in the arse end of nowhere!" I snapped back, the mortification of the whole evening still very fresh in my head.

"Oh for God's sake, Holly, you're a big girl now!"

"I'm well aware of that, Oliver, but I still think an apology would be nice."

"For what? Do you think I did it on purpose?"

"That's hardly the point."

"No, the point is that you forgot your fucking phone! How that has become my fault is beyond me."

"I'm not saying that it was your fault."

He had a point. I could hardly blame him for the fact that I'd left the house leaving my two key possessions behind.

"And who in God's name was that ignoramus that phoned me?"

"He's not an – he's just a friend."

"Oh really? Well he didn't sound like just a fucking friend to me. That's another thing, Holly – I'm getting all sorts of stick from you about Catherine but, to be honest, I haven't the foggiest idea what you're up to these days."

"What's that supposed to mean?"

"Oh, don't sound all fucking angelic now! I mean, you're sharing a house with that Harry guy and now this other prick comes out of the woodwork. How am I supposed to feel about that?"

"He's Harry's brother if you must know and there is nothing going on with either of them. How dare you imply otherwise!" My head was starting to hurt with the abuse he was throwing at me.

"How dare I? Have you any idea how obnoxious he was last night?"

"I'm sorry, but I didn't know he was going to phone you! Do you have any idea how embarrassed I was when he arrived to collect me?"

"Oh, he collected you, did he? What a fucking knight in shining armour!"

"Oh for God's sake, Oliver! Yes, he was actually." Even though I was tired, and my head was thumping, I couldn't let him twist this to be somehow Mark's fault. "And if he hadn't, God knows what would have happened. I'd no phone and I'd no wallet either. You should be thanking him today – he had to get a baby-sitter to mind his kids while he came and collected me – do you know that? If you thought anything about me at all, you should be thanking him. Now if you don't mind, I'm not in the mood for this today. I'm tired and I'm pissed off."

"What do you mean a baby-sitter? He has kids?"

"*What has that got to do with anything?*" I hissed back, looking over at Amber who was blissfully playing with plastic bowls on the kitchen floor. "I told you, he's just a friend! What, you're allowed a girlfriend but I can't have a fucking friend?"

"I'm entitled to ask!"

"No, you're not! You are entitled to nothing. It's all your fault that we are in this mess. If you had any idea what I've done to try and keep this relationship going! Well, forget it," I was crying now, "it's finished. I've had enough."

I terminated the call and burst into tears.

Next thing there was a little head of golden curls in my lap.

"No cry, Holleee!" A little hand patted my knee.

Shit, I'd forgotten all about Amber. I scooped her up into my arms, worried about how much of my bad language she might have heard.

"I'm sorry, honey! Holly is just being a big Silly Billy."

"Silly Holly," she smiled at me, reaching up one chubby hand to pat my cheek and I couldn't help smiling back.

Just then, my phone started to ring. I looked at the screen. It was Oliver. I pressed the reject button and looked at Amber.

"Do you know what, baby? I want you to promise me that when you're a big girl you won't listen to any rubbish from boys – promise?"

The poor child nodded happily, and I hugged her again as hard as I could.

And then I heard the front door open. My cheeks flared again with embarrassment. I had been dreading meeting Mark and had hoped that some extreme veterinary medical emergency might keep him at work for a week.

The journey home with him the previous night had been one of the most uncomfortable experiences of my life.

He'd glowered the whole way and I'd sat in silence beside him, trying my hardest not to cry. We were half an hour from home when I grabbed his arm.

"Jesus, Mark, the children!"

He sighed. "I know I'm not much of a father, Holly, but even I wouldn't leave them at home on their own."

"I didn't think you would!" I exclaimed, and then the realisation of exactly how much trouble he'd had to go to for me dawned on me.

"Who did you get?"

"I rang Dawn."

"Dawn? But what about Daniel?"

"The last time I checked she had a husband of her own?"

"Oh God!" I put my hand over my eyes.

"Look, I told her I had an emergency to go out to. Your sordid secret is still safe."

"It's not a sordid –" I started to object, but stopped myself. To be fair, it was sordid enough and I was very glad that he hadn't told her the real reason behind his emergency. "It's not sordid," I finished, "but thank you, I appreciate you not telling her."

"You're welcome."

And that had been literally the last word spoken between us.

After what seemed like hours we'd arrived back at the house.

306

Dawn had looked at me in surprise.

"Holly! I wasn't expecting to see you. Don't you look gorgeous?"

"Doesn't she just," Mark said drily. "I knew Holly would be coming home around this time so I rang her to see if she'd like a lift."

"Well, you certainly couldn't let her wander around the countryside looking like that!"

"Indeed." Mark wasn't even trying to conceal the sarcasm in his voice.

I knew Dawn was just trying to be nice but I felt like screaming at her to shut up.

By the time I managed to get her to stop babbling on, Mark had gone to bed and I hadn't seen him since.

And now he was home for lunch.

He walked into the kitchen to where we were sitting but, before I could even look up, Amber said her clearest words to date.

"Holly cry."

"Amber!" I hissed, before muttering, "I wasn't crying. I had something in my eye."

"Of course." He walked over to the fridge.

"Amber, if you're finished would you like to go and pick out a jigsaw?" I said.

She scampered out of the room and, taking a deep breath, I said, "Look, Mark, I want to thank you for –"

But before I could finish my sentence, he put down a set of keys on the kitchen table.

"I only came home to give you these. Fenton's wife is changing her car. It's yours if you want it."

I opened my mouth to object, but he put up his hand to stop me.

"Just take it. I'd rather you had your own transport when something like last night happens again."

I closed my mouth.

He turned to leave the room, and then stopped.

"And Holly, don't fool yourself. It will happen again."

And then he was gone.

Chapter 38

After the door shut behind him, the house was quiet. Amber was in the playroom taking out every jigsaw she owned and I didn't care. I had turned off my phone as I wasn't up to finding out what was worse, knowing Oliver was trying to ring me and not answering, or knowing he wasn't . . .

I had half an hour until we were due at the Mother and Toddler Group. So I did what I'd started doing with any spare minute I had, and brought down my laptop.

Though to be honest, even the babyline was getting complicated these days.

It had all started simply enough. I'd logged on as MarshaG to ask about my fictional three-year-old's messy poos. Having got a more comprehensive response than I ever could have imagined, I'd relayed all my findings to Mrs Fagan, advising firmly that she discuss any moves with her doctor first. After all, the last thing I wanted was to be logging on next week asking about a child who didn't poo at all . . .

And I would have left it at that. Except the next time I logged on there was a raft of enquiries wondering how I'd got on.

These enquiries ranged from Suki10 wondering if I'd gone to the doctor and Dingdongdell inviting me to some giant babyline coffee morning in Bewleys. Oh, and some other poster called Goatgirl was offering me a month's supply of "goat products".

There was nothing for it but more lies. So I replied that I'd consulted the doctor, started her on the lactose-free milk and that her poo was now second to none. And of course I'd thanked them all emphatically for their help but that I wasn't free the morning of the coffee meet-up as I was getting my ingrown toenail removed. I even told Goatgirl that my neighbour had a goat and that he'd kindly offered me lots of "goat products" but that I'd contact her as soon as I had a shortage.

And again, I should have left it there.

But well, I was lonely, and they were nice girls, and there was a bit of chat, and one thing led to another. To make a long story short, when I had to start keeping a notebook with notes on the character I'd created, I knew I'd gone too far.

Within a week, MarshaG had been developed to be the proud mother of four children. DS1 was five, and in school – I'd decided it was probably no harm to create him in case Jamie had any school issues – and of course the messy poo DD was three. And then, in a moment of madness, I'd decided that twins of four months would be useful – I mean, there was bound to be some mad new mother in the village that was going to have some crazy question for me. That was when things got really

310

complicated. But, the thing was, I had zero baby experience – the only baby I'd ever been within ten feet of was Dawn's Daniel, and I didn't think it would be realistic for one poor baby to have all the ailments that I might need advice on.

For example, I was about to head out now to the Mother and Toddler Group where some variation of baby argument was always underway: correct time to start solids, which car seat, which buggy, which formula . . . I swear, no wonder mothers with babies stick together – no one else could listen to that kind of obsessing, over and over and over again.

Then of course there had to be a father for all these children. I'd deliberated a lot over him. I wanted someone who wasn't around much. I'd toyed with a businessman type but, in the end, my evil streak had created a long-distance truck driver for poor Marsha.

I swear, the girls on the babyline thought I was a martyr altogether.

But I'd settled into my groove with MarshaG. I found that it was grand, so long as I kept one eye on my notes. I'd nearly given everything away once when I'd got the sex of the twins mixed up, but the babyliners had all given a virtual nod of understanding when I blamed baby-brain for the misunderstanding.

So it all ran along fine until I got involved in the discussion at the school gate about little Ben Thompson and the fact that, at one year of age, he still wasn't sitting up.

And MarshaG didn't have a one-year-old.

So there was nothing for it but to register a second time. SlippyDippy was created solely for her non-sitting-one-year-old DS, and the whole thing began again . . .

But the babyline had its funny times too. Last Saturday morning, when I'd eventually got the new playroom sorted and found a spare five minutes to myself, I'd logged on only to find a thread titled "Dishy Dentist on the *Late Late*".

It had to be . . .

It was.

Unlike my mother, the babyline ladies had no problem with how Chad had looked on Friday night. What they didn't say they'd like to do to my squeaky-clean, dazzling-gnashered brother! My mother would be drowning him in Holy Water if she knew. By the end of the discussion there were ladies offering to "slightly damage" each other's molars just so they'd have an excuse to make an appointment with my darling brother.

I sighed at the memory of that thread. Yes, it was definitely getting complicated. I closed the laptop and went to get Amber ready for going out.

"So where were you going all dressed up last night?"

We were walking down to the community centre when Dawn asked the question I'd been dreading.

"Oh, nowhere in particular," I answered, trying to sound coy, while really feeling like telling her to mind her own business. That damn dress – I felt like binning it at this stage.

"Eh sorry – but nobody wears a dress like that to nowhere in particular! I think there must be a man on the scene . . ."

I grunted without meaning to.

"Oh dear. Touchy subject?"

I sighed. "Yes."

"Did you have a row?"

312

"Kind of." She was going to guess I wasn't in good humour anyway so there was no harm in telling some of the truth.

"Was it over Mark collecting you?"

I had to laugh. Damn, this girl was good. I nodded.

"Oh but that's okay – it's good he's jealous!"

"Well, he has no reason to be." I hadn't the heart to tell her that short of shaving my head and sitting naked on O'Connell Street, there was very little else I could do to show Oliver how serious I was about our relationship.

"Oh, come on! I know you don't think so, but Mark is a very good-looking guy."

Automatically my hand went to my cheek as it started to flame at the memory of his kiss. I wasn't going to admit this to her, but she was right. There was no escaping the fact that I was starting to find one side of Mark very attractive. For example, despite my embarrassment the night before, I was very impressed at the effort he'd made to rescue me from a pub in the back end of nowhere. I mean, he'd literally swooped in like a knight in shining armour and the fact that my plight had even concerned him impressed me no end. I'd spent the most part of my life looking after myself and someone putting themselves out like that for me was definitely a novelty and it certainly didn't bode well that Oliver had been prepared to leave me to my own devices.

But there was a whole other side to him that made my blood boil. He was grumpy, aloof, cold and had worse mood swings than any woman I knew. He could be smiling and chatty one minute and an absolute asshole the next. He also had a bad habit of making me feel like an absolute fool and, God knows, I was well able to do that much myself.

"With a very dead wife whom he still can't speak about," I retorted, my quick inner review of all his bad points helping me to come back to my senses. "I doubt he'll ever go out with anyone again. And if he does, God help her, she'll never live up to Emma Fielding! Though I'm sure Tara Harper would give it a pretty good shot."

"Tara who?"

"Oh, his boss's daughter. Blonde, blue-eyed, face like a cherubic angel."

"And they're going out?"

"Not that I know of, but come on, how suitable would she be? She understands the business, the hours, and from the way she simpers at him at the moment he can do no wrong."

"Holly Green! Are you jealous?"

"No!" I almost screeched, embarrassed at my Tara-rant. "Mark Fielding is not, and never will be, my type. End of story!"

"Okay, okay, I believe you. But to be fair, it's not me you should be telling, is it? That poor man of yours is probably feeling a bit insecure – what with a hunky man swooping in to rescue you! Were you talking to him today at all?"

"Yep. I hung up on him. And then turned off my phone." Damn her, I was starting to feel now like I might have overreacted. I suppose if the shoe was on the other foot and some Amazon had swept in and bundled Oliver home in a jeep I wouldn't be too impressed either.

"Oh, come on. Give him a ring."

"No way." No, I wouldn't go that far. But I did guiltily take my phone out of my pocket and switch it back on.

If he rang, he rang.

By now we'd reached the Community Centre. All the usual crowd were there. Maureen Costello was in full flow at one end of the room, with two girls I didn't know already developing a glassy-eyed look from listening to her.

I got my coffee and sat down as far away from her as possible. I really just wasn't in the mood today. Now that my phone was switched on, the fact that it hadn't rung was really starting to worry me.

To make matters worse, all everyone was talking about today was that Christmas was fast approaching and how little they'd all done.

I felt like turning around and snapping at them that at least they knew what country they'd be celebrating it in and more importantly who with!

Listening to them, I felt even more depressed. I'd been looking forward to Christmas so much. It was going to be me and Oliver, walking through the snow in Central Park, ice-skating at the Rockefeller Centre. Lying, our limbs entangled, watching old movies and eating chestnuts roasted on an open fire.

Or whatever.

If there was a clichéd romantic Christmas situation to be imagined, I'd imagined it.

And now, everything was all up in the air again.

In three weeks it would be Christmas Eve. And my entire life was spiralling out of control.

"Hey, what's up with you today?" Ellen asked, noticing my doleful expression.

"Oh she had a little row with her boyfriend," said Dawn.

Great, now the entire female population of the village

knew my business. I was about to murder her for saying anything when inside my pocket my phone began to ring.

I took it out, and sure enough Oliver's name was flashing on the display. I no longer cared who knew anything about me!

"It's him!" I hissed at Dawn. "Keep an eye on Amber for me, will you?"

I dashed from the hall to whoops and calls of "Good luck!" from the assembled mammies.

I waited to get outside before answering.

"Yes?" I said, trying not to sound as if I'd just run fifty feet to answer the phone and that my heart wasn't hammering in my chest with anxiety. In fact, for a second I thought I'd overdone it and that my voice was too cold.

"I'm sorry. I really am."

Scratch that. Coldness was perfect. In fact, more was needed . . .

"For what exactly? For standing me up, or for shouting at me today?"

"Both. Honestly, Holly. It's just that it drives me mad, not getting to see you, not knowing what you're up to. You don't understand."

I almost melted with relief and felt like punching the air screaming 'He loves me, he loves me!' but I knew I had to keep calm for just a few more minutes . . .

"How could I not understand, Oliver? This situation is not much better from where I'm standing."

"I know, I know. Anyway, look, I want to make it up to you."

"You don't have to do that," I said, my voice softer now.

"I know, but I want to. How do you feel about a whole weekend away, just the two of us?"

How would I *feel*?

I'd feel like this was way too good to be true, *that's* how I'd feel . . .

I'd wonder how you were going to get away for a full weekend when you couldn't manage three hours last night . . .

"How would you manage that?" I couldn't keep the scepticism from my voice.

"Look, I'll manage. Now, what do you think?"

"When are you talking about?" Now that the offer seemed to be genuine, I was getting worried about the practicalities. After all, I had responsibilities . . .

"This weekend. I'm meant to be at a course in London, but what if we were to head down the country instead?"

This weekend. Shit. Mark would be on duty.

"Why aren't you saying anything? I thought you'd be thrilled?"

"I am, I am! It's just I had something else on. Let me see if I can rearrange it, that's all."

"Something else on? Well, if you don't want to go!" He sounded huffy now.

"I do! For God's sake, of course I do. I'll work something out, I promise!"

"Well, I'll see you then."

"Eh yes, I suppose you will."

I returned to the hall, deep in thought.

"Well?" came the chorus.

I'd forgotten that the entire room was waiting with bated breath to see if my relationship was back on.

"Everything's okay," I smiled. There was a communal sigh of relief from the mammies, who then went back to their respective conversations on weaning or whatever.

"You don't look like everything's okay," said Dawn, wisely noticing that I was not exactly jumping around the room with joy.

"He wants to take me away for the weekend," I said glumly.

"What? That's brilliant!"

"Not really. It's Mark's weekend on. What am I going to do?"

"You are going to go," said Dawn firmly. "We'll sort something out. I can mind them."

"Oh Dawn, I couldn't do that."

"Why not? Maybe you can pay me back sometime when me and Graham go away on a dirty weekend!"

"Yes. Yes, of course I would," I said lamely, knowing that there was every possibility that I wasn't going to be around for that.

"Well, that's sorted. Now you just have to tell Mark."

Yes. All I had to do was tell Mark.

My stomach lurched at the thought.

Chapter 39

"You're *what*?"

I winced at the look of fury on Mark's face even though I'd been totally prepared for this kind of reaction.

"Look, I understand it's my weekend to work, so honestly, if it's really a big problem, it's fine, I'll cancel." I was aware that I was babbling, but at this stage my whole body was shaking with pure nerves.

"I'm not talking about the fact that you are meant to be working – I'm just really surprised that, after last night, a seemingly intelligent girl like you would be, you know –"

Oh God, not this again.

"He's really sorry. Honestly, something came up and he just couldn't make it."

"Oh, something came up alright."

"Mark!"

"It's not good enough. He left you stranded, Holly."

"It wasn't his fault that I forgot my phone and wallet," I said defensively.

"So what about his wife? I'm presuming she knows nothing about what the two of you are up to?"

Hardly.

I shook my head. This was excruciating. It was none of his business but I was hardly in any position to tell him that after what he'd done for me last night.

"She's his boss, it's complicated."

"It always is, Holly. That doesn't explain why a seemingly intelligent girl like yourself would put up with being someone else's bit on the side."

Oh, for the love of God, stop with the intelligent girl stuff. And anyhow, you don't know the half of it.

"It's not like that!" I said.

"Right. I'll take your word for it. So when do you want to go?"

Was that it? Was the lecture over?

"Tomorrow evening?" I proceeded cautiously, not wanting to unleash a further torrent of abuse. "Dawn has offered to mind the kids."

I braced myself for his reaction, but he just nodded. "Right. I'll talk to Fenton – see if there are any surgeries we can push back till Monday. I'm sure Dawn doesn't want them all weekend."

"Right. Eh, thanks. I appreciate it. Really."

He didn't answer. Just as I turned to leave the kitchen I remembered and, deciding it couldn't possibly irritate him any more than he was irritated already, I asked, "Would it be okay if I took the new car?"

"I think you should. I'm not coming to collect you this time."

I rolled my eyes behind his back, but there was a spring in my step as I left the room.

A whole weekend with Oliver . . .

No grumpy Mark, no children, no housework, no cooking.

He could say what he liked, I couldn't wait.

As soon as I got the kids to bed that night I started the big preparation. My packing was mostly done, thanks to Dawn. After leaving the Community Hall that morning, she had insisted that we go shopping to the local town (where I'd purchased all the books). In the two hours we had before collecting Jamie, I'd purchased new underwear, a slinky nightie and a new black dress for dinner.

"You can't go wrong with a black dress," she assured me, "and don't go wasting your precious money on shoes. I have lovely shoes that should fit you and a bag that would be fantastic with them at home."

For a second I thought of my beautiful black Louboutins that I'd sent on to New York the morning I'd packed up my Dublin apartment.

That reminded me.

"Gosh, I'm here a month this Saturday!"

"Really? Well, we'll have to postpone celebrating your anniversary until Monday. I doubt you'll be wasting too much time thinking about us this weekend!"

Honestly, you'd swear I was going on my honeymoon, the giggles and innuendo that Dawn was spouting. But the excitement only added to the anticipation and it wasn't long before I was just as giddy as she was.

It was almost eleven before I finished exfoliating, moisturising and defuzzing myself, not to mention applying a liberal layer of fake tan. Then I painted my finger and toenails, getting lost in the absolute luxury of it all. However, when I went to pluck my eyebrows, I remembered I'd left the tweezers downstairs in the kitchen where I'd used them to take a splinter out of Jamie's finger. Yes, that was about all my tweezers got used for these days . . .

I tiptoed down the attic stairs and past the bedrooms. After all, I had no desire to meet anyone, in my dressing gown and slathered in fake tan. But as I crept past Jamie's room I heard some noises within.

I pushed open the door gently only to see Jamie jump from the floor into bed and pull the covers over him.

"Jamie? What are you up to?"

There was no answer so I walked over to his bed and gently tried to pull back the quilt. But he had a firm grip on it and all I could see was the top of his head.

"Jamie, what's going on?"

Again, there was no answer.

"Jamie, I don't want to go and get your dad, but if this is something I can't sort out then I'll have to."

He released his hold a little and now I could see his eyes, guiltily looking up at me.

"What's up, buddy?"

"Nothing. I'm fine. I'm going to sleep."

"Well, you should have been asleep ages ago. Now I'm going to give you one last chance to tell me what you were up to . . ."

He let go the quilt and I pulled it slowly back, gasping at what it revealed.

He was fully dressed in his school uniform. Right down to the neat knot on his school tie. With a sinking feeling in my stomach, I realised why he was always dressed for school when I went to wake him.

Why he was dressed for football last Saturday.

Why he was dressed for football every Saturday.

"Jamie, what's going on? You can tell Holly."

"Nothing!" he almost shouted. "I'm fine. I told you, I want to go to sleep now!"

322

"Well, do you want to tell me why you're dressed for school?"

He shrugged.

"Do you do this every night?"

He looked at me and seemed to decide that there was no point in lying, and nodded.

"Why, honey?"

"In case we're in a hurry, or in case you don't get up."

"When have I never got up, buddy?"

"Never."

"Have I ever even been a teeny bit late getting up?"

He shook his head.

"And, while I know sometimes it's a bit mad down there in the morning, we've never, ever been late to school, have we?"

He shook his head.

"So maybe we'll just put back on your pj's, and I promise not to make you late in the morning."

He nodded and I helped him back into his pyjamas.

Tucking him back into bed, I stroked his hair.

"You okay now, sweetie?"

He nodded.

"And if you were worried about anything, you'd tell me, right?"

He nodded again and, with a tiny smile, said, "I won't worry any more, Holly, I promise."

I kissed him, left the room and continued downstairs in search of my tweezers.

So distracted was I by Jamie's disturbing revelation that I walked straight into Mark coming out of the kitchen.

"*Whoa!*" he cried as I crashed straight into his chest.

"Oh shit! I'm sorry, I wasn't looking!" I looked in

horror at the white T-shirt that was stretched across his broad chest and hoped there wouldn't be a Turin Shroud-like image of my fake-tanned face on it in the morning.

"I could see that."

I went to walk around him, and then stopped. "Look, Mark, could I speak to you for a second?"

I could see his shoulders visibly stiffen but he turned and followed me into the kitchen where he stood, arms folded.

"If this is about your boyfriend –"

"It's not. It's about Jamie." I told him about what I'd just witnessed.

For a second he didn't speak, but his lips were set in a tight line and a muscle in his jaw flinched.

"Right. Well, thanks for telling me. I'll have a chat with him."

"Oh no, please don't! Well, not directly. I told him I wouldn't say anything. And I wouldn't have, but it's sort of something I thought you should know."

He nodded. "I'll deal with it."

"It was just so weird –"

"I said I'd deal with it!" he said sharply.

Something about his demeanour bothered me.

"You know, Mark, you don't look too surprised. Did you know he was doing this?"

He didn't answer.

"Okay. Right, well, you know now," I said. I spotted my tweezers on the counter, scooped them up and turned to leave the room.

"Look, Holly. He used to do this before. I thought he'd stopped but, to be honest, I haven't checked in a long time. With Amber and stuff, I wasn't really that worried about him."

"Well, have you any idea why he does it? This is not normal behaviour."

It was the type of behaviour that would send the babyline ladies into paroxysms of shrieking and analysis.

He seemed to think for a minute before answering. "I'm not really sure, he doesn't talk much, as you know. But, well, I think it's because Emma wasn't always as organised as you. It wasn't – well, it wasn't really her fault but, you know, sometimes she just wasn't able for it all. He worries a lot, that's all. I'll get to the bottom of it, I promise."

For a second I thought of Mrs Murphy and her intimation that all wasn't quite right with Emma. And of the time that Jamie had wondered who would bring him to training "when" I was sick.

"So, you'll get to the bottom of it then? Without having a go at him, or telling him I told you?"

"I promise. I'll suss him out while you're away. Can we leave it at that?"

I nodded.

This house just got stranger and stranger.

Roll on my dirty weekend with Oliver . . .

Chapter 40

"Oh dear God, no!"

This could not be happening. Of all the days, in all the year, how could Amber have chosen this day to wake up covered in spots?

But sure enough, the minute I entered her bedroom I could see them. Huge red spots all over her forehead, chest and arms, standing in stark relief against her pale skin. Her little eyes were in the back of her head and she started to cry as soon as she saw me.

"Hollleee, I sore!"

"Oh baby!" I ran to pick her up, guilty that my first reaction had been to scream in horror. "Holly will make you all better!"

Feckity Feckity Feck.

I took her up to my bed and sat her down beside me as I cranked up the laptop. I typed.

Child with red spots

It spat back at me.

Chickenpox

326

My heart sank.

This was not good.

Within minutes I had all the information I needed and had posted off a babyline request for any advice the girls could give me.

But they were never going to tell me what I needed to hear.

They were never going to say that those angry red spots would be gone by this evening. With a sinking heart, I resigned myself to the inevitable.

The weekend was off.

At eight thirty I rang Dawn.

"She has what?"

"Chickenpox."

"Are you sure?"

"Yes. I'm positive."

"Oh, Holly. What are you going to do?"

"Stay at home. What else can I do? You can't mind them now, that's for sure."

"But maybe –"

"No, Dawn. You have Daniel to worry about, and I know that she's probably not that contagious any more, now that the spots are out, but still I'm not risking it. Anyway, she's like an anti-Christ. I couldn't do that to you."

"Oh Holly love, I'm so sorry. Is there anything at all I can do?"

"Well, would you walk Jamie to school and maybe pick him up for me? I wouldn't ask but I don't want to take her out of the house."

"Of course. And I'll go to the chemist for you and get whatever you need."

"Great. A bag of Valium would be great!"

I put down the phone with a sigh, looking at my watch. I needed to cancel my hair appointment but the hairdresser's wouldn't be open yet. There was nothing for it but to get Jamie ready for school, a harder task with a needy Amber clinging to my hip.

The poor little child wasn't well at all and was feeling very itchy. As soon as Dawn had picked Jamie up, I ran a hot bath, and cutting the leg off one of my good pairs of tights, I filled the foot with oatmeal, tied it off, and put it in the bath. When the water had cooled to lukewarm I put Amber in and, lifting the tights-foot full of soaked oatmeal, allowed the milky liquid to dribble over her skin. It helped enormously with the itching and, after I had patted her dry, she actually managed to have a nap.

I'd asked Dawn to get me antihistamine in the chemist and, apart from keeping her temperature down, there was nothing left for me to do.

Well, nothing left for me to do, except try and figure out what in God's name I was going to tell Oliver.

I broke into a cold sweat every time I went to pick up the phone. He was going to go crazy. I had no idea how I was going to explain this one. The best I could come up with was that I had been stricken down with a horrible vomiting and diarrhoea bug. To be fair, his potential reaction terrified me so much, that was fast becoming a reality anyway.

At ten o'clock I dialled his number, but his phone was turned off. I tried twice more before sending him a text.

Pls ring me. H.

All through lunchtime I waited for the phone to ring. Eventually at almost two o'clock I got a text back.

In meeting all day, will ring asap. So excited. O

Oh God, this was a disaster. I quickly dialled his number but it was too late, the phone was off again already. God only knows what time he would get to turn it back on again. There was nothing for it but to wait.

Good job I'd all the washing and cooking done for the weekend, I thought glumly, because all poor Amber wanted was for me to sit down on the couch with her and watch Barney. And that's exactly what we had done for the whole day.

Dawn dropped Jamie home and I gave him his snack and put him in front of a different DVD in the new playroom.

Television was invented for days like this, I decided.

At five o'clock I heard Mark burst through the front door.

"Holly? Are you still here? Holly?"

"I'm in here!" I called from the TV room.

"Oh, good. I mean, I just wanted to say have a good time," he said, and for a second I thought I saw him blushing. Then he looked at me, still in my tracksuit, hair scraped back into a greasy ponytail. "Eh, why are you not ready?"

I gestured to the sick child asleep in my arms.

"Chickenpox," I said.

"What? Why didn't you call me?"

"There was no need, it's all under control."

"Oh bugger. Are you sure?"

"Yes. I'm sure."

"Did you take her to the doctor?"

"I really don't think there's any need. I've bathed her, she's on antihistamines and her temperature is controlled so I think I'm just going to monitor it for a while."

"Oh, right, well, you know the score. But hang on – you're not going to go now?"

"No, I'm not. But it's fine. Honestly. There'll be other weekends. I couldn't leave her with Dawn like this."

"But what about what's-his-name?"

"Oliver. His name is Oliver. And he doesn't know yet. He's in a meeting. I'm waiting for him to ring me back."

He leaned over me and pushed a stray curl out of Amber's eyes.

Now this tender Mark was one I could get used to.

"The poor little chicken," he murmured. "I'll be back in a second. Can I get you anything?"

"A cuppa would be nice," I smiled.

"Sure, back in a tick."

In ten minutes he was back, minus the cup of tea. He did, however, have a big fluffy blanket in his arms and he gestured to me to lay Amber down beside me on the couch. Then he tucked her in.

"Right," he said quietly. "Go up, get ready and get on your way."

"What? Mark, it's fine. Honestly."

"It's not fine, you go get ready."

"But I can't go and leave you like this!"

"My mum is going to be here in thirty minutes. I can stay till she gets here. The only thing I need you to do is make up the bed in the spare room – I just don't know where all the stuff is."

I looked at him in shock.

"You rang your *mother?*"

"Yes, that's what grannies are for!"

"Oh, Mark, I don't know what to say." I was genuinely speechless with surprise.

"Well, don't get too soppy on me now – you know

she'll have the whole house changed by the time you come back." He was trying to be gruff, but I knew he was pleased with my delight.

"Are you sure this is okay?"

"Absolutely, but Holly – and don't take this the wrong way – you smell of Calpol and God knows what. I think you should probably go and get changed, and maybe do something with your hair."

At that Amber stirred and opened one eye. I went to go to her but Mark got there first. He scooped her up and sat back down on the couch with her on his knee.

She looked up and smiled at him. "Dadda," she whispered before falling back asleep.

I smiled and for one bizarre moment it occurred to me that I'd far rather cuddle down on the couch with the two of them than get tarted up and drive miles to some fancy hotel.

Good God, Holly Green, how the mighty have fallen . . .

I wrenched myself away from the scene and ran up the stairs before I had any more ridiculous notions. I was definitely losing my marbles. How could the prospect of a weekend in a tracksuit with a sick child even marginally appeal to me? I put the thought out of my head before it formulated the answer I was afraid of.

In thirty minutes I was ready to go. Okay, so my hair was not professionally blow-dried, but I looked a whole lot better than I had done.

"Are you sure you're okay?" I asked anxiously again when I went back downstairs to where Mark and Amber were still cuddled on the couch. "Do you want me to wait until Jamie is in bed?"

331

"Holly. Go. Mum will be here in a minute. Actually," he paused, listening, "there she is now – let her in on your way out."

I opened the door to a kindly-faced woman, much younger than I'd expected.

"You must be Mrs Fielding," I said, suddenly embarrassed that this nice woman was giving up her time to allow me to go on a dirty weekend with someone else's boyfriend.

"And you must be Holly," she smiled. "I have heard so much about you from the children. And from Mark too, of course."

"Oh, nothing too awful, I hope." The mind boggled at what he might have told her about me. "Mrs Fielding, I'm so sorry to put you out like this. Really, I was happy to stay . . ."

"And I was happier to come!" she said, handing me her coat. Then she leaned towards me and in a conspiratorial whisper said, "He has never, ever, *ever* asked me for help before, you know."

"Really?" I was surprised.

"Really. In fact, my visits were actively discouraged, all this 'make sure you ring in advance' nonsense, but that's Mark for you." She winked at me, still smiling, and said, "I think you've managed to work your miracles on more than just the children. So go, enjoy yourself, and don't hurry back!"

I smiled my thanks as Mark came out into the hall, a sleeping Amber over one shoulder, holding my ringing phone.

"It's your – it's Oliver," he corrected himself, having the good grace to blush.

"Ha! You used his actual name – well done!" I was still smiling as I pressed the answer key.

"Hi, sorry, what? Was I looking for you? Oh yes . . ." I took a deep breath and made a conscious effort to smile. "I just wanted to say that I couldn't wait to see you!"

Chapter 41

By ten o'clock I was ensconced in the snug bar of a very, very nice hotel indeed.

"I told you I'd make it up to you." Oliver pulled me in closer.

"Yes, you did." I was too tired to talk, the stress and worry of the day finally starting to catch up with me.

"Hey, don't you go falling asleep on me now!" Oliver poked me in the ribs. "I'm nowhere near finished with you yet this evening."

To my shock I could feel myself groan inwardly. Not only had I had the day from hell, but I could hardly explain to Oliver that it was already past my usual bedtime and, really, all I wanted to do was go up to the room and fall into a deep sleep. For a second I thought longingly of my little single bed under the eaves at Meadowlands, and at this point I had to give myself a little shake.

"I'm not falling asleep – of course I'm not. But just in case, any chance of a vodka and Diet Coke?"

"Why, yes, of course, Madam," he bowed in mock

solemnity. "This weekend, your every wish is my command."

The next morning I was presented with a new problem. Despite the three vodkas I'd had to keep awake the previous night, and the subsequent vodka-fuelled workout that had gone on until the wee hours, I was wide awake at seven.

No, I groaned, it's too early!

I rolled over and closed my eyes tight, trying frantically to go back to sleep, but it was no good and before long my mind had started to race. I wondered if Mark was up, what kind of night Amber had had, how Jamie was coping . . .

This was ridiculous, there had to be a better way to spend this time than thinking about children that weren't even mine. I looked at the sleeping form of Oliver beside me in the bed and weighed up my options. I could wake him, but I decided against it, telling myself I should really let him sleep on.

Instead I tossed and turned until about seven thirty before creeping from the bed and taking my phone out onto the balcony of the hotel room. It was a still dark and starry but some faint streaks of dawn could be seen over the trees to the east. There were two wooden chairs on the balcony and I sat down on one, pulling the lapels of the huge dressing gown around me, drawing my knees up into its warmth. Taking out the phone, I hesitated for only a minute before starting to text.

Morning. How is Amber? Did she sleep? Is she very itchy? Did you give her the Zirtek this morning?

It took only seconds for the text back.

Mind your own business

Mark Fielding, you fecker!
I started to text furiously back.

Mark! I'm serious – how is she?

Back came his reply.

I'm serious too. She's fine. Go back to your break.

I started to text, then abandoned it, dialling his number instead.

"Yes?" he answered, his deep voice sounding surprisingly sexy. Though that could have been the speaker phone, I reasoned with myself as I could tell he was in the jeep.

"I can't sleep."

He started to laugh. "Is there not something else you should be doing then?"

"He's asleep." I looked through the glass door at the sleeping form of Oliver in the bed. "And anyhow, I'd rather know how Amber is, to be honest."

"Holly, that is slightly worrying."

"I can't help it! I feel so bad being away from her when she's not well."

"Well, don't. She woke really early feeling itchy but she looked a lot brighter and when I left she was snuggled in bed with her nana, reading stories."

"Now, Mark – is that the truth?"

"Holly. Go back to bed."

"I can't. I'm bored."

He laughed again. "Bored? Don't tell me you'd rather be here, surrounded by sick children, cleaning up after your grumpy boss, than holed up in a romantic hotel with lover boy!"

336

"Mmmm," I smiled into the phone, "the children wouldn't be so bad, but you're right – I'm not so fond of the cleaning-up-after-you bit."

"See, you're better off where you are."

"S'pose . . ."

"Go and wake that lazy lump of a boyfriend up – tell him he's wasting valuable time by sleeping."

"Huh, I don't think he'd thank me. Where are you on your way to?"

"I've three calls to make and I promised Mum I'd be home by eleven to give her a hand."

"Oh, so you'll come home early when your mum is there but not me – that's says it all."

"Eh, Holly, I *pay* you, remember?"

I burst out laughing. "Funny how I forgot that, isn't it!"

"I hope you're not complaining about your working conditions, young lady."

"Would I?"

"Well, you haven't been one to mince your words so far. But let's get back to the point – where are you exactly and why does your not-always-sweetness-and-light boyfriend not mind you yapping away on the phone to me?"

"He can't hear me," I giggled. "I'm out on the balcony. In *nothing but a dressing gown . . .*" I had the last bit hissed before I realised what I was saying.

"Oh right. Say hi to Tara – she's here beside me."

"She *what*?" I shot upright in embarrassment.

There was a roar of laughter. "I'm joking, but it's still strange information to give a man trying to drive, Ms Green."

"Mark! That wasn't fair!" Then I giggled in relief.

"Though I suppose you're right, sorry. If it's any consolation, it's bloody freezing out here so there's no chance of me taking it off."

"I really think we need to change this subject."

"Okay." I knew I should be embarrassed but the funny thing was that I wasn't. It seemed like the most natural conversation in the world to be having. "So where are you now?"

"Where I have been since the start of this call, parked outside Lady Hannah's, waiting for my nanny to stop twittering on about her state of undress so that maybe I can go and get some work done. Some of us have a sick child and a put-upon mother to get home to, you know."

"Oh crap – you should have said! I thought you were still driving."

"It's fine. I'm really just hoping that boyfriend of yours will wake up any minute and catch you on the phone to another man – now that would make my day."

"Mark Fielding!" I squealed. "What a dreadful thing to say! I'd be in all kinds of trouble then."

"Something tells me that wouldn't be for the first time."

"Isn't that the truth?" I admitted ruefully. "Anyhow, you better go or Lady Hannah will have a search party out looking for you."

"Yes. Will you be able to cope with the boredom when I'm gone?"

"I'll manage. I might see if I can find a newspaper in reception."

"Sounds fascinating. But, Holly?"

"Yes?"

"Get dressed first, will you?"

"Mark, I'm in a modern hotel – people walk around in dressing gowns all the time!"

"Whatever."

"Tell Amber I said hi – oh, and Jamie – don't forget Dawn said she'd take him to soccer – and tell her not to forget his drink bottle and –"

But he was gone. He'd actually hung up.

I smiled and looked again at Oliver still asleep. I knew I should really wake him, but I also knew what would happen when I did and God knows there was a long enough day ahead. So instead I pulled the robe around me, closed my eyes and sat for just another while before going in.

Chapter 42

"Hey! I thought we said no phones!"

I jumped and stuffed my mobile, on which I'd been texting Mark, back in my bag. Trying to look nonchalant, I stretched back out on the huge bed, hoping a wanton pose might distract him. It was Sunday afternoon and, to be honest, the constant need to appear wanton was starting to wear thin.

"Sorry, it was my dad," I lied hastily.

"Again? Oh, I don't know, Holly – I think you might be telling a fib."

My cheeks flared. "I am not! He keeps texting me about my mad mother and her crazy plans for Christmas and I don't know what to say to him."

To be fair, this much was true. I had received four texts from Dad already that weekend, the latest of which was requesting me to let my mother know if I was planning to bring a guest for Christmas Day as, if I was, there was going to be a need to buy a larger table with more chairs. I'd had to refrain from telling him to inform her that I was helping out at the local soup kitchen and to take me off the list altogether.

"You say nothing this weekend." Oliver crawled across the bed towards me – my plan to distract him unfortunately seemed to be working. "This weekend we worry about nothing or no one except ourselves." He kissed me, slowly and passionately.

"You're right," I nodded between kisses, guiltily resolving not to as much as look at my phone again.

"Anyhow, so what do you want to do with the rest of the day – swim, lunch or . . .?"

I wiggled out from underneath him. "Well, actually, we haven't time to do much. I kind of need to head soon."

"You what?" He recoiled in disbelief. "It's not even teatime!"

Oh God, I'd been hoping he needed to get back too, but the scowl on his face was definitely telling me he'd had no such plans.

"I know, but I need to get back."

"For what?"

Oh God, why hadn't I come up with a good excuse earlier? I could hardly tell him the real reason – that I figured Mark's mother had covered for me for long enough and that I also wanted to make sure that Amber was okay and that I was organised for the week ahead.

And that, despite the weekend being great, I kind of wanted to go home . . .

There was nothing for it but a half-truth.

"I promised someone I'd baby-sit this evening," I said.

"You promised someone *what*? Who?"

"Oh, what does it matter who? I need to get back. I didn't think it would be a problem. I thought you'd need to be back too."

"Well, it is and I don't. Now, tell me who – oh wait – it's that guy with the kids, isn't it?"

I nodded. It was the truth after all.

"Well, he'll have to do without you."

"Don't be ridiculous. I promised him. I can hardly let him down after what he did for me on Wednesday."

"Of course you can. What's he going to do? Think badly of you? So what? Why would you care?"

"Of course I'd care. Mark was very good to me the other night – he put himself out for me." And again this weekend, I thought to myself. "So, if I can do something to repay him, of course I will."

"For God's sake, Holly, you're such a Goody Two-Shoes!"

"Well, if that's what you think, so be it."

He looked at the resolve in my eyes and rolled his eyes.

"So when do you have to go?"

I shrugged. "Pretty soon."

"Mmm, pretty soon," he smiled, and started to creep over the bed towards me. "Sounds to me you might have time for just a little . . ."

I looked at him and, for the first time ever, I found myself able to resist his doe-brown eyes.

"No," I said, swatting him away with a pillow in mock-snootiness, "I'm afraid I don't, so you'll have to put that idea on hold for now."

"Eh, I don't think so," he said, by now pushing me back and pinning my arms to the bed.

Just as I waited for the usual feelings of lust to take over and sweep me into a maelstrom of passion, his phone rang.

"Shit," he said, rolling off me.

Where ordinarily I'd have told him to ignore it, I couldn't help feeling slightly relieved that it was his phone and not mine that was breaking the mood. When it transpired that it was Catherine and he now had to be home earlier than he thought, I wasn't even annoyed. It meant I wasn't the Big Bad Wolf for winding up the love-fest prematurely.

Phew.

Less than thirty minutes later, I was in my car, the fancy hotel already becoming a far distant memory. I reached down and switched the radio channel again in the hope of finding some good music that might coast me the last few miles home. It was hard to believe the weekend was almost over and that in a little under an hour I'd be back at No 12.

I couldn't help analysing the time we'd had. It had been a strange weekend. But then we weren't used to spending so much time together. It was bound to be different, wasn't it? And when everything else was sorted out, Catherine, Mark, Our Situation – when these stupid issues were a thing of the past, and it was just the two of us again, it was obvious that we'd be fine.

I'd probably been expecting too much from the weekend anyway, thanks to Dawn and all her talk of honeymoons.

Dawn! I put my phone on hands-free and dialled her number. She'd be dying to know all the gory details.

The phone rang, and rang, and rang.

Just as I was about to cancel the call, the ringing stopped. I presumed the call had been answered but yet no one had spoken.

"Hello? Dawn? Are you there?"

The answer was almost inaudible. It sounded more like a whimper or moan. For a second I wondered if Daniel had the phone, but even as this thought crossed my mind

I realised that a three-month-child was too young for that kind of caper.

I pulled in to the roadside and took the phone off speaker.

"Dawn? Dawn, is that you?"

I wondered was it my mobile reception but when I looked I had three bars.

"Dawn, can you hear me? Answer me! Is everything okay?"

There was another whimper and then the clear sound of sobs.

Jesus, she was crying!

"Dawn! Stop, please stop. Just tell me what's wrong. Is it Daniel?"

"We were going to have another baby," a voice not recognisable as Dawn's said eventually.

"Really? Oh, I didn't know – oh wait –" A cold feeling came over me. "What do you mean 'were', Dawn?"

But then there was just louder sobbing and crying and I couldn't make out a word she was saying.

Oh God, no – not another miscarriage. "Look, Dawn, I'm driving, but I'm on my way back. I'll be with you as soon as I can. Is there anyone else there? Where's Graham?"

There was no answer, but at least she'd stopped crying. Jesus, what was I going to do? I was still at least an hour away.

"Dawn, will you be okay till I get there?" Then I had a brainwave. "Dawn, will I call Mark? He could be with you in a minute?"

Mark would know what to do. I just knew he would.

"I'll be okay," she whispered again.

"I'll be there soon, sweetie – I promise!"

More silence.

"Dawn, I can't hear you, but I'll be with you very soon. I'm coming straight to your house."

I hung up the phone and put it back on the passenger seat, sighing deeply. I hadn't even known she was pregnant – I mean, Daniel was only three months old. She hadn't even mentioned going again so soon. I wondered how far along had she been. Not long surely? I couldn't see her as the type that would keep that kind of news to herself. But maybe with her history of miscarriages she would?

My heart sank. Poor, poor Dawn. Why did shit stuff like that always happen to the nice people? And there I'd been complaining that my weekend had been boringly blissful. I was utterly devastated by the grief in Dawn's voice. Darling Dawn, who I'd never seen without a smile and a giggle . . .

Before I pulled back out onto the road, I texted Mark to ask was it okay that I call in to her for a couple of minutes. The last thing I wanted was for him to spot my car three doors down and wonder why I hadn't made an appearance at home. He replied within an instant that his mother was baking with the children and that I was not allowed to come home for at least two hours.

At least that was something.

Oh God, what was I going to say?

For a minute I wished I could log onto the babyline. I'd seen a section on miscarriage and was sure there were some words of wisdom there that I could badly do with.

Whereas I'd seemed so close to home barely minutes before, now the miles seemed to drag. Eventually I pulled into Meadowlands and raced down the estate to Kinahans'.

There was nothing for it now but to wing it, I thought as I rang the doorbell.

I almost didn't recognise the Dawn that answered the door. She was pale and gaunt and her soft golden hair was tied back off a face that was totally devoid of make-up. Her eyes were sunken in her head, and red-raw from crying.

"Dawn?"

"Oh, Holly!" She flung herself on me, almost collapsing in giant, heaving sobs.

"Where's Graham? Where's Daniel?"

"Daniel's in bed," she managed between sobs, "and Graham . . ." She started to moan again.

"Oh Dawn, come on, I'm here now, it'll all be okay, I promise."

I was getting worried about her now. Should I call a doctor? Why wasn't she in hospital anyway? Fuck it, I wished I knew more about these things. "Dawn, you need to calm down, you're going to make yourself sick."

I managed to get her into the sitting room and cradled her on the couch.

She stopped crying and, staring into space, repeated her words from earlier. "We were going to have another baby."

"Oh Dawn, I know, but these things happen, and you'll have another."

She shook her head.

"When did it happen?"

"Last night," she gulped.

"Oh God, I'm so sorry."

"He was . . ." she could hardly get the words out, "he was . . . he was supposed to be in London."

I was confused now.

346

"Who was, honey? Graham? Was he here with you then?"

"*No he wasn't with me!*" she screamed, in a hoarse, bloodcurdling voice that I'd never heard from a human being before. "*He was with her!*"

I literally froze with the realisation that this was a very, very different situation from what I'd thought.

"Jesus Christ. What are you saying? That he was – no way, are you sure?" I wasn't sure I wanted to hear the answer.

"I'm sure," she nodded. "It's been going on for months."

I felt sick. Literally sick.

I had a million questions I wanted to ask her but I couldn't speak. The words just would not come out of my mouth.

"And you know what, Holly? The worst thing is I know her. She knows me. She knows. I mean what kind of selfish bitch is she?"

She was crying again, and all I could do was hold her, and rock her, and tell her that everything was going to be okay. When all the time, deep down, I knew that nothing would ever be okay again.

For either of us.

Chapter 43

"Welcome back, Holly!" yelled Jamie the minute I put my key in the door.

"*Holleeee!*" screamed Amber also, not to be outdone, her red spots looking considerably less angry.

"Hey, guys, thanks!"

Oh God, so much for sneaking in. I knelt down to hug them both. But they both resisted, instead taking a hand each and dragging me down the hall.

"*We have a surprise!*" Jamie was yelling again.

This was like a nightmare. All I wanted to do was go to my room, get into my bed and pretend this day had never happened. But instead I smiled glassily and let myself be pulled into the kitchen.

"Close your eyes!" ordered Jamie.

I did as I was bid, and then opened them to a giant screech of "*Surprise!*" from the children. They had made a huge banner for the wall with "*Welcome Back, Holly*" painted in bright colours and on the table was a huge cake with neon-pink icing and my name piped in blue.

"We missed you!" said Jamie.

"And that definitely goes for all of us," said a deep voice behind me. I turned to see Mark standing at the sink. "Promise me you'll never take any time off, ever again?"

I smiled as best I could, his words only reminding me that I was about to let this fantastic family down as well.

"Where's your mother?" I asked, looking around.

"Oh, she insisted on being gone before you got here. She left food in the oven for us, but thought we should have some time alone." He smirked. "If I didn't know her better I'd think she was trying to match-make!"

I smiled feebly.

"It's okay," he winked before whispering, "I told her you were on a dirty weekend with a married man!"

At that, I could take no more. Giant tears started to slide down my cheeks and I dashed for the roll of kitchen paper on the table.

"Jesus Christ, Holly, I'm joking!" Mark said, shocked at my reaction.

"Holly cry," said Amber, happy to be able to use her favourite phrase again, but Jamie looked petrified.

Mark immediately stepped in and started to shepherd the children out of the room.

"Oh Jamie, it's fine, it's just that no one ever cooked Holly such a nice cake before," he said brightly. "Now, why don't you two go wash your faces and hands and then we can sit down and once we've eaten up Nana's roast chicken, we can all have some cake!"

The two scampered out, Jamie casting me one last anxious look, and then there was silence. I couldn't turn to face him, nor could I stop the tears pouring from my eyes. So deep were my sobs that I found it hard to catch my breath in between.

"Holly, you have to tell me what's wrong. Did you have another row?"

I shook my head, trying to stem the tears from my eyes.

"Then what is it? Please, whatever it is, you can tell me!"

I shook my head.

"I can't," I whispered.

And then, standing in Mark's kitchen, kitchen paper rammed against my eyes, I broke down, all the tension of the past month, and the guilt of the Dawn situation bubbling to the surface.

And I cried like I'd never cried before.

I cried for Dawn and her ruined marriage.

I cried for Cain's wife and her ruined marriage.

And I cried for me.

(Mostly I cried for me.)

Then, through my tears, I felt two strong arms wrap themselves around me, turning me around. And I knew the situation had just gone from bad to infinitely cringey worse but I couldn't fight it. I leaned into Mark's chest and I cried, and cried again. And he hugged me, and stroked my hair and murmured into my ear.

"Holly, whatever it is, we can fix it, please stop crying, please."

"You can't fix it, Mark, no one can," I managed between sobs.

"I promise you, it can't be as bad as you think."

"It is!" I wailed. "I'm a horrible, selfish person, and that's just the truth!"

Through my distress I could feel his giant shoulders start to shake.

"You'd better not be laughing!" I wailed.

"I'm not."

"You are!"

"You're right, I am. But just a little bit."

"It's not funny, Mark, this is really serious!" I cried, pulling back to glare at him.

"I know, I know, I'm sorry, but that whole 'I'm-the-worst-person-in-the-world' crap just doesn't work with me. I could tell you stories about this house that would make your blood run cold. Now please, dry your eyes, and the minute we get the kids to bed, I'll make you a cuppa and you can tell me the whole story. Deal?"

"Mark, seriously, there is no point."

"There's every point."

"You're going to hate me."

"Well, if I do, then I do," he said, still smiling, "but I doubt it."

"Okay." I gave in and wiped my eyes with my sodden piece of kitchen paper.

"Eh, Holly, it just might take a bit more than that. I really don't want to make you cry again but, if you don't put on a bit of make-up, the children will be awake all night with nightmares."

Two hours later, the children were in bed and the house was quiet.

"Right, the dishwasher's done – I think I might just head up," I said as I tried to sneak from the room.

"Not so fast, Missus! Sit!" Mark pointed to the chair. "Now, tea or coffee?"

I groaned inwardly. At this stage all I wanted to do was go to bed and forget this horrendous day ever happened.

"Tea, please." I did as I was told and sat down.

"Now tell me the whole story."

I sighed. I was so exhausted.

"Mark. I don't know where to start. It's just all so complicated."

"Well, why don't you start at the bit where you're not really a nanny?"

Holy shit!

I looked at him in shock.

"I'm not a what?"

"Holly, I'm going to make this easier for you."

With that he got up from the table and left the kitchen. When he came back, he was carrying a huge brown cardboard box.

"This is one of three that arrived on Friday after you were gone."

I looked at the box, my heart sinking. I knew immediately that it was one of the three that I'd given to Seán to mind for me.

And it was open.

"Yes, it's open," said Mark. "I'm afraid I did that, well, only to one of them. I was expecting drugs, you see, and I had it open before I realised it was addressed to you."

And I had genuinely thought that this day couldn't get any worse.

Seán, you fucking eejit! I said I'd ring you in a month, not to send them in a month!

"Well, I had it open and had taken these out," he held up two of my business books in his hands, "and it dawned on me that either you were the most overqualified childminder in the world or," he replaced the books, "you have some very boring hobbies."

He sat back down in front of me.

"So get talking, Ms Green. I'm all ears."

Chapter 44

Was it any wonder that at three in the morning I was wide awake with not a hope of getting back to sleep? I'd been tossing and turning for hours, my poor brain unable to decide if it was better that I now had no secrets from Mark, or much, much worse.

He was just so unreadable. When I'd got to the end of my long and sorry tale he'd sat, deep in thought, for several minutes.

"So," he said eventually, "when you'd go for your break at Christmas, you were planning on never coming back."

"Yes," I whispered, unable to look at him.

"I see. And Oliver will be free to go with you then?"

"Well, he hopes so. I suppose there's always a chance that the promotions won't be announced before Christmas, but I'm hoping that won't happen."

"I see."

"Oh, stop saying 'I see' and just get to the point!" I snapped. "I know you're annoyed, you've every right to be. I don't blame you. This awful mess is all my fault and I can't even begin to tell you how sorry I am."

I'd had enough of this whole embarrassing topic, and certainly the memory of ending up in his arms earlier wasn't helping matters.

"My point," said Mark, a sharp tone coming into his voice, "is that we've been through all the Holly-is-the-worst-person-in-the-world bullshit. And I'm not saying yet whether you're right or wrong on that one. This is certainly a lot to take in. Two days ago I thought I had a superb nanny for the foreseeable future, now it appears I have a fugitive accountant for two to three weeks at most. The least you can do is give me a few hours to digest everything."

I'd nodded. "I'm sorry. There's nothing for you to digest. I'm going to start packing in the morning. Unless of course you want me to stay to help you find someone else."

"That won't be necessary. I have Harry to help me after all."

It amused me somewhat that, even without looking up, I knew that the muscle in his jaw would be clenching.

We were both tired. There was nothing for it but to say goodnight and head to bed.

And that's how the conversation had finished up. I flipped my pillow again and turned, but it was no good. There was no chance of me getting to sleep. Round and round in my head went all the dreadful things I'd done.

- I'd had an affair with a married man

- Now I was (albeit unwittingly) in an affair with a different man that had a girlfriend

- I'd involved the nicest man in Ireland in my scheme and now he was going to be murdered by his brother

- I'd betrayed my first ever best friend, who would hate me if she knew that I too was a "selfish bitch" who was knowingly in a relationship with someone who had a girlfriend

- And I'd lied to, and taken advantage of my boss, who'd entrusted me with his precious children. Alright, so they were easier to call precious thanks to me, but still, I wasn't to know that when I'd initially duped him

- And for the second time in six weeks (third time in six months – you go, girl!), I'd be leaving a job under a cloud

Oh Holly, your mother would be so proud.

It was ironic but for once, in crisis, I couldn't post on the babyline. Well, I could, but I'd have to create another new persona. MarshaG would never do anything as calamitously stupid as get herself into this situation. (Though, to be fair, with four kids under five it was unlikely that an affair would be high on her agenda.) In fact, I doubted I'd get any sympathy from anyone on the baby board. No, I'd have to search under 'Discussions' and hope that there was a board for 'Hopeless Women Who Ruin Everything'. Which wasn't outside the realms of possibility. After all, there was a board called 'Broken Hearts', where women wept and gnashed their teeth, melded together in one big moaning mêlée, about their failed relationships. In fact I'd noticed that while men occasionally posted on the babyline, they were never brave enough to show their faces on 'Broken Hearts'. They'd have been instantly run over by a mob of angry, bitter ex-wives and girlfriends baying for the blood of anything with testosterone.

In fact, in hindsight, I'd better stay away from 'Broken Hearts' myself. I was precisely the kind of female they ranted about the most. I'd read with interest one evening where a girl who'd bravely called herself 'otherwoman' had posted a thread asking for understanding on behalf of all "Other Women everywhere". She'd lasted about four hours and one hundred and sixty-two angry-bitch posts before she'd vanished, sobbing into cyberspace, never to be heard of again.

I wondered if Dawn was on the babyline, posting about her philandering husband.

Bloody Graham Kinahan.

How had I not spotted that one? Let's face it, it's not like I didn't know a two-timing rat when I saw one. I could write a thesis on them, for God's sake. In fact, I was quite surprised that I hadn't fancied him myself.

Or slept with him.

Or ruined my life for him.

Because that was the kind of thing women like me did, wasn't it? One thing was for sure, Dawn would have no time for me if she knew what I was up to. Of course she wouldn't. I was the Other Woman.

For the second time in a year.

Wincing in shame, I suddenly thought of Cain's wife, Melissa. Had she wept and moaned and screamed when she'd found out what he was up to? Had somebody had to hold her sobbing in their arms while she ranted and railed against the ruination of her life?

Why hadn't I thought of this before?

I'd known about her all along. I'd known and I hadn't given a damn.

I hadn't thought of this before because I'd thought of no one but myself.

You stupid, selfish girl.

Okay, so with Oliver it was different. I hadn't known until it was too late.

And he wasn't married.

And there were no children.

But he did have a girlfriend. A girlfriend that was there before me and I'd done very little that could be considered honourable since I'd found out.

I threw back the covers in disgust. I had to get up. Going round and round in a circle of self-hatred was getting me nowhere.

I crept down the stairs and into the kitchen, fished the hot chocolate from the back of the cupboard and then went to the fridge.

"Eh, what are you doing exactly?"

I jumped at the sound of Mark's voice and walloped my head off the fridge door.

"*Shite!* Why do you keep doing this to me?" I rubbed my head in indignation. "I'm getting some bloody milk for my bloody hot chocolate because I can't bloody well sleep!" I waved the purple tub of chocolate powder at him.

"Oh. That's fine. I thought maybe –"

"Maybe what? That I was trying to gas myself in the fridge? No, I wasn't, but I'm not promising my life won't come to that."

"That's not funny, Holly."

He was serious, but obviously couldn't not smile at the sight of me bashing my head off the fridge door once again in his presence. And once again, as luck would have it, in the bloody Garfield pyjamas.

Apart from the half-smirk on his lips, he looked awful.

Stubble peppered his jaw and he had huge dark circles under his eyes. "Make enough for two there, will you? I'm having sleeping issues myself."

"I suppose that's my fault too," I grumbled guiltily, finally retrieving the milk and pouring some into a saucepan.

"Right, that's it." His tone was sharp. "Sit down. I was going to have this chat with you tomorrow but as we're both here," he paused, looking at his watch, "3 a.m. seems as good a time as any."

Oh God, here it comes, I thought, as I sat down in front of him, feeling for all the world like I was sixteen again and had just been caught drinking by my dad.

A dressing-down from Mark Fielding and me in my Garfield pyjamas without so much as a screed of make-up on . . .

"It is not your fault that Graham Kinahan had an affair." Mark didn't waste any time getting to the point.

I grunted but that didn't stop him.

"As you know yourself, a lot of men have affairs, and well –" his face broke into a smirk, "they can't all be your fault." He paused to clear his throat. "Well, not quite all of them. Personally, I don't think very much of someone who never seems to be content with what they have. I'd also wonder how they could ever be trusted again. So no, your current relationship is not ideal but, for now, let's assume that Oliver is going to do the right thing and that all your dreams come true."

I nodded, but he was talking again.

"However –"

Oh shit, here it comes.

"I would like you to consider something."

Oh. I looked at him. "What?"

358

"I'd like you to consider staying on here for a while if for some reason things don't work out or, you know, if," he added hastily, "if Oliver needs to stay a while longer to sort things out."

"Oh Mark, I don't know." I immediately shook my head. I'd made up my mind, I was going – where, I didn't know – but I was going.

"Look, obviously this is not the job of your dreams, though frankly I doubt you're half as good an accountant as you are Domestic CEO but, still, if you need to hang around temporarily, I'd like it to be here."

"But, Mark, I've lied to you, I've lied to Dawn. How could you possibly overlook all that?"

He looked at me, and even though he was still smiling, a look of sadness suddenly came into his eyes. "On a scale of one to ten, I've heard worse lies, Holly."

Not the words I'd been expecting.

"Why are you being so nice to me? I don't deserve it." It was a genuine question – he'd have been well within his rights to turf me out and change the locks.

"Holly, you've got yourself into a bit of a scrape, but you haven't exactly killed anyone yet. You need to take your time, relax, take some time out – you can't possibly make intelligent decisions when your head is in this kind of state."

"I'm not in a state." I knew this was a lie as I said it.

"So when was the last time you cried on someone's shoulder? Any kind of tears, let alone the deluge you subjected me to?"

I shook my head. I'd no idea but it certainly hadn't been recently.

"So you'll think about what I'm saying?"

"I'll think about it."

"Good. Now, this might be completely your idea of hell, but Fenton is putting together a table for the Hunt Ball next Friday. Why don't you come with us? He pressed me to come last year but I said no. But, you know, maybe we could both do with a night out. It could be your going-away party. Maybe Harry might come and you could even ask Dawn if you like – might be a good chance to cheer her up too."

"Who'll mind the kids?"

"My mother said she'd take them to hers for the weekend. Come on, apparently it's a very glamorous occasion."

"I won't know anyone."

"You'll know me, and Harry, and Tara."

Ah, Tara. Of course.

"Let me think about it." The last thing I felt like doing at the moment was dressing up and going to a party. Though the competitive streak in me was poking its head up, whispering about being a good opportunity to show these country bumpkins the real Holly Green.

"I'll take that as a yes but, while I have you, there is one other thing you could do for me."

His look of embarrassment unnerved me.

"What?" I asked.

"Well, it's our debtors' list. You see, we're owed quite a bit but we just don't have the time to chase our debtors. Now, not that I'm saying that you've masses of free time, but you seem to have a bit of a business head on you, and you'd definitely scare them."

"I beg your pardon?" I couldn't help but be indignant at what he'd implied.

"Oh come on, that can't be the first time you've been called scary!"

"I am not scary!"

"Holly Green, you are singularly the scariest woman I have ever met – how have you not noticed that I'm terrified of you?"

"*You* are terrified of *me*!" I laughed aloud. "You're hardly brimming with good humour and positivity yourself, Mr Fielding!"

When I found myself batting my eyelashes, it hit me – there was no escaping the fact that I was flirting.

With Mark Fielding.

I mean, it was almost four in the morning, I'd no make-up on, no fancy clothes, and none of my lines had been rehearsed for hours beforehand . . .

But it was definitely flirting.

And it actually felt okay.

"I am a vet, Ms Green. If I liked humans, I would have become a doctor."

I grinned at him. "And I'm an auditor, Mr Fielding. If I liked humans I'd have –"

"Got a job minding children?" he finished for me, one eyebrow arched, a smirk on his lips.

He was flirting back!

"Touché!" I murmured. "But speaking of said children, I really should go back to bed – I doubt they'll be too understanding about this early-morning rendezvous at seven o'clock when they expect me to start tending to their every need."

"Yes," he sighed, looking at his watch, "I've to be on the gallops in exactly three hours."

"Good point."

"Yes."

We looked at each other, neither seeming to know what to say next.

So I got up.

"You'll think about what I asked?" he said hurriedly.

"The bad-debts thing? Of course I'll do it – I'll start tomorrow."

"No, not that – well, that too, but the other . . ."

"The ball?"

"No – the staying. I mean, you'll think about staying. Will you?" Now he was standing too, and for a moment I saw a younger Mark, so like Jamie when he wanted something, almost hopping from foot to foot with anxiety.

And, just like I'd say to Jamie, I said, "I'll see, Mark, I'll see."

And with that we went to bed.

Chapter 45

Despite my complete lack of sleep the night before, by half nine the next morning I was pounding on Dawn's front door. All the curtains in the house were still closed and there was no sign of life.

"Dawn, it's Holly. Let me in!"

After a few minutes the door opened. Even poor Amber stepped back in fright at the sight of Dawn, who looked even worse than she had yesterday. She was in her dressing gown, clearly hadn't showered and looked wretched. More worrying, I could hear Daniel roaring in his room.

"Oh Dawn!" I sighed. "Come on, let's get you sorted."

I manhandled her into the kitchen and stuck on the kettle. Then I brought Amber into the sitting room, plonked her on the cream couch and found a children's channel with non-stop cartoons to keep her busy. Before leaving the room I tugged open the huge curtains and opened a window. The whole house smelled musty and stale.

I strode back into the kitchen and sat in front of Dawn.

"Where's Graham?"

"He's at work now," she said. "But I wouldn't let him in last night. I don't know where he went."

"Okay. Fair enough. Look, I want you to listen to me, Dawn."

She looked at me, tears welling up in her eyes again.

"I want you to go upstairs and have a shower and get dressed. Moping around in a dressing gown is not going to work. You are going to put on some make-up too. I'm going to bring Daniel down, dress him and feed him. Then we are all going out for a walk. We're going to go for coffee and we're going to figure out what you need to do. Okay?"

"I can't," she whispered, the tears overflowing.

"Yes, you can. One step at a time. As soon as we have a plan, you'll feel better. Trust me. Can you do that?"

She nodded.

"Right, up to the shower. I'm going to grab Daniel."

We went upstairs where she reluctantly headed for her bedroom. Upstairs looked nearly worse than downstairs – there were puddles of laundry everywhere and again every window and curtain was closed.

I sighed. I needed to work quickly. Scooping up a distraught Daniel and propping him on one hip, I swung open his curtains and opened his window.

"Now that's better, isn't it?"

He looked up at me with giant sad eyes. Poor little soul, I thought, it's not your fault that everything is such a mess. I brought him downstairs, pausing first to listen outside Dawn's bedroom door, where to my relief I could hear the shower going.

Amber was mercifully well-behaved and still engrossed

in the cartoons and, by the time Dawn came back downstairs, I had Daniel fed and changed and on his play mat. I'd also raced around the house, opening curtains and windows and scooping up all the dirty washing. I'd one wash on and another waiting and the dishwasher was loaded.

"Hey!" I said when Dawn walked quietly into the kitchen. "You look much better."

"I can't go out Holly, really, I can't. I just can't face anyone." She looked at me with her giant sad blue eyes and for a minute I thought she was going to cry again.

"Okay. No problem. But you are going to let me cook you something to eat, and you're going to sit down and eat it while I fly up and change your sheets. Then we're going to have a chat, get our plan together and I'll take Daniel for the day while you go back to bed."

To my surprise she just nodded and sat down. Within minutes I'd rustled up an omelette and two giant mugs of tea and I sat down with her while she ate slowly and with difficulty – but she ate.

At last she pushed her plate away.

"Right, Dawn," I said, "I want you to take a deep breath and tell me everything you know."

At my words, fresh tears started to spill down her cheeks. I handed her a square of kitchen roll.

"Her name is Nicola and it's been going on for about six months," she finally managed.

"How do you know all this?"

"Well, he went to London on Friday afternoon, and when I went to phone him that evening, I noticed he left his phone behind." Her mouth broke into a crooked sneer. "The fool! I mean, it's such a cliché, isn't it? Anyhow I worried that he'd think he'd lost it in the airport and be going crazy trying to find it so I rang Charles, the colleague he was in London with – sorry – the colleague he was *meant* to be in London with – but he knew nothing about the trip. Which just didn't add up. Anyhow, I had the phone, and God forgive me but I've read enough books and watched enough silly TV to know that it mightn't be a bad idea to go through it. Bingo! I could read his emails and everything. He hadn't tried hard to hide anything really. He must think I'm a complete gobshite."

"So what are you going to do?"

She shrugged. "Well, that's just it. I don't know, do I? I mean," she gulped, clearly trying not to break down again, "what do I do? I wouldn't let him in when he got home last night, so God only knows where he is now. He's been trying to phone but I haven't had the energy to talk to him. What would you do?"

Oh crap, was I totally the wrong person to answer that question!

I sighed. "I don't know, Dawn, I really don't. But either way you'll have to talk to him eventually. No point in doing it when you're so tired though, so let me do your bed, then you get into it for a few hours and I'll take Daniel to Mark's with me."

"What if he comes back while you're gone?"

Before I got a chance to answer, her phone beeped with a text message.

"It's him," she said, looking at it. "He wants to come home tonight, to talk."

"Okay. So what do you want to do?"

"I don't know!" She started to cry again.

"Right, well, I think you should let him. I'll hang on to

Daniel and that might let him see you mean business. You're going to have to talk to him sometime."

She nodded.

"Now go and pack me a bag for Daniel while I do your sheets and then you must get to bed – you look like you haven't slept in a week. Then I'll head with the kids."

I pottered around for a while after she went upstairs to make sure she was asleep before I left. Then, packing up the two children, I headed down the street to Mark's.

"Oh my, don't you have your hands full today."

As always Bernadette Foley was hanging around near her front door.

"Hi, Mrs Foley, yes, lots of children today!"

"Nothing wrong with poor Dawn, I hope?"

"Oh no, Mrs Foley, but everyone needs a break sometime, don't they?"

"I suppose," she sniffed, peeved that I wasn't giving her more information. "After all, poor Emma needed more rest than most, didn't she?"

I paused, my key almost in the door. "I wouldn't know, Mrs Foley. I wasn't here then, remember?" My voice was sharp, but I was wondering what she meant.

"Oh well, I remember poor Teresa Murphy was worn out minding those children. I mean, I used to say to her that it was ridiculous, them with a perfectly good mother and father of their own."

"Really." I was torn between getting away from this awful woman and finding out more.

"Oh yes, but I was told in no uncertain terms to mind my own business! But I'm telling you, sick or not, that pair took some advantage of Teresa all the same."

"Sick?"

"Oh, I've said too much now. Anyway, what does it matter now, sure didn't God take her when he wanted in the end. All that worrying on Teresa's part couldn't do much about that, could it?"

I'd heard enough.

"Bye now, Mrs Foley."

I really hadn't the energy for this today. Not alone had I an extra child to look after, I really wanted to get stuck into ringing the list of debtors Mark had left for me that morning.

And I had plans for the evening . . . in the form of a Christmas tree I had ordered earlier that morning.

It wasn't a vast list, but some of the amounts and the length of time they'd been owing, were incredible. Mark had written notes in the margin as to the various disputes or other matters that might be delaying payment. I suspected that most, as with the majority of outstanding accounts I'd worked with, simply required a few timely reminders from a different voice in order to prompt payment.

As soon as I got Amber immersed in a jigsaw and Daniel down for a nap, I made a coffee and sat down with the phone.

I eased myself in gently with a few non-contentious-looking accounts.

An hour later I decided to call it a day. It had been relatively successful: three didn't answer their phones, two promised a cheque, and four promised to pay but looked for discounts. I'd knew have to discuss the discount element with Mark later, so I promised to phone them back.

Before I tidied up, I scanned the list one last time to see

who I might phone after lunch. One particular account caught my eye, mostly because it was such a large amount of money.

New Trafford Stud, Maynooth, Co. Kildare
Amount: 15,899
Outstanding: 120 days

I looked at the clock then, casting a quick glance at Daniel who was only just starting to stir, I picked up the phone and dialled the number.

"'Ello?" a voice with a thick Dublin accent answered.

"Hi, this is Raven's Hill Veterinary Clinic – to whom am I speaking?"

"Never mind who I am, what the fuck do you want?"

And then, with a crashing heart, I realised exactly who I was speaking to.

Chapter 46

"Not that way, Daddy!" Jamie shrieked as Mark deliberately hung the giant Santa upside down.

"Daddy, no!" Amber giggled.

I smiled at them all. This was exactly how I'd imagined this scene. The children's faces were alight both with joy and the sparkle of the lights of the newly erected Christmas tree. They ran from the bundle of decorations to the tree and back over and over again, only stopping to gaze at the fat Santas on the mantelpiece that I'd purchased while in Newbridge with Dawn the week before and the giant rosy-red stockings that hung below. I almost felt sorry that Daniel, asleep in his buggy in the hall, was missing all the excitement.

"I still think this is ridiculously early." Mark shook his head at the festive chaos around him.

"Bah, humbug!" I teased, poking his arm gently.

"Seriously, Holly, I'm a last-minute-Christmas-Eve kind of guy – this is madness."

My smile faded for a second as I remembered my real reason for the early preparations. No matter what happened

I wasn't going to be here Christmas Eve, and I'd really just wanted to see the children's faces when the tree went up.

"If that tree dies, you'll be the one putting up another one!" Now it was Mark's turn to tease me, as if sensing my sudden change of mood.

"I'll water it," I smiled, trying to shake off my moment of gloom. Tonight was not the night for it.

Anyway, I was glad I'd twisted his arm. The kids were ecstatic although I may have pushed the boat out a bit far with the preparations. Already there were presents under the tree and every now and again Jamie would re-examine the labels to see whose was the biggest. And Amber, poor little Amber, was just mesmerised by the whole experience. Her little arms reached up to the decorations and she had a strand of tinsel wound around her chubby little fist.

I gazed in happiness around the room and then felt Mark's arm around me.

"Thanks," he said.

"It's – it's fine," I stuttered, my face almost as red as the stockings.

"No, seriously, they're thrilled, and I'm not so sure I could have – well, you know, done this myself."

His arm was still around me and for a moment I leaned my head against his shoulder.

"They deserve it," I said quietly.

"Yes. It's just a pity you won't be –"

"Mark, don't." I moved away from his arm and went to start tidying up some of the empty boxes.

"Sorry, it's just – forget it."

"What's wrong, Daddy?" Jamie looked up.

"Absolutely nothing!" I interrupted gaily. "Now, who's for hot chocolate and marshmallows!"

"*Us!*" the two of them screeched in unison and Mark looked at me, relieved.

I smiled back at him, glad the tense moment had passed, and then without thinking went to the window again to peep through the curtains.

"Is his car still there?" he asked, smiling.

"I don't know what you mean." I blushed again.

"Don't think I haven't seen you peeping out those curtains all night."

I had to laugh. He was right. In between all our decorations chaos, I'd been stealing glances through the window at Dawn's house, to see if Graham had gone yet.

"Guilty as charged," I sighed, "but I'm just worried about her."

"Well, at least they're talking." Mark shrugged.

"Not sure if that is a good thing or a bad thing," I muttered.

"So you think she should kick him to touch?"

"Don't you? Thought you were all against that sort of thing."

"Well, I cannot understand how you'd have a nice girl like Dawn at home and still want to be playing away, but I can see how she can't just kick him out either. It's not that easy when there's kids involved." Mark gestured to a sleeping Daniel in the corner of the room. "Actually," he smiled, "if I remember correctly, you didn't find it that easy and there were no kids involved."

"That was different."

"Of course it was."

"It was, Mark! And I didn't just give in either, I'll have you know!"

"Of course you didn't!" He smirked again. "Anyhow,

let's change the subject. Did you think about the ball? I've asked Harry – he's said he'll go."

"Oh, yes. Okay. If Harry's going, I suppose I'll go."

"Oh, thanks a million!"

"Ha! Sorry, but you know what I mean. I'm not just going to go with a pile of boring old vets!"

"Boring old vets – Tara'll be delighted with that description. Anyhow, what about Dawn – did you ask her?"

"Not yet, but something tells me that'd be far too many happy couples in one room for poor Dawn right now."

"Well, happy couples and you and me." He smirked.

"And Tara."

"Oh yes, I forgot about Tara."

Like really.

"And don't forget Harry!" I added coyly in revenge.

"Oh yeah, how could I forget Harry?"

"Now, now – no nastiness – hang on – *shhh!*" I hissed, peeping yet again out the window. I grabbed his arm. "Look, the car is leaving. Way to go, Dawn! Not letting him stay the night!"

"Show me, move over!" He jostled me for position at the curtain.

"Hey! Aren't boring vets above peeking out behind curtains?" I teased him.

"It's the boring ones you'd want to watch," he whispered as we watched Graham's car slowly leave the estate.

By the time it had disappeared from view, I was hopping so excitedly from one foot to the other that Mark said, "Look, Holly, do you want to call up there?"

"What about the hot chocolate?" I almost didn't want to leave the Fielding Christmas extravaganza.

"I think I can manage."

"Well, I suppose I could bring Daniel home – do you mind? I won't be long!"

"Yes, it's okay. I'll put *our* children to bed then, will I?" Too late he realised what he said, and blushed. "By 'our' I mean the children of this house, obviously."

"Of course," I said solemnly, mimicking his usual response, "and if you do that little thing for me, I just might have a surprise for you tomorrow."

"What?"

"It's a surprise!" I teased. "Anyhow, it mightn't work out so I can't tell you now . . ."

"Right. Well, go on, but I'll be expecting an update when you get back. God be with the days when the whole housing estate could be murdering each other and I wouldn't know."

Within four minutes I was ringing Dawn's doorbell, a sleeping Daniel in his buggy beside me.

"Oh, Holly! That was quick. How did you know he was – oh, you were watching out the window! I should have known."

I studied her face carefully. She definitely looked better than she had that morning.

"So, what happened?" I asked, pushing past her with the buggy. "Should I put the kettle on?"

"Listen to you! You're getting more Irish every day."

"Dawn. I *am* Irish. Now get to the point. I'm assuming as he didn't stay that it didn't go too well?"

"Give me some credit. I was never letting him stay tonight. What do you take me for?" Dawn looked at me in horror as she put the tea bags in the pot. He's gone to his mother's. My idea."

"His mother's? Oh you cruel woman!"

"Well, I'm not having him dossing down in some hotel with God-knows-who while I figure out what to do next! Joan will be disgusted with him, so it won't do any harm to have her know exactly what's going on."

"Oh Dawn, you are a way tougher woman than I gave you credit for!"

"Holly, this is really, really serious. We might not ever recover from this. Do you know what? He blames my obsession with trying to get pregnant, says it was all I ever talked about, that I never spoke to him any more. You know, Holly, when we first met I was all about my career. I was even above him in the bank pecking-order. He probably thinks I've let myself go or whatever crappy phrase they use for the mothers of young children now. And yes, I could have gone back to work, put Daniel in a crèche but we agreed – *we* agreed that that wasn't what we were going to do. I thought he liked coming home to us, that he liked the fact that his dinner was made and that I wasn't arriving home, later than him, stressed to the nines with a cranky child. Clearly he changed his mind on all that – seems we're not enough at all."

"Oh." I didn't know what to say. It wasn't quite the standard my-wife-doesn't-understand-me line but not that original all the same. "What do you think? Could he have had a point? About the all-consuming motherhood bit, I mean?"

"Well, it was kind of all-consuming, but hardly a reason to go shagging somebody else. I mean, Daniel is his too – we didn't have him just for me! Look, Holly, I know I might come across as some kind of Stepford Wife and that the highlight of my day is serving dinner to my husband with a pretty bow in my hair, but I don't do things by halves. I gave up work to have Daniel and to look after him and the house, and that's what I do. When I worked, that was what mattered. No point in half-doing things."

I looked at the determined set of her jaw and suddenly felt a new kind of respect for Dawn, while also remembering guiltily how I'd mocked her housewife-iness when we'd first met. Turns out she was more of an achiever than me when all was said and done.

"So what are you going to do now?" I asked.

"I don't know. I really don't. I just wish it hadn't happened at all. To think that forty-eight hours ago I was planning another baby!"

With that she burst into tears and I dashed to hug her.

"Dawn, I'm so sorry, but it will be fine and I'm sure he feels just as rotten."

"I hope his mother kills him!" she managed between sobs.

"At least you haven't promised your boss you'd go to a ball with him on Friday night," I said in an attempt to distract her.

It worked.

"You what?" she cried. "Run that by me again!"

"Now calm down – it's some table Mark's boss is putting together and Harry is coming too. He actually suggested you come too, and maybe you should. It would be a distraction and might make that husband of yours a bit jealous!"

"Don't change the subject! I can't believe you're going to a ball with Mark Fielding and you're only telling me now!"

"Now hold on, the whole clinic is going, and I really think he only asked me and Harry to cheer me up."

I winced but it was too late.

"Cheer you up? About what?"

"Oh, you know," I tried frantically to think of something, "I hated seeing you so upset and I just got a bit weepy, I suppose."

"Ah Holly, you're such a sweetie." Dawn patted my arm. "But hang on! You cried, to *Mark*? And now you think he wants to cheer you up? Whatever happened to you two hating each other?"

"We never hated each other! Well, okay, we did, but we've called a truce now."

"Is that what they're calling it these days? And what does the dishy Oliver think about this ball?"

She had me there.

I hadn't told him and, to be honest, I wasn't planning to. He was to be away for most of the week so I wouldn't be seeing him until the following week, by which time he'd know about the promotions and we'd be finalising our plans.

"I haven't told him. There's no need – it's just a kind of Christmas party and he'd have no interest. I'm not even sure I do!"

"Well, what are you going to wear? Do you have anything suitable? Do you want to go shopping? I'll go with you. What are you going to do with your hair? Oh Holly, this is so exciting, are you excited? Why are you not excited?" Dawn, in typical Dawn fashion, was all ready to forget her own problems and instantly put my needs to the fore.

"I don't know what I'm wearing! I hadn't thought

about it. I suppose I'll have to get something as I've nothing with me. Do you really have any interest in going shopping with me?"

"Oh yes! Beats hanging around here, thinking about my marriage going down the tubes!"

"Oh, Dawn. It might not –"

"Stop!" Dawn held up her hand. "I literally can't think about it any more. Now let's make a plan for some serious dress-shopping. How about tomorrow? Do you want to go to town? Should we get the bus, the train – oh feck, what'll we do with the kids?"

"Hey, hey, slow down – we're not going shopping tomorrow – I've something else lined up for us. Now, tell me again – what bank did you work for?"

Chapter 47

"Explain to me again why exactly I'm sitting in a car with you, driving around in circles in the middle of nowhere?" Dawn could keep quiet no longer.

"Because you're my friend and you needed distracting. Anyway, your presence is vital to my plan."

"Aha! This famous plan again. When do I get to hear what exactly it involves?"

"Soon, Dawn, soon. I promise." I peered out the driver's window. "Now exactly what direction would you think that signpost is meant to be pointing?"

It was nine thirty in the morning and we were definitely lost. In typical Irish manner, the signposting was terrible and I really had no idea where we were. What was worse was that the two children strapped into their car seats in the back were starting to get restless. I looked at the hastily scrawled directions again. I knew that the address we were looking for was less than a mile from the town, so I turned the car and headed back towards Maynooth along a different country road.

And then, about two hundred yards down the road ahead, I spotted exactly what I was looking for.

Two large – like really large – gold eagles, spreading their huge wings atop two grandiose pillars.

"This is it!" I said excitedly as we drove towards them.

"How do you know? I can't read any name from here."

"Oh, trust me, I know."

We drove on until we reached the entrance and sure enough, there was a big brass plaque embedded into the wall with a name etched in large flowing letters: *Trafford Stud.*

Bingo!

The giant gates were closed, so I got out of the car and looked for the buzzer. Pressing it, I waited.

"Hello?" came a tinny female voice.

"Delivery." I was chancing my arm but to my delight the gates started to creak open.

"That was easy," I said to an open-mouthed Dawn as I hopped back into the car.

"Okay," Dawn could take the suspense no longer, "before we go any further I want to know exactly what's going on."

I quickly filled her in as we crunched along the gravel driveway. When we came to a fork I chose to keep right and we eventually pulled up to the front door of a huge ostentatious house.

I took a deep breath.

"Stay here pet, I'll be back in a minute."

"Good luck!" she hissed.

I walked up the three marble steps to the front door. I gingerly pressed the doorbell which was embedded in a giant brass gargoyle.

After a minute the door was opened by a small, squat blonde lady. She was heavily made up and dripping in expensive-looking jewellery.

"Yes?" she asked, in an attempt at a posh Dublin accent.

"I'm from Raven's Hill Veterinary. I'm here to collect a cheque," I said calmly.

"Is he expecting you?" She looked at me warily.

"Well, he's expecting *someone* . . ."

"Wait here," she said eventually, closing the door in my face.

I waited, and after a few minutes could hear a heavier footstep approach the door. Then it opened.

And there he was. All five foot two of him.

"Mr Baron," I said politely, "how lovely to meet you again."

"What the *fuck*?" he spluttered. "Dorry said you were from the fuckin' vets?"

"Oh, but I am. That's what I do now, Mr Baron. Debt collection."

"You fuckin' wha'?" His eyes narrowed into two tiny slits.

But this horrible little man didn't scare me. In fact, as I looked at him, I could feel a massive surge of anger and resentment rise within me.

It's all your fault, you despicable little shit!
Everything was fine until you had me fired.

Narrowing my own eyes, I took a step towards him.

"So if you could just give me that cheque, I'll be off."

"I'm giving you nothing," he spat. "I'll tell you what I told that prick Fielding – there's a recession and I've no fucking money to give him."

"Ah, but I think *we* both know that's not true, don't we, Mr Baron?"

"You just get back in your car, and fuck off to wherever you came from. I'll put a cheque in the post when I'm good and ready."

"I'd like it today please, Mr Baron."

"Well, you're not fucking getting it today!" he roared before slamming the door in my face.

I flinched at the force of the slammed door, but it was nothing worse than I'd expected.

"Time for plan B?" asked Dawn when I got back to the car.

"Yep," I answered resolutely, switching on the engine.

We drove back down the gravel drive.

"So how long would you think this will take?" asked Dawn.

"I really don't know." I was winging this bit. "But I suggest it's time we settle down and make ourselves comfortable."

Less than twenty minutes later we heard the first crunch of an approaching car on the gravel driveway.

"Here goes!" I took a deep breath.

I knew it was him as soon as I saw the flashy red sports car approach us.

And stop.

He had to stop because we were parked across the gateway, just under the two giant gold eagles.

The horn sounded straight away.

"Don't even look up," I hissed, head deep in my magazine.

"Oh Holly, I'm terrified."

"Shhh – he's coming!"

"Get the fuck out of my way!" Ger Baron roared as he approached our car.

I rolled my window down an inch.

"No," I answered politely. "We'll move when you give me what we came for."

He threw his head back with laughter, but it was laughter tinged with fury. "You'll be here for a while so."

"I think you'll find we're prepared for that, Mr Baron."

He looked into the car and I could see his eyes widen as he took in a sleeping Daniel, Amber happily watching Barney on a portable DVD player, and myself and Dawn with a pile of magazines, two flasks and a selection of bars of chocolate.

"We're *very* prepared. In fact, we're enjoying ourselves so much we really feel we could be here for the long haul. But as soon as we get that cheque, I suppose we'll have to be off." I smiled sweetly, before rolling my window back up and returning to my magazine.

Afraid to look up, I almost winced as I heard him roar outside the window.

"What if he breaks the window?" Dawn hissed again.

"He won't. I promise."

God, I *hoped* he wouldn't. To my relief, after a minute of ranting, he got back into his car and turned it in a hail of gravel.

We heaved a collective sigh of relief.

"What if he calls the police?" asked Dawn.

"Again, I don't think he will. But if he does, then we'll cross that bridge when we come to it. The bigger problem will be if we run out of Barney DVDs . . ." I gestured to Amber in the back seat and Dawn laughed.

"You said it!" she grinned.

An hour later we were still there. I was starting to wonder

what to do next when a big truck pulled off the main road and stopped when it saw we were blocking the way in.

A huge truck driver got out of the cab.

"What's going on?" he asked when I rolled down my window.

"I'm sorry – you'll have to come back. We can't move." I prayed he wasn't going to get angry.

"Ye whah?"

"We can't move."

"Are you broke down?"

I took a deep breath. "No. No, we're not broken down. And I'm really sorry, you obviously need to get in here, but, well, I'm not moving."

"Why not?"

"You'll have to ask Mr Baron that."

"Tell him!" hissed Dawn beside me.

"I can't," I hissed back. "That would be slander or something – we can't afford a lawsuit!"

The giant trucker scratched his head and then returned to his truck where I could see him take out his phone.

Within minutes there was a screech of tires and the little red car zoomed back into view.

"*Move that fucking car!*"

I could hear the angry words clearly through my closed window.

I rolled the window down an inch.

"You know what I need before I can do that, Mr Baron."

"I said move that car!"

"And I said no."

Eyeball to eyeball we glared at each other, each forgetting everyone else present. It was like the last six weeks had never happened.

"You were always a fucking bitch!" he spat.

"And you were always a lying, scheming excuse for a fraudster," I spat back.

"I'm going to fucking kill you."

I really hoped Amber was still immersed in her DVD. It was bad enough that Dawn was shaking like a leaf beside me.

"No, you're not, Mr Baron. You're going to get your chequebook and pay those two lovely men for the months of hard work they put into your horses." I looked at the fields beside the driveway. "I'm assuming the foals they saved are in those fields, foals you wouldn't have today if it wasn't for the Raven's Hill Veterinary team. For once, Mr Baron, do the decent thing."

"Bitch!" he said again.

"Prick!" I answered, matching his tone exactly.

And with that he returned to the car and, to my absolute relief and amazement, came back with a chequebook.

"You'll take half," he snapped.

"And have to come back and do this again next week? Tempting and all as that sounds, I think I'll pass thank you very much."

He glared at me again but the cheque he handed me was for the full amount.

"Now, get the fuck out of this man's way."

"Sorry, no can do yet."

"Why the fuck not?" he roared.

"Because this is a cheque, Mr Baron. Worth nothing until it's lodged."

With that I got out of the car and went around to the boot, and Dawn did the same. By now the trucker was looking at us in total amazement.

I opened the boot, thanking God that the car Mark had given me was an estate, and took out Emma's old bike.

"What the –"

Dawn took the cheque from me, fastened her jacket and hopped onto the bike.

"Won't be long!" she trilled as she cycled off. "I used to work in the Maynooth branch myself, so they'll be very nice and helpful to me!"

I turned to the truck driver.

"Look, I'm really sorry for the inconvenience but, please, let me make it up to you – have a cup of tea and a bun."

The truck driver looked at me open-mouthed and then burst out laughing.

"Do you know what, love, I will. I've never seen the like of this before. Sorry, mate," he turned to an apoplectic Ger Baron, "but these girls have made my day."

"Oh, shut the fuck up!" Ger Baron was now hopping up and down with rage. "I'll fucking stop that cheque, that's what I'll do!" he roared.

"No, you won't, Mr Baron," my voice was quiet and level, "or I'll be on to my friends in the Revenue and you'll rue the day you didn't give the measly fifteen grand to the vets."

All he could manage was another howl of "*Bitch!*" before he got into his car and drove back up the driveway.

I dreaded to think of poor Dorry up in the house and what she'd have to listen to for the rest of the day.

But more than that, I tingled with excitement when I thought of what Mark would say when he heard our story.

Chapter 48

I thought I'd burst with excitement when Mark came home that evening. However, I managed to wait until the children were in bed before I handed him the lodgement slip.

"What's this?" he asked.

"Read it."

"I am reading it, but what is it?"

"A lodgement slip. For fifteen thousand, eight hundred and ninety-nine euro."

"But it's lodged into the practice account!"

"It is."

He studied it again to see what he could be missing.

"Hang on – is this – no, it couldn't be . . ." He looked at me, frowning in total puzzlement.

"It is."

"But how?"

So I sat him down and told him the whole story, from start to finish.

"So you parked your car across his driveway until he gave you a cheque. And you brought a bike to cycle to the bank to lodge it."

"Yes, well, Dawn used to work in that branch, so she was able to pull a few strings."

He sat looking at the slip and for a second I thought he was annoyed.

Oh crap, I couldn't have messed up again, could I?

Then he stood up and came around the table to my chair.

"Stand up," he ordered.

Double crap.

I stood up.

With a whoop he wrapped both arms around me and spun me around the kitchen.

"Mark!" I squealed.

"You beauty!" he roared, still swinging me in a giant bear-like hug. "We have been trying to get that money for so long! You fucking absolute *beauty*!"

"Eh okay, you can put me down now." I was scarlet with embarrassment at his arms being around me once again, but not enough to actually force myself from his grip.

"Oh sorry!"

He released his hold and I slid to the ground.

But then, still whooping with excitement, he insisted on giving me whatever cash he had in his wallet – a surprisingly sizeable amount – as a bonus.

"Buy yourself something. Buy a dress, something pretty, something for you!" he said, for all the world babbling like an excited child.

And I took the cash. After all, I'd a funny feeling I was going to need it in Naas the next day . . .

Yes, I'd finally managed to persuade Dawn that my quest

for 'the dress' did not necessitate a trip to Dublin. Firstly, I was petrified I'd bump into someone I knew, and secondly I knew that, despite the brave face that Dawn was insisting on showing, she no more felt like a trip up to busy Grafton Street than I did. We also had the minor problem of having two children with us as really, with Dawn's current difficulties, getting them minded was a complication we could do without.

So Naas it was, although I predicted that I had not chosen the low-cost option. I knew from the Irish fashion magazines in Kutz n Kurls that there was one shop in particular – Mustique – that even Dublin ladies seemed to flock to, so this was to be our first port of call. Dawn was bemused at the fact that I was even considering a frock from Mustique as an option and I knew by her smirks that she was not buying my theory that it was only because I hadn't spent a penny on myself in so long.

However, to be fair, it turned out her tastes were as exclusive as mine and, despite all her teasing, she wasn't for letting me settle for a jumped-up bridesmaid's frock in some awful shade of peach or aqua either.

I longed to tell her about the Donna Karan navy silk gown still hanging in my wardrobe in Monica's Perry Street apartment, or the Herve Leger sequinned bandage dress that I'd also left behind, but I doubted she'd buy a nanny having such an extensive wardrobe of Saks Fifth Avenue purchases.

But it was nice that she shared my enthusiasm for finding the perfect dress, even if she didn't quite understand my desperation. I'm not really sure I understood it myself. It had a lot to do with the fact that for six weeks now I'd been seen in nothing except jeans and tracksuit tops and this was my chance to show everyone that I was capable of so much better. Even the night where I'd pushed the boat out and worn the Alexander McQueen dress I'd managed to get myself stranded and just ended up looking ridiculous. All I wanted was one night before I went where I got it right.

I tried to explain to Dawn how I felt.

"Ah yes, but to impress who?" teased Dawn again, as we pushed our two buggies through the hallowed double doors of Mustique.

But I didn't answer. I was too busy heaving a sigh of relief at finding the right shop. Even just seeing designers I recognised on the rails meant the magazines were obviously right – Mustique was the place to go.

"Have you *seen* the prices?" Dawn gasped in horror.

"Just don't look!" I hissed back at her as, head high, I approached the glamorous sales assistant, almost expecting a *Pretty Woman* moment of disparity. But to be fair, Lola, as she introduced herself, was to turn out to be very pleasant and helpful.

"A dress for a ball," she headed over to the rails, "and let me guess – you're probably an 8 to 10?"

I froze – suddenly rethinking my stance on this Lola girl. I might have put on some weight but not two dress sizes! Then just as I was about to voice my disgust I remembered she was referring to UK sizes – phew!

"Yes, that's right," I answered sheepishly.

"Any price bracket in mind?"

Dawn opened her mouth but I interjected with a firm "Price not a factor," before she could say anything.

What followed was a most enjoyable hour of sumptuous fabrics, jewelled hues and complete luxury. Even Amber was over-awed by all the different dresses and sat, remarkably well behaved, in her buggy for the entire process.

"Holly pwetty!" she even gurgled when I arrived out from behind the curtain in a pink frothy creation that I'd tried on to humour Dawn despite my protestations, but I had definite ideas of what I wanted and pink froth was not on the list. By now I'd tried on half a dozen frocks and while at least three would have been fine, I still hadn't felt that *wow* moment.

Chapter 49

"*Coo-eee, it's me!* Let me in, I want to see the end result!"

I smiled as I heard Dawn screech through the letterbox. She was definitely more excited than me about this night out.

Which was saying a lot, because I was pretty excited.

"Oh Holly," she gasped when I opened the door, "it's stunning! I mean, I know I loved it in the shop but I actually can't believe how good you look."

"Hey, easy now, do I look that bad normally?" I tried to pretend to be cross but I was delighted with her remarks.

When the helpful Lola had come across the shop floor with the forest-green David Meister dress, I knew instantly it was everything I was looking for. Cut on the bias from silk jersey, when I put it on it draped over one shoulder and scooped down very low on my back, skimming over my hips and flowing down to pool at my ankles. She had then brought out some gold sandals and a gold clutch bag and I instantly felt like a movie star.

"No, of course not, but you look so different – I mean – look at your hair!" Dawn gasped.

"Oh, yes, I've gone back to my roots." I turned to look in the hall mirror.

I was pretty pleased with my hair too. I'd finally had to make a decision about my precious highlights, and that morning, in Kutz and Kurlz, I'd kissed them goodbye and let Maisie take me back to my natural red colour. I'd then let her loose with a few hair clips and the result was a half-up, half-down tumble of curls over one shoulder. I had to hand it to her: it looked kind of alright.

And yes, there was no denying the fact that my mother might well have had a point – dark red hair suited me far better, making my brown eyes seem huge in my pale face.

In fact I was far paler all over on this night than I'd usually have been on such a night out. With my new hair colour, I didn't need the oceans of fake tan that I'd always have used before. Instead, I'd used just enough to take the blue hue from my arms and chest, the dark green dress suiting the alabaster, rather than tangerine, look.

"So, where's Mark?"

I turned back towards the mirror, in case Dawn saw me blush. It was crazy, but I couldn't wait for Mark to see me all dressed up. To be fair, he'd seen me at my worst enough times. But despite my panic to be ready before he arrived home, there was still no sign of him.

I rolled my eyes, "At work of course – he should be back shortly."

"Damn, I was hoping to catch sight of him in his tux."
You and me both.

"Any news about Graham?" I asked to distract from my second blush in as many minutes.

"Not really. Of course, he wants to come back. I've had his mother on the phone practically every day. I think she did everything short of sticking him on the Naughty Step when he told her what happened, but now of course she wants me to give him another shot."

"And will you?"

"Oh Holly, I don't know what to do. Of course I want to but what's to stop him from doing it again? I can't be with him twenty-four hours a day. I need more time. I need to know he's serious."

"Well, I think you're great – you've handled the whole thing far better than I ever could."

"I doubt that! You'd never let this happen to you, I know you wouldn't."

I hadn't the heart to disagree with her. After all, tonight was my night for forgetting every wrong thing I'd ever done, and having one night of fun.

The front door bell rang and, just as I stepped out into the hall, the phone rang also. Gesturing to Dawn to get the front door I ran for the phone.

"Holly, it's Mark."

"Mark! Why are you phoning? Please don't say . . ." My heart sank. I knew exactly what was coming next.

"Holly, I'm sorry, I really am, I might make it yet, but I'm still in Lady Smythe's. You go on without me. Is there any sign of Harry yet?"

"He's just arrived." I almost couldn't speak with disappointment.

"Well, Harry knows Fenton, so you'll be fine with him. If I can get there I will, I promise."

"Yeah, sure." I had my doubts.

I walked out to the hall where Harry was chatting to Dawn.

Harry let out a long wolf whistle when he saw me, then realised that there was something wrong.

"What is it?" he asked. "How can a girl that looks that good not be smiling!"

"He's not coming," I said, ridiculously feeling like I might cry.

"Typical," said Harry. "Not to worry, it just means we can have a bit of fun now!"

But for once, Harry's chatter didn't work. It had all been for nothing.

"Oh my God – you're really disappointed, aren't you?" Harry's eyes were wide with surprise.

I shrugged.

"Holly Green – snap out of it! We'll have much better fun without boring old Mark! Has Uncle Harry ever let you down yet?"

I smiled. He was right, it wasn't the end of the world, and in fact a night out with Harry couldn't be anything but a bit of fun. "You're right," I said, "and I have just the thing to kick-start the night."

I went to the fridge and took out a bottle of champagne. "Dawn, grab some glasses, and get one for yourself."

"Oh, I couldn't!"

"And why ever not? Daniel is with his daddy. Let's have a glass each and then you take the rest home with you."

"Daniel?" Harry asked.

"My son." Dawn blushed. "He's with his dad. We're – well – we're having some time apart."

"Oh, well, that definitely calls for some champagne!" Harry grinned.

"Harry!" I chided. "Dawn is far, far too young for you!"

"Ah yes, but she qualifies by not being available, which means her demands on me will be minimal – it's a kind of little-used sub-rule in my book."

I laughed again, looking sideways at Dawn to see how she was taking the teasing, but thankfully she was smiling. Good old Harry – a bit of male attention was exactly what she needed.

Before long, the bottle of champagne was gone and Dawn had dashed home to grab another.

"It's one we got for our last anniversary," she giggled. "I've had it in the fridge for ages waiting for an occasion."

"Well, I think this occasion is definitely as good as any," said Harry, with a hilarious air of solemnity.

Soon that bottle too was gone and it really was time we were on our way.

"Harry, we have to go!"

"There's plenty of time." Harry dismissed me with a wave of his hand.

"No, there isn't. Fenton is expecting us and Mark will go mad if he finds out we were late."

"He can hardly talk, he's not even going."

"It doesn't matter. Now, will you kindly walk Dawn down to her house, and I'll call a cab to get us to the hotel."

"Madam?" Harry proffered his crooked arm to Dawn who giggled in response.

"I can't walk down the estate on the arm of a man in a tux!" she squealed. "Bernadette Foley would have a coronary!"

"I will simply tell her that I am Mr Mark Fielding's new butler and that one of my duties is escorting drunken-abandoned-wives safely back to their marital home," said Harry.

In a chorus of giggles they wobbled their way from the house and I quickly rang a taxi.

Less than twenty minutes later we pulled up at the hotel.

"Wow!" I said as I spotted a crowd of ladies in beautiful dresses walk through the front door. "This is posher than I thought!"

"It's the Hunt Ball, my dear," said Harry, extending his arm to help me from the car. "It's like the Oscars, only far, far more competitive."

"But I've never hunted a day in my life! I shouldn't be here." I started to panic as I spotted several gentlemen in scarlet jackets, one even carrying what appeared to be a hunting horn in his hand.

"I believe bargain-hunting counts," Harry whispered in my ear and I laughed.

"I totally qualify so!"

My eyes widened as we entered the hotel, which had really pulled out all the stops in the preparation for the night. Huge Christmas trees were erected in the lobby, laden with heavy golden-and-scarlet bows. I resolved to tell Mark that we hadn't been the only ones with our tree up early.

We threaded our way through the crowds, acquiring two glasses of complimentary champagne from a waitress on the way, until eventually Harry spotted Fenton and Marian at the far side of the room.

"You must be Holly!" Fenton was a handsome older man with a huge smile. "We've heard so much about you – not least that you are the best debt collector this side of Sherwood Forest!"

"I think I was just lucky this week," I smiled. "But it's lovely to meet you too. Where's Tara?"

"She's with Mark, of course," said Marian, rolling her eyes. "The two of them stuck out in Lady Hannah's!"

"Typical!" Fenton boomed. "I don't know how many times I've warned him not to let her take advantage, but he won't listen."

"I think that's a severe case of pot and kettle, darling," his wife interrupted. "Holly dear, my name is Marian, and I know exactly how it feels to be stood up in the name of veterinary science."

I smiled. "Well, I've only been stood up by one of my dates," I said. "Harry has been doing a very good job of looking after me so far."

Just then a gong was sounded.

"Ah, we've to go to our seats! Good job, I'm starving!" bellowed Fenton.

"I might just powder my nose first – I'll follow you in," I said to Harry. "Make sure you keep me a seat!"

I fought my way against the crowd, heading for the ballroom and out to the ladies'. There really was a lot of style and I was glad I'd made such an effort.

Well done, Holly Green! I congratulated myself in the mirror. *Now get out there and enjoy yourself.*

When I returned to the corridor, it was empty save for one last tuxedoed man, striding away from me.

Oh my God, I would have recognised those shoulders anywhere.

"Mark?" I called.

He turned. My heart gave an inexplicable flip.

"You made it!"

Mark looked at me, still not saying anything, and then his mouth opened in shock.

"Holly? Is that you? Oh my God, you look amazing!"

"You don't look too bad yourself!" I smiled as I deliberately sashayed towards him, the champagne having well and truly kicked in by now.

"Seriously, you look absolutely stunning."

I blushed furiously underneath my make-up, but his reaction was exactly what I'd hoped for.

"Where's Tara?" I asked.

"Eh, well," he blushed, "I left her in Lady Hannah's actually – she's going to keep an eye on the mare while I'm here."

Good old Tara.

I looked up at him from under my heavily mascara'd eyelashes and offered him my arm.

"Shall we?"

Chapter 50

It was fast turning into the best night out I'd had in a long, long time. The ballroom, like the lobby, was dripping with luxurious decorations and every cream-covered chair had a huge scarlet-and-gold bow on the back. Giant candlesticks bedecked every table and the chandeliers that hung from the ceiling glittered like a million tiny stars. Fenton and Marian were delightful company and I'd the pleasure of sitting with Marian on my right during dinner. We'd shared a giggle about how utterly impossible vets were and she'd let me in on quite a few of Mark's secrets.

"Oh, he thinks he's all macho and hard," she winked at me, "but did he ever tell you about the time he fainted during a C-section?"

"Ah Marian, that's not fair!" Mark objected loudly.

"You fainted!" I said in disbelief. "I find that very hard to believe."

"Oh, he fainted alright," Marian rolled her eyes, "and broke two instrument trays on his way down."

"Tell her the full story!" Mark was mortified. "Tell her!"

"Oh yes," she rolled her eyes, "he claims he was under the weather that day, some kind of virus, but then he would, wouldn't he!"

I laughed again and turned back to my dessert. I shouldn't eat another bite – my dress was tight enough as it was.

"Are you glad you came?" Mark whispered as I put the last mouthful of chocolate éclair into my mouth.

I nodded. "Absolutely, it's just what the doctor ordered – they are such lovely people."

"Yes, if slightly economical with the truth." Mark was clearly still resentful about the fainting story.

"Oh, don't worry! I'm sure it happens to loads of vets!" Before I realised what I was doing, I'd patted his knee to comfort him.

Our eyes met and it was as if the air suddenly became charged with electricity. I pulled my hand back quickly but our eyes never wavered.

With a boom, a loud-voiced man with a microphone shattered the moment.

"Ah! It's the auction!" shouted Fenton.

"Now, Fenton, you are to keep your hands to yourself!" warned Marian.

I blushed, thinking I could have done with the same advice only seconds before.

Mark smiled as if reading my mind, and I smiled back before excusing myself from the table.

I paced the ladies' in an attempt to pull myself together.
Holly Green, you behave!

After all, I was here to put all my muddles behind me, not to acquire some more. But whether it was excitement or the fact that my dress was crushing my ribcage, my heart was still hammering in my chest and I didn't trust myself to return yet to the table.

"Holly? Whatever are you doing here?"

I froze, hoping I hadn't been admonishing myself out loud. Turning, I saw Maureen Costello exit one of the cubicles.

"Oh, Maureen, hi, don't you look wonderful!" I said, lamely trying to change the subject.

"Who are you here with?" She wasn't for changing any subject.

"Mark's boss put together a table, so he asked me to come."

"Oh right. Gosh, they must have been stuck for numbers if he had to bring his baby-sitter!" she trilled.

I literally wanted to thump her.

"And what about your boyfriend, is he here too?"

Damn her, how did she know about Oliver? Then I remembered that morning at the Mother and Toddler Group.

"No," I said, suddenly feeling all my earlier excitement start to drain away. "He's away on business."

"Oh, well, have a good evening. I have to say, you do scrub up rather well, though I am surprised at Mark, what with Emma not really being gone all that long."

She left before I had a chance to answer her.

With a slightly subdued step I returned to the table.

"Hey, what's up?" Mark looked at me, concern in his eyes.

"Oh nothing, I just met Maureen Costello in the toilet."

"Oh dear, what did she say to you?"

"She said you must have been desperate to make up a

table if you had to resort to bringing your baby-sitter to a ball," I said dolefully, deciding to omit her last barbed comment.

Mark threw back his head in laughter. "Oh, Maureen never fails to disappoint!" He looked at me. "You're not seriously letting that comment get to you, are you? You should have told her the truth, that you're actually my live-in accountant!"

I smiled. "Oh, she's probably a self-trained accountant with a PhD in vets' finances."

"Well, anyway, I was wondering if my baby-sitter would care to dance?"

I looked at him, for a second not knowing what to answer. I mean, it was a perfectly reasonable request. We were at a ball after all. But why then did I really feel I should say no?

He stood up and held out his hand.

"Please?"

I was definitely over-thinking this. I held up my hand and answered, "Yes, I'd be delighted."

The minute I stood up, I knew all eyes were on us. I supposed that I shouldn't care – after all, in a week I'd be gone from this tiny village and no one here would ever see me again. But I could feel the eyes of the entire table bore into my back as Mark led me onto the dance floor.

"Have I mortified you?" he asked as I made him take me almost to the far side of the room before I'd start dancing.

"A bit," I smiled, "but I'm sure I'll get over it."

"Good," he said, placing one hand on my bare back, making me shiver involuntarily. "You look amazing tonight, you know."

"Thanks," I said, suddenly unable to look at him.

"Don't tell me you've gone all shy on me?"

I didn't answer.

Mark put one finger under my chin and tilted my face upwards.

"Please don't be," he said. "I only enticed you out here because I really want to take this chance to thank you."

"To thank me?"

"Yes, for everything you've done for me and my family."

"Oh Mark, please, there is no way you should be thanking me. After all the lies and –"

He put his finger gently on my lips.

"Shhh, we're not going to mention any of that tonight. All I want to say is that, thanks to you, my home is somewhere I don't mind coming back to any more. And I doubt you'll ever know how much that means to me."

"Oh Mark!" I looked up at the sincerity in his eyes, not really knowing what else to say.

"And just one last thing . . . about that boyfriend of yours . . ."

Now it was my turn to reach up and put a finger on his lips.

"Not tonight," I said softly.

He nodded his agreement and I placed my head on his chest and we danced as if there was no one else in the room.

There was no escaping the fact that the mood between us had changed and I'm not sure which of us moved first but only seconds had passed before we were staring into each other's eyes again.

Every fibre in my being was telling me to walk away,

but I was frozen to the spot. As he reached down, I knew exactly what he was about to do, and I closed my eyes, waiting for his lips to reach mine.

Instead, they brushed my neck and he whispered in my ear, "Jesus Christ, Holly, I can't do this here."

I smiled and, taking him by the hand, led him from the dance floor, my legs shaking and my heart thumping in my chest. Within seconds we were in a secluded corridor in a passage that led off the ballroom and he had me in his arms.

"Mark, are you sure?" I managed, my breath coming in short gasps.

"Yes," he said quietly, "I've been sure for weeks."

And then Mark Fielding kissed me. And it was the most powerful kiss I'd ever experienced. The world seemed to spin around my head, and I forgot who I was, where I was, I forgot everything that didn't matter.

All that mattered, at that exact moment, was how utterly right that kiss felt.

I reached up to hold his face, his strong jaw peppered with stubble. And we kissed for what seemed like forever.

And when we stopped, he engulfed me in an embrace that threatened to take away whatever breath I had left in my body.

"Oh Holly," he whispered, "I'm sorry, but there was no way I couldn't do that."

"Well," I smiled, "at least I can blame the champagne in the morning, but I really don't know what your excuse is going to be."

And with that he took a step back from me, his face white.

"So that's what this is to you, is it? A drunken mistake?"

"Mark! That's not what I said – that's not what I meant!"

"Forget it," he snapped and before I could say anything else he had turned and was striding away from me.

Chapter 51

I stood there for a minute, in total shock.

Still reeling from the effect of his kiss, I couldn't believe that the spot where he'd been standing, only seconds ago, was empty.

What had I said that was so wrong? Surely he'd known I was joking? Could he really be that sensitive?

I started to make my way back to the table, dreading seeing him again. Would everyone know what had happened? I took a detour to the ladies', swearing that if I happened to meet Maureen Costello again, I was going to sock her one before she got to open her mouth.

In the ladies, I tried to formulate what I was going to say to Mark back at the table. Would I even get a chance to talk to him with everyone around? Surely he had to let me explain.

Did I want to explain?

What was I doing running around after someone that bloody moody?

You have a boyfriend! I screeched to myself, but for

some reason, the fact that Oliver existed somewhere in a parallel universe didn't seem important. All I could remember was Mark's kiss, and how utterly right it had felt. Even thinking about it now, despite its abrupt ending, still sent shockwaves through my body.

He had to let me explain.

I finally mustered up the courage to return to the table, but there was no sign of Mark.

"That bloody Lady Hannah!" Marian shook her head when she saw me. "Can you believe he had to go back?"

I looked from her to Harry. "He's gone?"

Harry nodded. "You didn't know?"

I shook my head. "No, I was in the ladies'."

"Apparently Tara rang him when he was away from the table."

Fucking Tara.

I sank down into my chair in despair.

Harry leaned close and whispered, "Okay, tell Uncle Harry what's wrong."

I shook my head again, looking at Marian and Fenton who were well within earshot.

"Okay, well, then, come and dance with me."

"No, Harry, honestly, I'm not in the mood."

"Then get that down you," he plonked a glass of champagne in front of me, "and get in the mood, because we are going to dance all night long!"

And we did. To be fair to Harry, he could be pretty persuasive, and it helped that he knew Mark so well. He bellowed with laughter when I told him what happened in the corridor.

"I cannot believe you kissed my brother," he howled, practically holding his sides with merriment. "I mean, I can believe he kissed you alright, but what were *you* thinking! He's a psychopath!"

"I know that now," I admitted glumly, "but it seemed like a good idea at the time."

He laughed again. "What I wouldn't give to be at your breakfast table in the morning."

"Oh Harry, that's a great idea, please stay! I'm not going to be able to face him on my own."

"Not a chance, my dear. Anyhow, he won't show up – he's probably going to have his head up a horse's arse for months now, just so that he doesn't have to face you!"

"Feel free to suggest that idea to him," I muttered.

"Right, that's it, too much chatting and not half enough drinking or dancing. I'm off to the bar – more champagne?"

I shook my head, I'd really had enough, but he vanished anyway. All I actually wanted to do was go home but there was no way I could leave yet.

Marian sat down beside me.

"Are you having a good night?" she asked.

I nodded. What else could I do?

"You're disappointed he's gone, aren't you?" she said softly.

I stiffened but said nothing.

"Oh Holly, that's only natural. You two seem to have become quite close."

"No, honestly, I'm fine. We're – we're not that close really." The memory of his kiss followed swiftly by that of his wrath came flooding back and for one awful moment I thought I might cry.

"Don't think too badly of him, Holly. He works very hard. Too hard, Fenton says, but we're terribly, terribly fond of him."

I sat looking down, not really knowing what to say.

"I've embarrassed you now." She patted my arm. "I'm not trying to interfere, my dear, but go easy on him. He has been through some terrible times."

Thankfully at that moment Harry returned with another bottle of champagne.

Gratefully, I held out my glass.

We made a very wobbly pair when we arrived back at Meadowlands sometime after three in the morning. I'd eventually persuaded Harry to stay the night – in any case he was in no condition to even think about heading anywhere further afield.

Now that we were back at the house, the enormity of what had happened suddenly seemed very huge indeed. I sank down on the couch beside Harry.

"Oh cheer up!" he said, putting his arm around me. "It'll all be fine, wait and see."

"No, it won't, Harry." I shook my head. "Things will never be alright again. You don't understand."

"Oh, what's there to understand? You were drunk, you kissed your boss. These things happen."

"But why do they happen so often to *me*!" I wailed before bursting into tears.

He started to laugh. "It's not your fault you've an addiction to men in authority!"

"But I think I really like him!" I said, covering my face with my hands. "I've tried to pretend I don't, I've tried to ignore everything I feel about him and then, tonight, I actually thought he might feel the same. But it's all gone wrong and I don't even know what I did!"

"You didn't do anything. That's Mark for you. Poor Emma was worn out trying to keep him happy."

"Poor Emma obviously never did put a foot wrong in her life!" I moaned. "She definitely didn't have the self-destruct button that I can't seem to get my finger off."

"Oh come here!" Harry pulled me in for a hug. "I'm just very proud that you can pronounce 'self-destruct' after the amount of drink we've just put away!"

I started to laugh, about to tell him that it had in fact been him that had drunk most of the champagne at the table, but then a voice behind us made me jump.

"So this is how it is now, is it?"

I swung around and looked over the back of the couch. It was Mark, still in his dinner shirt and suit trousers, looking like a madman.

"No!" I cried, struggling to get out from under Harry's heavy, and almost lifeless, arm, "Harry was just –"

"I could see exactly what Harry was *just* doing," he snarled, "and I don't know why I'm surprised at either of you."

"Oh Mark, put a sock in it," Harry sighed without even turning around. "You had your chance and you blew it. Get over it."

With a roar, Mark strode around the couch and I screamed.

"No! Mark, for God's sake, he's pulling your leg!" I sprang to my feet.

But Harry just slouched there, laughing. "Go on, big brother, you've been waiting to hit me all your life! Well, here's your chance to get it out of your system. You'll be hitting me for no reason, but sure that wouldn't matter to you. You've been flying off the handle for no reason for years now."

Mark's face was white with fury. "I want you out of my house," he said. "Now!"

411

"No problem, bro." Harry stood up, "I was just seeing your nanny home safely, seeing as you abandoned her. I'm not sure why you even bothered coming out tonight – all those people, drinking, having fun – it must have nearly killed you."

"Out. Now, Harry." Mark was barely able to speak. Then he turned to me. "And, as for you, I think a good night's sleep might be in order for you too."

"Oh, leave her alone for God's sake! What's she done only have a bit of fun? Oh I forgot, fun is a crime in this house, isn't it?"

"Oh stop! Both of you, please stop!" I was crying now, horrified at the scene in front of me. "Harry, just go! I'm sorry for making you come back."

"No." Harry was suddenly looking very, very sober. "You know what, Holly, I think I'd like to have a chat with my brother – so if you wouldn't mind leaving us alone?"

There was nothing I could do but leave them to it. Reluctant to go up to my room in case things got physical, I went across the hall into the playroom and lay down on the couch.

Even from there I could hear them shouting at each other, at first loudly and then more intermittently. I lay on the couch sobbing, until, despite my best intentions, I drifted off to sleep.

I'm not sure what it was that woke me some time later. For a moment, I had no idea where I was. The room was dark and someone had covered me with a blanket. I raised my head from its uncomfortable position on the arm of the sofa. I could barely make out the silhouette of a tuxedoed man on the armchair opposite me. Harry had obviously stayed. I wondered how it had ended between himself and Mark. For a moment, though, their argument was the least of my problems as suddenly the room started to spin around my head.

Oh crap, I was going to get sick.

With a groan, I threw back the blanket and ran for the downstairs bathroom, only just making it in time. Wave after wave of sickness swept over me as I clutched the toilet bowl. Then I felt someone scoop my hair back from my face and pat my icy-cold bare back in soothing circles.

"Oh Harry, this has to be the worst night of my life," I groaned as eventually the sickness stopped.

"I'm sorry to hear that."

Christ!

It wasn't Harry, it was Mark.

Oh bloody brilliant.

I flinched in horror at the recollection of what he'd just witnessed.

"Oh Mark, please go away – just leave me alone," I whispered, staying crouched against the toilet. There was no way I was turning to face him, looking the way I did.

"Stop being silly. Here." He handed me a warm, wet flannel and when I still wouldn't look at him he tilted my face up and wiped it softly. I could feel the hairs rise on the back of my neck at his touch, but I had no choice now but to look at him. And what I saw frightened me. His face was deathly white and drawn. In fact, he looked just as bad as I felt.

Which, funnily enough, made me feel even worse.

"Now, come on, you're freezing. You need to get out of that dress and into bed," he said, putting down the cloth.

I shook my head, afraid to leave the vicinity of the

toilet. The last thing I wanted to do was vomit all over his feet in the hall.

He went out and brought one of his T-shirts and a giant tracksuit bottoms back in to me.

"Put these on. I'll make you a cup of tea to take upstairs with you."

"I don't want tea."

"Well, you'll thank me in the morning, trust me." He left the clothes with me and went into the kitchen.

Slowly I climbed out of my beautiful dress, rinsed my mouth and, squirting some toothpaste on my finger, dragged it over my teeth. Then, when I was dressed in his over-sized clothes I decided that I just didn't have the energy to climb all those stairs so I padded back to the couch in the playroom and sat on it, the blanket now around my shoulders. He brought in two cups of hot tea and some toast, and sat down beside me.

"Thanks," I muttered.

"Holly, I am so sorry."

I cringed. "Oh Mark, don't. I don't want to talk about it."

"Well, I do. That brother of mine gave me some talking to when you left, and I'm not saying he was right on everything, but he was definitely right about one thing. You didn't deserve the way I treated you tonight. I completely overreacted."

I could feel the heat rise in my cheeks as the memories of the night flooded back, but I had to clarify one thing.

"I know my case is severely weakened by the fact that I just threw up all over the place but, Mark, I wasn't drunk when, you know, when you and I . . ." I stopped. It was all just too embarrassing.

"I know. It was unforgiveable of me, and I'm sorry."

He put an arm around me and I hesitated for only a second before curling into him, once again breathing in his unmistakeable smell. As he hugged me my heart started to thump in my chest again, but this time my dizziness was as much to do with confusion as passion.

"Have some toast," he said, giving my shoulder a quick squeeze, "and when you wake up in the morning, you'll feel a lot better."

He went to get up but I stopped him, saying, "Don't go yet."

"Holly –"

"Please."

So he didn't. And we sat there, me nibbling on toast, him stroking my hair.

"You should probably take all those clips out," he said softly.

I nodded, my eyes closing as he gently started to remove Maisie's hair-grips, one by one, stroking my hair softly as he did so. At the sensation of his fingers in my hair, my heart started to race. On and on he went, even when the last of the clips had fallen to the floor and there was no reason to continue stroking.

I turned my head slowly to look at him. His hand slid slowly round to cup my cheek and I closed my eyes, turning slightly to bury my lips in his hand. My heart was thumping in my chest and then, taking a deep breath, I turned to face him. There were no words spoken as we sat drinking in each other's faces. I raised my hand to his cheek and traced his cheekbone with my finger and then he turned and brushed his lips across my hand.

And then we both leaned in to kiss. At first softly, tenderly, our hands cupping each other's faces, then with more urgency. His hands moved to the back of my head, burrowing deep into my hair, but still mine stayed tracing his strong jaw, holding his beautiful face close to mine.

Again I was struck with how right kissing this man felt. Everything that had ever gone before now floated somewhere out of grasp of my memory.

My hands moved from his jaw down to trace his broad shoulders and huge expanse of chest. Through his dinner shirt I could feel every muscle and sinew of his strong body, as it strained against mine. And still we kissed, he with one hand still tangled in my hair, the other splayed across my shoulders. I flushed as his hand moved down my back, under the giant T-shirt and onto my naked waist. Subconsciously my fingers moved to the buttons on his shirt.

With every touch of his fingers on my body I arched closer to him. Our kisses became more urgent, and I knew that he wanted me as much as I wanted him. I had never felt such unbridled desire for someone. Not for Cain, and not for Oliver.

Oliver.

And then, with a sinking heart, I knew this could go no further. Before I could formulate another thought I noticed that Mark's lips had also ceased moving on mine and that his hand was now motionless on the small of my back. We both spoke at the exact same time.

"Mark – I can't –"

"Holly – I can't do this –"

I'd continued before I realised what he'd said. "I have a boyfriend – I just can't – wait – what did you say?"

"It's fine, Holly," he pulled me close, squeezing me tightly in his arms as he spoke, "I can't either. It's – I just can't – after Emma – it's, oh fuck it, I can't even explain –"

I sighed, holding him closely. "Oh Mark, I know. I understand."

"You don't, but it doesn't matter. You're right. It's not right what we're doing, it makes us as bad as –" He stopped, as if he couldn't say the words.

By now we were lying in each other's arms, my head on his chest, his arms wrapped around me.

"I should go," he sighed.

"Yes," I nodded.

But neither of us moved, and before long I had slipped into a deep sleep.

Chapter 52

When I woke again it was morning and Mark was gone. While I wasn't surprised, I definitely couldn't help but feel disappointed.

I sat upright on the couch, wincing as the memories of the night before came flooding back. The skin on my back burned at the memory of his touch and my cheeks flared at the thought of what had almost happened. Gingerly I stood up. To be fair to Mark, the middle-of-the-night tea and toast had worked wonders and I didn't feel half as sick as I thought I would.

I tiptoed to the window and looked out. The jeep was gone.

I folded up the blanket and went out into the hall, picking up my poor ball dress from outside the toilet door. I walked slowly, taking care not to trip over the ends of his giant tracksuit bottoms.

The house was shockingly quiet. I took a quick look into the sitting room but there was no sign of Harry and the blankets I'd given him the night before were still folded neatly where I'd left them. I wondered what exactly had happened between them when I'd left the room, but I was too embarrassed by the whole mess to pick up the phone and ring Harry to find out.

In any case, it was far too early to ring him, because he had to have been feeling a lot worse than me.

Taking another quick peek into the kitchen I noticed that the empty champagne bottles from the night before were gone and there was no sign of the glasses either. Mark must have tidied them away. I blushed at how he'd feel about us drinking so much before we'd even left the house. He probably didn't even know that Dawn had been there too.

Lucky Dawn! I envied her that her night's enjoyment had finished as early as it had. Just as I wondered what on earth I was going to tell her about the evening's drama, the front-door bell chimed.

With a groan I remembered that I'd promised her we would get a head-start on some Christmas shopping. It wasn't often we both had a day off without children. There was nothing for it but to open the door.

"Oh my God! What happened to you?" she shrieked.

"Do I look that bad?"

"Well, never mind how you look – I'm more interested in the fact that you're wearing Mark's clothes!"

Christ! The bloody clothes. I'd forgotten. My cheeks flared red.

"Oh – my – God. Tell me you did *not* sleep with Mark Fielding!"

"I –" I didn't know what to say. There was nothing for it but the truth. "Well, I did actually, but not the way you mean."

"Oh – my – *God*."

"Dawn! Stop saying 'Oh my God'!"

"Well, what do you want me to say?"

"Stop saying anything! Oh Christ, I need a shower and I need tea."

"You run and have your shower, and I'll put on the kettle." She shoved me towards the stairs, and then she stopped. "Oh my God, wait – is he, like, *here*?"

"Who?"

"Mark! Who do you think I mean? Oh God, it *was* Mark, wasn't it? Tell me it wasn't Harry?"

"No, it wasn't Harry, relax, he's still available. Actually, what am I talking about, they're both still available."

"Stop!" She put her hands over her ears. "I don't want any half-stories. Shower first, and then spill."

I plodded my way up the stairs and into my room. Sitting on the bed I slipped off the tracksuit bottoms and then pulled the T-shirt up over my head. I folded up the T-shirt and put it beside my pillow, for some unexplainable reason unable to let it go just yet.

You are a fool, Holly Green! I told myself sharply as I stepped under the shower.

Nothing but a bloody fool.

"Oh – my – God!" said Dawn predictably when I finished my story.

I'd left out bits, of course, like how his kiss had made me feel, how close we'd come to doing something we both would have regretted and especially the bit about how, no matter how hard I tried, I now couldn't get him out of my head. And about how, despite all the mess of the night, how right it had felt.

"So what about Oliver? Is he out of the picture now?"

Damn you, Dawn, I knew you'd ask that.

"Of course not," I snapped. "He's the reason that nothing happened. Well, he was my reason. Mark, on the other hand, is understandably still in love with his dead wife."

"Will you tell him?"

Will I tell him? Good question. No. I won't be telling him.

"I don't know, Dawn, probably not, it's complicated."

Like really complicated, like in an I'm-not-Oliver's-only-girlfriend kind of complicated.

"How long have you liked Mark? I mean, have you fancied him all along?"

"No! I mean, don't be ridiculous – I have a boyfriend, you know."

Who, to be fair, hasn't taken up too much of your thoughts in the last forty-eight hours . . .

"You would make a great couple, you know," Dawn said, her tone suddenly serious and quiet.

"No, we wouldn't! We'd kill each other. Anyway, even if Oliver didn't exist, there's no way he's over Emma – that's painfully clear. And I simply couldn't handle that hanging over me. I've lived in the shadow of my sister for years – there is absolutely no way I need another Marsha in my life, let alone a dead one."

"Oh, Holly."

"No, Dawn. It's fine. This is a ridiculous conversation. I have Oliver. I love Oliver for God's sake. Maybe Mark's first instinct was right, and it was all just a drunken mistake. Anyhow, I'm going to forget it. It was a glitch and God knows I'm well used to them."

"Well, how does Mark feel about it all?"

"Well, to be fair he made his feelings perfectly clear last night and he was gone this morning when I woke up." I smiled ruefully. "So I suppose that's an answer in itself."

"Would you not talk to him about it? It would clear the air at least. I mean it's going to be awkward – you live together for God's sake."

"Yeah, well, that's a whole other issue," I sighed. "I may as well tell you, Dawn – I'm going to have to leave here."

It was the truth – there was no way I could stay here now.

"Oh come on, it was just a kiss, don't be silly!" Dawn looked horrified at my suggestion.

Oh Dawn, it was so much more than a kiss . . .

"Dawn, I can't stay now. I just can't."

"You could if things worked out between you two."

"Dawn, there is no 'us two'. It's just never going to happen."

"Well, don't do anything hasty. Have a think about it and maybe talk to Mark tonight."

"There's nothing to talk about. Nothing."

"Well, I guess shopping it is so," said Dawn brightly, obviously seeing that a change of subject was needed. "So where's your list? And don't lie, I know you have one."

She was right, I did have one. I was so conscious that this was the children's first Christmas without their mother and I really wanted to help get them through it. I'd made so many plans that I was starting to feel sorry myself that I wouldn't be at Meadowlands to share the day with them.

Instead, all I could do was leave Mark with everything he'd need. I'd written down everything they'd mentioned

422

on their Santa letters and a lot more besides, and that was what I'd planned to get today and leave hidden in the loft.

The town was packed, predictably enough for two weeks before Christmas. I did my best to muster up some Christmas cheer but, what with the hangover and the remainder of the night's complications, it was very difficult.

I just couldn't get Mark Fielding out of my head. And I hated myself for it. For the indecision, the complication, the downright messiness of the whole situation.

Usually you crave this kind of excitement – what is wrong with you?

I had no idea.

For once even Dawn wasn't much help. She too was a bit morose as it started to dawn on her that their first Christmas with Daniel was not going to be everything she'd planned.

"What are we like?" she finally sighed as we fought our way through the crowds, raucous clanging festive music ringing in our ears.

"I know, I'm so sorry."

"I'm sorry too . . ."

A fat tear slipped down her cheek and I pulled her in for a hug.

"Holly Green – are you *laughing*?" she mumbled into my shoulder.

"Kind of," I admitted. Because it was true, I was laughing. I couldn't help it. A couple with less Christmas spirit you couldn't have found.

She started to laugh too. "This is crap. Let's just go home!"

"Okay," I nodded and we linked arms and headed back to the car.

When we reached the village, a mad idea entered my head. I got Dawn to stop the car at Brophy's butcher's.

"I just want to get some sausages for the kids."

I was lying. I'd had a crazy notion on the way home that it might be nice to cook dinner for myself and Mark – after all, the children weren't coming back until the next morning, and it would give us a chance to talk. Dawn was right, I couldn't leave things the way they were, and maybe a civilised meal would clarify everything, at the very least in my own head.

I had nothing to lose. Oliver had rung twice today but I'd ignored the first call and pretended I'd bad reception for the second.

I couldn't talk to him at the moment. I felt guilty, selfish, but most of all, very, very confused.

As we drove into Meadowlands, my nerves started to jangle at the thought of seeing Mark again but then ironically changed to disappointment when there was no sign of his jeep outside.

"You going to be okay?" Dawn asked.

"Yep." I nodded. "You?"

"I guess so." She gave a rueful smile. "What kind of a pair are we? Do you want to call over later?"

"Maybe not tonight, Dawn – I think I'm going to get something to eat and go to bed. I didn't get much sleep last night, as you know."

"Sure. Well, give me a shout in the morning. Graham is dropping Daniel back at lunchtime so I might need an injection of moral support."

I nodded as we went our separate ways. The house was cold and very, very quiet. There was no sign that Mark had returned at all during the day. Sighing, I headed to the tiny attic space beside my room with the bags of presents.

"There must be a light here somewhere," I muttered, fumbling about in the darkness with my hand. Ha! I found the switch and flicked it on.

Looking around I recognised all the boxes that Harry had carried up for me the morning we'd cleaned out Emma's study. Then I spotted the last, smaller box and remembered that it contained all the photographs. Out of pure curiosity I dragged it over and opened it.

I don't know what I was looking for really. I suppose I just wanted to torment myself with another peek at how Mark's life had been before the tragedy of his wife's death had turned him into such a cold, tortured soul.

The albums seemed to be in date order, and I picked one of the earlier ones first. In each shot Emma was the epitome of life, radiant and glowing and laughing. But in every one of those pictures, my eyes were drawn to Mark and the look of utter pride on his face. My heart twisting slightly with jealousy, I opened the next album. These seemed more recent; some of them included shots of the children. Again in every shot Emma had her head flung back, but in these Mark seemed tired, strained – obviously at this stage he was working every hour God sent him. In one particular shot, it looked like Amber's christening, his face was visibly thunderous next to Emma's animated laughter and I wondered what client he was worrying about.

Comforted by the fact that he looked grumpy even then, and slightly puzzled that in every shot Emma looked the picture of health, I closed the album, packed it back into its box, and made my way down the ladder to fetch the last of the presents.

Afterwards I wandered aimlessly around the empty house, picking up stray toys and straightening cushions. It was almost seven o'clock – surely he'd be back soon? I started to get dinner ready. I'd bought two nice steaks and had just about enough energy to peel potatoes for homemade chips. I'd have opened a bottle of wine but for the fiasco the night before.

Anyhow, I wasn't sure my stomach could take it.

At eight o'clock I could wait no longer. I started to cook, hoping that at any minute he'd come through the door to the smell of steak and onions wafting through the house.

You sad bitch.

By eight thirty, there was nothing for it but to cover his meal and sit at the prettily laid table, alone, and start to eat.

Bet you feel silly now.

At nine, I could keep my eyes open no longer. I got up from the table and started to scrape my dish into the bin. I heard the sound of the front door open and someone tiptoe down the hall towards the kitchen.

"Oh! I thought you'd be in bed," Mark said when he saw me.

"Sorry to disappoint you – don't worry, I'm going now," I said, putting my dish in the dishwasher.

I hadn't meant to sound so cross, but I couldn't help it.

"I wasn't trying to avoid you," he said. Then he spotted the place laid for him at the table and he winced. "Oh shit, I'm sorry, I didn't know –"

"Of course you didn't. Don't mind me, I'm just tired."

"Well, I'm still sorry – I ate at Fenton's, we had some stuff to discuss and, well, time got away from me."

"Mark, it's okay." I couldn't even look at him. It was so obvious that he'd stayed out for as long as he could in

426

the hope that I'd be in bed when he got home. Well, he could have what he wanted, I was going to bed. "You don't have to explain. I understand."

"What are you talking about?" He stepped in my way as I tried to leave the kitchen.

"You know what I'm talking about." I stood there, barely inches away from him and looked him straight in the eye.

"Oh."

"Look, it's fine, forget it."

He leaned back against the door frame and now it was his turn to avoid eye contact.

"Okay," he said. "You're right. I've been meaning to talk to you, and I suppose I was putting it off. I'm sorry, Holly, but –"

"It's okay," I interrupted quickly, "You're absolutely right. It should never have happened."

"It's not that –"

But I'd heard enough, I ducked under his arm and ran from the room.

Chapter 53

Rrrrrrrrrrriiinnnng
Rrrrrrrrrrriiiiiiinnng

I leapt at the sound of my phone penetrating the night. I pulled it quickly out from under my pillow to see Oliver's name flashing on the screen. Everything came flooding back to me and with a sinking heart I remembered that I hadn't returned his call the night before. Now he was going to be annoyed with me too.

"Oliver?"

"Hi."

"Look, I'm sorry I didn't call back, the phone was flat and I fell asleep and –"

"I have some news."

I shot up in the bed. "News? What news?" All the time my head trying to figure out what news he could possibly have at seven thirty on a Sunday morning.

"I'm on my way. We're going to New York, baby!"

"We're what? When?"

"Today?"

"What? Today? Wait – you got the promotion? But it's Sunday? You got promoted on a Sunday?"

"Hardly."

"Well then, what? Oh! You broke up with Catherine? Is that it?"

"Look, it's a really long story. I'll tell you all about it on the plane. How soon can you be packed? If we don't make today's flight we can stay somewhere in town tonight. The dream starts here, baby!"

"Whoa – what's a long story? That's it, isn't it? You've broken up with her, haven't you?"

"Jesus Christ, Holly, yes, I have." He paused. "Kind of. She broke up with me actually. Can you believe it, it's quite funny really."

I started to get a really strange feeling in my stomach.

"Oliver, I'm not finding it that funny to be honest. I need to know what happened. Now."

"Oh for God's sake, Holly, what does it matter? She found out, right? She found out about you, she went berserk and, well, threw me out. What does it matter?"

"She found out about *me*?" I almost screamed into the phone. "How?"

He started to laugh sheepishly. "I told you it was funny. Remember that night we stayed in Rathmoylan House? I put it on the wrong bloody credit card."

"Oh, Oliver."

"I know, it's a bit of a cliché alright but, come on, what does it matter? She went mad, so what? We never need to see her again."

"So no promotion?" I said slowly. I felt there was something I was missing – but my head felt like it was full of cotton wool and I couldn't think.

"Holly, come on! There you go again, stressing the negative! This time tomorrow we'll be in the Big Apple, in the US of A, just me and you. I kind of thought this might be a nice surprise." He sounded hurt now.

"It is, of course it is." I rubbed my eyes, wondering how much of this would have filtered back to the New York office by the time I got there. "Just give me a minute, Oliver, I need to think." My head felt like it was spinning.

Oh Christ. Mark. What was I going to tell him?

"Now hold on," I said. "I can't just get up and leave here at the drop of a hat."

"Why not?"

Yes, Holly, why not?

I was starting to realise that this might just be the answer to all my problems. This time tomorrow I could be back in New York, and this horrible nightmare would be behind me.

For God's sake – this whole stupid plan had worked.

I had what I wanted.

I had Oliver.

"Hey, you there?" Oliver sounded concerned.

"Yes."

"Don't tell me you're crying?"

"Yes," I said, now half laughing and crying.

"Well, look, I've a few things to tidy up this end, and then I'll be down for you. You'd better text me your address. I presume on this occasion it's okay to come to the house. Hairy is not going to punch my lights out or anything?"

"No. He's not here." With a sinking heart I remembered that Oliver thought I was living with Harry, not Mark. The same Mark who would be here, waiting for the children who were due home at lunchtime.

Oh God, the children – I couldn't go without saying goodbye to them.

"Look, I can't go until lunchtime – I need to pack and –"

"Right, well, I'll ring you when I'm on my way down."

When he hung up, I sank back down into the sanctuary of my warm bed, the now quiet phone still clutched in my hand.

Oliver was on his way.

This whole awful saga was almost over.

I would be gone from this house by lunchtime, never to return again.

I replayed his words over and over in my head, a habit cultivated over the last few weeks.

I will tell her.

I will go to New York with you.

Some day we will be together all the time.

He hadn't been lying. He was on his way.

And there I lay, curled in my small, single bed under the eaves, like a child, my arms automatically clutching my stomach, marvelling at the dull, nagging pain that was sending it into knots.

For God's sake, this is good news, Holly.

How long had I waited for this moment?

We're going to New York, baby!

I had dreamt of this moment, of Oliver telling Catherine calmly and quietly, telling her that they were breaking up, that he was leaving to go to New York. That there were no hard feelings, but that he was moving on.

But that wasn't what had happened, was it? He hadn't told her, she'd found out. She'd found out and from the sounds of it had thrown him out without further discussion.

Catherine Taylor found out her boyfriend was cheating and didn't want him any more. I almost laughed aloud. Never, in my wildest dreams, when I'd imagined this situation, had I thought for a second that my admiration would lie with Catherine, and not Oliver.

Fair play to her.

She'd done what I hadn't.

And that was it. The nagging feeling in my stomach was one of disappointment. I was disappointed that my moment had been somewhat sullied by one minor detail.

Oliver hadn't told her.

He'd been caught.

Oh for the love of God, Holly, what does it matter?

I swung my legs out of the bed and sat up. I had to pack. He was going to come and collect me.

I had to tell Mark.

Oh God, Mark.

I decided to wait until I heard him get up. There was no way I was going to go knocking on his bedroom door, that was for sure.

I showered and changed while I waited and put my make-up on.

I definitely needed make up for this.

When I heard movement downstairs, I went down. He was in the kitchen.

"Hi," I said.

"Hi. Tea?" he asked, turning towards the kettle.

"Mark, I need to speak to you."

"Oh. Right."

He didn't turn around. I was almost glad. It made it easier.

"I'm leaving," I said.

"Yes," he said, "I thought you might. Where are you going to go?"

"New York. With Oliver. Like we planned."

Still he wouldn't turn around. He stayed with his back to me, methodically dunking tea bags in and out of mugs.

"When?" His voice was quiet. I could hardly hear him.

"Today, as soon as the kids get back."

He stopped dunking the tea bag.

"I'm sorry," I said, "I know it's short notice, but, well, he's on his way."

"And what about his girlfriend?"

"She knows apparently. It's all over."

"You'd better get packing so."

Oh, turn around, you coward!

I felt like screaming at him. But I didn't. There was no point.

He was right.

I had packing to do.

Chapter 54

I went up to my room and sank down on the bed. It was all too much to take in.

Oliver was on his way.

To get me.

And I had to pack, but I didn't know where to start. I looked around the tiny room, at the entire contents of the last six weeks of my life. Coiling my laptop lead around my hand, I resisted the urge to open the babyline for the last time.

There was no point. I knew I should log on and bid MarshaG's farewells, but I wouldn't. I'd seen discussion threads before wondering as to the whereabouts of various absent users – perhaps there'd be one for me eventually.

I picked up the bundle of child-rearing books and placed them tidily one by one on the shelf beside the bed. I'd leave them for the next nanny. Though hopefully she wouldn't need them as much as I had.

But she would need some notes! I couldn't let her find out everything the hard way like I had! I scrambled around for some paper and a pen but just as I started to scribble down some hasty thoughts, there was a soft knock on the door behind me.

Without waiting for an answer, Mark came into the room.

"Have you got a minute?"

I sighed, and put my notes to one side.

"I need to talk to you about Emma," he continued.

To be fair, I hadn't expected him to say that. Still I didn't answer, but he didn't seem to care. He sat down on the bed beside me and began to speak.

"I absolutely adored her."

Okay, stop right there.

"You know what, Mark? You don't need to explain anything to me. It's fine. It's all worked out for the best."

But he wasn't listening. "I adored her. But not as much as I hated her."

I gasped. If he was trying to catch my attention, he had it.

"I remember the first time we met. She was a friend of Harry's."

"I know, Harry told me."

"Did he? Well, anyway, that should have warned me. I rarely went out with Harry but that particular night was his birthday. She came late. She used to work as a waitress in a little restaurant on Wicklow Street. Wanted to be an actress, you know, but it never really seemed to work out for her. Anyway, I saw her the minute she entered the bar, tall, blonde, quirky. Like no girl I had ever seen before. I'll never forget it, that feeling of '*I have to have her*'."

He gave a bitter laugh.

"It sounds stupid, but I've often thought since that it

was like that time we found a baby fox at home – me and Harry wanted to keep him but Mam wouldn't let us. She said he wouldn't survive in captivity, so she got Uncle Joe to bring him to the sanctuary. Of course she was right, but we gave her merry hell. Well, Emma was just like that baby fox. I knew she was out of my league, but this time I didn't give up."

I really hadn't time for this. I put my notes into my bag and stood up to start emptying the wardrobe.

"The funny thing was," he continued, "she didn't put up much of a fight. She seemed to be ready to step outside her bohemian lifestyle. She teased me so much about studying so hard. She thought I took everything too seriously. To Emma, life was one big joke. One big party. She still went out with her arty friends, sometimes not coming home till morning. But I had my finals coming up, so I would study and she would sleep. It didn't seem to matter as long as we were together. I would look over at her, curled asleep on the bed, knowing, even then, that it was all too good to be true."

This was the most words that Mark had spoken to me in all the weeks I'd been with him. Just my luck that he'd decided to chat when Oliver was on his way here for me. But there was no way of getting him to stop. So instead, I continued to take clothes off hangers, and he continued to talk.

"The night of my graduation ball, I was so excited. Because we rarely socialised with the college, I don't think anyone really believed she existed. I wanted to show her off. Well, she didn't disappoint. She wore this white dress. Emma didn't do high fashion. She was all floaty and fabulous."

436

I opened my mouth to say 'I know, I saw the pictures,' but then closed it again quickly. But he didn't notice.

"I can tell you, I was *the man* that night. I was so goddamn proud I proposed, and six months later we were married and living here in Duncane."

He swallowed before continuing.

"It was all my fault really. Like that poor little fox, Emma couldn't cope with captivity, with rural life. I knew within a week of moving here that we had made a dreadful mistake. But still I wouldn't give up. I just wouldn't admit that Mr Perfect Mark Fielding had messed up. So we ignored the cracks and next thing Emma was pregnant with Jamie. That changed everything for a while. It seemed to give her a purpose, something of her own to obsess about. We were so excited. And then he was born, and he was so perfect. It was all perfect for a while."

He seemed to be getting distressed now. I turned but he wasn't looking at me. He was still just sitting on the bed, staring down at his feet, his hands joined.

"So what went wrong?" I asked quietly.

"I had to work! That's what went wrong – I had to work. I was a first year vet. Fenton had specifically hired me to take over a lot of his clients. I couldn't say no." He laughed that bitter laugh again. "Okay, I could have said no to some stuff, but that's what I do – I work. It was always that way – like when Dad died – who else was going to take over? Harry? Not bloody likely with him off chasing the snow. It's what I do! I don't know what happened then. She got lonely, I suppose. Bored. She started heading back up to town the odd evening. I couldn't blame her, because she'd be on her own here practically all week. Then she'd head up for the odd night, then the odd weekend."

"And you let her?"

"What choice had I? I could hardly say no. I wanted to but how unreasonable would that have been? She said she was staying with her mother, but her mother was no better. Flaky to the core. I bet she didn't know where she was either. Well, wherever she was she'd come home and I'd know. I could smell the cigarettes, the wine, the cheap aftershave . . . I knew from her face, the way she couldn't look me in the eye . . . And of course Harry didn't help."

"*Harry*? No!" I couldn't keep the shock from my voice.

"Oh nothing like that," he said, "but he always took her side and I hated him for that. I was ridiculously jealous that they'd so much in common. He made a point of always saying I was unreasonable and 'anti-fun' and there never seemed any point in trying to persuade him otherwise."

"But Mark, why did you put up with that behaviour? If you knew what she was . . ." My voice trailed off.

"But what could I do? I suppose I could have kicked her out, but it wasn't all bad. We still got on well enough. It was harder though, with Jamie there. And she was a good mother. Not too organised, mind you – they might both be still in their nightclothes when I'd get home in the evening, but they'd have spent the day finger-painting, or just cuddled together. She adored that child. I remember coming home one evening to find her sitting on the stairs with him, just holding him in her arms and sobbing. Really crying like her heart was going to break. I got such a fright. I thought there might be something wrong, but no, she just kept saying that she didn't deserve him, that he was so perfect. Looking back, she must have had post-natal depression or something. I was just too bull-headed to pay much attention. I laughed at her, told her not to be so silly. She seemed better after that. She'd go out with Jamie all the time. Even when he could walk she'd have him in that sling. She started to chat to the neighbours, would go for coffee, and really seemed to settle down. Then she found out she was pregnant with Amber."

I couldn't believe what I was hearing. It was a fascinating insight into the woman whose pictures I had dusted, whose clothes I had tidied, whose husband had frustrated me so much I no longer knew what I felt about him.

"And that was when things took a plunge. She found that pregnancy so hard. Of course Jamie was up and about by then so she couldn't curl up with her book all day like she had with him. And no, I wasn't around a lot. But by then she had a few friends around the village, so I didn't worry so much. I should have. Shortly after Amber was born, the real problems started."

"Things got worse?" It was hard to believe.

"Oh yes. Things got worse alright. Up to this she'd always had a glass of wine in the evenings. Sometimes two, sometimes a bottle. I was okay with that, I reckoned she deserved to unwind – it couldn't have been easy at home here all day on her own. Being honest, anything that put her in a better mood and off my case was fine by me.

"Then, when I'd come home, it would be already poured. She was just letting it breathe, she'd say. Then one day I came home at lunchtime to find a half bottle on the table, her asleep with Amber on the couch and Jamie in a wet nappy in front of the TV. I went ballistic. Of course she cried and apologised and swore it had been a one-off but it was obvious that she just hadn't been expecting me."

In a flash I remembered his reaction that first afternoon when he'd come back unexpectedly to find me sitting on the floor in the kitchen, amidst chaos.

"Let me make something clear, Holly, it's never a good sign when someone tells you they weren't expecting you home yet."

And I'd thought he was just being an asshole.

"Oh Mark. I'd no idea."

"Neither did I, let me tell you. Well, that was the first almighty row we ever really had. We said the most horrible things to each other. We were both in denial really – she couldn't accept she had a problem and I couldn't accept that it was all my fault. The thing was, I just didn't know what to do next. And for that, I really hated her. She threatened to take the children back to Dublin, but how could I let her? By this stage she was drinking every chance she had – I couldn't let her take them. Okay, so I hadn't spent as much time with them as I should, but that doesn't mean I didn't love every bone in their bodies. Hell, I still loved every bone in *her* body! So I was trapped, terrified she'd leave, yet knowing it was not going to get any better if she stayed."

"Good God, what did you do?" I'd stopped all pretence at packing now and was just standing there, leaning against the wardrobe, clothes folded in my arms.

"What could I do? I tried to fix it. I really did. But it was so sad, so awful. I couldn't turn my back for a second. She even drank in the middle of the night when she thought we were all asleep."

"And no one else knew?"

"No. Well, Teresa Murphy used to help her out a bit with the kids, so she knew there was something up, but she never got to the bottom of it. The other girls in the village only saw her when she was in 'good form' as I called it. Doesn't mean she was sober, mind you, but Emma could be a good actress when she needed to."

"Mrs Murphy thought she was sick," I said quietly.

"I suspected that," he said grimly, "and that would have suited Emma just fine. She could call poor Teresa Murphy when she was too sick to get out of bed, or too drunk to drive the car. And it suited me to let Teresa believe the whole sickness thing, to be honest. I'd no interest in her knowing the truth – the next thing you'd know, the whole village would be talking about how the vet's wife was an alcoholic. Far better they thought she was sick." His voice caught.

With a start, his reaction to my drunken ardour at the Hunt Ball came flooding back and suddenly I was mortified. He didn't notice my discomfort though, and just kept talking.

"Those months were the longest of my life. I tried to get her help, I even booked her into a facility, told everyone she was on a holiday but, within six hours of her coming back, she was at it again. And I will never forgive myself for making her so miserable and not being able to fix her.

"Then, that last afternoon . . ."

His voice cracked and I crossed the room to sit on the bed beside him, my hand on his arm, but he continued, the words spilling out in a rush.

"That afternoon I was in Ballynoe Stud when Fenton drove in behind me, and he looked at me and I knew something was wrong. And I grabbed him by the shoulders and shook him and then he told me that the children were okay, that she had left them in the house for some reason – well, I suppose in her warped way she didn't want them in the car when she was – well, anyway, she was dead. And I was glad! That's the kind of person I am, Holly. She was dead, the children were okay, it was over and all I could do was thank God."

His head sank into this hands and I put my arm around his shoulders.

"Oh Mark, no one could blame you," I said softly, but he had calmed now, as if a huge weight had been lifted from him.

"Well, I'm not so sure, and it's something I will never, ever forgive myself for." He turned to look at me, his mouth set in a grim line. "But that's not my point, Holly. I need you to see why I can't ask you to stay here with me."

I looked at him blankly, as he reached out one hand and pushed my hair behind my ear.

"And I want to, God knows I want to, but I have no right to bring you into this situation. You don't belong here any more than she did. And I can never, ever put another human being through that again. I killed Emma, Holly, as sure as if I'd crashed into her car myself."

"Mark, you didn't!"

"I did! I tried to change her, and it didn't work. Just like you trying to change that loser you're with now won't work either – it never does."

"It's not the same thing at all," I almost laughed. "People change all the time."

"Well, let me tell you now, he has no interest in changing – why would he? He has everything exactly as he wants it."

"That's a ridiculous thing to say. Anyway, I can't back

442

out now!" I didn't like where this conversation was going at all.

"How is it ridiculous? Can't you see, it's never too late! Do you really want to end up like me, afraid to admit that you've made a mistake, stuck in something awful until it really is too late?"

"Mark, he's on his way!" I sprang to my feet. "He's left her, for me, and he's on his way and I should be packed and ready. He'll go mad if he gets here and there's a strange man in my bedroom!" I started to shove things into my bag. "It's not fair that you should try and ruin this for me!"

"I'm not trying to ruin it for you!"

"You are! You're just like all the rest of them. Oh, Holly has messed up again, typical Holly, that's all she does, you know, ricochet from one disaster to another. Well, this *isn't* a disaster! He's here. For me. How dare you assume that I'm just like you? Why can't you see that this is *exactly* what I want? Now, please, get out of my room and just leave me alone!"

He opened his mouth to say something, then at the look of outrage on my face he shut it again.

"I'm sorry," he said. "Of course you're right."

And with that he turned and left the room. I watched him leave, watched the door close behind him and then looked at my half-packed bags beside me. And then I put my head in my hands and cried like my heart would break.

Chapter 55

At exactly one o'clock I heard a car pull up outside and the excited voices of the children coming home. I went down the stairs slowly, my heart heavy.

Mark and his mother were at the front door and I knew from her expression that he'd told her.

"Holleeee!" Jamie roared when he saw me, and before I could even bend down there were two sets of arms wrapped around me. I sank to my knees and enveloped the two children in a huge hug.

"Oh guys, I'm so glad you're back. Did you have a good holiday? I've something to tell you . . ."

The front door slammed with a bang. I looked up. Mark was gone. I looked over the two blonde heads at his mother but she just shrugged her shoulders, smiling sadly.

"Holly is going on her own little holiday, and I wanted to say goodbye to you before I go."

"You're going away?" asked Jamie, a frown on his little face.

"I am, sweetie."

444

"But who's going to mind us?"

"Well," I looked up at Mrs Fielding, who nodded, "your nana, and maybe Dawn – and Daddy of course."

"But I don't want you to go. You said you'd never go!"

Jamie looked at me, his eyes wide in panic, and I actually thought my heart was going to snap clean in two.

How had I ever thought I could do this? I could hardly speak with the lump in my throat and I could feel the tears rise up behind my eyes.

"I never said that, sweetie, but, you know, you're going to be so busy – you'll have to help Daddy get the house ready for Christmas, and help Amber to be good, and –"

Just then the doorbell rang, and I knew it could only be Oliver. I looked pleadingly at Mark's mother who was over in an instant, taking an oblivious Amber and mournful Jamie into the kitchen.

I looked at the closed front door, and I could see Oliver's form through the glass.

He was here.

Taking a deep breath I opened the door.

"*Start spreading the news!*" he burst into song in a deep voice and then stopped at the look on my face. "What in God's name is wrong with you?"

"Nothing. I'm just . . . nothing," I said lamely. What could I say to him? That my heart was breaking at leaving this shoddy little house? That the thought of never seeing Mark again was tearing me in two, that leaving the children was something I still wasn't sure I could actually do . . .

The children.

I felt a wave of nauseating panic rise in my chest. My notes! I hadn't given anyone my notes! I ushered Oliver into the playroom and made him sit down on the bright green couch.

"Eh, what am I doing in here?"

"You're waiting for me. God knows I waited for you for long enough!" I snapped.

I rushed upstairs and got my notes. Then I stuck my head around the kitchen door and called Mrs Fielding out to the hall.

"Yes, love," she said.

"Oh, Mrs Fielding – I wonder could I give these to you, for the next –" I gulped, "for the next girl." I held out my tearstained scribbles. "I'm sorry, they should be typed – they're a disgrace really, but maybe I could email – or you could give her my . . ." I couldn't finish.

"Oh Holly, slow down, don't be getting yourself upset. Take as much time as you need."

"There isn't any time!" I wailed. "There isn't any because I need to be on a plane and nobody else knows – nobody else knows anything about this house!"

I could hold the tears back no longer as I spoke.

"I mean everyone thinks Amber is so bold, but she's not, she's really not, it's just that she had no one, no one to show her any love or discipline or attention – for Christ's sake she's only two! And Jamie," I gulped, "everyone thinks he's fine cos he's quiet but he's even worse – I didn't even really get started with him – he's missed his whole childhood so far – he's seen things no child should ever see, and now I'm leaving him too so he'll probably be even worse – and Mark – oh God, Mark!"

I started to sob now and Mrs Fielding could do nothing but hold me in her arms until I'd calmed down enough to be able to speak.

"What about Mark, Holly love?"

"Mark needs some help too because, well, he thinks he killed Emma and he didn't, he just didn't know what to do and he deserves so much not to carry that around for the rest of his life."

"Shhh, Holly, don't be upsetting yourself like this."

"I tried to make things better here, I really did, but now I've just made everything worse!" The sobs were uncontrollable now.

"Hush now, sweetheart, of course you haven't. Mark's a new man since you came. But, Holly, about Mark . . ."

I instantly knew what she was going to say but I wouldn't let her finish. "Oh please don't," I shook my head, "there really is no point. Oliver's here and Mark, well, he's not ready. So please. Don't."

This topic seemed to snap me out of my hysteria.

"I'm sorry, Mrs Fielding, you really must think I'm some kind of psychopath, but I've grown so fond of – of everyone . . ." My voice trailed off.

"I'll mind them all for you," she said softly and I nodded my thanks before going upstairs for my stuff.

"You okay?" Oliver squeezed my hand as I fastened my seatbelt.

I nodded, looking out the window at the house one last time. Bloody Meadowlands. Thank God Mrs Fielding had taken the children down to the village to see Santa who was today doling out presents from a grotto in Brophy's Butchers.

I could see Dawn's car in her driveway, but I'd chickened out of phoning her. I'd left a note instead, with my email address, if she wanted it.

But I doubted she would.

I'd let her down badly, more than she would ever know.

Somewhere in Dublin there was somebody else ranting and raving and crying and weeping because their boyfriend had been cheating.

With me.

This was not my finest moment.

"Eh, this is it, Holls. Me and you." Oliver squeezed my cold hand again and I managed a watery smile. "I know we could only fly to London today, but we'll get to New York tomorrow. Just think – you'll get to show me your favourite city!"

I nodded, guilty that I couldn't get more excited. Surely it couldn't be right that my heart felt like it was cracking in two? Sweet Divine God, why could I never just be happy with what I had?

I took a deep breath. "Yes, it'll be super. You'll love it there."

"Yes, well, I'll be with you – that's all I want right now."

I smiled at his excitement, tearing my eyes away from the window. There was no point in looking at the house any longer – there was no one to wave me off.

I was leaving just as quietly as I'd come.

Oliver swung the Audi out onto the main road, and it started to eat up the miles. The further away we got from the village, the easier it became to forget the trauma of the last few hours. And the further away we got, the more surreal the whole experience became. It was as if I were in a trance, on automatic pilot.

"You're very quiet," Oliver said eventually after we'd travelled in silence for several miles.

"I know, I'm sorry, I suppose it's just hard to believe it's all really happening."

"Well, it is, baby, just as we'd planned."

"Well, not quite," I smiled. "It's a pity about your promotion, but I'm sure you'll find a job in no time."

"Well, now," Oliver winked at me, "I'll let you in on a little secret there! I *got* my promotion, ten days ago, so the silly bitch can do nothing about that!" He started to laugh, not even noticing that I'd snatched my hand away.

"I beg your pardon?"

"The promotions were last week. I got manager, baby!"

"And why didn't you tell me?" I could hardly get the words out.

"Well, I was going to, of course, but I, eh, I had a few things to investigate first."

"What kind of things?"

"Well, you know, options."

"You mean you weren't sure about New York?"

"Oh Holly, enough of the inquisition! You're making a much bigger deal of this than it is!"

"I don't think I am, Oliver. The 'deal' was – the minute you got promoted, we went to the States – that's what we've been waiting for."

"I know, and that's what we're doing. For Christ's sake, Holly, you're never happy!"

"Stop the car!" I said quietly.

"What?"

"Stop the car!"

"For fuck's sake, Holly, what are you on about? We're halfway up the Naas Dual Carriageway – why would I stop the fucking car?"

"It's because she found out, isn't it?"

449

"Isn't what?"

"You're only coming with me because Catherine found out about us and whatever little plan you were hatching for Dublin has all gone down the tubes."

He looked at me but had the good grace to say nothing.

"Oliver, I want you to answer me. Is that the truth?"

"I had options in Dublin. It might be correct to say that they no longer exist, but you were always part of the plan. Dublin, New York – what difference does it make?"

"It makes a huge difference," I said quietly. "Now stop the car."

Chapter 56

I wasn't sure what was driving me more insane, the uncomfortable bench, or the really annoying tannoy overhead that only seemed to be announcing places that I'd no intention of ever travelling to.

And there were suddenly a lot of those.

I looked around me. Bus Áras was definitely no Grand Central Station, that was for sure. You'd be lucky to get a lukewarm can of Diet Coke let alone a Gin Martini in a frozen glass. Of course no matter where I'd been sitting the novelty would have worn off after almost two hours, but that was Sunday bus times for you. Beggers couldn't be choosers.

But the long wait had brought a strange kind of calm to my tired, stressed mind. For the first time in nearly thirty years, I knew I was doing the right thing.

And boy, was that a bizarre feeling!

I was sad too, sad that it had taken me so long to realise that sometimes the easiest thing to do is the right thing. What had Oliver shouted at me that time in the car on our way back from Ger Baron's?

451

"The point is, Holly, there's an easy way and a hard way to do things! It beats the shit out of me why you always pick the bloody hard way!"

God, that seemed like a million years ago. He'd banged his fist against the wheel that day too. But he'd definitely been angrier this morning. He'd called me every name under the sun, and he'd been right to. When I made him stop the car I had no idea what I was going to do. But one thing was for sure. It didn't involve Oliver Conlon.

Mark was wrong. People could change.

I'd changed.

I'd decided that women like Catherine were right not to accept cheating as a rite of passage. I thought about Cain's wife for a second and how she'd taken him back, and how, before long, Dawn probably would take Graham back too. But they had children and now, more than ever before, I understood that you would do ridiculous things to keep a family together.

Mark had.

I sighed.

So when I'd got out of Oliver's car and sat on the side of the Naas Dual Carriageway with all my luggage and wondered what step to take next, the first thing I'd decided was that I definitely wasn't going to New York. Well, not today anyway. Maybe after Christmas. I could always go back to Fontaines, see if Fat Tony's offer of a commis-chef position was still open. But I'd well and truly burnt my bridges at Grantham Sparks, that was for sure.

So for now, home to Mother it was. I eventually flagged a taxi and got it to bring me here to Bus Áras, where I knew I could catch a bus to Celbridge. My last humbling bus journey of this whole sorry saga.

She'd be surprised to see me. She'd definitely like my hair, though. She'd probably tell me I'd lost more weight but I'd explain it was stress. Damn it, I'd probably just tell her everything. This new me didn't lie. God love her, but the excitement would probably make her spontaneously combust into little pieces all over the new extension. Then she'd douse me with Holy Water and I'd get colic from all the turkey she'd be shovelling into me. And I would let her. I was actually looking forward to a good square meal – meat and ten veg – Mother's Christmas dinners were legendary. I'd decided I would even let her drag me to Mass because maybe asking the Good Lord to help with my recovery wouldn't be such a bad thing.

And then, as my ultimate punishment, I'd get to partake in the big Marsha homecoming. We'd get to listen to her tales of how many lives she saved, the kids would give piano recitals and it would all be one big stomach-churning display of perfection. Well, let's face it, it was nothing more than I deserved.

And anyhow, Marsha *was* perfect. It was high time I learnt how to be gracious and just accept that. The fact that she was perfect didn't make her responsible for the fact that I was not.

And Dad, well, of course he'd be delighted to see me. I'd snuggle alongside him on the giant couch and he'd hug me and tell me it was all for the best. Of course, when the dust had settled he'd worry about my getting another job – so would I, in time. But then maybe Chad might need a receptionist and sure at least I might get a good deal on some tooth-whitening.

Good old Chad, I knew exactly what he was going to say to me. He was going to laugh and ruffle my hair, and tease me, over and over again. "You worked as a nanny? And *then* you snogged your boss – I see!" Maybe after a few glasses of Kelly's famous Christmas punch I might fill him in on exactly what the housewives of Ireland wanted to do to him. But then, he probably knew, maybe that was what was making him look tired . . .

And that just left Kelly. Good old Kelly, her big eyes would widen even more and she'd take one look at me and ask me the question that I didn't want to answer. "It was that Mark guy, wasn't it? I knew you had a thing for him." And I wouldn't answer, because it didn't matter. But she'd know without my answering and she'd ring Paulo with some mad idea about designing a home linen collection in deepest crimson and calling it 'Holly's Heart' or some such rubbish. And of course it would be a runaway success.

But the best bit would be that she'd take me on a night out, and we'd drink and dance and go crazy like the old days. And I'd forget everything, and it would be great.

Until I woke up the next morning to find nothing had changed, that I was no longer in my little room in the loft, and that I'd never see Mark or the children again.

I'd texted Harry to say goodbye, dear darling Harry, and to let him know that I hadn't gone to New York with the "arsehole" and that instead was going to face the music at home. He'd texted back to say that he'd rescue me some night over Christmas from my parents and take me out for a drink. But I probably wouldn't go when it came to it. I'd caused enough trouble between him and Mark and I certainly wouldn't be ready to hear any news about Mark.

And next I texted Mark. I'd had to think about what to say in that one. In the end I kept it brief.

On the 3.45 bus to Celbridge. You were right. Thanks. Holly

Just then I heard the tannoy say "Celbridge, serving Leixlip, Maynooth . . ."

This was it. I switched off my phone and stood up, noticing it had started snowing outside the huge floor-to-ceiling windows.

The kids would be ecstatic.

For a second I imagined them outside building a snowman with their dad, pelting him with snowballs and then all piling back into the house for hot chocolate afterwards.

I stood for a second at the door and let the first flakes drift slowly down onto my closed eyes. It was as if I could imagine myself there with them, trying to find gloves to fit Jamie, fixing Amber's hat down over her curls, laughing with Mark at their antics.

"Celbridge, please." I handed my cash to the driver who just grunted.

I made my way down the narrow aisle to a seat near the back. I was suddenly very tired and closed my eyes as soon as I sat down. Within minutes the giant bus lurched into action.

"Bye, Dublin," I whispered before drifting off to sleep.

It seemed like only seconds had passed before the bus lurched to a stop. I opened one eye and looked out the window. Surely we couldn't be there already? I didn't recognise any of the by now snow-spattered landmarks but judging by the fact that no one was getting off, I figured we couldn't be there yet.

I closed my eyes and leaned back, waiting for the bus to pull off again. But it didn't and I could hear raised voices. I opened one eye to see a very tall man trying to make his way down the aisle.

And the very tall man was calling my name.

"There you are!" he cried when he saw me. "Get your bag – come on!"

"*Mark*?" I didn't trust my eyes. It couldn't be him. Could it?

"Holly, will you come on? This guy is not best pleased that I parked my jeep in front of him."

"You what?" This was like the scene where Mark had rescued me from the pub all over again.

"I'll explain in a minute – now hurry before he drives over it!"

Everyone else was staring at us by now so I sheepishly left my seat and Mark and I grabbed my bags from the overhead compartment. We must have biffed every single aisle-seat passenger with the bags on our way off the bus. I was mortified. Only when we were eventually standing on the side of the road did I turn to him.

"Mark! What in God's name are you doing?"

"Well, I was at the airport when I got your message – tried to get to Bus Áras in time but didn't – so I followed your bus route."

"You were at the *airport*?"

"Yes, looking for you. But then I got your text, so I had to hightail it out of there and try and catch you at the Bus Station. I know dragging you off a bus is a bit embarrassing but, trust me, Plan B was to search every house in Celbridge which wouldn't have been too enjoyable for me."

"You were at the airport looking for me?"

Mark Fielding. At the airport. Looking for me.

"Yes."

"But you said – I mean – why?"

"Well, something's come up. I'm looking for a project manager."

456

"Mark, this isn't funny – get to the point, it's freezing out here."

"Well, get in the jeep."

"No! I'm getting back on that bus!" I looked at the bus that was rapidly disappearing down the road. "I'm getting on some other bus," I finished lamely.

"Right then," he continued, "I was in Lady Smythe's the other night, you remember, after I 'abandoned' you at the Hunt Ball – and, well, she's offered me one of her yards, to build a clinic. I've discussed it with Fenton – actually that's what we were talking about last night when you assumed I was avoiding you, and he thinks it's a great idea."

"Really? Oh Mark, that's fantastic!" I was genuinely pleased for him.

"But I can't do it without you," he said quietly.

"You can." I looked away, brushing the now quickly falling snow from my jacket. "You could do it with Tara."

"Tara?"

"Oh Mark, come on. She's perfect for you. It's so obvious."

"Holly Green, I have no interest in Tara Harper in that way. I can't believe you think I do."

"Well, either way, I've learnt to know my limitations, and I think building a veterinary clinic is definitely out of my league. Now I have to go."

"No." He took a deep breath. "Don't go. The random job offer was Harry's idea. I obviously don't have his knack. But anyhow, now I'm going to take my mother's advice instead. I'd like you to come out to dinner with me."

"No, Mark."

"Please."

"Mark, nothing's changed. Not for you anyway. We've

been down this route and to the best of my recollection, it didn't go so well!"

"It didn't go well because I rushed it. I rushed it and then I panicked. And then when you got really drunk as a result of my panicking, I panicked even more. But I've stopped panicking now, I swear I have."

I couldn't help laughing at the manic expression on his face. He grabbed my hands and looked earnestly into my eyes.

"Look, I'm not exactly sure what you said to my mother before you left but she gave me a right talking-to. And I've been thinking about this. A lot. I mean, I put less thought into my marriage and, well, we both know how that turned out. But the thing is, well, the thing is you're not Emma and, well, I'm not the same Mark that I was back then. You've changed everything for me. We could be a team, I could do anything with you by my side." He paused. "What I'm really trying to say is I love you, Holly Green, and I'd like us to try again."

I couldn't believe what I was hearing.

I love you, Holly Green.

Mark was here and he loved me.

But surely it was too late? What about all my new resolutions? What if this was just another crazy idea?

"Mark," there needed to be a voice of reason here, "I don't know what to say. I was going to go home. I was trying to do the right thing. For once in my life, I was about to do the right thing."

"But this *is* the right thing, Holly, you know it is."

"But how do I know? I've thought so many times before that I was doing the right thing, and every single time I've been doing the completely wrong thing! I can't do that any more, Mark, I just can't!"

"Look, I don't want to rush into something and mess it up either. I've got the kids to worry about and God knows I've put them through enough in the last few years. So let's do it properly. Slowly. I mean, I've got it all worked out – move in with Dawn if you want. We can go to the movies, go for dinner, I don't know, whatever normal couples do. I know the nanny thing was never what you wanted so you can get a job, go back to finance, whatever – I don't care. Do whatever you want, but I am telling you, Holly, I am not prepared to hear you say no." He paused for breath and then said, "The night of the ball, despite everything going so horribly wrong in every way, well, I've never felt anything so right. And I don't need you to tell me you felt it too. Please say you'll give us a try, please."

Holy Cow.

Mark Fielding loved me.

Tears of happiness now started flowing freely down my cheeks and I nodded and whispered, "I will."

He grabbed me by the shoulders, "You will? You mean it?"

"I will, but maybe you should try kissing me again just to seal the deal," I smiled.

He gently took my face between his two giant hands and, as his lips met mine, I melted into the moment, ignoring the traffic hurtling past and the snow pelting down on us both.

"I think my bus is definitely gone," I whispered between kisses.

"Never mind the bloody bus," he whispered back. "That jeep is faced for home. Let's go."

www.thedomesticCEO.com
posted: 25.04.2012
post: 12
views: 634

Title: Midweek Staple

Welcome to another blog from the Domestic CEO (or plain old Holly Green as I used to be known . . .)

One thing I get asked for on my Facebook page time and time again is simple, tasty midweek suppers. This recipe below is one I kind of made up (nothing new there) and it covers all those bases in addition to being very healthy.

We cook stir-fry at least twice a week in our house and it's generally Mondays and Tuesdays that are allotted stir-fry on the planner. This is mostly because I buy all the fresh fruit and veg on Sundays but also because it's nice to at least start the week on a good note. Mark was sceptical at first as he said they used to complain to their mother about having certain dishes on certain nights (his brother, Harry, apparently still has nightmares about Bacon & Cabbage Wednesdays). But it works! At least you have a good idea of where you're at when getting home late on a busy Tuesday. To slightly alternate, it's usually Salmon Stir-fry on Mondays and

Chicken/Pork on Tuesdays, sometimes with wholegrain basmati rice or sometimes noodles. Usually Wednesday it's pasta (can you believe Mark is starting to cook?) and from there the week goes steadily downhill to the Saturday night steak treat!

So here goes with my recipe:

Tasty Mid-Week Salmon Stir-Fry

Two peppers (any colour you wish but I usually go with red & yellow as there's other green veg used in recipe)
Couple of cloves of garlic
I onion
Green beans/mange tout/sugar snap peas or combination of all
Bean sprouts if you're partial
Carrot sliced really finely
Peanuts/cashews/pumpkin seeds/sesame seeds
(and whatever else you like in a stir-fry)
2 salmon steaks
Soy sauce
Sweet chili dip
Harissa paste (if you can get your hands on it)
Rice or noodles

Method

Chop up all your veg.

Combine about I tablesp sweet chili sauce with a teasp of harissa paste in a ramekin.

Put your salmon steaks in an ovenproof dish and paint with sweet chili/harissa mix (note this totally gets

Title: The Special Dinner

So it's Mark's birthday on Saturday and, while I could book a table for two in a fancy restaurant, one of the perils of being the 'other half' of a vet on call is that the chances of being stranded at a table for two, alone & fuming, are never far away …

So I've decided to bring 'fancy' to Domestic CEO HQ instead.

Now if the thought of cooking a fancy dinner for two makes you recoil in terror, this is the blog post for you. Nobody is flush with cash these days and eating at home is infinitely cheaper than its more expensive counterpart. You're only paying for ingredients (which you get to choose yourself) and the cost and hassle of getting a baby-sitter is eliminated.

"But I can't do fancy!" I can hear you shriek.

Sure you can. Anyone can do fancy if they follow the three P's …

463

1) Planning

Don't wait until 8 p.m. on Saturday evening to start wondering about what you might eat. If you do this you can be guaranteed it'll either be beans on toast or a takeaway and I'm not sure which would be worse.

Think about your menu early in the week. This way you'll have time to research your ingredients (remember time is thriftiness's best friend) and explore just how fancy you want to go.

When you're picking your recipes, allow for the fact that some items won't be available in your local store so you may have to either go further afield, use a substitute, or simply pick something else.

When choosing your menu, try not to pick three courses that require your presence at the stove. You'll only end up hot and bothered – and not in a good way. A cold starter (pear, walnut and blue cheese salad for e.g.) is a good way to go as it means you'll arrive at the dinner table unflapped and still looking good. Something like soup is also ideal, though possibly not that seductive ...

And finally, remember, after your amazingly fantastic main course, you're not going to feel like getting up from the table to assemble a complicated dessert so one that's ready-to-go-just-add-ice-cream will be a blessing.

2) Preparation

Preparation is planning's Siamese twin. The golden rule is that the more you can do in advance, the better.

Anything that can be cooked or par-cooked in advance, do that morning and then cover and store. There's a strong case to be made for casserole-type mains (especially fancy ones, like stroganoff, bourguignon, coq au vin etc). These also generally improve with resting, so can easily be made the day before and then just heated up.

There is simply no case for an iota of veg-peeling after 5 p.m. on the night of the dinner. Prepared veg lasts perfectly well submerged in water.

Likewise your garnishes. Have your parsley chopped, your tomatoes concassed (i.e. roughly chopped and skinned) and your chives snipped and set aside in little bowls. There's a reason the professionals do this, and it's not to increase the wash-up. When I worked in Fontaines of New York, if your 'mise en place' wasn't set out to a tee, Tony Abadesso would *not* be happy . . .

Speaking of wash-up, advance preparation often means that a lot of the heavy wash-up can be done in advance of the meal, meaning you can leave the table guilt-free in a hurry, with only a few plates left for the morning!

If it's possible, set your table that afternoon. It might sound ridiculous, but it's too late to discover at 7 p.m. that the only candles you have are of the birthday variety.

3) Presentation
Sometimes it's not so much what you serve, but how you serve it. For my fancy dinner there's no way I'll be

taking out my Heston Blumenthal science kit, nor will there be a ballotine of ANYTHING on the menu, but there are certain tricks that can make even the simplest of food look, well, fancy!

Use your best tableware. The 'good china' is great – plain white is possibly even better but mismatched should only appear at kitschy afternoon tea spreads.

Don't just lob your food at the plate. Have a look at the images in your cookery books. It's as easy to put it on neatly as not. Wipe up spills with the corner of a wet cloth and don't drown anything in sauce unless it's called a stew!

Use what you have – ramekins, serving bowls, even shot glasses are all fantastic for adding that extra 'oomph' to the look of a dish.

Give a bit of height – serve your fish draped over a 'tower' of mash or champ (mash with spring onion). You don't need anything fancy to do this. If you don't have 'rings' then use a scone cutter or even a cup/mug to shape the tower. Then drizzle your sauce around the outside, scatter with chopped chives or tomato concasse and you'll think you're a chef.

Serving homemade chips? Don't just land them in a heap – make a neat stack (think Jenga) and it will look very impressive.

There are very few desserts that don't look better with a dusting of icing sugar and a strawberry/mint leaf combo on the side.

If serving a mousse/posset use a nice glass.

And finally, stick a petit four on the side of your coffee cup.

Before I go, I should mention the 'P' that you should try to avoid – Panic. If it all goes wrong, the worst thing that can happen is that you end up with that takeaway and a very funny story to tell the grandkids!

Enjoy, and do let me know how you get on!

Holly
xx

Don't forget to tune in on Friday for my promised Pack a Picnic from Scant Pickings Special! See you then!

POOLBEG WISHES TO

THANK YOU

for buying a Poolbeg book.

If you enjoyed this why not
visit our website:
www.poolbeg.com

and get another book delivered
straight to your home or to a
friend's home!

All books despatched within
24 hours.

POOLBEG

WHY NOT JOIN OUR MAILING LIST

@ www.poolbeg.com and get some
fantastic offers on Poolbeg books

rid of the 'fishy' taste that sometimes reminds you you've eaten salmon hours later).

Pop in oven at 180 degrees.

Heat up your wok.

Add in a dash of sesame seed oil (or whatever oil you use for cooking).

When it's really hot bung in your veg.

When veg starts to soften chuck in a few dashes of soy sauce (it'll make a cool sizzle).

Throw in some peanuts if you have them (or cashews if you're really feeling flush) and I usually bung in a few sesame seeds/pumpkin seeds too for added nutrition.

Meanwhile have your rice*/noodles cooking away.

*A note about rice here. Don't fool yourself with that cheapo white globby rubbish. Go and get yourself some good quality Basmati and slowly start introducing some wholegrain Basmati into the mix until your taste buds acclimatise to both the quality and nutty flavour. It's better for you and, honestly, you'll never look back . . . Lecture over, back to the recipe.

Your salmon should be done at this stage so you just need to plate up.

It's that simple, enjoy!

Holly
xxx

P.S. still working on that post I promised ye about the freezer stock-take – stay tuned!